REVENANT

Necrotic Apocalypse Book Two

D. PETRIE

MOUNTAINDALE
PRESS

ACKNOWLEDGMENTS

To my family and friends, thank you for your support.

To my DM who let me play Digby in that one campaign during quarantine, I'm sorry he derailed things that badly. But really, what did you expect?

PROLOGUE

The world has changed.

That was all Private First Class, Francis Mason, could think about as he trudged down the road toward California from Portland, Oregon, along with thirty members of his company. Trees surrounded the empty road on both sides. Just fourteen hours earlier, they had watched the entire city of Seattle vanish in a mushroom cloud. He still couldn't believe the last day had been real. It had all happened so fast.

Zombies.

Freaking zombies had invaded his homeland.

He felt stupid even thinking about it.

Then, he got angry.

The previous night had been spent guarding the quarantine line outside the city. He was certain they hadn't let a single one of those monsters through until just before the bomb fell when everything went sideways. Still, somehow the dead had spread throughout the country hours before that. Outbreaks had even started in other countries.

There was only one way that the dead could have gotten

that far so fast. They had help. It wasn't a mystery who it was either.

Skyline.

Mason clenched his jaw as the name echoed through his mind.

Those mercenary bastards had been the only organization operating within the city after the government signed away its trust to the highest bidder. Who else could it have been? On top of that, Skyline had sent their commander, a man named Bancroft, to the quarantine line to oversee the army's handling of the outbreak. It was like they just wanted to make sure everything went according to plan.

In the end, Skyline's mercs abandoned their posts and piled into their ridiculous, science fiction aircrafts and left. Mason couldn't forget the disdain on Bancroft's face as he looked back at the soldiers they left behind to hold the monsters back. The quarantine line fell apart after that.

Soon after, a strategic retreat became their only option, yet, no order came.

The brass didn't bother to recall the troops stationed around Seattle. What would be the point? The logistics of fighting an outbreak like that wasn't something that the Army or National Guard were prepared for. Instead, they just left Mason and his fellow soldiers to fend for themselves. As strange as it was, he wasn't even mad. They had an entire country to defend and there wasn't time to relocate or screen troops for infection.

As cold as it was, command had to consider the soldiers that had already been exposed as lost. There were complaints here and there among the surviving soldiers, but for the most part the horror of the situation was understood. Saving civilian lives was the priority. It had to be.

What kind of people would they be if it wasn't?

Mason pushed the thought out of his head to avoid thinking about his parents and sister in all of it. The county was falling apart around them, leaving countless dead already. Even worse, it was far from over. His throat ached as he tightened his grip on his rifle. There was nothing he could do.

With no retreat order, only a fraction of the soldiers on the quarantine line had survived. A horde of the dead, thousands deep, had seen to that. Their slathering jaws simply tore their way through everything and everyone in their path. Mason would have died there too if one of the sergeants hadn't taken it upon themselves to call the situation for what it was. Hopeless.

Now, as his group of mostly low-ranking soldiers marched toward the nearest base, Mason found weary faces everywhere. They had been forced to abandon their vehicles back in Portland. Things had gotten hairy there. A horde had come out of nowhere. They'd had sixty soldiers in their group at the time. Now, only thirty remained.

With a little luck… well, make that a lot of luck, they might be able to regroup. Maybe even do some good. Though, that was still a long shot. The dead were everywhere in the cities and the roads were a mess. Not a single car had been seen on the road they followed. To make matters worse, the sun was setting and spending the night in the woods with no gear wasn't high on the list. They would have to find somewhere to hole up until morning.

Mason checked his rifle's magazine, finding ten rounds. "This night is going to get worse before it gets better."

"What's that?" Private Parker asked as she walked beside him. She wore her rifle slung across her back with her hands in her pockets as if trying her hardest to look unfazed by the situation. She had lost her helmet at some point, revealing a somewhat matted mess of blonde hair. By regulations, she normally kept it secured with an elastic band, but it seemed she'd lost that too. Not that it mattered now.

"Sorry, I was thinking out loud." Mason tilted his rifle to one side. "I only have ten bullets left."

"Oh, I ran out back at the quarantine line." She hooked a thumb to her weapon. "This thing's empty. Not sure why I'm still carrying it." She turned to look behind her. "What about you, Sax, got any ammo?"

"Yes, in fact, I do." A slim man behind her tapped a finger on a magazine slotted onto his gear. "This one's full. I had the good sense to hide behind Mason when everything hit the fan. He has better aim than you do, so I didn't have to fire as much."

Parker stopped short and rummaged around in her pouches for something, eventually pulling a hand out only to produce a middle finger that she promptly presented to Sax. "I can aim this just fine."

"Ack." Sax immediately clutched his hands to his heart, as if receiving a fatal wound. He stumbled forward to lean on Mason's shoulder before letting out a weak cough. "I shan't recover from this deep emotional wound." He held both hands out to him, cupping one hand within the other as if holding something previous. "Please, Mason, I am not long for this world, but I ask that you deliver this message to my closest friend, Parker."

Mason rolled his eyes and reached for Sax's hands as if accepting what he offered.

"Thank you, sir, now I may rest in peace." Sax slid down, making a quiet gurgling noise in his throat.

Mason promptly held up his hand and flipped Parker off. "Private Sax wanted you to have this, it was his dying wish."

"Yeah, I deserve that." She shrugged and kept walking.

Parker and Sax had made it their mission to provide a hint of levity throughout the horrors of the last twenty hours. They had spent a fair amount of the march from Portland ranking the dateability of comic book characters. Eventually they both agreed that most were not good boyfriend material. More recently they had switched up to rating zombie movies in order of most realistic now that they had something to compare them to.

It was an odd, but strangely cathartic activity.

They had both gravitated toward Mason as things fell apart like a pair of stray cats that had shown up in his house without being invited. He didn't complain. Friends had become more important than ever. Despite their demeanor, Mason had noticed tears welling in each of their eyes at one point of another. The same could be said about himself. He just wasn't putting in as much effort as they were to comfort the people around them.

"Hey Tanner, what 'bout you? Got any ammo?" Parker stood on her toes to shout to one of the other privates. Several nearby men all shushed her. "Sorry, sorry." Parker ducked down to hide before whispering her question again.

"Yeah, yeah, sure. I have a few rounds left." Tanner, another private, answered without looking up. Mason couldn't help but notice sweat running down his pale forehead.

"You okay over there Tanner?" Sax's voice wavered. "You look a little moist."

"I'm fine, just tired." Tanner avoided eye contact. "Been walking all day."

Here we go. Mason tensed up as he stepped into the conversation. "Seriously, Tanner. If you need to check in with a medic, I think there's one still alive back there with the sergeant."

"I said I'm fine. Just leave me alone." Tanner walked a little faster.

"Okay, I'm just going to say it here," Parker looked him in the eye, "but don't be that guy."

"What guy?" Tanner took a step away from her.

Parker slapped her wrist with her other hand. "Don't be that guy in every zombie movie who hides a bite. We know how this thing spreads at this point."

"Get the fuck off my back, Parker." Tanner wiped sweat from his brow. "Why you gotta be such a bitch all the time?"

Parker stood there blinking at the sudden hostility.

"How about you roll up your sleeve?" Mason stepped in, catching a crimson stain on the man's cuff.

"How about you mind your own business?" Tanner folded his arms.

"Now you're the one being a bitch." Parker rolled her eyes at him.

"Seriously, Tanner, if you have an injury or don't feel well, you need to get yourself looked at." Mason stepped between them before things escalated.

"Yeah, don't be that guy," Sax repeated Parker's words.

Tanner placed his hand on his rifle and stared daggers at the three of them as their questions backed him into a corner. Some of the other soldiers around him were starting to get nervous too. Behind them, the sun fell in the sky, nearly disappearing over the horizon as shadows stretched across the empty road. Two of the other men switched on the flashlights mounted on their weapons. They kept their rifles aimed at the ground but held them at the ready.

"It's okay, Tanner, we just want to help." Mason stepped closer with his hands held up to try to defuse the situation.

"What's goin' on?" One of the few remaining officers near the back jogged up to investigate.

Tanner flinched as they approached.

"He's hiding a bite, sir." One of the other men held a light on Tanner's feet.

"Aw, crap." Sax stepped back as the officer got involved.

Tanner tried to argue but there wasn't anything he could say to change the situation. Mason stepped back as well, ready to react if the wounded soldier decided to raise his weapon.

"Alright, fine!" Tanner pulled his sleeve up to show a nasty bite. "Is this what you want? Should you just shoot me in the head now or do you want to wait 'til I turn?" His voice climbed into a shrill cry as tears began to fill the poor man's eyes.

Mason stared at the ground, not wanting to see what came next. If only Tanner had come forward earlier. They could have tried something. Anything. Now, there wasn't much anyone could do. They'd seen the process enough times already to know what to expect. A slow decline into death before reanimating.

Tanner shook his head and swore under his breath at Sax and Parker. Then, without warning, he spun on his heel and bolted for the tree-line. He collapsed before he made it ten feet. His body spasmed in the dirt for a solid ten seconds before finally going limp. Silence fell over the road, leaving the sound of leaves rustling in the wind to fill the void.

"That's… odd." Sax arched an eyebrow.

Odd was the right word. They hadn't seen a reaction like that before. Normally, people got tired and weak before quietly passing away. The sudden spasms were new. Mason squinted at Tanner's body as shadows settled over the road. It looked like he was still breathing.

"Check him out." The officer gestured to one of the privates shining a light on Tanner's body.

Mason readied his rifle, wishing he had more bullets as the sun vanished beneath the horizon to snuff out the last rays of light. He stood back to let the others investigate. One of them shined a flashlight down on Tanner's chest.

"He's still breath—"

Before the soldier could get out another word, Tanner twisted his body around and lunged. He hissed at the flashlight, showing a mouth full of shifting teeth as they reformed into two dozen crooked fangs. A rifle barked, putting him back down with a hole through his skull.

"What the hell was that?" Sax stepped closer to Mason.

"Maybe he was turning into one of those mutated ones?" He shook his head, not really knowing if that was possible. They had seen a few different types of zombies with a range of abilities back at the quarantine line, but they didn't know what caused the changes to manifest.

Parker moved closer as well. "Could be, but we've never seen one like that before. And how did he change so fast?"

"Whatever he was, he's dead now." The soldier shining a light on Tanner's corpse turned around just as a low growl emanated from the shadows behind him.

Everyone flinched as Tanner threw himself onto the man's back to sink his teeth into his victim's throat. Mason gasped as the bullet hole in his forehead began to close.

"Oh god, he's healing."

Unlike the zombies he'd seen before, Tanner didn't tear away any flesh. Instead, he tightened his arms around the soldier's body and adjusted the angle of his neck. A horrible sucking sound came from Tanner's mouth as his throat pulsed like he was swallowing.

"Is he… drinking?" Parker covered her mouth.

Everyone raised their weapons. It was too late for the man in Tanner's grasp. Mason's finger hesitated on the trigger of his rifle, all too aware that he only had ten rounds left. He didn't even know if bullets would work after what he just witnessed. Either way, they needed to make every shot count.

Tanner's eyes shifted from a dark brown to a dull orange, like embers dying in a fire. His pupils dilated and flicked around as everyone turned on their flashlights. Mason's hands started to sweat as all the color drained from Tanner's body and his ears elongated to form wicked points. Then he was gone. A blur of pale skin vanished into the night, dropping the bloodless corpse of his victim to the ground.

"Where did he go?" someone called out as they swept their rifle across the scene. More of the group followed suit, aiming their weapons in all directions. A chittering screech came from the other side. Panicked shouting followed.

"Shit, he's over there."

"How is he that fast?"

"What is he?"

"Is he even a zombie?"

"I don't know."

"Fu—" Mason swept his light back to where Tanner had been, finding his recent victim standing again.

The skin of their torn throat shuddered before knitting back together. A second mouth full of razor-sharp teeth lunged forward. Muzzle flashes lit up the night as everyone panicked. Elongated shadows strobed across the ground.

A pale blur the size of Tanner rushed someone nearby, only to backhand them. Mason tripped and fell back, dropping his rifle, as their body flew past him by nearly a dozen feet.

A scream tore through the night from the other side, cutting off with a sudden croak. Boots trampled the road and dirt around him, scrambling to escape the chaos. Mason scooted back on his rear, grabbing for his gun. His fingertips caught the butt of a weapon. It wasn't his. It was a sniper rifle. He hadn't used one since basic training. That was only eight months ago. It was good enough. His fingers slipped along the weapon, smearing drops of blood from its previous owner down one side.

Frantic flashlights streaked across the scene, searching for threats as rifles barked. Bullets peppered the ground inches from Mason's hand, throwing dirt in his face and mouth. He spat it out as voices shouted all at once. The friendly fire was almost as bad as the blood-sucking creatures that were hunting them. He struggled to get his bearings. Laying there wasn't an option.

Scrambling to his feet, a heavy boot slammed into his back. An inhuman screech echoed as the boot kicked off. Mason hit the ground again, coughing a lungful of air into the dirt. A masculine voice cried out from somewhere nearby.

Another creature rushed from the shadows, illuminated by the pink glow of a bloody flashlight resting on the ground. It weaved toward him, its jaws wide.

A shot rang out only a foot from his head, the noise assaulting his eardrums.

The creature fell back to the ground flailing. It wouldn't be down for long.

The soldier that had fired the gun didn't stop. Instead, they stepped over Mason's legs and flipped their rifle in their hands. They brought the butt down on the monster's throat.

The slender silhouette of Sax fell to his knees over the monster to bludgeon the creature in a desperate effort to keep the thing down. In the same instant, a hand clamped down on Mason's shoulder.

"Come on. We have to move!"

Mason flicked his head to the side, finding Parker dragging him to his feet. The silhouette of Sax slamming his rifle into the creature on the ground reflected in Parker's eyes. The soldier continued to bludgeon the thing as its body twitched and flailed.

Reaching up, Mason caught Parker's wrist and pulled himself upright. Dozens of inhuman howls filled the night, the creatures numbers growing with every victim they sunk their jaws into. Parker was right, they had to move.

"Come on." Mason reached for the shoulder of Sax's uniform and yanked him off the monster. "That's not helping."

"I don't know what to do." Sax's voice trembled.

"We run." Parker grabbed him by a strap on his body armor.

"She's right." Mason turned toward the woods. "We've lost here. All we can do is retreat. If we stay here, we're dead."

Sax nodded and fell in line as Mason started running. The image of Tanner latched onto the throat of his victim hung in his memory.

That was no zombie.

Nothing that had come out of Seattle had been that strong or that fast.

No, Tanner had become something else.

Something his mind wasn't ready to process.

The sound of screams trailed off behind them as they ran, replaced by nothing but chittering screeches as the creatures claimed their victims. It had only been thirty seconds and, already, there was no one left. Mason kept running, having no idea if he even had a bullet in the rifle he carried or where they might find somewhere safe.

The only thing keeping the creatures from pursuing them was the bodies of their comrades that they'd left behind. The thought of it turned his stomach, despite knowing there was nothing he could do. All they could do was keep moving. Just keep running. Keep surviving.

He tightened his grip on his weapon.

The world had changed.

CHAPTER ONE

Alex strolled casually through rows of grapevines in California's wine country with a rifle slung over his shoulder. It had already been two weeks since he and Becca had crash landed one of Skyline's kestrels outside Seattle with a ravenous zombie necromancer seat-belted into their passenger compartment.

It seemed like a lifetime ago.

So much had changed, making the future he envisioned after becoming an enchanter a little less bright.

The electric grid had failed almost immediately. The internet still functioned, partially, despite being a ghost town. Many sites continued to run, there just wasn't anyone posting. It was as if everyone had simply died within the first two days. Obviously, he hoped that wasn't the case.

There hadn't been much in the way of supplies in the kestrel. Just a few rifles, a helmet, and some body armor. The helmet went to Lord Graves. It had taken a great deal of trouble to get it on him without him biting off a hand, but they made do.

With the visor down, the ravenous lord of the dead was less dangerous. In the end, Alex and Becca had lured him into one of the weapon crates in the back of the aircraft and locked him inside. From there, it was just a matter of finding a truck to carry him, as well as something to eat.

An hour after getting Digby stowed, they realized their second problem. The ravenous zombie was also radioactive. The necromancer had absorbed a portion of the energy from the nuke that destroyed Seattle to stop the kestrel from being torn apart. Thanks to him, they survived the blast, though a poisonous aura lingered around the zombie from then on.

It was so strong that simply being within a few dozen feet of Digby caused radiation sickness to set in at least once every couple hours. Alex's Purify Water spell had gotten plenty of use, with its cleansing properties being the only way to remove the status. Becca's Regeneration spell had handled the rest.

In contrast to Digby's complications, Asher, his reanimated raven, had been well behaved. The deceased bird had been content to perch on top of the crate her master had been locked in. She didn't try to eat Alex or Becca. Not even when they set up camp and slept for the night.

With Henwick and Skyline thinking they had been caught in the blast that destroyed Seattle, it made sense to lay low and avoid contact with anyone, living or dead, until they had a better grip on the situation they faced. Fortunately, Becca's drone equipment had survived the crash, leaving her with two units. Without eyes in the sky, they wouldn't have made it as far south as they had.

The hordes had stuck to the cities, so avoiding zombies turned out to be easy. Alex had needed to kill a dozen the first day when they went to find a truck to transport his ravenous lord in.

He and Becca had gained a level from the encounter. It would have been better if Digby had been able to grow his horde, but with him locked in a storage crate, he wasn't able to provide much in the way of leadership.

It was only by sheer luck that they found the vineyard that they'd held up in for the last two weeks. They had literally passed a sign for the property on a quiet road they'd taken to avoid the cities. The place was huge, secluded, and abandoned. The perfect place to hide while they figured out what to do next.

On top of that, the property's previous owner had recently taken their own life, leaving a convenient meal for their ravenous necromancer. That had been a load off Alex's mind, since fresh human corpses were limited.

Unless someone was willing to go hunting.

Alex plucked a grape from a vine and popped it in his mouth. He probably should have washed it first, but after reaching level five and putting his extra point into constitution, a little pesticide wasn't going to hurt him much. He would have preferred to put the point into strength, like he'd done with the others so far, but both he and Becca had been struggling to stay healthy since the crash.

Having Digby and his radioactive status around had forced him to increase his constitution just to avoid the constant nausea that came along with radiation sickness. Now, he only got sick a few times per day rather than every other hour.

Alex shrugged and ate another grape. *I'm sure having a high constitution will come in handy later on.*

Swallowing the treat, he pulled an old skeleton key from his pocket. He didn't actually know what it went to, it was just something he'd found in the vineyard's main house. All that mattered was that it was made of iron. That way it would function with the Detect Enemy spell he'd extracted from one of Skyline's guardian rings back in Seattle.

Much like his other abilities, it wasn't anything powerful, just a simple enchantment that would cause any object with a high iron content to grow cold in the presence of hostile creatures.

There hadn't been many enemies roaming the property, so there hadn't been much need for magic in the last two weeks. Alex had cast his three spells with gusto regardless, hoping to learn something new.

As dark as the world had become, he still marveled in the abilities that Digby had given him. Knowing that the Heretic Seed's Skill Link passive could discover a related spell from simply performing a task well, Alex had made a point of putting maximum effort into everything he did, even if it was just cooking or cleaning. A few chores were a small price to pay for magic.

Unfortunately, it seemed that hiding in the vineyard didn't net much in the way of interesting tasks for the Seed's system to discover new spells. On top of that, it soon became apparent that ranking up the abilities they already had required each use of the spell to matter in some meaningful way.

Casting things repeatedly without a real need to did nothing but waste mana. With that, the only spell that he had been able to improve had been Purify Water, which had gained a weak healing property at rank B. At least there was an upside to constantly getting radiation poisoning.

Focusing on the ring floating at the edge of his vision, Alex watched as it snapped to the center of his view to expand into his status window.

STATUS
Name: Alex Sanders
Race: Human
Heretic Class: Enchanter
Mana: 132/142
Mana Composition: Balanced
Current Level: 5 (378 experience to next level.)

ATTRIBUTES
Constitution: 22
Defense: 18
Strength: 19
Dexterity: 18
Agility: 20
Intelligence: 21

Perception: 18
Will: 22

AILMENTS
None

AVAILABLE SPELLS:
DETECT ENEMY
Description: Enchant any iron object with the ability to grow cold in the presence of hostile entities.
Rank: D
Cost: 10MP
Range: Touch

ENCHANT WEAPON
Description: Infuse a weapon or projectile with mana. An infused weapon will deal increased damage as well as disrupt the mana flow of another caster. Potential damage will increase with rank. Enchanting a single projectile will provide a greater effect.
Rank: D
Cost: 15MP
Range: Touch

PURIFY WATER
Description: Imbue any liquid with cleansing power. Purified liquids will become safe for human consumption and will remove most ailments. At higher ranks, purified liquids may also gain a mild regenerative effect.
Rank: B
Cost: 10MP
Range: Touch
Additional Effect: Mild Healing
Additional Effect Duration: 10 seconds

PASSIVE TRAITS:

ANALYZE
Reveal hidden information about an object or target, such as rarity and hostility toward you.

MANA ABSORPTION
Ambient mana will be absorbed whenever MANA POINTS are below maximum values. Rate of absorption may vary depending on ambient mana concentration and essence composition. Absorption may be increased through meditation and rest. WARNING: Mana absorption will be delayed whenever spells are cast.

SKILL LINK
Discover new spells by demonstrating repeated and proficient use of non-heretic skills or talents.

TIMELESS
Due to the higher than normal concentration of mana within a heretic's body, the natural aging process has been halted, allowing for more time to reach the full potential of your class. It is still possible to expire from external damage.

Looking over his stats and abilities, he still wasn't anywhere near as powerful as Digby. Even Rebecca had better spells, and she was only level two. Despite that, he felt strong. He had always known that he was weaker than most, but now, things had changed. It wasn't like he'd suddenly gained giant muscles or bulked up, but more like his body had become more solid.

In comparison to a normal person that had made a point of hitting the gym, he was still a little weak. Though, that was changing. With another few levels, he would get there. It wasn't just strength either, but his other stats as well. His balance, endurance, and control over his actions had all improved. Even his aim was better. Again, he was still a little below average, but he sure as hell wasn't as uncoordinated as he was before.

As much as he wanted to focus on the enchanter's central stat, will, he thought it might be better to fill out the attributes he had neglected for most of his life. There would be time to maximize his class later but, for now, he liked the feeling of being able to throw a punch.

After all, it didn't matter how powerful of an enchanter he might become if he got killed before he could get there because his defense was too low. Especially after he'd quit wearing the Skyline body armor that he'd salvaged from the kestrel.

In the first week after they'd reached the vineyard, Alex had dressed ready for combat twenty-four-seven. His tactical gear looked badass but after a few days, he'd tossed it aside in favor of something more comfortable. Fortunately, one of the rooms in the vineyards main house had a selection of clothing that was close to his size. It was mostly Hawaiian shirts, vintage tees, and cargo pants, but they were better than nothing. Plus, he could appreciate the irony of such a casual style becoming his apocalypse attire.

"You detecting any threats over here?" A Skyline-branded drone descended into the row of grapevines to pull Alex out of his thoughts.

"There's something faint." Alex gripped the iron key in his hand, feeling it cool against his skin.

"Great, I'll head up and see if I can spot it." The drone rose back into the sky.

Alex watched it go, wondering if he would ever see Becca again. It wasn't that she was planning on leaving, just that she hadn't left her room in the vineyard's main house since they arrived. Most days, he simply left a plate of food outside her door only to find it empty a little while later. It reminded him of cat-sitting for his neighbors back in the apartment building he'd lived in before the curse hit.

I hope someone is still feeding that cat. Alex lowered his head, trying not to imagine the poor thing scratching at the apartment door, begging for food that would never come.

"Found it." Becca lowered back down to hover just over his head. "About a hundred feet away."

"Is it alone?" Alex pulled his rifle from his shoulder.

"Yeah, it's just one zombie wandering around."

"Perfect, lead the way."

Alex followed Becca's drone down the row of vines until he came upon the corpse. Hiding behind the leaves, he analyzed the monster.

Zombie, Common.

He released a sigh of relief, confirming that it wasn't something more dangerous like a glutton or a devourer. It would be strange for an uncommon or rare zombie to wander so far from a city, but still, it never hurt to check. More importantly, the monster wasn't ravenous. If it was, he would have needed to enchant his weapon to add power to the shot in order to put it down faster. Instead, he slung his rifle back over his shoulder and stepped around the grapevine.

"Hey there." He gave the corpse a welcoming wave before gesturing to the direction he came from. "Right this way."

After a hollow moan, the zombie reached out and staggered in his direction.

"That's right, we'll take good care of you." Alex began walking backward.

"How many does this make?" Becca's drone floated casually beside him.

"Ah, seventeen, I think." Alex tilted his head to one side.

It didn't make sense to kill the creatures. Not when Digby could use them. They couldn't stay in the vineyard forever. Eventually they would need to venture out, and to do that, Alex's deceased lord would need a horde ready to move when the time came.

He was just glad the zombies were easy to bait. Apparently, he was fairly appetizing. It would have been nice if Digby would help but of late, he had more important things to do.

"Do you think seventeen is enough?" Becca's voice wavered. "You know, for Dig to keep us safe out there?"

"Yeah, but I should try to head out a little further to get a few levels before we think about moving." He glanced at the lens of her camera. "You could come too. At least you have a solid attack spell. I certainly feel better with you out here in person to watch my back."

"Maybe." Becca gave her usual non-committal response.

Alex didn't push the subject, opting to focus on the walking corpse following him back to the vineyard's main house. The building was a three-story home with an attached winery, complete with the largest wine cellar imaginable. A storehouse sat off to the side with a cargo van parked beside it. The structure looked like it had once been a barn with a hay loft before being repurposed. A simple wooden ramp led up to a wide window up top near the roof.

Checking to make sure the zombie wasn't catching up or lagging too far behind, Alex backed up the ramp and crawled in through the window. Becca floated in behind him as he placed a hand on a railing overlooking a storage area.

A chorus of moans came from the space below as sixteen zombies reached up for him.

"I know, I know. I look tasty, I get it." Alex carefully traversed the loft until he reached the other side of the building, where a shovel leaned against the wall. He grabbed the handle and waited. His newest guest peeked in through the window a moment later, after successfully navigating the ramp. "Welcome to your new home. It's not much, but you won't get rained on."

The zombie staggered toward him, passing an opening in the railing.

"Okie dokie, down you go." Alex placed the shovel against the monster's chest and gave it a shove back over the edge of the loft. The zombie let out a sudden snarl as it fell. Alex dropped the tip of the shovel to the floor and peeked down while leaning on the handle.

Becca hovered beside him for a moment. "Okie dokie?"

"What?" Alex shrugged at the drone. "I was trying to be friendly."

"You just shoved a zombie off a ledge, I don't think being nice matters at this point." Becca floated back out through the window they'd entered through.

"Maybe, but being friendly can't hurt?" He returned his shovel to the corner and followed her out.

"I guess, but they're dead. They don't care if you're nice to them." She stopped in front of the main house.

"I know, but it makes me feel better about locking them all in there." He hooked a thumb back at the storage building.

"Sure." She swiveled toward the grapevines. "Anyway, we only have another thirty minutes of daylight left. You want to call it for today?"

Alex looked out over the horizon as pink and orange light filtered through the clouds. He'd seen more sunsets in the last two weeks than he'd seen in years. Things had moved at a faster pace back then. Now, though, life as he knew it was just bittersweet memory. He took in a long breath, letting the scent of soil mix with the aroma of grapes.

"Nah, I think I'm going to do one more pass of the vineyard before quitting."

"Suit yourself. I'll do a flyover and see what I can find." Becca climbed into the sky until her drone was nothing but a dark speck in the pink light of the setting sun.

Alex slung his rifle over his shoulder and reached for the iron key in his pocket. With the threat detector in hand, he strolled off down the rows of grapevines.

Maybe I should try some wine again later. Alex grimaced at the thought.

He'd never been much of a drinker before the world ended, and he knew nothing about wine. It just seemed like a waste considering there was an enormous cellar full of the stuff beneath the winery. He'd been trying to get accustomed to the taste, but so far, it hadn't grown on him.

He sauntered along absentmindedly as he considered what

sort of rations might pair best with the vineyard's oldest bottle. That was when he stumbled upon a group of three zombies standing beneath a tree. Like most of the dead, they wore the standard dirty garments, as always. However, something was off.

"Oh damn." He nearly tripped over a stray vine before checking his iron key to discover the detection spell had worn off. Alex flicked his eyes back to the trio of monsters, expecting them to stagger toward him. For a second they reached out only to retreat back into the shadow of the tree.

"That's odd?" He couldn't help but notice how pale they were as he wondered why they were keeping their distance. Normally, they would stagger toward a lone human without hesitation. "You guys feeling alright?"

"Oh good, you found some." Becca dropped down to hover beside him.

"Yeah, but something's off. They aren't attacking." Alex cast his Detect Enemy spell again, feeling the key in his hand turn ice cold in an instant. He immediately focused on the group to ask the Heretic Seed's analyze function for answers. It labeled all three creatures the same.

Dormant Revenant, Common, Hostile.

"What the hell is a revenant?" Alex took a step back.

"What?" Becca swiveled to observe the trio.

"That's what the Seed called them."

"I don't like the sound of that." She drifted a few feet back to float behind him. "Why aren't they trying to eat you?"

"No idea. They look like they want to, but don't have the confidence to attack."

"Maybe you should just take them out rather than trying to lure them back to join the horde." Her camera made a sudden clicking noise, before she added a confused, "Oh, weird."

"What?" Alex slid his rifle off his shoulder.

"They aren't dead."

"What do you mean they aren't dead? How could that be possible?" Alex cast Enchant Weapon on his gun.

"I don't know, but according to infrared, they're warm and my directional mic is picking up heartbeats."

Alex raised his weapon and addressed the group. "Excuse me."

"Still trying to be friendly?" Becca scoffed.

"If they're alive, maybe they can understand us."

One of the revenants growled and swiped at the air, stepping forward as the shadow it stood in stretched in the light of the setting sun.

"Okay, maybe not." Alex took aim at the closest monster, realizing something strange. There wasn't a wound or blemish in sight. On top of that, their teeth were sharper, almost like fangs. Their ears were even tipped with points, reminding Alex of the old film, Nosferatu, with its unique and monstrous vampire.

"Sorry about this." He squeezed the trigger and put a round straight through the monster's chest. The revenant fell flat on its back.

"You should have gone for the head," Becca commented.

"I'm not that great a shot yet, need to improve my dex for that." He retargeted on one of the others, putting a round in its throat. "My enchantment messes up their mana system though, so it should keep them down long enough to get close and finish them off."

"How strategic…"

"Kind of." He switched to the third creature just as the sun fell below the tree-line.

The revenant let out a sudden screech before rushing forward.

"Oh shit." Alex pulled the trigger, this time putting an enchanted bullet through its eye. The round exploded out the back of its head. He bent over panting as soon as the last target was down. "You sure you don't want to get out here and cover my back in person?"

Becca didn't answer, opting to fly over to the corpses and shine a light across the scene. "What the hell are they?"

"Maybe some kind of mutation that we haven't seen before?" Alex crept toward the first creature he'd shot to finish it off.

"That could explain how they were still alive." Becca dipped down to float just over one of their heads. "How long does your enchantment mess up a zombie for?"

"Usually several minutes, unless I hit their brain. Then they stay down for good."

"And what if they aren't zombies?"

"Not sure. I've never tested it on a heretic or a guardian to see how long it messes up their mana flow for."

"Shit, you might have an answer then." Becca darted away from the corpses. "They're healing."

"That's imposs…" Alex trailed off as he witnessed the wounds he'd inflicted begin to repair themselves. It was as if the creatures had an ability similar to Becca's Regeneration spell, in that it activated automatically while unconscious. His breath froze in his throat as the bodies began to twitch. Including the one that had been shot in the head.

"Oh god." Alex backed away.

"Headshots don't work." Becca spun to face him with her camera before coming to the only conclusion that made sense. "Run!"

Alex was moving before the first of the monsters got back to their feet, only looking back to analyze one of the things again in hope of learning more.

Active Revenant, Common, Hostile.

Active? Alex leaped through one of the rows of vines as an ear-splitting screech shattered the silence behind him. *Hadn't the Heretic Seed labeled them as dormant just a second ago?* The sound of feet hitting dirt behind him chased the thought from his mind. Something had definitely changed, but there wasn't time to think about it. He sprinted at full speed, wishing he'd put his extra point into agility.

"I am not getting killed here." At least his high constitution had boosted his endurance.

"Get back to the house." Becca's drone swooped down. "I'll meet you there."

"That's where I'm heading."

A vicious chittering came from his right and left as well as behind. He knew enough to understand when he was being hunted. The sound of vines snapping closed in on him. Clutching his rifle, he stumbled into the open area in front of the main house, nearly falling over in the process. He spun around and leveled his weapon at the shadows behind him.

There was nothing there.

The floodlights on the house illuminated the lawn. Alex said a quiet 'thanks' to the generator in the basement that kept the place running. A screech echoed from the left. He flicked his rifle to the side. Another sound came from the right, causing him to sweep his aim to meet it. He switched his weapon's select fire to full auto as silence fell over the vineyard once again.

It didn't last.

From the right, a revenant tore through the vines just as a second skittered into the light on the other side. The third burst right through the middle, splattering crushed grapes across the lawn.

Alex fired in a frantic spray, carving an arc through the air around him. Mana infused bullets punched into the first two creatures as the third lunged at his throat with a mouth full of razor-sharp fangs. He fell back, bringing his rifle around and squeezing out the last few rounds in the magazine. They tore through the revenant's gut. The monster slammed into his shoulder, throwing him to the side before rolling away with the momentum.

The three unknown enemies lay on the ground, their limbs twitching. Somehow, they were still alive. Their wounds popped with sputtering squelches, as if their disrupted mana flow was attempting to reassert itself to heal them again.

"Out of the way!" Becca burst through the front door of the house with both hands raised.

Mist condensed in the air above one of the downed creatures to form an icicle. She dropped one hand as if guiding the frosty spike to her target while simultaneously forming a second shard of ice. The first icicle slammed through the throat of her target, followed by another that impaled the second. Becca raised a hand again, sending a third dagger of frost into the last of the creatures. They continued to flail and screech.

"I'm not done." She threw up her hands and hurried three more icicles into her targets. She kept going until she was out of mana.

"Are they—"

"Dead?" She panted. "No, but they should be soon. My guess is they can survive fine with something as small as bullet fragments lodged in their bodies, but they probably won't fare well with a big ass spike of ice holding their wounds open. If they can't regenerate the damage, it will take its toll and they should succumb."

"Like driving a stake through a vampire." Alex tried not to think about how crazy that sentence sounded.

"I guess." Becca leaned on the porch railing that wrapped around the house.

Alex reloaded his weapon and leveled it on the closest of the revenants, waiting for them to stop moving. It spasmed with one last twitch before finally falling still.

3 active revenants defeated, 432 experience awarded.
You have reached level 6.
926 experience to next level.
You have 1 additional attribute point to set.

"Thank god." He lowered his gun and dropped his point into constitution. "What in the apocalypse were those?"

"I have no idea." Becca stared at the corpses.

"Whatever they are…" Alex trailed off as he looked in her direction. He spun away from her a second later, realizing that she wasn't wearing any pants. "Ah, yeah, so—"

"Yes, Alex, I'm not wearing pants. I haven't for days." She stepped off the porch and wandered over to the corpses, apparently not caring about her attire. "I wasn't expecting to have to rush out of the house to rescue anyone and thought you'd prefer that I not waste time to throw something on."

"Thanks for that, I guess." He shrugged. "But, um, why?"

"I haven't worn anything but pajamas for months, as I have been locked in my apartment back in Seattle. I'm not comfortable in jeans yet." She crouched down to look at the revenants. "Plus it's the apocalypse, who's going to tell me to put on pants? I do what I want."

"You have a point." Alex let out a laugh. "I just hadn't thought of the apocalypse as pants optional."

"I know, right? Who knew?" She stepped back up the stairs and placed her hand on the door of the house. "On second thought. Examining corpses really does call for a more formal attire. I'll be back. Do me a favor and go get Dig. He needs to know about this."

Alex turned to the wine cellar's entrance and swallowed. He hadn't gone down there for a few hours. He glanced back at the three bodies on the lawn, worried they might get up again. A chill slithered across the back of his neck as he shook off the fear. He'd already received experience for them. There was no coming back after that. With the revenants dealt with for now, he trudged off toward the cellar.

"I suppose we can't let him stay down there forever." Alex pushed through the door.

A cool darkness greeted him as he descended the stairs into a long room filled with racks of bottles. Alex walked past the shelves, stopping occasionally to examine a label here and there. The closer he got to the room at the far end of the cellar, the more he lagged at the racks of alcohol.

Finally, he claimed a bottle from a shelf and stepped toward the door at the end of the aisle. He sighed as a hungry moan emanated from the other side only to be followed by a blood-curdling scream.

Light spilled from the crack beneath the door. He hesitated as he placed his hand on the door handle and a desperate word bled through the wood to meet his ears.

"Braaaaiiiiiinnnnnssss…"

CHAPTER TWO

"Braaaaiiiiiinnnnnssss..."

Digby scoffed at the absurdity of the video he was watching on the tablet that Rebecca had salvaged from the crashed kestrel. "That's ridiculous. I would never behave like that, even if I was trying to eat someone's brain."

Digby looked up from his place, sitting on a sofa with his knees tucked close to his chest as Alex entered the small room he'd been staying in at the back of the wine cellar. The boy was wearing another one of those ugly floral shirts he'd found in the manor. "Oh, perfect timing, come sit. I have questions."

"Ah, sorry, I can't right— "

"Nonsense, have a seat." He patted the cushion next to him. Asher gave a happy caw from her perch on the back of the sofa. She'd always seemed fond of the boy.

Digby had spent the last two weeks researching the modern world through the lens of every zombie movie that Rebecca had been able to procure from the information network she had access to. In the process, he'd learned an enormous amount about the world, from society and technology to culture and curse words.

His current movie wasn't as good as some of the videos he'd watched in the last week, but it wasn't the worst. His favorite had been a comedic one from his homeland starring a skinny bloke and his chubby friend. He found it amazing that humanity could see so much humor within the horror of the situation. Something about that spoke to him.

The videos also helped him understand the relationship humanity had with death. Sometimes their outlook was bleak and nihilistic, while others held on to hope. He enjoyed the latter far more. Being depressed was no fun.

At the very least, he was learning more about how they might survive in their current situation and rebuild for the future. Plus, watching movies was better than staring at the wall doing nothing for hours.

With each video he devoured, he'd also accumulated a ridiculous number of questions that he lacked the context to figure out. Fortunately, he had an apprentice to fill in the blanks. Together he and Alex had spent hours watching and rewatching scenes as he bombarded him with questions. Judging from the boy's waning enthusiasm, it wasn't his favorite activity. Despite that, it was necessary. Especially since he had barely seen Rebecca since they arrived at the vineyard.

Digby had been ravenous after they'd crashed and spent a couple days trapped in a crate after escaping Seattle. He was just glad that his apprentice had found an edible corpse when they reached the vineyard. He had been watching movies and laying low ever since.

"No, seriously." Alex remained in the doorway. "We need you to see something outside."

"Alright, what do you need, boy?" Digby paused the movie playing on the tablet with a stylus, since he had trouble working its screen with his left hand. The claws on his right hand didn't work at all.

Alex's shoulders fell. "I should probably give up on getting you to stop calling me boy."

"Probably." Digby tossed the tablet on the cushion beside

him and stretched his legs before placing his lone foot on the floor. A peg-leg of crystalized blood touched down beside it. The missing limb had actually subtracted a full eight points from his attributes, bringing back the unstable balance he'd had back when he'd first thawed out in Seattle. He would have to either add points as he leveled up or find a replacement foot. He eyed Alex's left leg for a moment.

"Hmm, looks to be about the right size."

"What?" Alex blinked.

"What?" Digby pretended like he hadn't just been thinking about cutting off his apprentice's foot to replace his own. He gave the boy an innocent smile. Obviously, he wouldn't really steal someone's foot, or at least, he wouldn't steal body parts from someone he liked. Standing up, his knees cracked loud enough to send a shudder through Alex's body. "Sorry, I guess I've been sitting in the same position for longer than I realized."

"You don't get uncomfortable like that?" Alex winced as another one of Digby's joints popped.

"Strangely, no. One of the perks of being dead, I guess." Digby reached for the coat that he'd tossed over the arm of the sofa. He watched his maximum mana on his HUD jump up the moment he shrugged it on.

MP: 163/213

Checking his appearance in a mirror leaning against one wall, he gave thanks to the fictional Goblin King that had been the garment's previous owner. The coat's collar wrapped his neck with a wicked curve, reinforcing his image as a powerful necromancer. Combined with the horned formation of his bone armor that sat upon his forehead like a crown, and the gauntlet of interlocking plates that covered his right hand, he was starting to like the way he looked.

Of course, he was still missing his nose, but that was still the least of his concerns. He pushed a few locks of white hair from his face and straightened the vest he wore under his coat before standing tall.

"Return of the Living Dead, huh?" Alex interrupted his attempt to admire himself in the mirror as he gestured to the tablet sitting on the sofa.

"Indeed, how did you know?" Digby patted his shoulder to call Asher up to her perch. The deceased albino raven flapped up to his shoulder with an affectionate caw. Digby gave her head a pat.

"Return of the Living Dead is the only series I know of where the zombies actually say brains." Alex turned back the way he'd come and headed for the cellar's exit.

"Exactly, it's completely unrealistic." Digby followed, limping behind him. "I was just thinking that I've never felt the need to moan the word brains whilst pursuing prey." He scoffed. "Utterly ridiculous."

"Can't argue with that." Alex shrugged. "It was never my favorite. I saw it when I was fourteen at a friend's house."

"That's oddly specific." Digby arched an eyebrow.

"My friend found it in his brother's room and wanted to watch it because of the nudity. Seeing a naked lady was a big deal at that age." Alex let out an awkward laugh. "I was super uncomfortable about it, so the memory stuck with me."

"I should say so. It might be the fact that I'm dead, but the fascination you people have with each other's bodies is laughable. Although, that's coming from someone whose only interest in another person's body is whether I can eat it or not. So maybe don't take my word for it." Digby dragged his feet as they approached the door, realizing he hadn't set foot out in the open for over a week. "Anyway, what did you need me to see outside? Skyline hasn't found us or anything, right? I don't want to get caught now that we've made a clean getaway."

"No, nothing like that. Just a bunch of revenants." Alex kept walking.

"What's a revenant?" Digby stopped short.

"That's what we're hoping you can help with." The enchanter climbed the steps of the cellar.

The air of the vineyard had a pleasant earthy aroma that had a calming effect on Digby, though he wasn't sure why. Rebecca was waiting for him on the porch of the main house, tying her hair back in a haphazard manner with a loop of stretchy string hanging from her mouth. She walked to the far end of the space, probably avoiding the radioactive aura that he was still emitting. He hoped it would go away when he decided to use the stored energy he'd absorbed to enhance a spell.

Three pale corpses lay in the grass with shards of ice melting in their wounds.

"That's new." Digby eyed the bodies.

That was when a loud screech echoed in the distance followed by a second cry ringing out from the other side of the vineyard.

"I'm not going to like this, am I?" Digby stared out over the rows of darkened grapevines.

"No, Dig, you're not." Rebecca stepped away from the railing, glancing at what he assumed was the mana value on her HUD.

"Shit, those three must have drawn two more with all their screeching earlier." Alex pulled his rifle off his shoulder and backed toward the house.

"I'm a bit confused." Digby raised one claw as if to press pause on the situation.

"So are we." Alex rushed over to the storage building that he'd been keeping a small horde in. "We just got attacked by those three and it sounds like more are on the way."

"Alright then." Digby spun back toward the wine cellar. "I'll be cowering in my room where it's safe. Anyone care to join me?"

"I don't think it's safe down there." Alex got ready to open the storage area's gate. "These things don't seem like the type to let a few doors stop them."

"Yeah, they're fast as hell." Rebecca retreated toward the front door of the house.

"Oh joy." Digby rolled his eyes and tested his weight on his injured leg. "We fight then." He checked his HUD to make sure he'd absorbed enough mana to fill up to his max after putting on his coat.

COVEN
DIGBY: MP: 213/213
ALEX: MP: 149/149
REBECCA: MP: 56/141
ASHER: MP: 34/34

"I'm low on mana." Rebecca vanished through the door of the manor only to holler back as she rushed up the stairs. "I'll support you from the air." A drone flew out one of the windows of the second floor a moment later.

Without skipping a beat, Digby nodded to Alex, giving him the go ahead to open the storage building. The enchanter disengaged the latch before pulling the gate open. A horde of zombies poured out. Digby cast Control on each, bringing his minion counter up to seventeen while dropping his mana down to one forty-five points remaining.

The many teeth were ready.

Digby raised his right hand and opened his maw. The shadowy gateway to the dimensional space of his void that held the remains of everyone he'd eaten appeared in his palm. He cast Forge, sending tendrils of black blood creeping along the fingers of his bone gauntlet until they reached his claws to form five razor sharp talons. His mana dropped another twenty points.

With that, he was ready for anything.

"They're coming from the south." Rebecca's drone drifted by overhead.

"Alright, let's see what these things are capable o—Oh, holy hell!" Digby's jaw hit the ground as a half dozen pale forms burst from the grapevines at a full sprint. He'd seen a few movies over the course of the week where the zombies could run. Those had been the scariest. The only weakness his kind had was that they were slow and uncoordinated.

"Get in the air." He nudged Asher off his shoulder, sending her up where it was safe. He had dropped a couple more points into her perception since the battle in Seattle, but her defense was still lacking. She was a little too frail to be useful in a fight. Once she was safe, he drew back his claws and sent his horde into the fray with a wild battle cry.

"Rend!"

To his surprise, the entire group of enemies simply blew past him and his minions without giving any of them a second look.

"Wait, what?" He analyzed the foes to learn more.

Active Revenant, Common, Neutral.

Digby spun around and arched an eyebrow as the creatures raced past his minions in the direction of his tender apprentice. Alex put three down with a barrage of enchanted bullets, his rifle clicking empty a second later.

"Oh no." Digby cast Burial, finally having access to the bare earth required for the spell now that he'd left Seattle. Dirt swelled beneath the feet of one of the revenants, opening a hole roughly the size of an average grave. It fell into the pit, taking a second down with it as it flailed. The earth filled back in to trap them both beneath six feet of dirt. Digby let out an approving laugh at the effectiveness of the spell, having finally gotten a chance to test it on an enemy.

The last revenant stopped short, turning back to him. The Heretic Seed updated its relationship toward him to hostile now that he had attacked.

"That makes sense." Digby opened his maw beneath the creature's feet and forged a blood shard that shot up through its chin to burst from the top of its skull. "That wasn't so bad now."

Digby hadn't been aware of the conflict with the three revenants that Alex and Rebecca had killed while he was down in the wine cellar, leading him to watch his HUD in curiosity of how much the foes might be worth. He arched an eyebrow a few seconds later when none came.

"What's this now?" He approached the creature that he'd impaled on a spike of blood. It twitched for a few more seconds before finally going limp.

1 active revenant defeated, 114 experience awarded.

"Crap, they're healing." Alex reloaded his rifle and backed away from the three creatures he'd shot a moment before.

"What?" Digby's face fell as all three began to twitch. He watched in horror as their wounds knit themselves back together like someone had cast a Regeneration on them. "That's not fair."

"I know." Alex recast Enchant Weapon on his gun. "Even with magic, I can only keep them down for a few seconds."

"New plan then." Digby turned back to his horde. "Rend them to pieces. But leave me the heads." It was always good to have a spare skull to create Cremation bombs with in a pinch.

All seventeen zombies piled onto the creatures before they were able to get back up. Digby couldn't help but notice the hunger inside him stir, as if the revenants were somehow still edible despite their condition.

He gave the order to feed, surprised when his zombies dug in without hesitation, proving his theory true. Alex recoiled at the sight, still not used to seeing the dead eat.

3 common revenants defeated, 342 experience awarded.

Another few seconds went by before another message came in.

2 common revenants defeated, 228 experience awarded.

He assumed it was from the two creatures he'd trapped beneath the earth and brushed his hands together as if finishing up a job well done before repeating his declaration of, "That wasn't so bad."

"We have more incoming." Rebecca's drone passed by overhead. "From the west and east. Can't confirm the numbers, but there's a lot."

"Seriously?" Alex complained as he swallowed a mouthful of purified water, probably to quell the nausea caused by the mix of radiation and the sight of Digby's horde feeding.

Another twelve revenants sprinted from behind the vineyard's manor before six more burst from one of the rows of vines. Grape leaves littered the ground in their wake as they chittered and screeched. Digby could feel the vibrations of the stampede through the ground with his remaining foot. He checked his mana.

MP: 85/213

His eyes bulged; he'd already blown through two thirds of his magic. If it wasn't for the Goblin King's coat, he would have been almost out already.

"New plan!" Digby spun back toward the house and beckoned to his apprentice. "Retreat!"

Alex nearly tripped over himself as he scrambled toward the manor. Digby grabbed two of the severed heads from the lawn that his horde had left for him and hobbled his way to the porch. He cursed his peg-leg the entire way up the stairs.

Glancing back, he ordered his horde, "Rend them all! Don't let a single foe through!"

With that, he leapt through the front door and slammed it closed as soon as Alex was safe inside.

"What's the plan here?" Rebecca leaned her head over the railing of the second floor above.

"Don't die!" Digby stepped back into the manor's entry hall.

Rebecca let out an annoyed huff before ducking into her room upstairs again to watch the battle from the bird's-eye view of her drone.

"Do you think the horde can win?" Alex backed up beside him as the sound of inhuman screeching mixed with the hungry howls of Digby's zombies outside.

"Probably not." He tossed one of the heads he carried to the floor to use later and prepared to throw the other as one of the revenants outside approached the front window. Several experience messages flashed across his vision. He lost track of how many. Digby glanced at the minion counter at the corner of his HUD as it ticked down to a flat zero.

Rebecca shouted from her room upstairs. "Get ready!"

Before her words were finished, the sound of shattering glass came from the sitting area to the left. A revenant tumbled into the room, righting itself in an instant like a cat.

"Watch the windows." Digby stepped in front of his apprentice with his claws at the ready. The creature lunged only to get a talon buried in its chin. With a hard twist, Digby snapped the blood forged claw from his finger to leave it lodged in his foe's brain. "Try healing that."

Alex's rifle barked behind him, along with more glass breaking. Digby spun back to the nearest window, finding another two enemies climbing through. He tossed one of the heads he'd brought inside to his clawed gauntlet and cast Cremation. Green fire consumed the flesh around the skull. He let it cook for a second to ignite the contents inside before lobbing the macabre explosive at the pair of revenants. The skull screamed with pressure, bursting on impact to splash emerald fire across both creatures.

Pale skin cracked and popped as their strange regenerative ability attempted to keep up with the damage. They toppled to the porch outside the window shortly after, unable to fight off the flames. It was as if their healing ability had somehow run out of power. His mind put two and two together.

They need mana just like us, and they run out just as easy.

Digby spun to tell Alex what he'd realized just as his rifle clicked empty. His apprentice flew through the air a second later, landing on a small table that smashed under the weight of his wiry body. A revenant threw itself onto the fallen enchanter in an instant.

"No, you don't." Digby limped to his apprentice's aid and drove a talon into the back of the creature's skull, snapping the claw off in its brain. The wound pulsated as the foe spasmed. A few seconds later it fell limp across Alex's lap. That was when the sound of more glass breaking came from the second floor. Digby's head snapped up toward Rebecca's room.

A sudden crash followed, like a body hitting a wall. Digby leaped toward the stairs as Alex kicked the revenant's corpse off of his legs. They raced forward as a pale form slammed into the railing above. It tipped over the side to crash into the floor below with a damp splat. Digby stared down at the icicles sticking out of its body. Rebecca stumbled out of her room above, limping down the stairs while clutching one arm. A gash ran down her shoulder.

"God damn it." She winced just before a shimmer of magic swept over her body. Digby caught her mana value drop by ten as the wound began to close, leaving her with enough left for one or two more healing spells.

Asher landed on the railing above, cawing at the window behind them, apparently having flown in through the broken one upstairs in Rebecca's room. Digby thanked her for the warning and snatched the other severed head he'd brought inside with him off the floor. He lit it up with Cremation before he even looked at the threat.

His eyes widened as soon as he turned around, finding another four revenants climbing through the fire on the porch from his last spell. Their pants caught fire, but they didn't stop, letting their healing ability repair the damage to their legs while they attempted to climb through the broken window. The remnants of a bullet wound on one of their heads vanished, replaced by pristine flesh. They must have been the ones that Alex had been shooting at.

Taking advantage while they were grouped close together, Digby tossed the flaming skull in his hand. It exploded in a cascade of emerald fire to engulf three of them. Digby lunged forward to slam his remaining talons into the chest of the last of the creatures. He broke them off with a hard crack before slamming his peg-leg into its chest to kick it back into the growing fire.

"Is that… all of them?" Alex panted, leaning on the railing that led to the second floor.

Everyone stood still, listening for more. The sound of burning wood filled the silence as the blaze on the porch continued to spread across the front of the house.

"I think so." Rebecca let out a breath when nothing else came.

"Thank all that is holy." Digby checked his mana.

MP: 55/213

He cringed. "That was close."

The fire behind him spat and popped as it climbed up the dry wood of the wall. Digby cringed again, realizing it had already spread too far to be put out by just the three of them. Slowly, he turned back to Rebecca, expecting her to scold him for throwing fire around willy-nilly.

Instead, she just sighed and turned back upstairs. "I'll get my things and meet you out front."

"That might be a good idea." Alex rushed up the stairs behind her to retrieve whatever he didn't want to burn.

Digby glanced down at the experience massages that he'd been ignoring.

You have reached level 19.
3,487 experience to next level.
You have 1 additional attribute point to set.

"Well, at least that's something." Digby swept his eyes across the room. The corpses of several revenants littered the floor, along with broken glass and furniture. The carnage made him feel a little better about setting the house on fire. He stared into the blaze, watching as the emerald flames licked at the wall, their color shifting to a more natural orange.

"It was nice while it lasted," he let out a breathless sigh, "but we can't stay here."

CHAPTER THREE

Digby gestured toward the entrance to the winery's cellar where he'd been staying for the last week. "Might I interest you in an underground abode for the night? It's actually quite nice. Some might compare it to a comfortable grave."

Both Alex and Rebecca stared at him whilst standing in front of the burning remains of the house they had been living in. Neither of them seemed enthused about his offer. The pair had soot smeared on their faces and clothing. A satchel lay at each of their feet containing the entirety of their worldly possessions.

"I see you were able to grab your things before the fire reached your rooms."

"Thanks for helping by the way." Rebecca narrowed her eyes at him.

"Well, someone had to stand guard in case more of those revenants came around for a visit, and that just so happened to be me since they don't attack unless provoked." Digby dropped his hands to his hips and puffed out his chest.

"That is true, actually." Alex admitted. "And hey, I'm level eight now, so there's that."

"Yeah, and I just reached seven." Rebecca knelt down to inspect one of her drones as her stomach growled audibly.

"Here, eat something." Alex tossed her a package of food from the stock they had salvaged from the kestrel. "You just jumped up a bunch of levels and your body's working overtime to increase its stats. You're probably starving."

"That's an understatement." She tore the package open and wolfed down its contents, reminding Digby of his own nonexistent table manners.

"Easy, now. Else I might mistake you for one of my zombies."

The ravenous woman glared at him but said nothing.

Digby had gained a level as well, but had decided to hold off until he'd eaten something to allocate his extra point. Considering the fact that his void was nearly empty after raising the rest of his attributes, he didn't want to press his luck. The last thing he needed was to go ravenous because he spent his extra point. He didn't want to get locked in that crate again.

Thinking about food, Digby turned back the few intact corpses on the lawn that hadn't been burnt to a crisp and nudged at the nearest one with his peg-leg. "What the hell did you lot pick a fight with here?"

Corpse: Revenant, 114 MP required to animate.
Animate corpse? Yes/No

"Other than something costly to animate, that is?" Digby crouched down to examine the corpse after refusing the Heretic Seed's offer to resurrect the creature.

"Wish I knew." Rebecca shifted her irritated stare from Digby to the revenant, letting him off the hook for burning down their temporary home.

"Could they be a new mutation?" Alex crouched down at Digby's side.

"No, they're definitely not zombies." Digby reached out and grabbed hold of the monster's hand.

"How can you tell?" Alex stepped closer.

"Well, first of all," Digby proceeded to bite off a fingertip, "they're edible."

"Aww, jeez." Alex looked away. "Warn me before you do that."

"Sorry, I thought you'd be used to it by now." Digby shrugged as he chewed and considered the possibilities. As troublesome as the creatures had been to deal with, having an edible lifeform other than humans was actually a blessing. Ever since discovering the mutation path of the Ravager, he had been wondering how he would be able to get stronger.

His options were powerful, but they all had a steep cost that he wasn't sure he wanted to pay. Hunting innocent people for resources hadn't been high on his list. Then again, if those innocent people had already become monsters on their own, that would certainly expand the menu. The only question was, where did these revenants come from?

That was when the obvious answer hit him.

"Skyline." His mouth fell into severe frown as he spoke the word.

"What?" Rebecca stepped closer.

"It's the spell." Digby looked up at her. "The one that they needed my help to cast. It has to be. Henwick had said that the curse could be modified to create something stronger that they could control." He poked one of the corpses with a claw. "I'm willing to bet that these are what they were trying to create."

"That would make sense." Alex nodded.

"If that's the case, it would explain why all online activity came to such an abrupt stop only a day after Seattle." Rebecca pulled her laptop from the bag at her feet before sitting down in the grass. The screen lit up her face as she opened it. "In the first twenty hours of the curse's outbreak, there was still plenty of internet activity reporting that zombies were everywhere and spreading. Then, around dusk on the second day, it all went quiet, like everyone just vanished."

"Or died," Alex added.

"Indeed. Considering how much trouble these revenants gave us, if they have gone widespread then anyone without magic wouldn't stand a chance. The creatures would be able to end humanity almost immediately."

"So that's it then." Becca scrolled through some information. "Henwick and his people must have hijacked the curse somehow and made an edit to create a different monster when infected."

"Is that even possible?" Alex stood back up.

"Probably. The Heretic Seed that created all this appears to be some form of lost technology." Rebecca stared off into the middle distance. "Who says the curse can't be hacked? Especially by an organization that has apparently been studying magic."

"Damn." Alex flicked his eyes back to Digby. "But how would they do that without you?"

"Hmm." Digby ran his left hand across Asher's feathers as she pecked at one of the corpses. "I've been thinking about that since Henwick said he didn't need me anymore, and the answer is stupidly simple. All he would have to do is recruit a new mage with that Guardian Core system of his and get a zombie to give them a nibble. When they reanimated, they would be just like me. A zombie with access to magic and a pure mana balance."

"Except for the fact that all their attributes would drop to zero and leave them a mindless mess." Rebecca added. "You only regained your intelligence because the Heretic Seed awarded you ten points of experience for every year you spent frozen in the Arctic."

"There's a mutation to get around that." Digby opened his maw and shoved in one of the revenant's hands. "The Path of the Leader will give you seven intelligence and let you recall some of the memories you had as a human. And I'm sure whatever tier is above Leader has more ways to bring someone up to speed too. All Henwick would have to do is execute a bunch of people and feed his zombie mage a steady diet of hearts and minds."

"How many people would he have to kill?" Alex winced in preparation for the answer.

"Oh, several dozen, possibly a hundred or more." Digby closed his maw, taking the revenant's arm off at the shoulder.

"That sounds like an acceptable sacrifice for Skyline." Rebecca sighed, wrapping her arms around herself as if she was cold.

"Indeed. They're the real monsters here." Digby moved on to the deceased revenant's other arm.

"Wait," Alex chimed in. "You said that online activity stopped around dusk; do you mean here in the U.S. or everywhere?"

"Everywhere." Rebecca glanced at her laptop. "Online activity went dead just as the sun was setting in their time zone. I thought it might have been because it was harder to see and thus more dangerous, but now I'm thinking it has something to do with these things."

"That sounds about right." Alex stared out across the vineyard. "The Heretic Seed labeled the three I stumbled upon earlier as dormant. They were still hostile, but they seemed to be held back by something. Once the sun went down, they attacked and the Seed relabeled them as active."

"So they're nocturnal. Maybe that's what Henwick meant by creating something stronger but easier to control." Digby tapped a claw on his chin. "These things must have weaknesses that his people can exploit, like sunlight or something related to the daytime."

"Let's just hope we can do the same." Rebecca snapped her laptop closed. "If these things have come this far from the cities, then they are probably everywhere."

"Indeed, the Heretic Seed lists them as common, so there must be a lot of them out and about." Digby nodded.

"I hate to say it, but we should take Dig up on his offer and spend the night in the cellar. We'll head out at dawn since this place has been," Rebecca glowered at Digby, "incinerated."

"I said I was sorry." He avoided making eye contact.

"No, you didn't," she pushed back.

"Oh yes, you're right. I didn't." Digby shrugged without adding an apology.

"We should head in then." Alex picked up his bag and made his way to the cellar door. "We can come up with a plan in the morning."

"A plan for what?" Digby furrowed his brow.

"Ah, to, you know," Alex slowed to a stop and turned back to him and Rebecca, "stop Skyline, and like, save the world?"

"Why would we do that?" Digby stood back up.

"Because they did all this?" The enchanter sounded confused.

"Well, yes, but I don't see what part of this makes it our responsibility to deal with." Digby gestured to the corpses on the ground.

"Then what do we do about all this?" Alex dropped his bag

"We do nothing." Digby nodded at his own suggestion.

"What?" Alex looked to Rebecca for an opinion.

"Dig has a point." She tilted her head to one side before tipping back in the other direction. "Things might be different if this was a week ago. If we had magic before all this happened, we could have slowed the spread or tried something to stop the curse. But at this point, Skyline has already won."

"Not to mention Henwick has had eight hundred years to grow stronger." Digby shrugged. "I'm no pushover, but I'm certainly not a match for him."

"True, but we are leveling fast." Alex stared at the ground. "And I'm getting stronger."

"That's nice. But look around." Digby swept a hand through the air. "There isn't a world left to save. What good would picking a fight with Skyline do now?"

"I don't know." Alex shrugged, showing his naiveté.

"All we can do is take things one day at a time." Rebecca yawned. "And what we need now is somewhere new to stay that can be fortified. Not to mention food. We can't just live off grapes and wine."

"You're half right. It's not enough to just to find somewhere safe and survive. No, we have to find a home. Someplace that we can claim as our own. Skyline may have won, but that doesn't mean we've lost." Digby stood a little taller, trying to give them some hope. "I have no intention of hiding and scrounging for crumbs when we have the power to carve out a place for ourselves in this world. All we need to do is find somewhere worth our efforts."

"That's it?" Alex didn't seem to get the message.

"For now." Digby nodded before raising a claw. "Once we have the basics in hand, we can see about increasing our power. I may not be keen on starting a war with Henwick, but that doesn't mean I'll let us be caught with our pants down."

"And how do you suggest we do that? Just go out hunting and hope we level up?" Rebecca leaned back on her hands.

"Yes, but also," Digby stared up into the night sky, "remember how I told you that the Heretic Seed spoke to me back in Seattle after that brute of a man, Manning, crushed my skull?"

"Yeah." Rebecca and Alex both nodded.

"Well, something it said got me thinking." Digby lowered his gaze back down to his fellow heretics. "Where is the rest of the original Seed's monolith?"

"Didn't you say it exploded?" Alex furrowed his brow.

"It did, but that doesn't mean it's gone." Digby placed his gauntlet over his heart. "There is a shard embedded in my chest, along with another one that had been stuck in Henwick's arm. So my question is, where is the rest of the damned thing? If Skyline was able create their Guardian Core from just one fragment, what could we do if we found more?"

"Would the other pieces even be functional?" Rebecca leaned forward.

"I don't know, but when I spoke to the Seed it didn't even know what it was, or who created it. When I asked, it suggested that we might find out more if we found more of its pieces. The way I see it, someone created our rings and they had access to the monolith. So I'm thinking if we can gather enough pieces, we might be able to do the same."

"You want to create more heretics, then?" Rebecca stared down at the runes on her finger left behind by the obsidian ring that had given her magic.

"Indeed." Digby grinned. "If we can stay hidden and grow our numbers along with our powers, then we might have something to work with if Henwick ever discovers us."

"So we, what? Go to England?" Alex pointed in a seemingly random direction as if gesturing to Digby's homeland.

"Maybe not." Rebecca flicked her eyes up to Digby. "It's been eight hundred years since the Seed's monolith exploded. The fragments could be anywhere by now. They might not even be in Europe anymore."

"True, but I'm betting there's a clue out there somewhere." Digby shrugged. "But again, that little treasure hunt will have to wait, considering I just burnt down our house here."

"I'm starting to see a pattern." Rebecca rubbed at her temples. "You better not burn down the next place we find."

"I'll try." Digby gave her a crooked grin that implied that he was making no promises. "We'll just have to find a place worthy of me."

"I'd settle for anywhere with a bed right now." Alex yawned.

"Speaking of, I'm going to try to catch a few hours of sleep before dawn." Rebecca picked up her things to bring them to the cellar.

"Good idea. I wouldn't mind watching a couple videos before we have to leave." Digby sauntered toward the door behind her.

"Oh no you don't." Rebecca spun and jabbed a finger in his direction. "You're staying outside."

"Well, I never…" Digby stomped his peg-leg.

"You said it yourself, someone has to stay outside and keep watch, and the revenants don't attack you without being provoked."

Digby's face fell. "I did say that, didn't I."

"Besides, I don't want to have to wake up Alex every couple hours to purify water for me because being too close to you is giving me radiation poisoning. As it is, I've had to blow my extra points on constitution."

"Ah, yes, that is also true." Digby stared down at his radioactive body.

"Indeed." Rebecca said in a tone clearly meant to sound like him.

"She does have a point." Alex backed her up.

"Alright, fine, but someone needs to bring me my tablet, so I don't get bored out here." Alex disappeared into the cellar, returning with what he'd asked for. "Thank you, boy. I'm sure I will have plenty of questions by the time you wake up."

"Yay." The enchanter blew out a heavy sigh as he headed back inside with Rebecca.

Digby swept his gaze across to the burning manor before dropping his eyes to the revenant corpses that littered the lawn.

At least there was something to eat.

CHAPTER FOUR

Digby sat in the grass as the embers of the vineyard's destroyed manor burned themselves out, leaving a smoldering shell remaining where the once-grand building had stood. He and Asher ate what they could of the revenants that hadn't been burnt in the blaze.

Finding one of the creature's legs in relatively good condition, he clapped his hands together and cast Forge on the corpse. All at once, the body's blood supply flooded to its leg where it formed a razor-sharp blade that severed the extremity just below the knee to leave a well-formed replacement part. He had reattached a finger once, so why not a foot?

Hmm, now I just need a place to put it.

Digby dropped his eyes down to his peg-leg and opened his maw to shove his foot inside. He braced himself and snapped the gateway shut to sever everything he didn't need. It wasn't comfortable, but it didn't really hurt either. Sitting down, he placed the revenant's foot against what was left of his shin like he was putting on a boot. Once he had everything lined up, he cast Necrotic Regeneration to stick the two together. A moment later he stood back up.

There now, that should do it. Digby winced, realizing that something felt off. Brushing the sensation to the back of his mind, he took a step forward only to have the foot wobble and snap off like it hadn't fully attached itself.

"The hell?" Digby tumbled to one side, getting a puzzled look from Asher as she picked at a brain a few feet away. He rolled over and reached for the missing foot again. "Alright, let's try this one more time."

Another three attempts were met with the same result. The foot simply fell off as soon as he put any weight on it, sending Digby tumbling down each time. Eventually he just Forged another peg-leg and threw the spare foot into the grapevines in frustration.

"I didn't want a monster's foot anyway." Digby sat in the grass and stewed for a bit before thinking about the problem more. "Why didn't it work?"

It wasn't the first time he'd reattached something he'd lost after finding a replacement from a corpse. That was when he remembered how he'd lost the foot. That holy knight back in Seattle, Manning, had lopped it off with a sword carrying some sort of spell that purified curses. He ground his teeth at the thought, realizing that the injury may have been more severe than he'd realized.

It was possible that the wound wouldn't allow for him to reattach a new foot that was already inflicted with the curse, or worse, he might not be able to repair the damage at all. He made a note to find an untainted human that wasn't in need of both feet to check to be sure.

Eventually, he just let out a breathless sigh and glanced to the circle floating at the edge of his vision to call his status window up.

STATUS
Name: Digby Graves
Race: Zombie
Heretic Class: Necromancer

Mana: 220/220
Mana Composition: Pure
Current Level: 19 (3,487 experience to next level.)

ATTRIBUTES
Constitution: 17
Defense: 23
Strength: 21
Dexterity: 21
Agility: 14
Intelligence: 27
Perception: 21
Will: 25

AILMENTS
Radioactive

"Hmm." He still had a way to go before he would reach his next level, reenforcing his concern about encountering anyone from Skyline. There was no telling how powerful Henwick or his vassals had become over the years. As it was, Digby was missing a foot and ran out of mana every few minutes. He just wasn't capable of sustaining significant offense yet.

After polishing off what he could of the revenant's corpses, he dropped his extra point from his last level into agility. Standing up to stretch, he felt a little more balanced. It was still a long way off before he could walk or run normally again, but he was getting there. After attempting an uncoordinated jog across the lawn with mixed results, he brought up a list of the mutations available to him. At least they gave him a slight advantage over Henwick's guardians.

MUTATION PATH, RAVAGER, AVAILABLE MUTATIONS:
SHEEP'S CLOTHING
Description: Mimic a human appearance to lull your prey into a false sense of security.

Resource Requirements: 10 flesh.

TEMPORARY MASS

Description: Consume void resources to weave a structure of muscle and bone around your body to enhance strength and defense until it is either released or its structural integrity has been compromised enough to disrupt functionality.

Resource Requirements: 25 flesh and 10 bone.

Attribute Effects: +11 strength, +9 defense

Limitations: All effects are temporary. Once claimed, each use requires 2 flesh and 1 bone.

HELL'S MAW

Description: Increase the maximum size of your void gateway at will.

Resource Requirements: 30 viscera.

Attribute Effects: +3 perception, +6 will.

Limitations: Once claimed, each use requires the expenditure of 1 MP for every 5 inches of diameter beyond your maw's default width.

DISSECTION

Description: When consuming prey, you may gain a deeper understanding of how bodies are formed. This will allow you to spot and exploit a target's weaknesses instinctively.

Resource Requirements: 10 mind and 5 heart.

Attribute Effects: +3 intelligence, +6 perception.

AVAILABLE RESOURCES

Sinew: 6

Flesh: 5

Bone: 4

Viscera: 6

Heart: 6

Mind: 6

Digby frowned. He still had a way to go there as well. He shook his head. There was no sense worrying about it now. With nothing left to eat, he beckoned to Asher and headed over to the winery's delivery van sitting to the side of the storage building. He doubted Rebecca and his apprentice would sleep for long considering their situation, but he assumed he still had time to watch something on his tablet.

It wasn't that he was lazy—well, he was—but also, he really was learning a lot. Not to mention, it helped him avoid looking foolish. There was nothing worse than saying something in front of his accomplices, only to find out that he was using a word wrong or had made an assumption based on his eight-hundred-year-old education.

Of course, his intelligence was much higher than it had been before he'd died. Though, after comparing the attributes that Rebecca had started with to his own and Alex's, his theory that he hadn't been that sharp to begin with was beginning to hold true. As he understood things, it seemed like twenty was a good estimate of what a strong value would be for any normal human. Realizing that, his intelligence was merely a bit above average. Still, he wondered what would happen if he continued to place his points there. Would it change him if he began to approach a genius level?

Digby shrugged off the question and crawled into the delivery van, taking off his coat before tossing it in the back. He turned back and patted the floor beside him. Asher flew in behind him with a happy caw. Together they settled into a corner behind the driver's seat, leaving the rear door open to keep a lookout for enemies. Before starting another video, he brought up his feathered minion's status as well.

Name: Asher
Race: Zombie (Avian)
Mutation Path: Leader

Mana: 34/34
Mana Composition: Pure

ATTRIBUTES
Constitution: 0
Defense: 0
Strength: 2
Dexterity: 0
Agility: 8
Intelligence: 6
Perception: 3
Will: 4

AILMENTS
Deceased

He wasn't able to see her void's contents, but he hoped she was close to reaching the next mutation within the Leader's path.

With nothing else to think about, he gave Asher's head a pat and leaned back to pass the time until dawn.

A few episodes of a depressing zombie drama later, a yawning Rebecca appeared at the open door of the van. Asher cawed at her intrusion as she tossed a bag in the back. Alex emerged from the cellar a few minutes later, carrying one of her two drones. He set it down beside the van and went back to grab the other as Rebecca went to work.

Digby scooped up Asher and crawled out of the van while the rest of his coven prepared the vehicle for travel. The sun was just beginning to peek over the horizon to shine across the fields of grapevines. Digby watched as the clouds refracted an ephemeral glow. They would have to find somewhere equally majestic to call home. He smiled. Yes, they would need to find somewhere worthy.

It took a little over an hour for Rebecca to outfit the van the way she wanted it. A battery salvaged from the kestrel they'd escaped Seattle in was hooked into the back, giving them about a week of electricity to run her equipment and laptop. Apparently, it could regain its charge by being left out in the sun for a day or so. Both of her drones were set into a dock that she and Alex had strapped to the roof. They covered them with a tarp after Rebecca mentioned she was concerned about Skyline noticing them with a satellite.

As Digby understood it, humanity had placed machines above the clouds that could watch anything going on below. The idea that someone could be observing anything anywhere was terrifying. Though it seemed that people had gotten used to the idea. Despite that, it made sense to stay out of sight as much as possible.

Digby busied himself while they worked by wrapping several bottles of wine from the cellar in refuse bags. According to Alex, the plastic material would keep its contents dry even if submerged. Once they were wrapped up tight, he slipped a few dozen bottles into his maw for safe keeping.

As a zombie, he no longer had a taste for alcohol, or anything else for that matter, but he figured the bottles might prove valuable for trading if they ran into other humans. All they would have to do was wash them off and unwrap them.

One of the activities he'd busied himself with over their time at the vineyard had been practicing placing things within his void and calling them back out. There was an element of focus and concentration involved. Currently, he had a fifty percent success rate as half the time he produced random bones that he'd eaten. He assumed his ability would improve with his attributes, possibly perception.

It was a little weird to store things in what was essentially his dimensional stomach, but if he could get better at retrieving items, he could consistently carry large quantities of supplies and weapons without being weighed down. Alex had called it his necrotic bag of holding. Most people would have found the idea disturbing, but then again, no one had to know where he stored things.

The sun climbed higher, reminding Digby that they were on a clock. He checked the time on his tablet. It was already seven in the morning.

"So where are we off to?" He limped his way back to the van as Rebecca and Alex were finishing up. "You both know the area better than I."

"I figure we could head south for now." Rebecca blew a lock of dark hair from her face after getting her laptop stowed. "But we should stick to the coast."

"Good idea." Alex hefted a plastic bag holding several water bottles. "We'll have to head inland in a few places to avoid the cities, but we should be able to find something secluded somewhere near the sea that might make for a new home."

Once the van was ready to leave, Rebecca slipped a set of body armor on over her shirt and climbed into the passenger seat, ready to head out into the unknown. Alex purified a couple bottles of water to combat the effects of Digby's poisonous aura before taking his place at the wheel. The enchanter was still wearing one of those ugly floral shirts that he'd found in the vineyard's manor.

Digby shook his head. Honestly, there were some things that he wished they hadn't been able to save from the fire.

With the two of them in place, Digby hopped in the back and sat down against the wall. Asher perched on a bag beside him. There were no seats in the cargo area of the van, but Digby didn't really notice any discomfort from remaining on the floor, so it seemed like the best place for him.

Together, the three of them took one last look at the vineyard through the windshield as Alex fired up the engine. In the interest of setting the right mood, Digby thrust a clawed finger out toward the horizon.

"Drive on, my boy, and may we find our new home soon."

He promptly fell over as soon as the van started moving.

CHAPTER FIVE

Becca sipped a bottle of magically purified water, watching her poisoned status vanish as the van headed south. They'd already been on the road for an hour and weren't any closer to finding anywhere that could be fortified.

The internet had become less user friendly as things began to shut down, but she was still able to look up and mark a few locations that might work. Unfortunately, their options were slim. Their big problem was that the majority of suitable buildings were located in the cities where the population prior to the curse was higher. Her expectation was that the monsters would follow suit.

Pulling over for a break outside of Sacramento, Becca launched a drone for what she intended to be a quick flyover to get an idea of the situation. At first glance, the city looked empty, though, after heading deeper, she found both zombies and revenants. A horde of around one hundred of the dead milled about in the open while a smaller number of the newer monsters kept to the shadows that were available.

Becca did a quick estimate in her head based on a guess of the city's pre-apocalypse population. The horde was big, but nowhere near the size of the ones she'd seen back in Seattle. There should have been more. The obvious question hung in her mind. Where did all of the people go?

Thinking about it logically, it wasn't that hard to figure out.

The revenants were certainly more deadly, so it stood to reason that once Henwick hijacked the curse, they would have killed more people than the zombies. Add to that the revs' weakness to sunlight, and the only thing that made sense was that they had gathered somewhere dark during the day. She swallowed hard as she piloted her drone between the buildings. They were probably full of the strange, new creatures. The city's population had to be somewhere after all.

Turning her drone around, she headed back to where she saw the horde only to stop short when she rounded the corner of a building.

"Shit!" She froze as a kestrel filled her laptop's display.

"What's the matter?" Digby sat up in the cargo area behind her.

Becca flicked her eyes to the corner of her drone's display to make sure she had activated its optical camouflage. She blew out a sigh of relief, finding the indicator on. She turned the laptop so the others could see.

"No." Digby recoiled the instant he saw the image.

"What is Skyline doing there?" Alex leaned toward her.

"Do they know we're here?" Digby glanced to the back door of the van with a frantic look in his eyes.

"I don't think so." Becca checked a map of the area. "My drone is a couple miles away. We're close, but not in visual range."

"Well, what are we waiting for? Call your drone back and let's get the hell out of here." Digby slapped the back of Alex's seat. "Start driving."

"Wait." Becca held up a hand as the kestrel began to descend over the horde of zombies she'd spotted earlier.

"What are they doing?" Digby ducked lower to get closer to the screen.

"I don't know." Becca tapped the sticks of the drone's controller to the side, moving it into a position where they could watch.

Skyline's aircraft slowed to hover six feet above the horde. Becca furrowed her brow as the ramp at the rear popped open. A man in full armor walked down, clipping a safety line to the roof as he leaned out over the zombies. Another one of Skyline's people stepped into view to hand him a long pole with a loop of wire at the end.

It was similar to one of those sticks that animal control would use to capture a rabid dog with, except this one had an additional line at the other end that was secured to the interior of the kestrel. The man leaning out the ramp took the pole and slipped the wire around the head of one of the zombies. Becca zoomed in on the monster, finding a formation of bone on its forehead similar to the horned crown that Digby had grown as part of his armor.

"That's a brute." The necromance tapped on the screen, tipping it back in the process.

"I thought brutes were bigger?" Becca adjusted the angel of the laptop's monitor.

"Sometimes they are." Alex chimed in. "But they have two different mutations available. One makes them big while the other just gives them armor. Digby and I fought a bone brute back in Seattle while you were still trapped in your apartment."

"Okay. And what about that one?" Becca pointed to the screen as Skyline's men slipped another wire around the neck of another zombie.

Digby stared at the screen for a second, watching as several other zombies started trying to free the recent captive. "That one's a leader. It looks like it just compelled the others to protect it."

"They aren't having much luck." Alex noted as the zombies failed to remove the wire.

Once both of the monsters had a line secured around their necks, the kestrel ascended, pulling its captives off the ground to dangle beneath it. Becca watched as the aircraft climbed to past her drone. She waited a few seconds to keep her distance before following.

"Careful, Becky." Digby gripped the back of her seat. "Don't want to get spotted."

"Don't worry, the camouflage is active." She brought her drone up to the top of a building where the kestrel seemed to be heading.

"That can't be good." Alex blew out a sigh as a few more of Skyline's men came into view, standing on top of the building next to a cargo container the size of a minivan. One of the men pulled a lever on the side, opening a hatch on top of the container. The kestrel moved in to hover over the opening. Once it was in position, the lines holding the two uncommon zombies released their captives. Both of the monsters dropped straight into the container.

"They're taking in specimens?" Becca considered the possibility.

"What would they want with a pair of uncommon zombies?" Alex tapped on the steering wheel.

"I don't know, but we best be making ourselves scarce before they realize we're here." Digby retreated into the rear of the van. "I'm sure we would make for valuable test subjects as well."

"Agreed." Becca pulled her drone back. "And this gives us another reason to stay out of the larger cities. If Skyline is out here, then they're sure to be visiting other heavily populated areas as well."

Tension filled the van as they waited for the drone to return. Skyline wasn't laying low after dooming the world; no, they were working on something. Alex was right. Whatever it was, it couldn't be good.

They got moving as soon as the drone was secure back in its dock on the roof and covered completely by the tarp. It was unlikely that one of Skyline's teams would spot them, but playing it safe seemed to be the best course of action.

With a little luck, if they were noticed, they would look like any other group of survivors. There were bound to be people still out there, after all. Even with the revenants hunting at night, there should still be people alive somewhere. The world would never be the same, that much was a fact, but the curse would have to try a lot harder to completely erase the human race from the planet.

Becca practically held her breath for the next few hours, only relaxing when they were far enough from the cities and well on their way into the more secluded portions of California. Pretty soon the road was surrounded by nothing but trees on both sides, with mountains passing in the distance.

"How about we check that place out?" Alex pointed to a sign reading 'Gray Fox Campgrounds.'

"Maybe." Becca did a quick search to find out what the area had to offer. According to the photos and reviews that were available, it looked secluded enough that they could spend a few quiet nights. Plus, there was a lodge with a camping supply store where they might find some much-needed gear and supplies. She smirked at the fact that Yelp reviews were actually serving a purpose in the apocalypse. "Gray Fox Campground it is. It's as good a place as any to resupply and figure out our next move." She leaned back over her seat. "How's that sound, Dig? You feel like doing some camping?"

"What?" He sat up straight in a sudden movement as if insulted. "What sort of peasant do you take me for? We have a whole world to pick from. Why would I want to sleep on the ground?"

"You don't even sleep." She shook her head. "And there's a lodge, so don't worry; we'll have a roof over our heads."

"Plus, it's already three in the afternoon," Alex tapped on the clock set into the van's dash. "If we don't find somewhere soon, we might run out of daylight."

"Yeah, better to not take chances. Not to mention you guys might have to clear out some revs while it's still light if the place has any current guests." Becca closed her laptop and put her feet up.

"What do you mean by you guys?" Alex arched an eyebrow at her.

"I'm staying in the van." She pointed toward the roof. "Drone operator, remember. I'll watch your backs from here."

"Oh no you won't." Digby stood up, causing Asher to fall from his lap. "No apprentice of mine is going to sit in here and let their magic waste away."

"I don't remember agreeing to be your apprentice." Becca made a point to look out the window rather than make eye contact with him.

"I beg your pardon. You have a responsibility as a heretic to cultivate your power. Even if only to protect yourself." Digby held on to the ceiling to avoid falling over again. "Clearing out a few revenants will do you good."

"Yeah, yeah, I hear you." Becca sunk into her seat as Alex took the next exit. It wasn't long before the van slowed to a stop surrounded by trees.

"Everyone out." Digby practically leapt from the van, stumbling as if he'd forgotten about his missing foot. He stabilized himself and called to Asher. "Go stretch your wings."

The albino raven nodded her beak and took off into the trees.

Becca reluctantly hopped out of the van, also stumbling when she touched the ground. She had been sitting for too long. Once she was stable, she closed the passenger door only to have a wave of vertigo sweep over her when she looked up at the trees. She immediately leaned against the van. There was something comforting about having a wall behind her. She stared at her HUD and waited for the feeling to pass.

MP: 177/177

Having something constant to focus on helped.

The campground was silent, save for the wind blowing

through the leaves and the occasional chirp of birds. Most importantly, there wasn't a rev or zombie in sight.

The lodge rested further ahead, seemingly empty. Becca pulled a smart phone from her pocket and accessed one of her drones. She wasn't about to walk in anywhere blind. Pulling the tarp from the roof, she launched one unit and set it to hover a hundred feet above her location to give a bird's-eye view of their surroundings. It would also give them a warning if it picked up any motion around the building.

Satisfied with her precautions, she took a step away from the van. She didn't get far before Digby and Alex blew past her like a couple of children.

"Keep up, Becky." The necromancer didn't even look back as he hobbled toward the lodge's shop.

"I'm gonna see if they have archery equipment." Alex kept pace behind him.

Becca shook her head at them both before following.

The lodge was large enough to house a well-stocked supply store and some administrative offices. The building's exterior was designed to look like a log cabin and the inside was decorated with the standard kitsch that one would expect. To her surprise, there wasn't a single monster in the building. She arched an eyebrow. It was strange that nothing was wandering around.

She checked the feed from her drone, sending the surveillance unit up another few hundred feet, finding the rest of the campground empty as well.

"Hmm, we couldn't be that lucky. Could we?"

The place should have been occupied when the curse hit, but other than a few vehicles parked here and there, she saw no sign that anyone had been through recently. There was always a chance that everyone had made a break for the coast in an attempt to escape. She nodded to herself, finding her explanation plausible. She would have to convince Digby and Alex to do a sweep of the surrounding cabins, just in case.

A sudden crash pulled her out of her thoughts and sent her

jumping a foot in the air. She immediately rolled her eyes, catching Digby standing next to a broken display full of hunting knives.

"Who wants a dagger?" The deceased necromancer claimed a blade with a white handle, carved to resemble a bear, probably because it looked expensive. The zombie tucked it into his coat.

"I could go for a knife." Alex slung a bow from an archery display over his shoulder before practically running to claim a blade of his own. The enchanter looted the largest bowie knife available and attached its sheath to his belt next to a combat knife that he'd already been wearing.

Despite her best efforts, Becca smiled when she noticed the display next to her. Several hatchets, a couple axes, and best of all, a few machetes hung from hooks. She promptly picked up one of the oversized blades and held it in Alex's direction. She then prepared her best Australian accent.

"That's not a knife. This is a knife."

"That's sweet." The enchanter immediately discarded his previous knife and claimed not one but two machetes from the rack next to her. Becca couldn't help but notice the unbridled joy in his eyes as he did. An uncoordinated display of pretend martial arts followed. It was sometimes hard to believe he was close to the same age as her.

Becca grabbed a simple backpack and loaded it with everything she thought might be useful. A hatchet, flashlights, batteries, matches. It all went in her bag. She grabbed a first aid kit, only to hesitate before adding it to the mix. Oddly enough, she wasn't sure if she had a use for medical supplies anymore. With her Regeneration spell, Band-Aids didn't have much purpose.

Glancing to the corner of the Heretic Seed's interface, she brought up her status window.

Name: Rebecca Alvarez
Race: Human
Heretic Class: Mage

Mana: 177/177
Mana Composition: Balanced
Current Level: 7 (988 experience to next level.)

ATTRIBUTES
Constitution: 25
Defense: 20
Strength: 19
Dexterity: 23
Agility: 20
Intelligence: 25
Perception: 28
Will: 21

AILMENTS
None

SPELLS
ICICLE
Description: Gather moisture from the air around you to form an icicle. Once formed, icicles will hover in place for 3 seconds, during which they may be claimed as a melee weapon or launched in the direction of a target. Accuracy is dependent on caster's focus.
Rank: D
Cost: 20MP
Icicle Size: 15 x 3 inches
Range: 15ft

REGENERATION
Description: Heal wounds for yourself or others. If rendered unconscious, this spell will cast automatically until all damage is repaired or until MP runs out.
Rank: B
Cost: 10MP
Duration: 50 seconds

Range: 30ft

Becca frowned at her two spells. Both were solid abilities, but Digby might have a point about her hiding in the van too much. It had been two weeks since she'd become a heretic and she hadn't discovered anything new. She shook off the thought. At least she was getting stronger physically.

With the experience she'd gained the night before, she'd been pushed up past most of the lower levels at an alarming rate. Honestly, it almost felt like cheating. After spending so long locked in a luxury apartment, she hadn't exactly stayed in shape, but now, that was starting to change.

Becca picked up one of the machetes, feeling the weight of it in her hand. Loosening her grip, she let it slip through her fingers only to rotate her hand to catch it again. She tossed it back and forth a few times, noting the improvements in her coordination and speed. It wasn't anything superhuman, but her movements seemed to flow better than before. She could even type faster.

That wasn't even the best part.

Having put her recent points into perception, Becca had noticed a significant increase in the capabilities of her senses. Her hearing was sharper, her eyesight was better, and her skin felt more sensitive. Of course, there were some drawbacks. Her enhanced sense of smell didn't make riding in an enclosed space with Digby any more pleasant. The zombie could use a bath. There had been moments that she could almost taste him in the air. Even worse was Alex, who seemed to think his farts were quiet enough that no one would notice. Well, surprise, she noticed.

Becca's growling stomach pulled her out of her thoughts. She was still starving after gaining so many levels. She snatched a package of camping rations and shoved it into her bag. Afterward, she searched for anything else she could eat that wouldn't spoil. When her pack was good and full without being overloaded, she attached the last of the machetes to one side and hoisted it to her back.

With supplies handled, she joined Digby near the register where the zombie was picking out a walking stick from a bin. It was probably the most sensible thing he'd looted yet, considering his situation. She let him be and pulled several maps of the area from a rack by the point-of-sale system. It was only a matter of time before the internet completely failed and she wouldn't be able to navigate the way she had all morning.

Unfolding one of the maps, she placed her smart phone down beside it and oriented it with the feed from her drone. The area really was quite secluded. She pulled a pen from the register and marked off a few places that might be worth checking out. With a little luck, they might have time to visit one of them before nightfall. She dropped her pen a second later when a message scrolled across her HUD.

SKILL LINK

By demonstrating repeated and proficient use of the non-mage skill or talent, navigation, you have discovered an adjacent spell.

CARTOGRAPHY

Description: Send a pulse into the ambient mana around you to map your surroundings. Each use will add to the area that has been previously mapped. Mapped areas may be viewed at any time. This spell may interact with other location dependent spells.

Rank: D

Cost: 30MP

Map Area: 5 miles

Limitations: If cast while inside a structure, cartography will only map the interior of that structure rather than the surrounding area. Cartography is unable to map any area blocked by any form of door or barrier.

Oh good, finally, a use for you.

"Holy fuck." Her mouth fell open as she finally gained a new spell.

"What's that now?" Digby eyed her sideways.

"I just learned a cartography spell." Becca flicked her eyes to the door. "I'll be right back."

Without another word, she raced out of the lodge and held out both hands. She was casting the spell before she'd even thought the word. A gust of wind blew in, carrying dust and leaves in a circle around her as a strange light gathered between her hands. Becca felt the pull of her mana, stronger than when she'd cast her other spells. The orb of light swelled, taking on a pattern of shifting color, like oil floating on the surface of a puddle.

Then, it burst.

Motes of light spread out all around her, like dandelion seeds on the wind. The effect faded seconds later just as a glowing circle appeared on the ground before her. The shape expanded until it was over ten feet wide with her standing at its center. A translucent image spread out from her feet, even rising up from the ground to display a topographical map of the area, like some form of advanced augmented reality.

"Oh wow." She marveled at the practicality of the spell.

Upon further investigation, she found that she could manipulate the image at will. She swiped to the side intuitively, causing the image to slide in the same direction to show blank space that hadn't been mapped yet. She could even scale the display up and down, or zoom in on individual points to view them in near-perfect detail. It was amazing.

The only things she couldn't see were the interior of the lodge or of the cabins that littered the campground. With a thought, the display vanished. It returned again just as easily, and without needing to recast the spell.

"I am going to get so much use out of this." She was practically salivating at the prospect of creating a perfect map of everywhere she went. "This is even better than a satellite. I wonder what it will be capable of when it ranks up."

Becca returned to the lodge to show Digby and Alex what she'd discovered. She opened her map on the floor of the shop as soon as she was inside, expanding it as large as it would go before walking to its center.

"Hey Dig, what do you think of this?" She threw out both hands with pride.

Both Digby and Alex starred in her direction for a few seconds before speaking.

"Umm, Becky, should we be concerned about your mental stability?" Digby tilted his head to the side.

"Yeah, are we supposed to be looking at something?" Alex asked while standing in one of the mountains of her display as if it wasn't there.

"You can't see it, can you?" Becca deflated.

"See what?" Digby stepped closer, leaning on his new walking stick.

"Nothing, it's just a…" She trailed off. "Never mind. I learned a spell that maps the area. It lets me create a massive augmented reality display of a five-mile radius. You're just going to have to trust me that it's impressive."

"I'm sure it's quite something." Digby brushed her discovery aside before slapping a brochure down on the checkout counter. "While you were out there waving your hands around at your imaginary map, I have also discovered something fantastic."

"It's not imaginary," Becca growled before snatching the brochure from the counter. "What's this?"

"That, my dear Becky, is our new home." Digby took a bow as she read the front on the brochure out loud.

———

Hearst Castle
  You're Invited to an American Castle!
  Visitors Center Opens at 8am Daily
  First Tour of the Day Begins at 9am

"Ah, okay?" Becca looked up from the brochure. "This some sort of museum?"

"No, it's a castle." Digby's face fell. "And we are going to claim it as our own."

"Sure, but…" Becca glanced down at the paper then back up to the agitated necromancer. "I'm sorry, why?"

"Because it's a castle." Digby snatched the pamphlet from her hand and opened it to show a photo of an extravagant Mediterranean-style structure. "This says it was once only accessible to celebrities and famous guests. And I can't think of a more worthy place to claim as our new estate."

"Yes, but why there?" she repeated her question.

"Because it's a castle!" Digby stomped his peg-leg. "I can't believe I have to explain this. What better structure could you ask for? It's sure to be built like a fortress."

"Maybe if it had been built back in your day. But buildings now aren't constructed with defense in mind. I'm sure it's a beautiful place, but it's no fortress."

"I still say we investigate it." Digby stuffed the brochure into his coat and marched toward the exit, turning back for a moment before pushing through the door. "And when we do, I'm sure you'll take one look at it and never want to leave."

Becca glanced to Alex for his opinion, immediately regretting the impulse.

"He might have a point." The enchanter shrugged.

"Oh, of course you would want to live in a castle. You were swinging those machetes around pretending to be a knight just a minute ago." Becca released a heavy sigh.

"That's accurate." Alex's face turned a little red. "But the castle is secluded, and it could actually work out. At the very least, it's worth checking out."

"Fine." Becca made her way toward the door of the lodge. "We don't have anywhere better in mind, so why the hell not." She held out her arms in an exaggerated shrug just as the smart phone in her pocket vibrated to let her know that her drone had picked up movement. "Oh shit."

"What?" Alex froze.

"We're not alone." Becca rushed out the door toward the van.

Digby stood out in the open near the vehicle, leaning on his walking stick, oblivious to whatever danger might be coming. A second of quiet went by just before the necromancer's head snapped to the side and a gunshot shattered the silence of the campground. Digby hit the ground like a common corpse, a dark spatter of necrotic gray matter covering the side of the van.

Becca and Alex stumbled forward, both skidding to a stop. She swept her vision from the van to the lodge, then back again, unsure which direction they should run. Her indecision left them both out in the open.

A masculine voice echoed through the trees.

"Don't even think about moving."

"Shit." Becca cursed herself. "I knew I should have stayed in the van."

CHAPTER SIX

"What happened?" The familiar face of the Heretic Seed's copycat manifestation leaned over Digby as the sound of waves and the smell of the sea surrounded him. He was back in the imaginary space that he'd appeared in the last time his brain had been damaged.

"Gah!" Digby leapt up with a sudden jolt.

The recreation of the boat he'd spent eight hundred years in floated gently in an endless ocean. The Heretic Seed's crimson eyes stared at him while wearing his own face like a mask, reminding him what he'd looked like back when he'd been alive. Back when he had a nose. It really had been a nice nose. He shook off the thought, remembering what had just happened to him.

"I was shot!"

"That's not good," the Seed commented, matter-of-factly. "Is there anything——"

"Shut up!" Digby cast Necrotic Regeneration to repair the damage to his brain and send his consciousness back to his body in the outside world.

"Rude." The Heretic Seed folded its arms.

"No time to talk." Digby leaped up to his feet as the sun reflecting off the ocean grew bright enough to blind him. He closed his eyes.

A moment of darkness passed with no way to tell how long it actually was. Then he snapped his eyes open. The taste of dirt filled his mouth as his vision came into focus. The horned section of bone that had wrapped his skull as part of his bone armor lay a couple feet away. It must have been broken off when the bullet struck his head, though the missing piece was beginning to reform as his regeneration spell finished its work. Still, whatever firearm had shot him must have been stronger than any he'd been attacked with before to do that much damage to his armor.

Digby resisted the impulse to stand up. He had just been shot in the head by an unknown assailant. It seemed prudent to play dead until he understood the situation. Besides, maintaining the element of surprise had always proven useful in the past.

"Put your hands above your head and lay down on your stomachs," a voice shouted from somewhere beyond Digby's view.

Rebecca's voice came next, sounding like she was struggling to stay calm. "Don't shoot, we mean you no harm."

"We'll be the judge of that," the masculine voice responded. "Now, what were you doing with that zombie?"

A foot stepped into Digby's field of vision as the unfamiliar man walked toward him. He glanced up without moving his head. The man was wearing a black, combat-style boot under a pair of trousers with a pocket on the knee. He wore a plaid shirt on top. His entire outfit, minus the boots, was available back in the lodge's shop, Digby was sure of it. They were all items that he'd rated as not extravagant enough to steal. The man must have gotten there before him and looted a few of the less fancy items.

Setting the man's fashion sense aside, the gun he carried was a problem. Digby had seen a weapon like it before in a couple videos. He assumed from the large scope on top that it was designed for sniping.

That must have been what shot me.

To make matters worse, two more people, another man and a woman, stepped in behind the first, each wearing a similar outfit and carrying weapons of their own. The woman held a large revolver. She had another two pistols strapped to her thighs and a shotgun on her back. Apparently, the revolver and pistols weren't enough. The man beside her was less muscular than the one in front and held a more standard rifle.

"Um, ah, that's not, um, or, he is." Alex struggled to form a coherent sentence.

"Oh hell, you are not helping." Rebecca sighed.

"Sorry."

Digby ignored his apprentice's apology and focused on the ground next to his assailant's foot to open his maw. He was pretty sure he could impale the man with a quick blood forge before anyone could attack.

"I asked a question," the man repeated. "What are you Skyline assholes doing here with that zombie?"

Digby immediately closed his maw at the mention of Skyline. Even more important was why these people would have an unfavorable opinion of the mercenary group. An enemy of his enemy could be a friend after all. He could always impale them later if he needed to.

"Skyline?" Rebecca's voice climbed an octave, clearly following a similar line of thought. "We're not with —"

"Don't try to lie, I recognize that body armor."

"You do?" She responded with a question before adding another. "Are you military?"

"You can file that under things we're not telling you," the woman standing at the back added in an almost sing-song tone, waving her revolver back and forth with each word.

"You're not helping, Parker." The slim man glowered at her. "Mason has it covered."

The woman lowered her head, letting her revolver drop a little. "Way to tell them our names, Sax."

"Oh shit, sorry." They both stopped talking.

The man in front, apparently named Mason, let out a long sigh before addressing Rebecca again. "We were military two weeks ago, back when there was still a military to be a part of. Now we're just surviving, no thanks to Skyline."

"Okay, you don't like Skyline, I get that," Rebecca said. "That's actually good. We don't either."

"Are we supposed to believe that?" Mason arched an eyebrow.

"It's true," Alex chimed in. "We had to fight our way out of Seattle before the bomb dropped. We took some gear off a few of Skyline's mercenaries."

Mason fell silent as if considering the story. It was enough to give Digby confidence that the trio wouldn't shoot anyone without at least talking first. It was about time too. He was sick of lying in the dirt.

"Can I get up now?" Digby rolled over.

"Holy fucking shit!" Mason shrieked as he leaped backward.

"It talked!" Parker nearly dropped her revolver.

"Witchcraft!" Sax shrieked and jumped backwards.

"Yes, yes, the zombie talked." Digby pushed himself off the ground, being careful not to make any sudden movements that might seem aggressive. "Why is everyone always so surprised?"

"Damn it, Dig." Rebecca placed a hand to her forehead. "You could have at least let me prepare them before you got up."

"Sta—stay where you are." Mason leveled his rifle at Digby's head.

"Don't bother." Rebecca gestured to his gun. "You can't kill him with that."

"He's one of those things then? The other zombies, the ones that heal?" Parker pointed her revolver at Digby.

"Or it's witchcraft." Sax added, this time without shrieking.

"Shut up, Sax. I keep saying, none of this is witchcraft." She elbowed him in the shoulder. "It's clearly some sort of government experiment."

"Why would the government want to make talking zombies?" he spouted back. "Only witches would want to do that."

"What would witches want with talking zombies?" She let her aim falter.

"To act as minions?" He shrugged.

"Could you two, please." Mason held up a hand to put a stop to their side conversation.

"He's right, you know. It is witchcraft." Digby picked up his walking stick and had a good lean, ignoring the weapons pointed in his direction.

"I'm sorry, what?" Mason's face fell.

"Okay, I'm going to summarize the best I can." Rebecca stepped forward, keeping her hands up. "This here is Digby. He was a victim of a curse that was placed on him by a necromancer eight hundred years ago."

"A necromancer?" Mason furrowed his brow.

"Yes, it's a mage that uses death magic."

"I know what a necromancer is. I've played Dungeons and Dragons before," Mason snapped back.

"Really?" Alex's eyes lit up as if he'd found a kindred spirit.

"Yes, but none of that shit's real."

"Unfortunately, you're wrong about that." Rebecca continued. "Because Digby here died, reanimated as a zombie, and ended up frozen in the Arctic, only to be discovered and shipped to Seattle for study centuries later. That was two weeks ago. Obviously, he woke up and all of this happened." She gestured to the world around her.

"You're saying that this guy caused the apocalypse." Mason raised his gun back up.

"It wasn't my fault." Digby stepped forward, ignoring the weapon.

"It was a little your fault," Rebecca added before continuing. "But it doesn't matter who started it anymore. What matters is who spread it and who created the revenants."

"What's a revenant?" Parker spoke up.

"That's what we call the zombies that can—"

"They aren't zombies." Digby interrupted as everyone looked at him with puzzled expressions. "What? They aren't. Revenants are much worse, and I won't have you giving my kind a bad reputation by misnaming them."

"Of course they aren't zombies," Sax agreed with enthusiasm. "They're vampires."

"Exactly," Digby nodded, "they're vampi—wait, what?"

"No, they aren't." Parker sighed as if dredging up another old conversation.

"They drink blood, don't they?" Sax glowered back at her.

"They do?" Digby cocked his head to one side.

"You didn't know that?" Mason eyed him.

"Clearly not," he snapped back.

"We didn't let any get close enough to find out before killing them," Alex added, clearly trying to make it sound like it had been easy.

"Well, they do," Sax insisted. "Which is why I say they're vamps."

"Nah, if they were vamps, they would be sexier." Parker shrugged off the claim as Sax let out a groan.

"What do you want them to do, sparkle?"

"Oh my god, we are getting nowhere with this." Rebecca drove a stake through their conversation. "The point is that the revenants were created by Skyline in some sort of play at world domination. And yes, I totally realize how insane all of this sounds, but Skyline only intends to save people that are loyal to them. They modified the original curse that created the zombies into something more lethal that they could control somehow. I know your gut is saying that I'm lying or crazy, but it's all true. Take it from someone who knows what it's like to be on your side of this conversation before. I used to be one of Skyline's drone operators, and when I stumbled onto all this, I was just as freaked out as I'm sure you all are now. I deserted and joined up with Dig here when I learned everything that they had planned." She pulled her smart phone from her pocket and lowered a drone down to hover beside her so they could see it. "I stole a few surveillance units before leaving. Now, we're on the run just as much as anyone else."

"Jesus." Mason's eyes bulged, understandably having trouble accepting the facts as they were laid out before him.

"Okay, most of that was batshit, but I told you Bancroft and the rest of those Skyline ass-hats had something to do with this," Parker chimed in from behind him.

"Bancroft?" Digby's ear pricked up. "Who's he?"

"I've heard of him." Rebecca glanced back at him over her shoulder and gestured to the phone she held at her side. The device was angled so that Digby could see its screen. The words Veritas Analysis Active appeared on the screen. She continued speaking without skipping a beat. "I haven't met Bancroft, but I believe he's Skyline's top commander, right?"

"Right, and I have met him." Mason lowered his gun. "Sort of."

Digby glanced at the screen of Rebecca's phone.

True, 97% accuracy.

"What do you mean, you sort of met him?" Digby probed.

"Bancroft was at the quarantine line around Seattle where the three of us were stationed. I only saw Bancroft in passing, but he and his mercenaries abandoned us just as the dead began to overrun our forces. I'll never forget how he just walked into one of those giant drone aircrafts and left. It was like every-thing had gone according to plan."

True, 97% accuracy.

"That sounds about right for Skyline." Rebecca glanced back to Digby for confirmation. He nodded to let her know that

Mason had been honest. Her shoulders relaxed. There was a chance they could trust these soldiers.

"Who's this guy then?" Sax gestured to Alex.

"The boy is my apprentice." Digby stood tall.

"Apprentice in what?" Mason looked at Alex sideways.

"Magic." Digby tapped his walking stick on the ground like a wizard's staff.

"Again, that crap isn't real," Mason repeated.

True, 97% accuracy.

Clearly, Mason didn't believe them. They were going to need a demonstration.

"Show them your power, Alex." Digby gestured to the open space between them and the lodge. He continued to hold out his hand for a full ten seconds before turning back to the enchanter behind him. "What's the problem?"

Alex shrugged. "I don't have any spells that create an impressive effect for anyone to see. You want me to make some water glow, sure, I can do that, but if you want proof of magic, then you're barking up the wrong tree."

Digby closed his eyes and rubbed at what was left of the bridge of his nose. "Alright, Rebecca, could do an icicle or something?"

"Sure." She raised one hand as mist converged into a spike of frozen water. Dropping her hand back down, she plunged it into the earth. All three of the newcomers' jaws dropped in unison as the group fell silent.

A long pause went by before Sax spoke up. "Witches!"

"Damn, I hate to agree." Parker gave an exaggerated shrug. "But yeah, that's witchcraft right there."

"Indeed." Digby let a smug grin creep across his face in an 'I told you so' sort of way.

"I don't really know how to deal with…" Mason waved his hand around in the direction of the icicle. "…that. But fine, magic is real. We just had our entire unit massacred by one of those, what did you call them?"

"Revenants?" Rebecca nodded.

"Fine, yeah, those things." He slung his rifle over his back. "One of the men we served with turned and attacked whoever was closest. Everyone they bit just got up and did the same. Unlike before, with the regular zombies in Seattle, the change was instant. It was just blind luck that the three of us got away alive."

True, 97% accuracy.

Mason was starting to come around.

"Does that mean you aren't going to shoot me again?" Digby narrowed his eyes at the soldier.

"For now." Mason shrugged. "At least you're not part of Skyline."

True, 97% accuracy.

"Excellent." That was good enough for Digby to relax. He brushed some dirt from his coat before adding, "And I will accept your apology."

"I'm not apologizing to a zombie that was wandering around in our campground. You might as well have been carrying a sign saying, please, shoot me in the head." Mason argued.

"Would it have killed you to resist your kind's violent tendencies long enough fire a warning shot?" Digby narrowed his eyes at the man before dropping his gaze to Mason's left foot. "Actually, what's your shoe size?"

Mason looked confused for a second before he glanced down at Digby's peg-leg. He snapped his eyes back up and flicked them to Rebecca. "Is this guy for real?"

"Yeah, he's always like this." She deflated. "It's exhausting."

"Oh, I'm sorry, Becky, would you like me to put you back in

the tower that I rescued you from?" He placed one hand to his ear. "Wait, what's that? It exploded? How horrible."

"Okay, okay." She sighed and turned back to Mason. "Look, I know how Dig comes across. He might be a monster, but when push comes to shove, he's a better person than most humans."

Digby opened his mouth to make a snide comment, but closed it again as her words hit him. For a moment he thought his heart might begin beating again. He cleared his throat and spun away from the group to face a large cabin that sat near the lodge.

"We should take this conversation indoors where we're less exposed." He began walking toward the cabin. Rebecca agreed and stuck close to his side, letting Alex bring up the rear. She held her phone's screen so both she and Digby could see if anyone behind them made any sudden moves.

"Hey you, hold up," Mason called out.

"My name is Lord Graves, not hey you." Digby kept walking.

"Seriously, we're not done here."

Digby ignored the request in an attempt to assert some element of dominance. He wasn't about to let Mason tell him what to do. Not to mention the sudden hostility was suspicious.

"I mean it, don't take another step." Mason's tone grew severe as the sound of guns being raised met Digby's ears.

"What's the problem?" Digby started to turn around but stopped the instant he caught movement in the cabin's window. It had looked like a person ducking out of sight.

Oh, I get it.

He looked back over his shoulder. "Who do you have hiding in the cabin, Mason?"

"No one. We're alone."

Rebecca held her phone so Digby could see.

False, 97% accuracy.

He and Rebecca nodded to each other in understanding.

Digby threw caution aside and limped up the steps of the log cabin. With a thought, he opened his maw in the palm of his hand to forge a new set of talons for his bone gauntlet. He froze as soon as he threw open the door.

He'd been right. The soldiers weren't alone.

No, they weren't alone at all.

CHAPTER SEVEN

Digby stood with his clawed hand raised, ready to tear apart whoever was hiding inside the cabin. After Mason's poor attempt at deception, he was sure the soldier was hiding something. His jaw dropped as soon as the door swung open and he found out what it was.

"Oh shit, Dig." Rebecca bumped into his back as he stood in the open doorway, their shadows stretching across the room to cover a group of terrified people.

A quick count revealed seven children, two young men, two women, and an old lady. Digby immediately dropped his claws to his side and tried to pretend that he hadn't been ready to murder the group a second before. With a lack of options, he stood there like a fool with a crooked smile on his face as the survivors huddled on the other side of the cabin behind the elderly woman.

"Ah… hello." He tried to be friendly.

That was when the old bag cracked him on the face with a cane.

"Gah!" Digby fell backward, landing on Alex who had been standing at the bottom of the cabin's steps.

"I got the bastard." The old woman grabbed at Rebecca's wrist. "Quick, Mason. Shoot them."

"Hey, stop that." Rebecca swatted at the old woman's hand to free herself from her attacker's arthritic death grip. "And don't shoot. We didn't know you were hiding civilians."

"Yeah, well, we are." Mason and the other two soldiers approached with their guns raised. "We traveled all the way down here from Seattle, most of it on foot. We picked up a few strays along the way."

"And you thought you'd take it upon yourselves to protect them?" Rebecca finally twisted herself free of the old woman's fingers.

"What's wrong with that?" Mason glared at her. "There might not be a country left to defend, but we're still soldiers, we might as well fulfill our duty with whatever time we have left."

"And we thank you for it." The old woman stepped down one of the steps to jab Digby with her cane. "Now shoot this monster in the face."

"Get away from me, you old crone." He rolled off of Alex and hid behind his apprentice.

The elderly woman's face fell as soon as he spoke. Mason lowered his gun, signaling for Parker and Sax to do the same as he addressed the old woman. "That's enough, Miss Foley. We can take things from here."

She let out an annoyed harrumph before turning back to the cabin door. Digby relaxed only to tense back up when she spun back around and jabbed Alex with her cane, hitting him square in the crotch.

"Ah god, why me?" Alex curled up into a fetal position, making it difficult for Digby to continue to hide behind him.

"Thank you for keeping them in line, Miss Foley." Mason inclined his head to the ancient woman.

"You're welcome, son." She gave Mason a bright smile before heading back into the cabin.

"She's worse than a revenant." Digby pushed himself up from the ground.

"Agreed." Alex took a few deep breaths. "She hit me hard enough to give me an ailment that shows up on my HUD."

"Really?" Digby stepped aside so Rebecca could help his apprentice up, glancing at the boy's name listed as part of his coven on his HUD, finding the word 'Nausea' beside it.

"I'm okay, it will pass." Alex got to his feet.

"Why wait?" Digby gestured to the canteen that the enchanter carried.

"Oh yeah." Alex cast a quick purify spell and took a sip of water. "Thank god for witchcraft." He immediately stood back up like the assault had never happened.

"What did you do?" Mason eyed him suspiciously.

Alex held out his canteen to the soldier. "If you have anyone that's injured, have them drink from this. The magic isn't that strong, but the water inside will heal minor stuff."

Mason took the container and handed it to Parker. She smelled it for a second before shrugging and tipping it back. Her eyes widened the instant she swallowed, doing a double take at the canteen. She immediately pulled up one pant leg and removed a bloody bandage from her shin. A wound, a few days old, began to heal slowly.

"That is… something else. The water is even cold." She immediately headed into the cabin to offer a sip to a couple of the survivors that had minor wounds.

"That will cure most ailments and has a slight regenerative effect that will wear off in a minute. But I can cast the spell again whenever you need it." Alex stood tall as he explained it. "I'm an enchanter. I can't do anything as impressive as Becca's icicle, but I have my uses."

"Will that water cure a zombie bite?" Mason arched an eyebrow.

"Yeah. It gets rid of everything from curses to radiation poisoning." Alex glanced to Digby. "Oh yeah, you're all going to want to drink some of that if you stay near Lord Graves for too long."

"Yes, he took a high dose of radiation when the bomb fell

on Seattle." Rebecca jumped in to explain. "So, he is quite poisonous to be around right now. There's no immediate danger but let us know if anyone starts feeling sick while we're here. They'll be fine as long as we're proactive about cleansing them."

"Oh." Mason took a giant step away from Digby as Sax covered his genitals with both hands.

"Anyway." Digby rejoined the conversation. "I think we've proven that we don't mean you or your people harm. And we will be happy to move on in the morning. So if you don't mind, we will find somewhere to spend the night and get out of your hair."

"Actually, why don't you come in and share information with us? It looks like we might be a little…" Mason glanced at one of the other survivors as a wound on their forehead began to close. "…out of our depths on what's really going on, and we would be grateful if you could fill us in."

"And if you step out of line, we can just send Nana Foley and her cane after you again," Parker added.

"Lovely." Digby groaned as he followed Mason into the cabin.

With a fragile alliance in place, Digby and Rebecca went over everything that had happened back in Seattle as well as everything about the Heretic Seed. There was always the risk that someone there might be captured by Skyline, but there wasn't much point in keeping anything to themselves. Henwick pretty much knew it all anyway.

The only thing they kept hidden was that a shard of the Heretic Seed was lodged in Digby's heart, since that was the only bit of information that still eluded their enemies.

In return, Mason went over the events of the last two weeks that they had spent laying low at the vineyard up north. Apparently, a soldier named Tanner that they had served with turned into a revenant and killed the rest of their unit after they'd retreated from the quarantine line.

From there, the three soldiers traveled south. They picked

up a few survivors here and there, all of which had already lost someone in their lives. Digby caught the occasional hateful glare from a few people after they learned that he had brought the curse that had caused the death of their friends and loved ones. Despite that, their spirits were high overall. Clearly, living through an apocalypse had sped up the mourning process.

For most of the survivors. There was some resistance to the idea that magic was real and that the end of the world had been brought about by a curse. After a few demonstrations, they began to get on board with the idea. Some even made requests. Alex's spells quickly became the favorite for the simple fact that Purify Water added a refreshing chill to any liquid.

Most of the children stayed away from Digby. The fact that he looked like an undead monster probably had something to do with it. After watching Rebecca and Alex interacting with him though, some of the adults started to come over out of curiosity.

The old woman, Miss Foley, had lost her husband of fifty years the week before. Most of the children were orphans. Linda, one of the women caring for the youths, had just moved to California with her fiancé a month ago, but had lost him two days into the apocalypse. She was clearly still working through her grief but didn't mind talking about his death if it would help everyone to understand the situation better. It took some time for her to stop staring at Digby's missing nose, but the information she provided proved valuable.

Her story happened a couple days after Seattle. Her fiancé had been bitten by a zombie before nightfall but had been able to hold off the change longer than most. Though his strong constitution meant nothing when the sun set.

According to Linda, it had been like someone had flipped a switch. She had understood at the time that there was no way to save him, but she never expected him to turn so fast. He became a revenant as soon as the night set in. She only survived by locking him in the car they were driving and leaving him on the side of the road.

When her story was finished, Digby made a point to thank her and offer her his condolences. He was sure the words of a zombie would carry little weight, but still, losing a family member was never easy.

The other woman in the group of survivors, a twenty-eight-year-old waitress, stayed on the other side of the cabin. According to the others, she hadn't interacted with anyone else much either.

Of the two young men, only one introduced himself. He was a college student named Troy, who was on his university's football team. It was strange to hear the boy talk about the sport as if it had been a loved one that had also perished in the last couple weeks along with everyone else.

Digby had asked him a number of questions, mostly to find out more about the modern world's education system. Even with his slightly above average intelligence, he had trouble understanding the concept of student loans. Both Troy and Alex had taken on a debt that would take decades to pay off. The practice sounded insane.

The other young man, Marcus, nodded from across the room when Troy called his name. He seemed friendly enough but had his hands full helping Linda care for the seven children in the cabin. There were certainly more orphans than Digby would have been able to handle. Watching the pair of surrogate caregivers work set off an uncomfortable ache in his chest. After a few minutes, he had to look away.

Once they had talked to everyone that was willing, Digby was able to form a clear picture of the effects of Henwick's altered curse. It seemed that during the day, it didn't behave any differently, but at night, anyone bitten by either a zombie or a revenant would turn into one of the new creatures almost instantly. The same went for anyone bitten during the day that had not yet changed until sunset. They simply turned revenant the moment the darkness set in.

On top of when and how fast the change occurred, these new monsters didn't devour their prey. Instead, they merely drank them dry, apparently sustaining themselves on blood alone. This behavior had the unfortunate effect of causing their numbers to grow rapidly due to the fact that the bodies they left behind remained intact and able to turn. Zombies were almost merciful in comparison, considering they prevented more than half of their victims from changing by eating their corpses.

Based on Rebecca's math, the numbers weren't good. With the rate that the revenants passed on the modified curse at night and their overall superior physical capabilities, it seemed like they would outnumber the zombies by nearly ten to one. The only saving grace was that the creatures went dormant during the day, making it safer to travel out in the open since they had a tendency to hide inside buildings. Not to mention their physical prowess and healing capabilities apparently went way down during daylight hours.

After sharing information and learning what he could from the survivors, Digby retired to the lodge building. It didn't make sense for him to stay with the others, considering they would all wake up with radiation poisoning if he did. Plus, having a zombie in the room with them would probably cause more than a few restless nights. He had no intention of eating anyone, but still, he was a predator. He wouldn't want a fox in the hen house either.

Rebecca and Alex stayed in the cabin since it had actual beds and was large enough to accommodate everyone. Each of them agreed to take a shift on watch along with Mason and his people. Now that no one was pointing guns at them, the three soldiers seemed trustworthy enough.

With that, Digby made himself a nest out of sleeping bags from the camping supply store and grabbed his tablet from the van. It still had enough charge to get through a couple movies. He could plug it into the van when they left in the morning.

A couple hours later, the credits of another video rolled. Digby checked the time.

Still a while before sunup.

He closed out of the movie he'd been playing and started

up its sequel, letting out a chuckle at the cover image of a shirt-less hero with a chainsaw for a hand. He glanced at his missing foot.

I wonder if I could put a chainsaw on there.

Digby shook his head at the notion.

Probably best not to. I'd just fall over and cut off my other foot.

Just as he settled back down, a voice came from nearby.

"What are you watching?"

"Gah!" Digby dropped his tablet from his lap to find a child of around twelve with messy hair staring at him. "What the hell are you doing here?"

"Couldn't sleep." The boy shrugged like it should have been obvious.

"So you thought you'd go bother the man-eating-zombie next door?" Digby picked up his tablet to make sure it wasn't broken.

"Do you want to see a magic trick?" The child held out both hands, palms up. A bright, red ball sat in the center of one.

"What?" Digby watched the object in his palm as he closed his right hand around it.

"Which is it in?" The boy closed his left hand as well without either hand touching the other.

"I don't care." Digby looked away before letting his atten-tion drift back and adding, "Fine, the ball is still in your right hand."

"Nope." The child laughed as if Digby had just embar-rassed himself, opening his right hand to reveal that it was empty, save for a sliver of red peeking through two of his fingers.

Digby leaned forward to peek at the underside of his hand, finding the rest of the squishy ball sticking out. "That's not a very good trick."

"Whatever, I'm still learning." The child pouted and shoved the ball into his pocket.

"Good, then go practice that trick someplace else." Digby tried to get back to his video, only to be interrupted again.

"Do you really eat people?" The kid leaned forward with a curious expression.

"Of course I eat people, I'm a zombie." Digby paused before adding, "But I only eat bad people, and corpses I find that are already dead. And now that I can eat revenants, humans are pretty much off the menu."

"So you've killed people before?" He leaned away as if staying out of reach.

"Some. When there wasn't a choice." Digby deflated a little before snapping his attention back to the intruder. "What's your name, child?"

"Hawk." The kid sounded excited.

"And how did you slip out of the cabin, Hawk?" Digby narrowed his eyes at the child.

"Everyone was asleep." He shrugged.

"Wasn't anyone keeping watch?"

"Parker and that guy that was with you are, but they were looking out the window."

"Hmm, probably more worried about keeping things out rather than watching for escapees," Digby assumed.

A moment of silence went by before Hawk started up again. "What's it like being dead? How do you do magic? What's up with your hand? How did you lose your foot? Does it hurt? What's—"

"I'm sorry, I feel like you've misinterpreted my willingness to entertain children here." Digby inched away. "So if you could please be so kind as to leave me be."

"Oh." The boy dropped his eyes to the floor.

"Oh, indeed." Digby settled back down. "Sorry. I'm not the friendly sort of zombie, and I've never had much tolerance for children."

"Can I watch your movie?" Hawk ignored him, sounding hopeful.

Digby closed his eyes for a second, reminding himself that the child had most likely lost his entire family and was probably in need of comfort wherever he could find it. Shouting at him or dragging him back to the cabin may not have be the best decision. Even if it would provide him with some peace and quiet. Finally, he forced a musty sigh from his lungs and opened his eyes. He reached forward and propped up his tablet so that Hawk could see without getting too close. At the very least, the boy could answer whatever questions he might have.

"Fine, you may sit quietly and watch this video, after which, you will go straight back to the cabin and sleep. And don't blame me if you get nightmares."

"Okay." Hawk grabbed a sleeping bag from the shelf and settled in.

"Not so close." Digby shooed the child away a few more feet. "I'm poisonous to be around. As it is, you'll need my apprentice to cleanse you when you go back to the cabin. If you start to feel sick, you'll have to head back before the video ends."

Hawk scooted away whilst remaining quiet.

"That's better." Digby tapped the play button with his stylus and leaned back. Within fifteen minutes, Hawk was asleep.

Digby pushed himself up as quietly as possible and relocated himself to a chair at the other end of the building to keep the child from falling ill while he slept. Waking up with radiation poisoning would be a bad way to start the day.

After checking to make sure the poor wretch hadn't stirred, Digby hit play on his tablet and settled back in until morning.

CHAPTER EIGHT

After finishing his most recent video, Digby wandered around the lodge's camping shop as boredom began gnawing at his idle mind. Checking the time, he stretched his deceased body with a series of loud cracks and headed for the exit. The sun would be up soon.

Stepping out the door of the lodge, Digby found Asher perched in a tree, pecking at the corpse of another bird. He decided to let her be and check in with the others at the cabin. Before he made it more than a few feet, he was met by a flustered Alex.

"Hey, have you seen a kid around? We're missing one."

"What?" Digby feigned surprise. "Are you telling me that you lost a child on your first night keeping watch?"

"I know, I know." Alex's eyes darted around the area as he started to panic.

"Oh. relax." Digby let his apprentice off the hook. "The child's inside the lodge."

"Thank god." Alex released a heavy sigh.

"Did you find him?" Parker stepped out from the door of the cabin.

"Yeah, he's asleep in the lodge."

"Whew. That's a weight off my mind." She hopped down the cabin's steps.

Mason came out next, along with Sax. They both carried a flashlight and were armed with pistols. Apparently, they had run out of bullets for their rifles and had resorted to borrowing guns from Parker's arsenal.

Mason banged on the door of a smaller cabin, with Rebecca answering a second later. The mage probably had trouble sleeping with so many people in one room, considering she was used to having a room to herself. She rubbed sleep from her eye as she pulled her phone from her pocket.

"What's going on?" Digby leaned closer to Alex.

"There's something hostile nearby." He held out the iron key he'd been using for his enchantments. Digby touched it with the skin of his left hand. Despite having a low sensitivity to temperatures, he could tell that the key was deathly cold. Whatever was coming, it was close. He checked his HUD.

MP: 220/220

Digby stepped back to give the soldiers room to spread out. He groaned a moment later when the old woman that had whacked him with her cane the day before stepped out.

"Mason, dear, come back inside. It's not even dawn—"

"Get back in the cabin, Miss Foley. It's not safe out here." He swept his flashlight across the camp site.

Digby took one step back toward the lodge just as the sound of branches breaking came from above. Mason and the other two soldiers raised their weapons to shine their lights into the trees where a pale form was visible through the leaves. Digby squinted up, having trouble making out much detail through the branches. Then he saw a hand curl around one of the tree trunks.

"Holy hell!" He stumbled backward.

It was huge.

A second hand passed through the leaves a dozen feet from the first. Then finally, a pale, bestial face emerged in the middle.

"Open fire!" Mason ordered as gunfire lit up the night.

All they did was make it mad.

The creature dropped from the trees, cracking the earth under its weight. It was the size of the cargo van they'd arrived in. With a sudden swipe, both Parker and Sax were thrown nearly twenty feet, hitting the wall of the lodge hard enough to shatter one of the windows nearby. A spatter of crimson coated the ground where they fell. Mason fired, peppering the massive revenant's pale skin, each wound knitting back together, barely slowing it down.

Miss Foley let out a terrified scream seconds before an enormous hand snapped around her waist. The creature tore the elderly woman from the cabin stairs like a rag doll. Her scream came to an abrupt halt as the beast shoved the woman into its enormous jaws. Jagged teeth closed on her neck and shoulder. Her ancient husk fell limp, dangling from the monster's mouth.

Digby could sense the flow of blood passing through the beast's throat as it swelled and contracted to drain the woman. For an instant, he froze, staring into the beast's dull, orange eyes. Its features were a mix of human and something else. A face like something out of a nightmare stared back, its snout-like nose sniffed at the air while its elongated ears twitched. A mass of rippling muscle covered every inch of its strangely slender body, like it was built for speed as well as strength. A wiry mane of gray fur draped its shoulders and upper back.

Digby focused on the creature.

Active Revenant Bloodstalker, Uncommon, Neutral.

Somehow, the creature had mutated.

"Oh Christ." Mason struggled to put pressure on Parker's side as blood ran through his fingers. Her hand reached out for one of her pistols, slipping across the handle of the weapon.

Rebecca stood frozen, her legs trembling as Alex cast Purify

Water. The enchanter tossed his canteen to Sax, who was closest. The soldier choked down a mouthful of water and pushed himself out of the dirt. A gash ran down his face, healing at a snail's pace from the spell's meager regenerative properties. He raised his pistol and fired, putting a bullet in the creature's head.

It hunched over, slamming a massive, clawed hand into the dirt for support. A muffled screech came from its mouth just before it dropped the elderly woman's body. Its eyes snapped in and out of focus before returning to normal as the bullet wound began to heal.

Digby tore his gaze away from the revenant. Mason and his people had accomplished nothing with their weapons. Someone had to take charge. Throwing out his hand, he opened his maw and cast Forge to send a black spike of crystalized blood into the beast's flank. The shard shattered on contact, unable to penetrate the revenant's hide. He lit the solidified fluid up with a Cremation to drive the creature away from the cabin.

"Rebecca!" he shouted to snap her back to the present. "Heal the wounded."

Her eyes darted around the scene before she ducked back to Mason's position to take care of Parker.

"Enchant the weapons, boy!" Digby called out to send Alex into action, placing an enchantment on everyone's firearms.

"Shoot one at a time to slow it down. Make every hit count," Digby ordered as the soldiers got back to their feet.

Firing on the beast would do no more than distract it and disrupt its regeneration, but it would buy time while Digby scrambled to think of a way to kill the beast. Before he could reach a solution, he remembered the child sleeping in the lodge. He snapped his head back to the supply store's window, catching Hawk's face peering through the glass.

"Stay inside!" he shouted, along with a wave of his hand to tell the boy to get down. Asher cawed at the child as well from her place perched on top of the roof. Digby beckoned to her, calling the raven down to land on his shoulder as he gave a command. "Guard the child." He nudged her off in the same instant, sending her flying toward a window that had been broken earlier when Parker had been thrown into the wall next to it.

Mason stepped forward and fired a shot from his now-enchanted pistol, blowing a wide hole in the revenant's chest. It fell forward, taking another bullet to its head. The creature's whole body spasmed and thrashed, flailing hard enough to crush anyone unfortunate enough to be hit by a stray swipe. It shuddered and twitched until it regained control over the mana flow that powered its healing.

With its body lashing out, something silver around the beast's neck snapped, sending a piece of metal flittering through the air to land near Mason.

"Dear god." His mouth fell open as he shined his light to the silver tag laying by his feet.

"What?" Digby snapped back, not appreciating the interruption.

"That's Tanner." He tightened his grip on his flashlight.

"Who the hell is Tanner?" Digby furrowed his brow.

"He served with us. He was the one that killed what was left of our unit." Mason raised his light to the remnants of a tattered shirt that draped the creature's muscular chest while scraps of fabric bearing a camouflage pattern hung from its waist and thighs. "That's an army uniform. How the hell did he find us?"

"It may have followed you," Digby answered. "The Heretic Seed called him a bloodstalker when I analyzed it. There's no telling what sort of mutations might be available to a creature like that."

Mason fired again, stopping Tanner from attacking, if only for another few seconds. "This isn't going to work."

The revenant regained control, this time faster than before, like it had built up a tolerance to Alex's enchantments. Tanner raised up to let out a blood-curdling screech that rattled the windows of the lodge.

That was when a second cry came from underneath it.

Digby's eyes bulged in horror as the body of the old woman snapped its arm forward. Her movements were fast and jerky as she got to her feet. Her arthritic joints cracked and popped as she moved, no longer in need of a cane. Miss Foley darted toward the lodge and the waiting meal inside. Digby tried to block her path, but the newborn revenant weaved to the side, sprinting past him toward the door.

"No!" Digby lunged, stumbling on his peg-leg. He cast Burial an instant too late, opening a grave in the ground behind the elderly creature as it crashed through the door of the lodge. The empty grave closed back up as Digby found his balance again. He kicked off with his remaining foot and hobbled toward the lodge, only looking back to give an order. "Keep Tanner busy!"

"Where are you going?" Rebecca pulled Parker back to her feet as Digby blew past them.

"Saving a brat."

Children made Digby uncomfortable, but that didn't mean he was going to stand by while one became dinner for a revenant. All he could do was trust that the others could handle Tanner without him.

CHAPTER NINE

"Damn it, Dig." Becca reached out as the irritating necromancer disappeared into the campground's lodge. She immediately ducked back behind the van as Tanner stomped around on the other side to swing at Alex and Mason. She peeked around the corner to cast an icicle.

"Shit!" Becca shrank back as Tanner slapped the shard of ice out of the air, breaking it into glittering pieces. "What do I do?"

MP: 127/177

She had plenty of mana, but didn't have any spells that could actually hurt the thing. Her icicles weren't fast or sharp enough. All she could do was distract it. Her legs shook. Spinning around, she pulled open the door of the van.

"Where are you going?" Mason reached a hand toward her just as she had a moment before when Digby had abandoned them.

"I'm not doing any good out here." Becca hoisted herself into the back of the vehicle and closed the door. The entire van rocked as something heavy struck the side, leaving a claw-shaped dent. "I wish I was back in my apartment."

She shook off the longing she felt for the prison she'd lived in for years and grabbed her laptop. Seconds later, her drone's HUD populated the screen. She checked its armaments, finding a pair of breaching charges.

"That's better than nothing."

Becca snatched up her system's modified game controller and thumbed the sticks to launch. The view through the screen climbed, showing her the van below. She darted over the revenant, making sure to keep out of its reach. With a little luck, she might be able to drop one of the charges close enough to its head to do some damage. She just needed to hold it still.

Becca tapped a key on her laptop to shine the drone's light down, aiming for the monster's eyes. It let out an annoyed screech.

"That got your attention." She hit the release command, dropping one of the breaching charges on the revenant's head.

Tanner darted to the side as the little plastic cylinder bounced off his shoulder. She pulled the trigger on her controller. A moderate bang came from just outside the van. The revenant lurched to the side, slamming into the side of the vehicle hard enough to put a four-foot dent in the metal. Becca ducked her head, trying to pretend that she wasn't in the middle of the fight. That she was someplace else, far away.

Raising back up, she brought her drone around. Tanner looked pissed, but his shoulder was none the worse for wear. The tissue simply knit itself back together. Even the wiry fur grew back.

"Damn!"

Becca glanced at the drone's HUD, then checked her own. She had one breaching charge and plenty of mana.

"What the hell can I do with that?" Her magic was useless, and she'd never get her remaining explosive close enough to do any real damage. The only thing she could think of was to try to dive bomb the monster's face, though that would almost certainly cost her the drone. She wiped sweat from her forehead just as Alex and Mason leaped out of the way of a heavy swipe. Tanner's claws missed them by inches.

"Crap." There wasn't a choice.

Becca whipped the drone down and darted at Tanner's head with her finger on the breaching charge's trigger. "This better work." The beast's jagged teeth were the last thing she saw as a set of malformed claws streaked through the drone's feed, cutting it to black.

She flinched and closed her eyes as she pulled the trigger.

Then there was nothing.

"Where was the kaboom?" She opened her eyes. "There was supposed to be a moderate kaboom." Becca's face fell as she read the words scrolling across the black screen of her laptop.

Unit lost.

"No!" The drone had been destroyed before the signal to detonate the charge could be received. "No," Becca repeated at the realization that she had wasted an irreplaceable resource for nothing.

The revenant chittered outside, sounding so close she could almost feel its hot breath on the back of her neck. She debated connecting to her other drone, unsure what she could even do. Her only other option was to go outside and start throwing icicles until she was out of mana, but that didn't seem like the best plan. Without a better idea, she gritted her teeth and connected to her last drone.

The laptop's HUD came to life, displaying a notification that seemed out of place. Becca nearly went cross-eyed when she realized the text wasn't being displayed by the computer's screen, but by the Heretic Seed's interface.

SKILL LINK
By demonstrating repeated and proficient use of the non-

mage skill or talent, remote operation, you have discovered an adjacent spell.

SPIRIT PROJECTION

Description: Project an immaterial image of yourself visible to both enemies and allies.

Rank: D

Cost: 20MP

Duration: 10 minutes

Limitations: Projected bodies are unable to touch physical objects and can be disrupted by any spell that might disrupt your mana flow. While controlling a projection, a caster's body will be vulnerable and unable to move or cast spells.

Aren't you a little too alive to become a ghost?

Becca stared at the text, questioning how it could help her fight. Then it hit her. "I can be a distraction."

She cast the spell without hesitation, feeling her mana flow as her vision blurred. A sudden wave of disorientation hit her, causing her fall limp to the floor of the van. The world stopped spinning a second later. Reaching back to rub her head, Becca realized that it didn't hurt. She glanced at her HUD.

MP: 107/177

The twenty mana for the spell had been spent.

"Weird." She sat up, not feeling any different. That was when she noticed her body lying on the floor beside her.

"Oh fuck, I'm a ghost." Becca sprang back up, reaching out to lean on the wall of the van. "Aw crap!" She let out a sudden shriek as her hand passed through the metal surface.

Tumbling to the dirt outside, she sat back up. The ground felt strange, like it was just a membrane of energy holding her up. Standing, she noticed she wasn't leaving any footprints.

"There you are!" Mason dove behind the van for a moment of safety. "I thought you'd abandoned us."

"I'm just trying to figure out a way to help." She glanced back and forth.

"Can't you attack with magic, or something?" Mason ducked his head as the revenant screeched from the other side of the van.

"My icicle spell is too weak." She stepped out from behind the van. "But I just learned one that might help."

"Wha—"

Becca ditched Mason behind the van just as the revenant went after Alex. The enchanter scrambled back, nearly tripping over Sax. The monster would be on them in seconds.

"Hey!" Becca ran straight up to the pale creature, putting her trust in the Heretic Seed's magic. "Come on, let's go."

Tanner spun in her direction, clearly more interested in a closer target. With a swipe of his clawed hand, the revenant carved a gouge in the ground. Becca spun out of the way, making it look like she'd dodged. In truth, the monster's fingers had passed through her leg. Fortunately, Tanner hadn't seemed to notice.

"Becca, be careful!" Alex's voice shook. "You're too close."

"I'm fine. I can't hurt this thing, but I can distract it long enough to keep you all alive a little longer." She stood her ground, feeling a bit of the confidence she used to have sitting behind a monitor, miles away.

Becca ducked another swipe before rolling under the beast's legs. The revenant grabbed at her feet, catching nothing but air. Alex and the others tensed every muscle in their bodies as she appeared to narrowly escape certain death several times. She would have explained what was really happening, but there wasn't enough time. Instead, she settled for letting everyone think she was brave for a few proud moments.

Weaving to one side, Becca scoffed as a claw whipped by her face. It was easy to get carried away, once she got used to the idea that she wasn't in any real danger. Of course, that was when she tripped over the only thing that was still tangible to her projected body, her own feet.

"Shit!" Becca stumbled to the ground, landing flat on her back.

Tanner didn't skip a beat.

The revenant dropped down, opening its jaws to sink its teeth into her throat. Shouts came from the others watching her demise, their voices trailing off as Tanner pulled away a mouthful of earth. Bits of dirt trickled from the monster's jaws, falling through Becca's face to land back on the ground. The revenant stared at her for a second before reaching out a hand to claw at her chest.

"Damn." She sighed as the creature's fingers passed through her.

The revenant immediately lowered his head to roar straight in her face, covering the ground in drool. She was glad none of it could stick to her. Tanner gave her one last frustrated swipe that tore apart the ground where she lay. Then he pushed off, to refocus on the rest of the group.

Becca cursed her feet for getting in her way. She really should have put more points into agility. Her short-lived diversion was finished. All she could do now was hope someone else could pick up where she left off. She shoved her illusionary body off the ground and turned to the lodge.

"Where the hell are you, Dig?"

CHAPTER TEN

Digby practically fell against the broken door of the lodge, throwing it open with his weight and momentum. Shards of glass from the window dropped to the floor on his way through. He followed the chittering screech of the elderly revenant as Asher responded with an aggressive squawk.

A battle raged, his beloved pet pecking and scratching at the old woman's face. The raven barely kept out of reach as Hawk huddled up against the wall where Digby had sat earlier in the night. The boy clutched his knees to his chest with tears streaming down his face at the sight of the monster that the old woman had become.

"Not one more step!" Digby stomped his peg-leg as he drew the dagger he'd looted from the camping store that afternoon. The elderly woman spun to face him with the agility of a dancer just as he plunged the blade down into her chest. The revenant fell, flailing on the floor. Digby could feel traces of mana flowing through what little blood she had remaining in her body as it struggled to heal the wound around the blade buried in her chest. Eventually, the thrashing came to a halt, leaving the old woman to rest in peace.

"Are you alright, my boy?" The staccato pop of gunfire echoed through the trees outside as Digby rushed to the traumatized child. He reached out to touch the boy's shoulder, shrinking back before making contact.

"I'm fine." Hawk pulled his eyes away from the corpse on the floor to give Digby a nod, wiping his eyes and putting on a brave face.

"Good, good." Digby wrapped one of the loose sleeping bags that covered the floor over around the child before beckoning to Asher. The zombified raven flapped over to land on his clawed hand before he set her down on Hawk's lap.

"Okay, boy. You stay here and be quiet, you hear? My friend Asher has been well-fed, so she won't hurt you, and she likes to be held so go ahead and keep her close. If anything happens, she'll keep you safe."

The revenant outside let out a wild cry, followed by the sound of something fleshy slamming into the wall of the lodge. Digby snapped his sights back to the windows. His eyes narrowed as a pale blur passed by outside. He flicked his attention to the old woman's corpse.

Corpse: Revenant, 112 MP required to animate.
Animate corpse? Yes/No

He nodded to the prompt, sending a wave of emerald energy slithering across the body. Miss Foley's eternal rest would have to wait a little longer. He glanced at his HUD as his maximum mana fell along with his remaining value.

MP: 53/108

It was a heavy sacrifice, but he wasn't sure if any of his other spells would do much. He was glad he'd taken the risk as the revenant's traits flooded his vision.

BOND OF THE DEAD

As a zombie animated directly by a necromancer, this
creature will gain one attribute point for every 2 levels of
their master. These points may be allocated at any time. 9
attribute points remaining.

NOCTURNAL

As a zombie created from the corpse of a deceased
revenant, this zombie will retain a portion of its attributes
associated with physical capabilities. Attributes will
revert to that of a normal zombie during daylight hours.
+8 Strength, +8 Defense, +4 Dexterity, +8 Agility, +5 Will

MINOR NECROTIC REGENERATION

As a zombie created from the corpse of a deceased
revenant, this zombie will simulate a revenant's regenerative ability. Regeneration will function at half the rate of a
living revenant. Minor Necrotic Regeneration requires
mana and void resources to function. This trait will cease
to function in daylight hours when there are higher
concentrations of life essence present in the ambient
mana.

Try not to get this one killed.

I make no guarantees, Digby silently commented on the Heretic
Seed's message as he dropped five of his new minion's bond
points into strength and another four into intelligence. He
turned back to Hawk once he was finished.

"Alright, Miss Foley and I are going to go assist everyone
outside." He nodded to Hawk and gave Asher a pat on the
head. "Keep him safe, girl."

The brave child nodded and held Asher tight.

Having taken care of the boy, Digby stood back up and
limped back toward the fight. The old woman's corpse slapped
a hand to the floor, pushing herself up to stand behind him.
With his new minion in tow, he shoved through the broken door
of the lodge and into the scene of desperation that awaited him.

Outside, Mason and Sax were down. Parker stood over

them, aiming her shotgun at the creature. Her other guns were scattered around the campground. The revenant stalked closer, no longer slowed by Alex's mana infused bullets.

Digby's apprentice stood beside Parker, pulling an arrow from a quiver he'd looted earlier. He nocked it to his new bow as mana flowed through his body, sending an entire enchantment into a single projectile rather than the weapon that fired it. The arrowhead glowed an angry red as he let it fly. The shaft buried itself in the beast's thigh with a hard thunk.

The creature's flesh swelled and bubbled, taking the whole spell in all at once until a chunk the size of a fist exploded from its leg. The revenant fell to one knee but remained stable. The wound was severe, but it wouldn't slow it down for long.

Rebecca burst from the back of the van, launching a pair of icicles. They shattered on contact against the beast's hide. Alex fired another arrow just as the wound to the creature's leg began to close. Another meaty chunk exploded from the revenant's shoulder.

Digby checked his companion's status on his HUD.

COVEN
DIGBY: MP: 53/108
ASHER: MP: 34/34
ALEX: MP: 50/165
REBECCA: MP: 67/177

Alex's arrows were working, but he didn't have enough mana to keep them coming. A few more was the best he could hope for. Rebecca wasn't faring any better. Digby clenched his clawed hand. They were losing. He beckoned to the reanimated revenant behind him and opened his maw on the ground next to it.

"Touch the darkness." He pointed down to the shadow by his feet.

The corpse of Miss Foley complied, crouching to place her hands in the black fluid that seeped from his void. Casting

Forge, he sent tendrils of necrotic blood coiling around his minion's hands to form a razor-sharp claw attached to each finger.

Digby raised a hand toward his enemy and uttered one word.

"Rend."

Miss Foley rushed forward, clawing the earth in a path that took the zombie around to the enormous revenant's back. His minion was slower than she had been when she was alive, but she was fast enough to leap to the creature's neck. Claws swiped and flesh tore as Tanner flailed at the distraction. A crimson spray erupted from the revenant's throat as the elderly zombie raked its fingers across its neck. The old woman bit down, leaving a set of false teeth buried in the top of Tanner's head when she pulled away.

"Do we have any more weapons?" Digby retreated to the parked van to let his minion work. Alex and Rebecca held their fire, falling back to his position as well.

"There's a breaching charge on the ground over there." Rebecca threw her hand out to point at a mass of broken plastic that looked like it had been a drone earlier in the fight. She tossed a regeneration spell at Mason to get him off the ground before adding, "I tried to blow Tanner to hell, but he took out my drone before I could get in position to detonate it. The explosive isn't large, but it's enough to do some damage if we can get it close enough."

Digby flicked his eyes back to her. "Can you set it with a timer so it can be placed by hand?"

"I can but you'd blow your arm off when—"

"I don't intend to be the one holding it." He cut her off and hooked a clawed thumb back at his minion.

Rebecca's eyes widened as she slapped Alex on the shoulder. "Cover me."

The enchanter complied, taking aim and firing another arrow while Rebecca leapt for her broken drone. She ripped a small cylinder free from the wreckage and tapped at a few buttons on the side before tossing it to Digby. Catching the object, he noticed a crimson display on one end that read sixteen. It ticked down to fifteen a second later.

Realizing he was holding an active bomb, he limped forward to summon his minion. "Return!"

Alex fired off his last enchanted arrow.

The corpse of Miss Foley let go of Tanner all at once, dropping to the ground to land on her back. With a sudden crack and series of pops, the zombie twisted her body to skitter across the ground like a spider. Digby thrust out the breaching charge in his hand to place it in the elderly minion's gummy jaws. The counter on the side ticked down to six.

Digby stabbed a finger out in the direction of Tanner's face and gave his command.

"Rend and tear."

Miss Foley's corpse snapped eyes back to the oversized creature, locking on the revenant's head. She darted across the dirt before leaping back up to the beast's neck.

"Three seconds." Rebecca counted down.

Digby thrust out a hand to focus on his minion. With the last of his mana, the elderly zombie burst into emerald flames. Tanner slapped at the woman's corpse as she dug her claws into his flesh. Digby dove behind the van along with Alex as a muffled pop sent chunks of burning tissue raining across the campground. Tanner screamed, dropping the headless corpse of Miss Foley to the dirt where it burned. The beast's skin bubbled and spat as portions of its skull showed through its blackened flesh.

That was when the creature stopped healing.

"He's out of MP!" Digby shouted, sensing the revenant's mana flow crawl to a stop. "Take him down!"

A pistol barked, but only once. The fight had taken its toll, leaving Mason and the others injured and out of ammunition. Digby slammed a fist against the van in frustration as Tanner let out a furious cry. The revenant barreled past him, stumbling into a tree as he ran for the safety of the forest. In seconds, the beast was gone.

Digby wasn't sure if he'd fatally wounded it or not. He locked his vision on his HUD where an experience message would normally appear after a kill.

Nothing came.

"Damn it!" He punched the van again, putting a ding in its side with his bone gauntlet. He glanced down at his missing foot. There was no way he could give chase. Not to mention he was nearly out of mana as well.

Parker and Alex tended to the wounded. Mason looked like he'd pull through. Sax, however, had lost a lot of blood. Rebecca stumbled over to him, having just enough mana for a single spell. She cast Regenerate on the fading soldier, bringing some color back to Sax's face.

Digby lowered his head, unsure if he was able to call what they'd accomplished a victory. What Tanner had become, a revenant bloodstalker, was so much stronger than anything he'd faced before.

If the world is full of those things… Digby stomped down the thought before finishing it.

He raised his head back up, finding Hawk stepping through the door of the lodge. The boy held Asher close to his chest like a cherished pet. Eventually, Digby let out a chuckle. With the world the way it was, it was victory enough. Tanner may have escaped, but the dawn would be there soon. They just had to take advantage of the time and get as far away as possible.

Maybe the castle from the brochure would pan out.

Parker helped the injured back to the cabin to recover. The rest of the survivors stood aside to watch as Alex and Rebecca healed both Mason and Sax. With no ability other than those that killed the living or manipulated the dead, Digby stood watch outside. Asher pecked at the charred remains of Miss Foley's corpse before flapping up to his shoulder. He gave the raven a scratch on her chin.

Hawk crept up to his side. "Is that…?"

"The old bag that attacked me with her cane?" Digby let his shoulders fall. "Indeed."

The boy glanced between the corpse and him. "You turned her into— "

"I did." Digby paused as a shudder passed through the boy. "I had to."

"I know." The child sounded hurt.

"I may not have known her long, but something tells me that this is what she would have wanted. I couldn't have chased that monster off without her help. And it's thanks to her that you and everyone else are still breathing." Digby glanced down at the boy. "Do you want to say something for her?"

Hawk stared at the woman's charred remains for a moment before nodding. "Thank you for being here." He let a tear escape before wiping it away with his sleeve. "I miss you."

"I don't." Digby shrugged, earning a sharp look from the boy. "What? I didn't know her." He tried to soften his gravelly voice. "But you're right. She will be missed by those whose lives she impacted, and from what I can tell, there were many." Digby reached out and cast Burial, watching the earth part to accept what was left of the woman. "Rest in peace, you old crone."

"You're kind of a jerk, huh?" Hawk looked up at him.

"I am what I am." Digby turned away to find Rebecca behind him. Mason stood beside her. The soldier's clothing was ripped and stained, but he looked to be in good health thanks to a few healing spells.

"Mister Graves?" He spoke up.

"Lord Graves," Digby corrected.

Mason let out a sigh. "Okay. Lord Graves."

"Yes, Mason?" Digby raised his head a bit at the sound of his self-given title.

"What are your plans?" The soldier's voice grew serious.

"My apprentice, Rebecca, and I will be traveling south a ways further. We've a location in mind for a new home and would like to reach it by sundown. We had only intended on stopping here for the night. So don't worry, we'll be out of your hair soon."

"Yes, about that…" Mason slipped his hands into his front pockets with his thumbs poking out as if he wasn't sure what to do with them. "Parker, Sax and I talked it over and, provided the rest of the group is onboard, we were wondering if you would like some help on your way."

"Help?" Digby shook his head. "Not really, we should be fine on our own."

"Yes, I see that. But what I mean is, can we come with you?"

"Why would you want to do that?" Digby furrowed his brow. "Why would a group of soldiers protecting children and other random survivors want to travel with a monster and his heretic companions? Not to mention you would have to drink purified water to stave off my poisonous aura."

"Look, Graves." Mason's gaze darted around before finally making eye contact. "The world as we knew it is gone. That thing, Tanner, would have killed us all if you hadn't been here, and I'm not so delusional to think that our lifespans are going to add up too much out here on our own. I won't pretend to understand the power that you three have, but I'm not dumb enough to think we can survive without it on our side. So, yes, if you three don't mind, we would like to travel together, even if we have to keep our distance to stay out of your aura."

"I wasn't able to save everyone." Digby gestured to the patch of disturbed soil by his feet.

"But you saved more than I could have alone." Mason lowered his eyes to Miss Foley's grave.

Digby scratched his chin for a moment. Then he scratched Asher's chin. Then he flicked his eyes to Rebecca. "What do you think?"

She shrugged. "I think we will need the extra hands to help fortify that ridiculous place you want to live in."

"They could slow us down," Digby countered.

"They could." Rebecca nodded.

"We won't." Mason shook his head.

Digby glanced to Hawk who was watching the exchange with a strangely hopeful expression, then he returned his attention to Mason. "I make no guarantees to keep your people safe or fed. And you'll have to pitch in when need be."

"That's fair." Mason nodded.

"Good." Digby extended his left hand to shake. "Then it's a deal."

Mason recoiled for an instant, his eyes falling to Digby's cold, dead finger. If his instincts were telling him to run, he didn't. Instead the soldier held out his hand in return. Digby grabbed hold, letting out a satisfied laugh as the soldier shivered at his touch. "Welcome aboard."

Rebecca leaned closer to Mason. "You're going to want to wash your hand. I don't think I've seen Dig wash since I met him."

"Bah." Digby waved away her comment. "I had Alex spray me with a hose back at the vineyard."

"Yeah, when?" She arched an eyebrow.

Digby raised a couple claws to count the days.

"Nope, never mind." Rebecca held up both hands. "I don't need to know."

"That's probably for the best." Digby lowered his claws to his side.

"Yes, great." Mason wiped his hand on his pants. "So where is this place that you have in mind to settle?"

Digby reached in his coat to retrieve the brochure for their new home and strafed around to stand beside Mason.

"Well, my friend, how do you feel about castles?"

CHAPTER ELEVEN

Shortly after dawn, the group of survivors loaded everything they could fit into a few of the cars that were parked off to the side of the camping supply store. Digby sauntered around them trying his best to appear confident, despite the gnawing fear that he might get them all killed.

Rebecca grabbed a number of small radios from the shop and handed them out to each of the vehicle's drivers. Alex called the hand-held communication devices walkie-talkies, which Digby liked. It was an accurate term. Plus, it sounded funny.

Next, he and Rebecca reviewed a map of the area to pinpoint the castle's location. It wasn't far to travel from the campground. Just ninety miles. They would make it there by noon if the roads were clear.

As usual, Digby settled into the back of the vineyard's van to watch videos on his tablet until he was needed. The next few hours passed by uneventfully, save for several bathroom breaks. They were forced to stop at nearly every gas station they passed to break in and use their facilities. Digby groaned each time. He wasn't aware that children had bladders the size of peas.

Rebecca made a point to cast her new cartography spell every time they stopped. She even hung herself out the window of the van to cast it a few times. Not that there was much to create a map of in the area, considering there had been nothing but trees and rolling hills lining both sides of the road for the last hour.

Fortunately, there were no revenants to be seen, probably all hiding somewhere dark until sundown. Digby still hadn't worked out why sunlight would have any effect on them. The only activity out and about were a few zombies here and there. Digby left them as they were, lacking the room to transport any new minions in the vehicles available. He suggested ditching a few of the children to free up some space, but the idea didn't go over well with the others. Obviously, he had been joking… for the most part.

After getting back on the road, Digby returned to his video library.

"How many movies are you going to watch?" Rebecca leaned around the back of the passenger seat.

"Probably all of them." He looked up at her over his tablet.

"I hate to sound like my parents, but too much screen time will rot your brain. Or at least, rot it more than it already is." She smirked.

"My brain is fine, thank you very much." Digby glowered at her. "And are these the same parents that sold you as a servant to Skyline?"

Rebecca flinched before turning back around. "Yeah…" She forced a chuckle. "They may not be the best source of advice, I suppose. But still, you might want to switch it up and watch something else. I could download you some documentaries so you can learn more about the world. I only started you with zombie movies because they were relevant to our current situation and I thought you might relate well to them."

"Hey, Lord Graves?" Alex chimed in.

"Yes?"

"Who do you root for when you watch a zombie movie?

The humans or the zombies?" Alex eyed him in the rearview mirror.

Digby thought about it for a second. "Both."

"How does that work?"

"I don't know. But no matter what happens, there's always a happy ending." Digby gave him a grin.

"That's an… interesting outlook, I guess." Alex nodded and continued driving just as Rebecca slapped a hand on the side of her seat.

"What?" Digby flinched.

"I need hard drives." She sat up straight.

"What for?" Alex looked at her sideways.

"For documentaries." Her eyes widened. "No, more than that. I just realized that Dig's tablet is currently the world's largest offline collection of humanity's accomplishments. The internet will fail completely at some point, and someone is going to need to preserve everything they can." She slapped herself in the forehead. "Oh shit, if it fails now, the only thing that will survive is a crap ton of zombie movies."

Alex let out a snort. "I can see it now, future generations learning about their past by watching High School of the Dead."

Digby laughed. "Yes, that one was weird."

"Oh no…" Rebecca covered her mouth with one hand as she realized how badly she may have doomed future civilizations. Her sudden crisis was interrupted by one of the walkie-talkies.

"Hey, this is Linda back in the rear car. We're going to need another bathroom break."

Rebecca picked up. "Can it wait? We're only around…" She paused, looking at what Digby assumed to be her imaginary map. "…six miles away from the castle. There will be restrooms there."

A moment went by before Linda responded. "Umm, no, I don't think we can wait that long."

Hawk was audible in the background. "Sax told you not to eat that yogurt at the last gas station."

Parker could be heard moaning as well.

"I did tell her that." Sax joined the conversation over the radios from one of the other cars.

"I thought you were messing with me," Parker argued. "It's not like yogurt needs to be refrigerated."

Several shocked voices from the other cars responded at once. "What?"

"Umm, Parker, dear?" Sax chimed in with a nurturing tone. "Do you somehow not know that yogurt goes bad if left out?"

"What?" Parked moaned again, sounding frustrated. "No it doesn't. My uncle packed one for me every day when I was in high school, and I left it in my bag until lunch. I was always fine."

"Parker?" Mason responded over the radio. "How have you survived this long?"

"Oh, shut up and pull over already." She howled loud enough that Digby might've been able to hear her from the rear car, even without the walkie-talkie.

He grabbed the radio. "You're going to have to hold it, Parker. We're not far from our new home."

"No way. We have a both ends situation brewing," Parker announced over the radio to their entire caravan.

"Gross." Digby's face fell at the description.

"Um, I did not sign on as a driver to deal with this kind of mess," Linda added.

"Okay, we can stop up there." Alex gestured to a road sign that read Hearst Castle Visitor's Center. The castle itself was another five miles up an enormous hill.

"Fine." Digby growled into the device. "Pull into the next right."

As soon as the van stopped, Parker ran past the window toward the building. Mason and Sax followed a second later with pistols drawn to guard their digestive challenged comrade.

"They never show that part in the movies." Digby shook his head.

"I'm sure you're glad you don't need to use the bathroom right now?" Rebecca leaned over her seat.

"Indeed."

"Having a bottomless void is pretty convenient," she commented.

"You could always get bit and join team zombie." Alex leaned on the steering wheel.

"True." Digby gave her a grin. "There's always room for more of the dead on my side."

"No thanks." Rebecca glowered at the both of them before popping her door open. "I'm going to cast my cartography spell. You two want to come guard me while Parker destroys the bathroom?"

"No thanks," Digby repeated her own words back to her. "You can guard yourself. Just icicle anything that looks particularly dangerous. You need to level up anyway."

"He's right, you know." Alex leaned toward her.

"Ugh, fine, I'll defend myself." She rolled her eyes. "But come with me anyway just so I feel better."

"Okay." Alex pushed out of the van as well.

"Have fun, you two." Digby sat back as soon as he was alone, though he pushed his tablet aside. They would be pulling up to the castle shortly. There wasn't much sense in starting another video. Asher cocked her head to the side next to him, as if wondering why he didn't go out with his fellow heretics. "Oh, don't look at me like that. It's not like I'll get bored without them."

Another minute went by. Then he popped open the rear door of the van and slid out to find the two of them standing by the front of the building. He was a little bored.

"How long does it take to cast a cartography spell?" He leaned on his walking stick as he watched Rebecca raise her walkie-talkie to her mouth. He couldn't hear what was being said but she turned back to him a moment later.

"That was Mason. We've got revenants inside."

"Of course we do." Digby limped his way forward. "Told you we shouldn't have stopped."

"Too late now." Alex followed as they approached the visitor's center.

"I'll get the drone in the air." Rebecca headed back for the van.

"You can do that from your phone." Digby beckoned her along. "We might need your icicles."

She hesitated for a moment as if her shadow was pinned to the ground. Eventually, she complied and followed behind. Digby took the radio from her and addressed the entire group.

"We have some revenants in the building, everyone stay in your vehicles." He let go of the walkie-talkie's button before pressing it down again. "Alright, Mason, where are…?" He trailed off as he caught a glimpse of a few human-like forms through the building's glass doors. "Never mind, I see them."

Pushing into the visitor's center, the situation became clear. Mason and Sax stood in front of a door marked restroom, both holding a pistol in the direction of five enemies. At first it was hard to tell the creatures apart from zombies. Though, upon closer inspection, their pale, unblemished skin and pointed ears made it clear. Beyond their appearance, they moved at the same lethargic pace as Digby's deceased brethren. An analyze confirmed it.

Dormant Revenant, Common, Neutral.

He glanced up, finding a skylight stretching across the center of the roof all the way to the back of the building. A beam of sunlight cut the room in half. The revenants remained on their side as if they didn't want to cross it. They reached out, their hands breaching the light.

Digby squinted. The light didn't seem to hurt them. It was more like they just didn't like it. He thought back to the revenant's racial traits that had appeared when he'd animated

Miss Foley. The description had said that their abilities would stop working during daylight hours. That must be what the Heretic Seed's analysis meant when it labeled them as dormant.

Looking at them now, their behaviors were nearly identical to those of zombies. He wondered if given enough time, they would brave the sunbeams to reach their prey on the other side of the room. His question was answered a second later when one of them stepped forward into the light.

"Hold your fire." Digby raised a hand to Mason who was adjusting his aim. "There might be more around, and the sound might be a problem." He gestured to Rebecca. "Besides, we have a mage who can handle a group this size quietly."

She groaned and cast Icicle, dropping a frozen shard down from above. It plunged into the head of the first revenant.

"See, hunting isn't so bad." Digby leaned on his walking stick like a sorcerer training an apprentice.

"Yeah, I know." She dropped another target. "I just feel more comfortable in the van and don't like squandering my mana." Another three Icicles put an end to the creatures.

5 dormant revenants defeated, 60 experience awarded.

"Okay, you happy now? I have less than half my MP left." Rebecca dropped her hands to her sides. "Also, way to screw up the experience, Dig."

"What do you mean?" He arched an eyebrow.

"I only got sixty for that." She let out an annoyed huff.

"Yes." Digby thought back to when he and Alex had fought a few enemies back in Seattle. "The Seed awards experience based on the level of the highest heretic involved in the conflict."

"It also subtracts a percent depending on the distance between you and the target," Alex chimed in. "So if an enemy dies from a minion or something and we're not in the area, we lose points."

"That's unhelpful." She deflated.

"Tell me about it," Digby scoffed. "I got nothing back in Seattle when we killed Manning, since you weren't a heretic when you finished him off with the kestrel's guns. That would have been a lot of experience too."

"It was better than letting him cut off more of your limbs." Rebecca gestured to his peg-leg.

"I wonder if there's a way to avoid the penalty for having a higher-level heretic with us?" Alex scratched at his head. "I mean, back at the vineyard when you were still down in the cellar, the Seed based its rewards off my level. So maybe it's better if you don't come in with us unless we really need you. Maybe it stops counting you if you aren't aware of what's happening."

"Oh by all means, I'll wait in the van next time then. The revenants don't register as hostile for me until I start attacking them anyway."

"I think I'd still prefer to have some back up, though." Rebecca commented.

"But you will get stronger faster alone." Digby pointed at her before glancing back to where Mason and Sax stood guard outside the restroom. "How long is Parker going to take in there?"

In an attempt to make use of his time, he walked over to the revenant's bodies on the floor and opened his maw to shove one of the creature's arms in. "At least there's something to eat while I wait. I was starting to run low on blood after forging so many spikes the last two days." He closed his maw, taking the revenant's limb off at the shoulder before moving on to another.

Both Mason and Sax gasped and looked away. Of course, that was when Parker stumbled out from the bathroom. She took one look at Digby as he butchered a corpse like a common hog and immediately turned green. She slapped a hand over her mouth and pushed back through the bathroom door before witnessing anything more.

"Maybe not the best time for that." Rebecca placed a hand to her forehead.

"I'll be done in a few minutes." Digby severed a leg with horrible squelch.

"Oh god." Sax covered his mouth and headed into the bathroom as well.

Mason simply closed his eyes and placed hand hands over his ears.

Digby smirked. "Better get used to it, fellas. You wouldn't want me to get hungry, now would you?"

After shoving what he could of the revenant's corpses into his maw, Parker and Sax returned from the restroom. He immediately placed his hands behind his back to conceal the fact that they were covered in blood. With some quick thinking, he cast Blood Forge to convert the mess into a convenient set of talons for his bone claws. The spell even pulled everything off his left hand.

"There. No need to even wash up." He grinned at his creation.

"Lovely." Rebecca walked over to the visitor center's eatery in search of food. "We should take whatever we can find while we're here."

"Keep alert though." Alex held out the iron key he carried. "My detection spell isn't picking up anything close, but this thing's a little cool so there's got to be a few revs or zombies out there somewhere."

"That makes sense." Rebecca pointed up to the skylights. "I'll keep the drone up there so nothing sneaks up on us. If anything comes out of the woods that surround the road, I'll know."

Looking through the shelves, they found the majority of the supplies already gone. Digby wasn't sure how much the establishment would normally keep on hand, but it seemed like there should have been more. It was as if someone had already come through and taken most of what had been available.

Digby glanced at his HUD as the others continued the search.

MP: 219/220

Huh? Digby stared at the number, wondering why he hadn't regained enough to reach full yet. His rate of absorption varied slightly depending on the balance of the ambient mana around him, but it had never been taken that long before. He had been sure at least five minutes had passed and he usually gained a point every few seconds. Being down twenty points, he should have reached full again over two minutes ago. He hadn't noticed a change in his absorption rate the night before, which only raised the question, what changed?

Digby thought back over the last two weeks. He hadn't used much magic while they laid low, so he hadn't noticed anything then either. He raised his eyes up to the skylight above.

Could it be the sun?

Thinking it over, it made sense. Light brought life to the earth, so it wouldn't be unreasonable to assume that its presence would alter the balance of the ambient mana during the day, flooding it with more life essence. With his pure death balance, the shift in mana composition might be leaving him with less to work with. He might have noticed the difference sooner, but he'd barely cast any spells the entire time he spent hiding in the vineyard's wine cellar.

Digby glanced at Rebecca's mana listed under his coven's information on his HUD. She had been below half earlier. Doing a little more math, he judged that she was absorbing essence twice as fast as he was.

That's not great.

Apparently having a pure mana balance, while powerful, came with its share of downsides. Digby tensed, realizing that he might share a bit of the revenant's weaknesses during the day. He would have to be careful how much mana he used while the sun was up. Before he could draw any more conclusions, his thoughts were interrupted by an alert that sounded from Rebecca's smartphone.

"Shit." Her eyes bulged at the screen as soon as she pulled the device from her pocket.

"What is it?" Mason stepped forward.

All the color drained from her face as she looked up from her phone. "We have incoming."

CHAPTER TWELVE

"What do you mean, we have incoming?" Digby was sure he didn't want to hear Rebecca's answer.

"It's a horde." She swiped her fingers across the screen of her phone.

"From which direction?" Mason ran toward the door and pulled a pistol from a holster.

"Shit," she cursed again. "Every direction!"

"How is that possible?" Parker staggered over, still looking under the weather.

"They must have all been in the trees lining the road. They've surrounded us." She dragged her finger along the screen of her phone, causing the drone hovering above to climb and widen the view. Her hand started to shake. "Oh god. There's thousands of them coming."

"Are they zombies or revs?" Sax took up a position by the door as Parker tossed him her shotgun.

"They're out in the daylight, so probably zombies."

"Is there time to get the cars out?" Mason reached for his walkie-talkie.

Rebecca went silent for a moment, glancing to him before

dropping her eyes down to her phone. "Yes, but we'll have to split up to divide the horde's attention. It's thinnest to the south. So you three should head that way. As long as you're careful, you can make it without help and you'll pull some of the zombies away to keep the rest of us from being overrun. The horde is thicker to the north but having Dig will make it safer." She looked up to him. "You can control up to twenty, right?"

"Yes." Digby nodded.

"You'll have to use them to clear a path."

"I can do that."

"Good, let's move. We'll take the rest of the survivors to the north with us and meet up with you three when the horde passes."

"Got it." Mason led Sax and Parker out to pile into one of the cars.

The rest of the survivors pulled up behind the vineyard's van. With a boost from Alex, Digby climbed onto the roof. The caravan was moving just as the first members of the horde reached the parking lot. Alex ran the first few down with the van to clear a path for the rest of the cars. Digby held on tight as the vehicle passed over the deceased obstacles. Glancing back, he caught Mason's car heading in the opposite direction.

Revving its engine, the van lurched forward toward a wall of zombies that were beginning to converge on the road. Digby checked his HUD.

MP: 220/220

He cast control until his minion count hit twenty, reaching the final rank for the spell on his last cast.

SPELL RANK INCREASED
Control Zombie has advanced from rank A to S. Base duration has increased to 60 minutes. Plus 50% duration due to mana purity. Total duration: 90 minutes. Total number of controlled zombies increased to 30. Mana cost

reduced to 2. Target's Intelligence bonus is increased to 10.

NEW SPELL DISCOVERED
By reaching the maximum rank for the spell Control Common Zombie, you have discovered the spell Control Uncommon Zombie.

CONTROL UNCOMMON ZOMBIE
Description: Temporarily subjugate the dead into your service regardless of target's will/resistance. Zombies under your control gain +2 intelligence and are unable to refuse any command. May control up to 1 uncommon zombie at any time.
Rank: D
Cost: 50MP
Duration: 10 minutes (+50% due to purity, total: 15 minutes.)
Range: 10ft (+50% due to purity, total: 15ft.)
Limitations: Commands are limited by target's intelligence. This spell is ineffective against the living.

"Hell yes!" Digby immediately cast control another ten times, cackling at the fact that each use now only cost him two points to cast. He just wished there were a few uncommon zombies in the mix to take control of as well. Though, he didn't have time to analyze them all in hope of finding a leader or glutton amongst them.

"Make a path!" he shouted to his new servants, getting an immediate response. The extra ten intelligence for each made an impact as well, creating an even greater level of cooperation amongst the dead. One zombie wearing a military uniform actually saluted before pulling a pistol from a holster and firing into the oncoming horde. Their aim was terrible, but still, a zombie with a gun was terrifying.

The engine of Mason's car roared as Parker hung out the

window, firing into the mass of bodies as they drove away in the opposite direction. Sax held onto her shirt to keep her from falling out. The distraction proved wise as they pulled away a solid third of the horde as the dead broke off to pursue the vehicle.

With the help of Digby's minions, the vineyard's van pushed through the crowd before they were able to block the road off completely. The rest of the cars followed behind, reaching a position of relative safety at the outer edge of the horde. Alex kept driving to make sure the horde remained behind them. Digby looked back at his thirty minions holding the line like a phalanx of soldiers.

Rebecca's drone dropped down to hover beside him as her voice came over its speaker. "Can you hold them back?"

He nodded. "It looks like my horde has things under control for the moment."

"Good. I had my doubts, but you seemed to have handled the situation." She almost sounded surprised.

"I ranked up my control spell too." He sat with his head high on the roof of the van. "Now we just have to circle back to pick up Mason."

"Of course." Rebecca let an awkward pause pass by. "If he makes it, we'll meet up and head on to the castle."

Digby arched an eyebrow. "What do you mean, if he makes it? I thought the horde was thinner in that direction?"

A few seconds of suspicious silence went by before she responded. "It is."

"Then why wouldn't they make it?" Digby turned to look at the drone, only to have it pull its camera away. He tightened his hand on the van's roof rack. "Becky. What did you do?"

"I made a judgement call." Her voice sounded cold.

"Damn it, Becky, don't give me vague answers." Digby slapped the roof of the van. "Why would they not make it?"

The drone spun back to face him. "Because there's three brutes in that direction. The big kind."

Digby froze.

Three?

With his current abilities, he was confident that he could beat a brute, but three? That, he was less certain of. Rebecca's intent was obvious. If they wanted to escape, sending a decoy in the opposite direct made the most sense.

"No!" Digby let go of the van's roof rack and rolled to the side, tumbling from the vehicle. He cast Necrotic Regeneration before he hit the road. There was no way he would be able to land without taking damage. Not with his missing foot hindering his agility. A few bones cracked, but the magic went to work immediately. Digby slammed his peg-leg down as he shoved himself upright and stared in the direction Mason's car had gone.

The dead filled the road.

He glanced at his mana.

MP: 110/220

It was going to have to be enough.

"This is no time to play hero," Rebecca shouted from her drone. "We need you."

Digby ignored her and hobbled forward. "Stay here and make sure everyone gets clear. The dead won't hurt me if I go alone."

"That will only last until you get between them and their food," she shouted over the growing moans on the surrounding zombies.

Digby hesitated. She was right. He shook his head a second later and shoved past a pair of zombies. "I'll cross that bridge when I come to it."

With that, he broke into a jog, his peg-leg hitting the road in a steady rhythm. He wasn't fast, but he was faster than the rest of the horde. Unfortunately, that meant that he couldn't take his thirty minions with him. They would never keep up. He had to go alone.

As a zombie, Digby couldn't argue with the logic of Rebecca's judgment. The needs of the many came first even if it meant sacrificing a few. That was how a horde worked. His undead instincts screamed at him that she was right.

Then why was he still playing hero?

Digby let out a mirthless laugh.

Hero? Me? "Bah!"

There was nothing heroic about what he was doing, no matter what it looked like. No, it was just simply fear. He couldn't lose Mason and his soldiers. If he did, then who the hell would lead the other survivors. Him? Fat chance. *I'm no leader.* Beside his heretics, what human could actually follow an undead monster? Even if they did, he simply wouldn't know what to do. That thought was far more terrifying than a few brutes.

Digby shoved past one zombie after another, struggling to progress as the horde grew thicker. There was a limit to what he could do. If he tried anything violent, they would surely tear him apart the moment they labeled him as hostile.

"Move!" He shouted a Compel, sending a ripple of compliance through the horde. The effect faded in seconds. "Damn."

There was nothing he could do. He was too slow and not nearly powerful enough. The horde pushed back, halting him in place. Digby felt his strength fade as his confidence began to falter. It surged back up as he caught a glimpse of a hulking form in the crowd walking on all fours like an animal.

A brute.

Digby didn't even hesitate before casting his new spell. His mana dropped a full fifty points as a zombie brute was added to his HUD under his list of minions. The massive zombie stopped in its tracks to look back at him.

"Join me!" Digby beckoned to the beast, watching as it used its weight to push through the horde. He clasped his hands together along with a villainous grin. "Good, good."

With the monster on his side, the odds were a little fairer. Then again, there was still a horde standing between him and his accomplices. Without a better option, Digby shrugged and climbed aboard his newest minion's back. The brute didn't have the agility to walk upright or weave through the crowd, but it could certainly make haste in a straight line.

"Onward!" Digby let a ridiculous cackle slip as he thrust a claw in the direction of Mason's car. Zombies flew out of the way as the brute galloped head first into the horde like a runaway bull. "That's it now, don't let a single one stop you."

From his elevated position, Digby spotted Mason's vehicle. He tensed as he noticed the other two brutes Rebecca had told him about closing in on the car. He wasn't sure if he could make it in time.

"Faster!" Digby kicked his brute with his one good foot as if he were riding a horse, getting a groan in return right before a sudden burst of speed. "Yes, that's right, we're almost—"

Digby's victorious cry was cut off as his minion stumbled. The beast really didn't have much in the way of agility after all.

"Wait, no shit." Digby tumbled from the brute's back, rolling onto the road where the feet of the horde closed in around him to blot out everything. Digby tucked his body into a ball, hoping that he wouldn't be trampled. He covered his head to protect his brain. The last thing he needed at the moment was a trip to see the Heretic Seed. He was sure that snarky, red-eyed jerk would have something to say about his idea to ride the brute.

Looking around, his minion wasn't anywhere to be seen. It must have kept going without him, having never received an order to stop.

"Well, that's just great."

Searching for a way out, he caught a glimpse of light to his left. Digby let out a grumble as he resigned himself to crawl for safety. To his surprise, it seemed that the zombies had still not marked him as hostile. He wasn't sure why. He would have expected that his brute would have trampled a few of the dead that had been in their way.

"Oh well, not something I'm going to worry about now." Digby continued to crawl until he emerged from the horde in the grass to the side of the road. He pushed up and started running as soon as he was clear.

"Alright, now where the hell is Mason?"

———————◆ ◆————————

Mason slammed his foot on the break as a hulking, dead form stepped into the middle of the road. The zombie was three times the size of a normal human and covered from head to toe in slabs of muscle.

Parker fell forward over the center console. "What the hell is that?"

"Shit, it's one of those big guys. I saw a few back at the quarantine line in Seattle." Sax searched his pocket for a shell to load into Parker's shotgun.

"It's a brute." Mason let out a grunt. "Dig filled me in on the different types of zombies last night when we were sharing information." He turned to Parker. "How are you on ammo?"

Still laying on her stomach over the center console, she snapped the cylinder from the side of her revolver to check. "A few rounds left."

"Shit." Mason checked the rearview, finding dozens of zombies closing in. There were more behind the brute blocking the road in the direction they were facing. Another of the over-sized zombies appeared, closing in from the other side in a pincer maneuver. For a second, they looked like they were holding ground as if waiting for a signal. Mason furrowed his brow. "They almost seem to be working together."

"I thought the mutated ones were usually out for themselves." Parker pushed herself up and returned to her seat in the back.

"So did I," Sax added. "The ones on the quarantine line were almost as aggressive to each other as they were to us."

"Something's different." Mason backed the car up, bumping

two of the zombies behind the vehicle as he attempted to angle the car to get around one of the brutes.

"Why the hell didn't Becca warn us?" Sax looked back in the direction the van had gone. "That drone jockey must have seen the brutes approaching. They're huge, there's no way she missed them."

"I'll ask her if we survive." Mason hit the gas and swerved.

One of the brutes leaped to the side, stumbling into their path. Mason slammed on the breaks and spun the wheel before putting it in reverse. The tires squealed as he backed over a random zombie and turned the car around. Dropping the pedal to the floor, the vehicle sped forward only to be rocked by the impact of one of the brutes as they body checked the front, right wheel well. A meaty hand slapped down on the hood. ·

"Shit!" Mason spun the wheel again and pumped the gas, trying to rock the car free as if it was stuck in a snowbank. Growing up in New England, he'd driven in less than ideal conditions before. Granted, a zombie horde had not been one of them.

The other brute slammed down on the trunk, stopping the car dead in its tracks. The horde crowded in on all sides with dozens of hands pressing against the windows.

Sax leaned to Parker. "Remember when you said you had a few rounds left?"

"Yeah."

"Does that mean you have at least three?"

"Shut up. Don't talk like that." Mason shot his friend a serious look. "We're getting out of —" His words were cut off when his door popped open. With a frantic grab, he caught the interior handle and pulled with all his strength. The sound of dozens of moaning voices bled through the crack of the door. A zombie on the other side dragged its cheek across the window, leaving an oily smear as it wrapped its other hand around the door handle outside.

"No you don't." Mason pulled the door closed just enough

for Parker to lunge forward across the front passenger seat and hit the auto-lock button on the door.

"Jesus, since when do they know how to open a car door?" Sax pulled on Parker's shirt to help her get back to her seat.

"It must be a leader. Dig said they were a little smarter than the rest." Mason slumped back in his seat to catch his breath once the door was secure.

"What do we do now?" Sax moved away from the windows in the back as the light outside was blotted out by the horde climbing the rear of the car.

"Shit if I know." Parker huddled up beside him.

"Everyone be quiet a second." Mason stared into the eyes of the brute leaning on the hood of the car as its meaty hand dented the metal. "Why aren't they breaking the windows?"

"Maybe they don't want to screw up the resale value." Parker let out an awkward laugh that was entirely inappropriate for the situation.

"Oh yeah, 'cause an early nineties Ford Taurus is really going to sell well in today's market," Sax snapped back, clearly trying to distract himself from their imminent demise.

That was when a third brute forced its way through the horde, shoving at the surrounding zombies. As soon as it had a little more room to move, it started pushing at the other brute.

"What the hell is it doing?" Sax clung to the back of Mason's seat.

"Maybe it wants us all to itself." Parker clung to him.

"No." Mason gripped the wheel. "I think it's helping us." He stepped on the gas, pushing the car forward a few inches. The brute continued to fight to clear a path as wild cackles erupted over the radio.

"Keep pushing." Digby laughed again. "My brute will set you free."

Mason floored it, spurred on by the necromancer's victorious howls over the radio. Zombies fell to the side out of the way, while some disappeared under the hood. His heart soared as the edge of the horde came into view. The car bumped and lurched as it ran over the last few zombies, finding Digby standing in the road beyond the horde with his pet raven sitting on his shoulder. His brute tumbled out of the mass of zombies behind them before pushing itself up on all fours to return to its master.

Stomping on the breaks, the car skidded to a stop. Digby didn't even step aside. Instead, the necromancer stood tall with his walking stick held to the side like a wizard's staff. The tail of his coat billowed in the breeze of the open road as he cackled like a madman.

Parker stared at the wild zombie. "That is one confident dead man."

Mason shook his head. "Yeah, he's something alright."

CHAPTER THIRTEEN

Digby held his ground as Mason's car burst through the horde of zombies. He could have stepped out of the way, but he thought his presence would be more impressive if he stood tall like the hero on the cover of one of his favorite movies, the one with a chainsaw for a hand. He suppressed a flinch when the car screeched to a stop only a few feet in front of him.

Whew, that could have gone badly. He was glad his deceased body didn't sweat anymore.

Mason leaned across the passenger seat to open the door. "Get in, before they catch up."

"Nonsense." Digby gestured toward the brute beside him, remembering how strong the mutated zombie was from the time he'd fought another of its kind back in Seattle. "I'd have to leave my new minion behind."

Just as the words left his mouth, the other two brutes carefully pushed through the horde. Digby couldn't help but notice how gentle they were with the rest of the dead. It was almost like they were being careful not to injure any of the common zombies in the mix.

That's odd. He shook his head and patted his oversized

minion on its hunched shoulder. "No matter. Rend them to pieces."

His brute took off at a gallop, straight into the beast on the right. The pair bowled into the zombies, throwing corpses into the air. The brute on the left turned back to join in the brawl as it too disappeared into the mass of walking corpses. Digby wished he hadn't been forced to leave the rest of his thirty common zombies back with the van, but he wouldn't have been able to reach Mason in time if he'd waited for them. As it was, he'd barely made it himself. A memory of nearly being trampled flashed through his mind.

A ferocious roar from within the crowd echoed off the surrounding hills, sending a jolt of fear through Digby's spine. There was a chance he didn't have as good a handle on the situation as he'd thought. He glanced at his HUD.

MP: 60/220

Digby cringed at the value, realizing how little he had left.

"On second thought, I will take you up on that ride." He pulled Asher from his shoulder and tossed her in the back of the car with Parker and Sax. Before dropping himself into the passenger seat, Rebecca's drone darted past him. She circled around to stop in front of him.

"Damn it, Dig. I was in the middle of explaining things when you ran off."

"Keep your pants on, Becky. I'll meet back up with you as soon as we're free."

"It's too late for that." Rebecca sounded frustrated.

"What, why?" Digby flicked his eyes back to the drone.

"Because we needed you here. The horde is bigger than I thought."

"How?" Digby slapped the roof of Mason's car causing both Parker and Sax to jump in the back.

"There were more in the woods on either side of the road, thousands of them. They closed in on us and blocked our path as soon as you ran off. Your horde slowed them down but there were too many."

Digby spun to scan the tree-line, finding a steady stream of corpses wandering into the light. Squinting, he found that they had already blocked the road further down as if springing a preplanned trap. He and Mason weren't escaping that way. Digby glanced to the minion list on his HUD, finding the thirty common zombies right where they belonged. He snapped his head back to the drone.

"How have you been overrun? My minions are all still functioning. They would have sacrificed themselves before letting the caravan get boxed in."

"They've been..." She paused. "I don't know how to describe it. It's like they've been taken prisoner."

"What?" Digby turned back toward where his controlled brute was as the horde began to spread out. He froze the second his minion came into view. The other two mutated beasts were holding it down, like they were trying to stop it from moving or fighting back. It was almost as if they didn't want to hurt it.

Digby focused on one of the brutes to activate the Heretic Seed's analyze ability.

Zombie Brute, Uncommon, Neutral.

"Rebecca, have you tried analyzing any of the zombies?"

"No, I know what they are, why would I...?" The drone hovered in place for a moment. "Oh weird, they're all neutral."

Digby checked another few zombies, finding their relationship status to be the same.

"We have to go!" Mason leaned out the car window.

"One minute." Digby waved a hand at him before marching toward his captured brute. "Alright, alright, who's in charge here? I'd like to negotiate."

Confused moans answered him.

"Fine, let me dumb this down." Digby rolled his eyes at the horde. "Which of you teeth are leading the many?"

A lone zombie slipped to the front of the group.

"That's the one that tried to open my door." Mason stepped out of the car as zombies surrounded them on all sides. Sax got out behind him, clearly concerned as they became trapped within a clearing at the center of the horde. Parker climbed out next, holding Asher in her arms. Digby narrowed his eyes at the zombie that had stepped out of the crowd.

Zombie Leader, Uncommon, Neutral.

"Alright, I'm not sure how you are controlling these brutes, but tell them to get off my minion."

The zombie let out a moan in the direction of the two beasts holding his brute down. The pair let go.

"That's better." Digby beckoned to his minion to return to his side. "Now, what's all this about?"

The zombie leader let out another moan, this time adding a Compel that Digby could understand.

The many, safe.

It followed with a more cryptic message.

Prey, safe.

With that the leader turned back into the crowd and the horde began walking as one.

"It's like they're trying to herd us." Mason glanced around, clearly uneasy with the situation. He stepped forward as the clearing they stood in moved along with the horde.

"What do we do?" Sax crept along beside Parker.

"We go with them." Digby shrugged, going with the flow. "There's obviously someone in charge. Let's find out who."

"What if it's someone from Skyline?" Mason lowered his voice as if he was worried one of the zombies might somehow report back on him. "Didn't you say that you think they have a necromancer on their side? That they must have created their own to manipulate this curse?"

"Indeed." Digby leaned on his walking stick as he moved

with the horde. "But I have a feeling that if this was Skyline's doing, they would have just torn me apart."

"That's it then, we have no choice but to let them take us wherever they want." Parker deflated as Asher flapped back up to Digby's shoulder.

"Seems that way." Digby nodded, submitting to the horde's collective will. A few minutes later, the vineyard's van came into view, the crowd of zombies flowing around it until it too was contained within the clearing. Rebecca and Alex leaned up against its side. Digby wasn't sure if he should be glad to find them or not, knowing they were just as trapped as he was. "I see you two got caught in the net as well."

"Yeah, the horde came up from both sides of the road." Alex's shoulders fell. "We all got caught. Even the other cars. There's no way to drive through the crowd."

"The weird part is that the whole horde is non-hostile," Rebecca added. "All they seemed to care about was that we got out of our cars. They backed off once they got our doors open."

"Dig thinks they're taking us to their leader." Mason stepped forward, avoiding eye contact with Rebecca. Digby couldn't help but notice the muscles in the soldier's jaw tighten as soon as he saw her.

"Why did they want us out of the cars, then?" Alex wrapped his knuckles against the van. "They could have surrounded us and forced us to drive in the direction they wanted."

"It was for safety." Digby scanned the crowd of walking dead that surrounded them, finding a few of his common minions in the mix. Each was held by at least two other zombies to keep them from fighting back. "They were afraid we might run over some of them. Which was probably valid. They want to protect their own. Hence why they haven't injured any of my minions."

"That's a little out of character for them?" Rebecca started walking as the clearing at the center of the horde pushed forward, forcing everyone inside to do the same.

"Not really." Digby shrugged. "They are the many. Meaning they know they are strongest together. With the curse being hijacked the way it has been, they probably sense that finding more of their kind might be a problem if their numbers are allowed to dwindle. Therefore, they will want to protect their own. Every zombie lost is a tooth that can no longer bite."

"Okay. That's a weird level of understanding." Parker followed behind Digby.

"Again, not really." He glanced back at her. "Zombies are actually quite timid. The well-being of their horde usually comes first. They will still sacrifice a few of their numbers in pursuit of prey, but mostly they will try to protect their own. It's not their fault they want to eat people. They need food and you all taste good. The fact that they are holding back now speaks to whoever is controlling them."

"What do you mean?" Mason kept pace.

"None of these zombies are under a spell. So the fact that they haven't attacked such easy prey means that they consider your survival beneficial to their horde. Whoever is behind this group has gone through a lot of effort to make the dead understand their intent."

Digby paused as the rest of the survivors came into view. Linda, Hawk, Troy, and everyone else were trapped within a bubble of life within the crowd of the dead. Their holding area merged with his group's as they continued to walk. The zombies gave them a perimeter of free space to walk in without making any motion to attack. After twenty minutes of following the road, the humans began to accept the idea that they might not be eaten. At least, not right away.

Digby didn't mention the constant hunger that radiated from the horde. Instead he just warned them not to get too close. The dead were holding back, but still, it was best not to tempt fate. The only ones that were truly safe were himself and the minions under his control. The horde released his subjects when he ordered them to stop struggling and cooperate. His brute was allowed to move freely as well. Once his minions were loose, he had them line the perimeter of their space, to ensure that none of the untamed zombies got bitey.

"How long are we going to walk for?" Hawk dragged his feet as it became clear that the horde was taking them further and further from the visitor's center.

"You can ride my minion if you want?" Digby motioned to the oversized zombie. Its back looked grimy.

"Never mind." Hawk lowered his head.

"Joking aside, how long are we going to walk for?" Alex chimed in.

"It's been over an hour." Rebecca checked the time on her phone before flicking the screen to move the drone that hovered above them. She cast her cartography spell a second later. "I hate to say it, but I think the horde is taking us to your castle, Dig."

"What?" He stopped short.

"It's the only thing in this direction." She let out a mirthless laugh. "I think someone has beaten you to claiming the place."

"We'll just see about that." He picked up his pace as the road climbed higher up a large hill. A few minutes later, the castle came into view in the distance. Digby let a wild grin creep across his face.

The place was more than he could have hoped for.

Two gorgeous white spires bracketed the front of an enormous Mediterranean castle, sitting high on a small mountain. The view from the place must have been fantastic. From its top, a necromancer could survey the lush greenery and rolling hills of the surrounding territory. Not to mention it would be impossible for an opposing army to march on the castle without being spotted from miles away.

The building was surrounded by well-maintained trees, giving the place a pleasant atmosphere. It was the sort of place a zombie like him could kick back and relax. As they got closer, he spotted several columns of stone, reminiscent of the architecture of ancient Rome. Statuary littered the property along with several smaller buildings that would function well as barracks in the future. It was almost hard to believe such a perfect place still existed in the strange world that he'd been thrust into.

"Still think my choice of destinations is ridiculous, Becky?" Digby looked up at the castle, unable to stop smiling. He might have even salivated if he could.

"Won't matter if we don't survive the walk there." She gestured to the horde that surrounded them.

"Indeed." He refreshed his control spells for his minions as their zombie guides came to a stop.

Digby struggled to see over the crowd, catching the zombie leader from before slipping through the horde toward the front. A few other zombies, probably leaders as well, joined them. He lost sight of them soon after. Then, suddenly, the entire mass of over three thousand zombies began to part, forming a narrow path that led up to the castle's front. Parker reached for her revolver, but Digby held out a hand to tell her to keep it lowered.

He squinted down the path, finding a man walking toward them. At first glance, he was elderly, with white hair and a beard. A cane tapped the ground beside him as he sauntered through the narrow passage of the dead at a casual pace. It wasn't until the man got closer that Digby noticed something else.

He was dead.

Zombie Master, Rare, Neutral.

Even stranger, another two men, both alive, stepped into the path behind him, both armed with hunting rifles. They held their weapons at their sides, as if making an effort not to appear aggressive.

"Hello there." The zombified man spoke in a pleasant, albeit raspy voice. "Apologies for the way in which you were brought to this location. I'm sure you are all afraid, but let me assure you that no harm shall befall…" He trailed off as soon as he met Digby's gaze. "What's this now? Are you perchance undead as well?"

"I am." Digby kept his answer simple as Asher let out a caw from his shoulder.

"Oh my, thank the lord. I knew there had to be more like me out there." The elderly dead man glanced around at the other survivors that stood behind Digby. "And you have already found humans to protect, that speaks well of your character." He thrust out a hand, offering it to shake.

"I, ah, yes." Digby stared at the zombie master's hand without taking it. Something about him rubbed him the wrong way. Maybe it was the fact that he still had a nose on his face.

"Oh, sorry, how rude of me." He inclined his head and placed his hand across his chest. "I am Rufus." The zombie master raised his head and gestured to the dead around him. "And this is my horde. I would like to extend an invitation of friendship and shelter."

Digby arched an eyebrow. "Shelter?"

"Yes." Rufus swept a hand back toward the castle.

"You are offering us shelter, in there?" Digby's eye twitched.

"I am." Rufus stood tall.

"And that castle is your property?" Digby suppressed a growl.

"It is, in the sense that I am inhabiting it, along with several humans, and that I am protecting this area with my horde."

"I see." Digby paused. "And there's no chance of you vacating the premises?"

"Ah, no." Rufus's face fell. "That isn't likely."

"Well then, I am Lord Graves." Digby forced his most polite smile and placed his hands together. "And on behalf of myself and the rest of my subjects, we accept your offer of hospitality."

"Since when are we his subjects?" Parker whispered to Alex.

The enchanter whispered back behind his hand. "At least he doesn't call you boy."

"Fantastic." Rufus perked back up, ignoring their whispering. "The human race is having a tough time of late, so it's important that they find safety as soon as possible." He glanced to the brute and the thirty zombies that Digby had claimed as his minions. "Would you be so kind to release the rest of our kind from your influence?"

"I would if I could." Digby feigned disappointment. "Unfortunately, there is no way to cancel my ability. It will, however, wear off on its own within a few hours." He exaggerated the limit, having the intent of recasting the spells a few times to keep his minions under his control. He would have to let the brute go though, since he wouldn't absorb enough during the day to offset the fifty points that his uncommon control spell would cost.

"I do apologize for commandeering your zombies, but I had been under the impression that my subjects were in danger." He layered on a bit of guilt.

"That's understandable." Rufus nodded.

"Indeed." They both stood awkwardly for a moment before Digby started up again. "Anyway, why don't you take us into your stronghold? My subjects have had a long journey and are sure to be exhausted. Many of them are children, you see. Forcing them to walk five miles in the hot sun was a bit much. Isn't that right, child?" Digby grabbed Hawk by the sleeve and yanked him closer.

"Ah, yes, my Lord." The kid followed along with his claim, mimicking a British accent similar to Digby's as he did. It seemed he was a quick study. "We are ever so tired. My feet be covered in blisters, they are."

"Indeed, child." Digby squeezed his shoulder to let him know he was laying it on a little thick before shoving the boy back to where he was.

"Oh, of course." Rufus signaled to the men standing behind him. "These are Mathew and James; they have been with me since I became aware of what I am. Your people will be safe under their care. If everyone would be so kind as to follow them, there is plenty of room in the castle and they will be quite comfortable."

Digby looked back to the nervous group of survivors and nodded before flicking his eyes to Mason while tapping the walkie-talkie clipped to the belt of his coat. The soldier nodded back, clearly understanding to contact him at the first sign of trouble. They headed off to follow the path through the horde, leaving him behind with the elderly zombie master. Only Rebecca and Alex remained at his sides.

"Shall I give you a tour so that we might get to know one another?" Rufus gestured back toward the castle with his head held high, clearly proud of the home that he offered.

"Yes, we shall." Digby followed as Rebecca and Alex fell in line behind him. "I'm quite curious; what made you choose this location as your home?"

"It's a castle, do you need more of a reason?" Rufus leaned on his cane as he walked through the passage of zombies.

"That makes sense." Digby gave Rebecca a smug look as Rufus set foot onto the stairs leading up to the front gate.

"On top of the obvious comforts that a property such as this provides, it is well suited for a large number of humans to survive with little worries. Not to mention, those new creatures that showed up don't come anywhere near it."

"The revenants, you mean?" Rebecca stepped up the stairs behind him.

"Revenants?" Rufus glanced back at her.

"Yes, that's what we call them."

"I suppose that has a ring to it." Rufus continued on. "We don't know why those creatures stay away from this property, but for some reason they don't come any closer than the visitor's center back there."

"Interesting." Digby made note to look into the phenomenon with the hope of duplicating it.

"I don't know how any of this would be possible without that advantage." Rufus nodded as he reached the top of the stairs and paused to let Digby and his accomplices survey the property.

The castle was truly a magnificent find. Beautiful architecture surrounded them. There was even a pool. A few humans swam in the tranquil blue water in the shadow of a row of stone columns and shrubbery. A few more people occupied the grounds. A couple were even working to convert the property's floral gardens into some sort of agricultural space. Probably to produce food.

With multiple guest houses littering the castle's grounds, there was no shortage of space for everyone. Even more amazing was that the people within the palace all appeared relaxed. Excited faces shined as Mason and the rest of the survivors that Digby had brought with him filtered into the area. It was as if they were simply glad to know more people had survived and made it to this paradise. They didn't even seem scared of Digby.

"As you can see, my offer of comfort and shelter is real." Rufus placed a hand on his shoulder. "I can't imagine what you and your people have been through, but they can relax here." The elderly zombie smiled and turned toward the large doors of the castle. "Now, let's get inside and talk some more."

With that, Rufus led the three of them in. Digby suppressed the urge to pocket every item of value they passed. The castle was simply packed full of treasures. Some of them shiny, sending a surge of excitement through Asher that Digby could feel across the bond they shared.

"Stretch your wings, my dear." Digby clicked his tongue at his pet. The raven took flight at his command, soaring through the high ceilings of the castle's hall.

Tapestries hung along the walls as they entered one room after another, each grander than the last. A group of teenagers played at one of many green tables within one room. They took turns hitting balls with the tip of a stick, trying to knock them into one of six pockets surrounding the table. According to

Rufus, the game was called billiards. It looked fun. Digby would have to make Rebecca and Alex play with him later.

As they passed by, the people within the castle gave Rufus a variety of greetings, each seeming to hold the elderly zombie in high regard. They didn't even bat an eye as Digby passed. He couldn't help but find it odd that the presence of the dead roaming their home was somehow treated as normal. It made him wonder what Rufus had done to enforce that level of acceptance.

Beyond the game room and grand entryway, there was a dining hall that looked like it had been pulled right out of the castle he'd been cursed in centuries ago. The only difference was that this one was somehow more extravagant, with intricate stone carvings on every surface. An enormous fireplace marked the center of the space.

They continued on, passing by a room featuring another pool. It was beautifully tiled; however it was also empty, with no water filling the space. A sign sat in the doorway.

Sorry, this room is currently under maintenance.

Dry or not, Digby was still impressed that the castle had not one but two swimming pools.

Finally, Rufus brought them to a grand library with wall to wall books. Every inch of the wooden shelving was covered in more ornate carvings. Hell, even the vaulted ceiling had been painstakingly decorated. Digby's eyes widened. Just how rich was the Hearst family that built the place?

"It is impressive, isn't it?" Rufus sat down in one of the many sofas that filled the room to form multiple sitting areas for people to read.

"Indeed." Digby nodded, trying to hide the astonished expression on his face. "I was just thinking about how amazing the Hearst family must have been."

"Surprisingly, not very." Rufus tilted his head from side to side. "It was really built by one man. He was rich enough, but his character lacked the virtue to match. I've read enough about the building to know that this wasn't a place built by generosity and kind words. Maybe that was one of the reasons I chose it. There's something satisfying about repurposing a monument to excess into a last bastion for human survival. It doesn't hurt that I get to watch so many people relax and work for the future within its walls."

"About that." Rebecca sat down on the sofa on the opposite end from Digby. "How is it that the people here are able to relax with a few thousand zombies surrounding them?"

"Yes." Digby leaned forward. "I am curious as to how you are able to control so many zombies at once with your Compels. I'd like an explanation of what the abilities of a zombie master are. Not to mention how you became one."

"Of course." He held up his hand as if to slow their stream of questions. "And I am curious about you as well. I haven't encountered a zombie capable of overriding my Compels the way you have." His gaze dropped to Digby's clawed hand before traveling back up to his horned crown. "I've never seen any of our kind with mutations from more than one path."

"Ah, yes." Digby flexed his talons. "You seem well informed on the plethora of abilities available. Is that a perk of being a zombie master as well?"

"It is." Rufus held his cane in front of him to lean forward. "When I became aware, I already seemed to know about the mutation paths and understand what types of zombies I could Compel. I don't know everything, but I'm better informed than most. As a master, my Compels are stronger than an ordinary leader and they work on uncommon zombies as well. That's how I keep the horde in line. There are a number of leaders mixed in that I Compel into reinforcing my commands and keeping the others under control. With that, everyone stays happy."

"And how did you become aware, if you don't mind me asking?" Digby leaned back while resting against the sofa's side as casually as possible, in an attempt to avoid his questions seeming like an interrogation.

Rufus broke eye contact for a moment, looking down at the

floor before answering. "I'm not really sure. I just did. When I became aware, I already had a horde following me."

"Really?" Digby tried to hide the suspicion that the zombie was lying. "How did you meet up with your people then? They must have been pretty scared of your horde at first."

"Actually, no." Rufus met his eyes again. "I had left my horde behind in a building to get a few minutes alone while I figured things out. That was when James and Mathew found me." He laughed. "I can only imagine how it was for them, stumbling onto me pacing back and forth while talking to myself. After asking me some questions, they understood my value immediately and we formed a partnership. I was just lucky they didn't shoot first."

"Lucky indeed. It would have been easy to end you if they found you alone." Digby gestured to the old zombie's cane to remind him how frail he looked, still annoyed by the ancient creature for beating him to his claim.

"Unfortunately, you are correct," Rufus admitted with a self-deprecating chuckle that irritated Digby even more. "I am far from my prime."

"What if a member of your horde goes ravenous?" Alex sat down between Digby and Rebecca, breaking the tension.

"Thanks to those, what did you call them, revenants?" Rufus nodded as if confirming his memory. "My horde has been well fed. I send them out to hunt during the day while these creatures are inactive. Once they have eaten their fill, there isn't much danger of them going out of control. Though, I still advise the people not to get too close to any of them without good reason or having me around. Beyond that, all I have to do is visit the horde and reissue Compels a few times per day. That seems to keep them in line."

"And with you around, the people are given safety in a dangerous world. That's why they seem so friendly and respectful toward you." Digby leaned back in his seat, wondering how the people would feel if they knew how many humans Rufus had to have killed and eaten to become self-aware. "The survivors must feel quite indebted to you."

"I like to think of it as... doing my best to help the people of this new world." The elderly zombie grimaced. "It isn't a debt. And I don't ask them for anything in return. I will continue to defend and protect them so that they may focus on what's important, themselves."

"How honorable." Digby let his suspicion taint his tone, causing Rebecca to clear her throat to tell him to shut up and change the subject. "Anyway, to answer your questions, I am a zombie ravager."

"I wasn't aware such a mutation path existed." Rufus sat up straight.

"It's sort of hidden." Digby shrugged, trying to sound nonchalant about achieving something that no other zombie had done. "It's a combination of other paths. A jack of all trades, if you will. As far as I know, I'm the only one." He debated leaving out the fact that he and his accomplices could use magic but decided against it since he couldn't be sure that Mason or the others wouldn't let something slip and get him caught in a lie. "Plus, the three of us can use magic."

"Magic?" Rufus blinked twice, before settling in to hear a recap of what had happened so far.

Digby recounted everything. Skyline. Henwick. The Heretic Seed. Everything. Again, the only bit he left out was the shard lodged in his chest. When he was done, the elderly zombie sat quietly for a full thirty seconds before speaking.

"I don't really know how to respond to all that." Rufus furrowed his caterpillar-like eyebrows.

"I assure you, it's all true." Digby looked him in the eyes.

"I know, I believe you." He held up a hand. "It all explains so much, but the idea of it all is just so monstrous. To think that an organization like Skyline exists and could carry out such a plan to end the world like they have. It just makes what we have here in this castle so much more important. These people need to remain free."

"I'm glad you see it that way." Digby lowered his head. "That's why the best thing we can do is lay low and build a stronghold to call home. As long as we don't give Skyline a reason to come knocking, they should leave us be for a while. That should be enough to ensure our survival for the time being. Once we've built a more stable situation, we intend to head out in search of a resource that might help us learn more about our power." Digby kept his plans vague, not wanting to mention anything about their search for the rest of the Heretic Seed's fragments.

"I understand." Rufus hesitated before standing up. "I should tell all of this to my people as well. I have twenty humans here under my care. They need to know what's really happening out there. And I'm sure you all will want some time to get settled in."

"Yes." Digby stood up. "Now if you would just point me in the direction of the castle's finest room, I will be claiming it as my own."

"You're welcome to take the master suite. It's located between the castle's towers and has the best view. You can reach its floor by heading up the stairs over there. There are enough rooms up there for each of you."

"That shall suit my needs nicely." Digby started to turn toward the stairs, stopping a second later. "Why is it that you have not taken the master suite as your own?"

Rufus leaned to one side on his cane. "You're not the first to ask me that question. The humans that live here with me have wondered as well. James has told me enough times that I should. He says that a leader should stand at the top. The others have even left it empty in case I change my mind."

"Then why didn't you?" Digby arched an eyebrow.

"It didn't feel right. I'm not a master of anything despite what my mutations call me. I'm only here to protect the people of this castle. For that reason, I have taken up residence in the lower levels. I don't need anything more."

"Well, your loss." Digby beckoned to Asher who had

perched on top of a bookshelf and marched up the stairs without another word, leaving Rufus behind.

Rebecca jogged up the stairs behind him as soon as they were out of earshot. "Were you trying to start a fight, or something?"

"Oh, please. How can you not find that decrepit corpse's humility irritating?" Digby rolled his eyes.

"I thought Rufus seemed… kind of nice." Alex ducked as Asher flapped over his head to land on Digby's shoulder. "He's like a sweet old grandparent, except, you know, dead."

"Don't you start fawning all over that fraud too." Digby stomped his peg-leg on the stairs. Asher let out a caw to reinforce his point.

"Fraud?" Rebecca's voice climbed an octave.

"Yes, fraud." Digby spun back to her. "I'm not sure how long I could sit and listen to him go on and on about protecting humanity, knowing how many people he's obviously killed to get where he is. I wouldn't be surprised if the people in this castle are not the first survivors to grace its presence, if you know what I mean."

"You think he's been eating people that come here looking for shelter?" Rebecca hesitated on the stairs, clearly questioning her safety.

"Maybe, maybe not." Digby held up a claw. "But I'll tell you one thing, there's no way in hell he doesn't know what he's done to get to where he is. I'm sure he knows exactly how many people he killed before becoming aware."

"Does it matter at this point?" Alex followed up the stairs. "We're here now and we're safer than we were at the vineyard."

"Oh yes, real safe. There's only a few thousand zombies outside just waiting for Rufus to decide he's done playing nice." Digby stomped his way on the top floor of the castle and into a hallway. "I can only control thirty-one zombies at a time, including uncommons. He can Compel thousands just by manipulating the leaders in the mix. His power is limited only by the number of dead in his clutches. Even if we were to take him out, his horde would still kill everyone here out of hunger the moment his control waned."

Rebecca scoffed. "It might be a little early to be thinking about assassinating him."

"I'm not saying that we should, I'm just making a point. What could we hope to do against his horde's numbers?" Digby threw open the door to the master suite, stopping dead in his tracks at the breathtaking view through the window. "Good god."

Rebecca stepped alongside him. "So I take it we will be staying here regardless of your feelings toward Rufus."

He nodded with his mouth hanging open as he surveyed one of the finest rooms he'd ever set eyes on.

"You assume correctly."

CHAPTER FOURTEEN

Mason stomped up the stairs that led toward the castle's master suite, clenching his jaw despite the fact that things were starting to look up.

After two weeks on the run, he was about ready to take it easy for a few days. He wasn't sure what to make of Rufus or the few thousand zombies surrounding his new home, but the people there seemed happy and safe. Sax and Parker had made a point of investigating the castle as much as possible, finding the place on the up and up. Even better, the castle's inhabitants needed the manpower that his group provided, making them an appreciated and valuable addition.

None of that mattered right now, though.

No, right now, he had a bone to pick with a certain drone jockey.

Marching past the master suite that Digby had claimed, Mason raised a fist to the door of the room next to it. At the last second, he hesitated, stopping himself from banging too hard. After taking a moment to think about it, he slammed his knuckles to the wood anyway. The reaction on the other side was immediate. The sound of someone jumping, accompanied by a sudden shriek. A door being closed came next. Then, finally, a seemingly calm voice.

"Come in."

"I have a bone to pick…" Mason wrenched the knob, and shoved into the room, finding Rebecca sitting on the floor amidst her laptop and several pieces of the drone that had been smashed by Tanner the night before. She was wearing a pair of jeans and a hoodie with the word Skyline on one side.

"I'm sorry, can I help you?" She looked up at him from her place on the floor.

"I, um," Mason lost his train of thought, unsure if he should crouch down to her height or stay standing. He shook off his confusion and restarted. "Why didn't you tell me there were three of those brutes waiting for us when you sent us in the opposite direction after the horde swarmed us?"

"I didn't know—"

"Bull." He cut her off. "I've seen drone feeds before, and there's no way you didn't see those things. We could have been killed."

"You weren't, though; the brutes weren't hostile." She shrugged and looked back to her laptop.

"But you didn't know that." He gritted his teeth. "So again, why didn't you tell me?"

She let out a long sigh. "Because someone had to keep the brutes from catching up to the rest of us."

He growled back, "So you did see them?"

"Yes," she answered matter-of-factly.

"And you, what? Thought you'd just throw us to the wolves?" He scoffed, remembering how Skyline had abandoned the soldiers stationed at the quarantine line in Seattle.

"I'm sorry you don't agree, but what would you rather I had done? Let some of the civilians die?" She kept her tone even as if it had been an easy decision. "Putting your team in danger instead of the others left the possibility of survival for more people."

"You could have gone yourself." Mason clenched his fist.

"You and Dig could have handled those things without a problem."

"Maybe, maybe not." She tilted her head from side to side.

"You'd have a better chance than us, but of course you'd have to stop hiding in the van and come out and fight." Mason stared down at her.

"The hell is that supposed to mean?" Becca's face flushed, telling him he'd hit the nail on the head.

"You think none of us have noticed that every time things get rough, you vanish and bring out a drone? I mean, and I can't believe I'm saying this with a straight face, but with your magic, you are one of the strongest combatants we have after Dig. Plus, you can literally perform miracles with your healing spell." He held a hand out toward her. "Do you have any idea how frustrating it is to have one of your best pieces taken off the board?"

"I am not anyone's pawn. I left that behind when I ditched Skyline. And you are not in charge here, army boy." She narrowed her eyes at him.

"I'm not saying I am. But neither are you. And I can't have you sending me and my friends off to die because you're too scared to fight." He called her out.

"You think I'm too scared?" She scoffed. "I'm sorry to burst your bubble, but I didn't send myself or Dig out to fight the brutes because we are simply more valuable."

"What's that supposed to mean?" He threw out both hands beside him.

"It's basic tactics. You don't risk losing your strongest units if you don't have to. It's as you said, I can perform miracles and Dig is our best fighter. Even Alex fills a vital role. Those abilities are more valuable than anything else right now. If we had gone instead and gotten killed, then where would you all be? What happens if Tanner tracks you down again? We need to be thinking about every potential fight that lays ahead of us, not just the ones that happen in the moment."

"You sound just like your friends at Skyline." He growled his words through his teeth.

"I…" She folded her arms and turned away from him. "I can't help it, that's how I was trained. A tactical advantage is still an advantage."

"I understand that." Mason crouched down, trying to get through to her. "But things are different now, and you don't work for Skyline anymore. The lives of soldiers like me, Sax, and Parker matter. We're people, not tools."

"I know that." She avoided eye contact.

"Then could you…?" He trailed off, noticing something odd. There was a perfectly good desk and chair in the room. So why was she sitting on the floor? Unless she couldn't sit in the chair? He glanced at her hands, realizing that she hadn't touched her laptop or any of the drone parts on the floor while they had been talking.

Mason arched his eyebrow, before reaching out to place a hand on her shoulder only to have his fingers pass through her.

"Crap." She lowered her head and sighed before winking out of existence like a ghost.

Where is she?

Mason flicked his eyes around the room, settling them on the door of a closet. *There.* Standing up, he rushed across the room and pulled open the door, finding the real Rebecca sitting at the bottom, blinking. He averted his eyes when he realized she wasn't wearing any pants. "Oh sorry, I didn't realize… I should have knocked."

"It's fine." She pulled her knees up to her chest. "I don't care."

"Ah, sure, but why exactly are you not…?" He tried to wrap his head around the reason she would be hiding in a closet without any pants.

"They're uncomfortable." She looked up. "Skyline kept me in an apartment alone for years. I haven't worn jeans for months and I didn't pack any pajama pants when I left."

"What do you mean, they kept you alone?" Mason shook his head.

"I mean exactly what it sounds like." She shrugged. "Their drone operators see things that could be considered sensitive. It's easiest to keep them isolated so that they don't have any leaks. Plus it keeps their assets dependent on them and develops a sense of detachment with other people."

"Shit, Becca." Mason crouched down again, getting an idea of how traumatized she might actually be. "Why would you agree to that sort of life?"

"It wasn't up to me," she snapped back. "My parents signed me into Skyline's training program when I was thirteen. Working for them was all I knew."

"And that's why you didn't think anything of sending me off to slow down the brutes." Mason deflated, feeling the anger drain from his body.

"I wasn't wrong. Tactically, that was the best option. It doesn't matter if I was scared or not." She shook her head.

"That may be true, but you had no right to take the choice away from us or my people. It's alright if you're scared, but if you had explained things fully, we may have agreed and gone with your plan regardless of the risks."

"I…" She trailed off and leaned her head back against the wall. "That's fair. I didn't have to withhold information, and I was scared." She scoffed at herself. "Of course I was. I haven't set foot outside in years, let alone fought the undead in a zombie apocalypse. I'd be insane if I wasn't terrified. Maybe that's why the Heretic Seed gave me this projection ability. So I can stay safe and keep the world at a distance."

"Thank you." Mason let out a calm breath.

"For what?" She looked up at him.

"For admitting that much." He stood up and grabbed a blanket from the bed before handing it to her. "I'll be honest, I came up here thinking you were another one of Skyline's assholes that only cared about themselves, like Bancroft. I was thinking you were as inhuman as the rest of them. But I get it. Magic or not, you are just as screwed up as the rest of us."

"Gee, thanks." She rolled her eyes.

"Now how about you get out of the closet?" He stepped away from the door to give her room. "And maybe try putting on some pants."

"Oh, shut up." She snatched the blanket and wrapped it around her shoulders. "I can sit in the closet if I want."

"I suppose that's true." He shrugged, feeling a little bad for getting mad at her without knowing what she'd been through. She was as much a victim of Skyline as any of the people they'd hurt. He softened his voice before adding, "Maybe put some pants on though."

"Quit with the pity." She tugged the blanket up so that it covered her head like a hood. "I'll get over my crap on my own. I don't need someone to fix me." Becca let out a growl before grabbing the door and pulling it shut.

"Alright then." He leaned closer to the closet so she could hear him through the door. "You come out when you're ready."

"Just get out of my room already."

Mason stood there for a second, unsure of what to say. Eventually, he decided to let her be. If she wanted to hide, then that was okay. He'd said what he had come to say.

"I'll see you later, then." Mason turned and walked out the door.

I'm starting to see why she and Digby get along.

In some ways, Becca was just as prickly as the deceased necromancer. Skyline may have done a number on her psychologically, but treating her with kid-gloves wasn't going to help. She would either come around eventually or she wouldn't.

He glanced back at the closet as an image of her sitting there in her underwear flashed through his mind. A wave of heat swept across his scalp. He immediately shook off the image and shoved his hands in his pockets to head back down stairs.

"Maybe Parker and Sax will want to play a game of pool before turning in for the night."

CHAPTER FIFTEEN

"Open up, boy!"

Alex sat straight up in bed at the sound of Digby banging on his door.

Asher's cawing followed.

Oh good lord, what time is it? He glanced out the window of the castle's upper floor as the sun rose in the distance. He felt like he'd only just gone to bed.

At least he waited until the sun was up. Alex rubbed his eyes. It had probably taken everything the zombie had to wait that long. Patience was not one of Digby's virtues.

"Come on, get up." The necromancer banged on the door again, this time louder, as if using his bone gauntlet for impact. "We have a busy day ahead of us."

"What?" Alex stumbled to the door and pulled it open a few inches, looking out through half closed eyes while wearing nothing but a pair of boxer shorts. "What time is it?"

"I have no idea, but the sun is up." Digby pushed into his room. "There isn't a moment to waste. Now put some clothes on, I'll wait." Asher flapped off of the zombie's shoulder and landed on the back of a chair.

"Alright, sure." Alex shrugged and pulled on a pair of cargo pants he'd looted from the campsite two days ago. There wasn't much point in arguing. Besides, he had agreed to support the necromancer in exchange for the Heretic Seed's power. So really, this was part of his job. He slipped on a white tank top and threw a Hawaiian shirt over it. "What are we doing that's so important?"

"It's time to explore the castle grounds and get the lay of the land." Digby grimaced at his shirt but refrained from commenting.

"Can it wait until after breakfast?" Alex stretched, layering on an exaggerated yawn for effect.

"No time." Digby tapped his one remaining foot on the floor.

"Why the hurry?" Alex rubbed his eyes.

"Because I don't sleep, and I've been getting restless hiding in my room."

"Why didn't you explore the castle last night then?"

"I would have, but I didn't want to run into you-know-who." Digby gestured down the stairs with his eyes.

"Who is you-know-who?" Alex yawned again.

"Rufus, that's who," Digby snapped back.

"Oh, I get it." Alex nodded, beginning to see where the necromancer's mind was going.

"Indeed, that's why we need to have a look around." Digby leaned on his walking stick. "That decrepit old corpse is bound to have a few half-eaten skeletons stuffed in a closet somewhere. All we have to do is find them."

"That sounds like more of a Becca job to me. She's better at gathering intel than I am." Alex started for her room.

"True, but I already knocked on her door and all I got was a rude gesture from an illusionary projection." Digby gave Alex a friendly smile. "Fortunately, I can always count on my loyal apprentice."

Asher gave an affectionate caw to back him up.

"Yay." Alex feigned excitement as he pulled on his boots.

"Oh, don't get sarcastic, boy." Digby jabbed him in the shin with the end of his walking stick. "We have important work to do. The safety of every human within these walls may depend on us uncovering whatever nefarious plan that zombie master might have in store for them."

"You know, Rufus might just be trying to help, like he says." Alex tied his shoelaces.

"Might I remind you of the scores of people he's eaten?" Digby held out both hands as if holding up the weight of a hundred corpses.

"True, but haven't you eaten a bunch of humans as well?" Alex eyed him sideways.

"Yes, but it's not that bad when I do it." The necromancer folded his arms.

"That's probably not the best argument." Alex stood up, ready to go.

"Look, if I have to watch one more person thank that deceased fraud for his help, I might vomit." Digby glanced to the side. "Provided I could vomit, that is."

"Let's head down to the dining hall and see what they have for food first. You can start your investigation there. If we go about this in a friendly and casual way, someone is more likely to let something slip." Alex avoided making eye contact while tying his other shoe, hoping Digby wouldn't catch on to the fact that he just wanted food.

"Good thinking, my boy." A crooked grin spread across Digby's face. "Actually, we could go around and ask everyone what they need to improve their lives here. That would kill two birds with one stone. We could learn what shortcomings the place has and present the appearance of trying to help."

"That makes sense." Alex nodded. After spending some time with Digby, he was learning how best to handle him. The zombie may have come across as a villain, but there was good in him. With the right encouragement, he could do a lot to help others.

"Brilliant, that would really win me some points with the

settlers here, and potentially dig up some dirt on Rufus." Digby spun toward the door and beckoned to Asher. "Let's be off then."

"Okay." Alex grabbed his canteen and followed as the necromancer rushed out the door toward the spiral staircase that led to the library. Alex raised his hand to tell Digby to be careful on the stairs with his peg-leg. He cringed as a sudden crash came from the stairwell followed by frantic cawing.

Yeah, this is going to be a fun day.

Alex sighed and followed down the stairs, making a point of holding onto the railing.

Once Digby had regenerated a few broken bones from his fall, they went on to the kitchen. The space was old but had been retrofitted with all the modern conveniences of a commercial facility, complete with an extra-large refrigerator. The brochure had mentioned that the castle was available for private parties, so it made sense that its food-prep facilities would be up to date. Alex checked the fridge, finding it cold and well-stocked.

"Hey, they have power."

"That's interesting." Digby flicked on a light switch. "Hmm, the lights upstairs didn't work, and I couldn't charge my tablet."

"Maybe they've shut down some zones to save power." Alex made a note of the contents of the fridge. Several cartons of egg substitute, large packages of bacon, and a variety of sliced meats filled the shelves; some of it had expired. He shut the door and turned back to Digby. "There must be a generator running somewhere."

"We'll have to look into that as well."

After checking the fridge, Alex looked through a few cabinets, finding a plethora of pre-packaged danishes and muffins. It was better than nothing, though Alex held off until they could find someone to ask permission first. He didn't want to go ahead and start eating food that he hadn't brought. If they said no, then he still had some rations up in his pack.

It wasn't long before an older woman wandered into the room.

"Jesus!" She jumped two feet in the air when Digby approached her, which was impressive considering she was somewhat larger than average. Alex ran to her aid, apologizing for the sudden shock.

"It's alright." She fanned herself as she sat down. "I thought I was getting used to seeing corpses wandering the halls. Sorry to overreact."

"No need to apologize." Digby seemed to be making an effort to be on his best behavior. "I realize my visage is not ideal."

"Nonsense. This is a new world." She stood back up. "I think the standards of beauty are going to need an update. Honestly, that's a little overdue to begin with." She reached for one of the containers of pastries. "I'm Kate. Let me get you something to eat, you all must be starving." She glanced at Digby. "Sorry, I don't have anything for zombies on account of, well, the obvious reasons. But there are plenty of danishes and a few other baked goods. We also have bacon and eggs in the refrigerator over there." She pointed across the kitchen to the oversized appliance.

"Are you sure I can have some?" Alex hesitated before reaching into the container.

"Of course." She grabbed a danish and took a bite only to talk with her mouth full. "We salvaged everything we could from the cafe in the visitor's center. There was plenty there and most of it should keep for about another week or so. Some of it has already spoiled though, and we won't be able to eat it all before the rest goes bad too."

"Can you point me to a frying pan? I can make you an omelet or something." Alex helped himself, munching on a danish while he grabbed a carton of fake eggs from the fridge.

"Oh, you don't have to." Kate pointed to one of the lower cabinets in contradiction to her words.

"It's just as easy to make two." Alex shrugged and turned on the stovetop.

"I would help, but," Digby gestured to himself, "best to keep the dead out of food preparation."

"Plus you don't wash your hands," Alex added.

"I wash." Digby paused. "When I get messy."

"There is a sink over there." Kate eyed him suspiciously while folding her arms. "And we have soap."

"Oh fine." Digby placed Asher on the back of a chair and went to the sink to wash up. "My hygiene aside, I hate to be the one to ask the obvious question," Digby dried his hands on his pants, "but what will you do once the food spoils?"

"We aren't really sure." Kate shrugged. "I have been keeping an eye on our supplies and we have plenty for now. But at some point, we're going to need to head out and get more. Unfortunately, that's one thing that Rufus' zombies can't do for us, and things have happened so fast that we haven't had time to even think about going ourselves. I suppose the first thing we should do is gather some basics. Flour, sugar, rice, canned goods, and stuff like that."

"Couldn't Rufus just head out with his horde to keep them on task and organize the effort?" Digby leaned against a counter, making a point of keeping his distance from the woman so as to keep his poisonous aura from having too much effect. "The dead may not have much intelligence, but they can be organized to some degree. Surely, they could pull a wagon. All Rufus would have to do is load it up."

"That's true." Kate finished her danish and hopped up to get a couple plates. "But if something ever happened to him, we would lose the horde's protection. And you saw for yourself how easy it would be for someone out there to get the wrong idea. A group of survivors might just shoot him and move on."

"That's true." Alex took a couple strips of bacon from the pan and set them aside before pouring in a generous amount of egg substitute.

Kate got up and grabbed a plate from a cabinet. "I know

that some of the other folks here are working on setting up a garden, so that's something. But obviously it won't produce anything right away."

"Maybe we could find some plants that are already producing and transplant them here." Alex tilted his head to one side as he tossed in some shredded cheese and chopped bacon into the pan before folding a layer of egg over onto itself. He slid the omelet onto a plate and passed it to Kate before starting a second one. A notification from the Heretic Seed popped up as he poured more of the egg substitute and placed the frying pan back on the burner.

SKILL LINK

By demonstrating repeated and proficient use of the non-mage skill or talent, cooking, you have discovered an adjacent spell.

HEAT OBJECT

Description: Slowly increase the temperature of an inanimate object. Practical when other means of cooking are unavailable. This spell will continue to heat an object until the caster stops focusing on it or until its maximum temperature is reached.

Rank: D

Cost: 10MP

Range: 6in

Maximum Temperature: 300 degrees Fahrenheit

Alex furrowed his brow at the description. He had been doing all of the cooking for himself and Becca for the last two weeks, so it made sense that the Seed's Skill Link trait would give him something eventually. Although, he wasn't sure how useful the spell would be, beyond helping out when they didn't have access to a stove.

Shutting the stovetop off, Alex shrugged and cast the spell on the frying pan full of fake egg. It was hard to tell if anything was happening at first since the pan was still hot, but after focusing on it for about a minute, his eggs began to cook faster. He immediately stopped focusing to keep his breakfast from burning. It was definitely going to take practice before he got some sort of temperature control down.

"Everything alright, boy?" Digby eyed him suspiciously, clearly sensing the mana moving through his body.

"Cooking spell." Alex shrugged. "Just discovered it."

"That's... helpful." Digby nodded without sounding too impressed before turning back to Kate to steer the conversation back to his investigation. "But anyway, who is setting up the garden?"

"You'll want to find James then." She took a bite of omelet. "The garden was his idea."

"That's one of Rufus' men, right?" Digby sat down at the table. "He was there when we were brought in yesterday?"

"I guess so." She finished her breakfast. "I wouldn't say that Rufus has men though. He isn't really in charge or anything."

"Oh, I was under the impression that he was the leader of this settlement." Digby tapped a claw on the table. "Would you be able to tell us who is?"

"It's more of a group effort right now. No one has really taken charge. We're all just working together." She scraped a last bit of cheese from her plate. "I guess most of the decisions have been made by James and Mathew. They consult with Rufus on everything though, and they keep the rest of us informed."

"That's good to know." Alex finished cooking and served himself.

"Yes, thank you very much for talking with us," Digby stood back up and held out a claw to call Asher back to his shoulder, "but we should be off to see who else needs help around here."

"But—" Alex glanced down at his freshly made breakfast that he'd just sat down to eat. His stomach growled.

"No time to waste." Digby marched toward the door.

Alex proceeded to shovel the omelet into his mouth before glancing around for a dishwasher.

"I'll take that." Kate grabbed his plate and stacked it on her own. "Least I can do is clean up."

"Thanks." Alex inclined his head before rushing in the direction Digby had wandered off to.

"Good luck." She gave him a smile.

After his rushed breakfast, Alex caught up to Digby, who was heading down every stairway he could find, assuming that a generator would be located on the sub levels. Alex followed along, not knowing where the best location for that kind of equipment would be. Eventually, they noticed a sound coming from outside and followed it out a door and into a fenced in area behind the castle.

A huge generator filled one corner of the space while an even bigger tank sat on the opposite end. A steady rumble came from the generator. To Alex's surprise, Digby understood more than he expected. The zombie remarked at the gauge of the fuel tank, mentioning that it was half-full and that they should try to find more propane to fill it.

"How do you know about this stuff?" Alex furrowed his brow.

"Salvaging fuel for generators comes up in a lot in your movies." Digby tapped at the fuel gauge. "To be honest, I'm always shocked by how much you all depend on electricity. I didn't have it, and I survived fine for most of my life."

"Yes, but then how would you charge your tablet to watch those movies?" Alex countered.

Digby's face fell. "We'll have to prioritize getting fuel, then."

"That would be a big help." A voice commented from behind.

Alex jumped back against the propane tank while Digby shouted and toppled over, still having trouble balancing with his missing foot. Asher flapped in the air squawking before dropping to the gravel that filled the fenced area. James stood a few feet away, looking somewhat pleased with himself.

"What the hell is the matter with you?" Digby hoisted himself back up, using his walking stick.

"Sorry. I couldn't resist. It's not every day you get to startle a zombie." James was an average-sized man in his mid-forties with a friendly presence. He wore a two-week beard and a polo shirt.

"That doesn't mean you should." Digby glanced down at the man's foot, narrowing his eyes. "On a related note, what's your shoe size?"

"Sorry for barging in here and messing with your generator." Alex scratched at the back of his head, trying to redirect the situation before Digby cut off someone's foot.

"That's okay." James walked over to the fuel gauge. "I was just about to check how much fuel was left. But did I hear you right? You two are thinking of heading out for propane?"

"That, among other things." Digby picked Asher up so she could perch on his gauntlet. "It seems it's too risky for Rufus to head out on his own. Fortunately, myself and Alex here are a bit more durable."

James glanced down at the necromancer's missing foot. "Are you now?"

"To a degree, yes." Digby tapped his peg-leg with his walking stick.

"If that's the case, we could really use the help." He stepped back and shrugged. "Honestly, you're catching us at a bad time. We only took over this castle a week ago, so we're still figuring things out. I've been handling the supplies and deciding what to do with our little settlement here. Matt, who was with me yesterday, is trying to keep the people organized. As it turns out, surviving the end of the world is harder than the movies make it seem."

"Tell me about it." Digby chuckled.

"It's especially bad when you don't have anyone with any training. I myself know a little about plants on account of running a dispensary before the collapse of civilization. So if you need a solid weed garden, then I'm your guy. Anything else is probably out of my expertise. Matt worked in tech support, so combined we don't have that much to offer. The rest of our group isn't much better. If we hadn't run into Rufus when we did, I'm sure we'd be one of those vampire zombies out there by now."

"You mean the revenants?" Alex arched his eyebrow at the term vampire zombie.

"Is that what your people named them?" James leaned his head to one side and if considering the word.

"That's what they are called according to the magic that we possess." Digby rolled his eyes. "And those things are certainly no zombie. Calling them that gives the rest of us a bad name."

"Revenant it is then." James held up both hands, backing down. "I have to say though, the magic thing is a little hard to take in."

"I can understand that." Alex nodded. "The number of things that I have had to accept as facts in the last two weeks has been ridiculous."

"I bet." James glanced at the deceased raven perched on Digby's clawed gauntlet.

"To be honest, I hadn't even heard of Skyline, let alone expected an organization run by magic users bent on world domination to exist." Alex shrugged.

"About that." James arched an eyebrow. "How worried should we be about these Skyline people?"

"No idea," Digby chimed in. "They've pretty much won at this point. So whatever they do from here is up to them. All we can do is try to stay out of it for now. Fortunately, they aren't a big enough organization to search the whole world for us. Odds are, they will leave us be as long as we don't do anything to make them take notice."

"That makes sense." James went silent for a few seconds. "I don't know what a group as small as ours could do against an organization like that. So yeah, staying off their radar is going to be important."

"Exactly." Digby attempted to snap his fingers, with little success. "But that doesn't mean we have to live in poverty. Right now we should focus on doing what we can to make this castle as comfortable for everyone as possible."

"I can't argue with that." James got down to business. "When you're ready, we should organize a supply run. Matt and I would be happy to go, if your group would be willing to protect us. If I'm not mistaken, you have some military personnel with you as well, right?"

Digby nodded. "Having a bit of magic will help too."

"I hope so. We need to pick up more propane and gas, probably some food items too. Maybe first aid as well."

"Perfect, we could head out today since it's still early." Digby grinned. "We might not find everything we need right away, but it would be good to get a lay of the land for future reference."

"Sure, I'll grab Matt and meet you out front in, like," James checked his wrist despite the fact that he wasn't wearing a watch, "an hour?"

"That will do." Digby gave the man a nod and headed back out to the front of the Castle.

Alex said a quick goodbye to James and followed just as Becca tracked them down.

"There you two are."

"So you've decided to join us then? I thought you would be still in bed, considering your rather rude reaction to me knocking on your door earlier." Digby leaned on his walking stick, looking smug.

"Yeah, thanks for that by the way. I was hoping to sleep in a little, but my poisoned status showed up right after you left. I guess being in the room next to yours is still too close." She glowered at the radioactive zombie. "I really wish you would just use that stored power already."

"Nonsense, I might need it for something." Digby turned up what was left of his nose in protest. "Adding the power I absorbed might lend me enough oomph to deal with that Tanner fellow if he tracks us down again. It's best to save it for when I need it."

"Whatever." She shook her head and held a hand out to Alex. "Can I get a cleanse?"

"Sure." He pulled his canteen, casting Purify Water before handing it over.

She downed a mouthful and handed it back. "Okay, now that I don't have to worry about dying of radiation sickness, I have something to show you both."

"What?" Alex put the cap back on his canteen.

"I know why the revenants don't come near this place." She spun away toward the front of the castle.

"Really, how?" Digby followed close behind.

"I stumbled upon it while I was looking for you." She stopped in front of a decorative fountain and raised her hand to a tall statue at its center. The figure looked Egyptian in origin and had the head of a lioness sitting atop the body of a woman. A disc sat upon her head.

"And?" Digby stared at Becca as if expecting more.

"Just analyze it, Dig." She dropped her hand to her side.

"Alright." The zombie stared up at the stature.

Alex shrugged and did the same, focusing on the stone figure.

Statue of Sekhmet: Ancient, Legendary
MASS ENCHANTMENT: Due to belief and admiration
shared by a large quantity of people, this item has gained
a power of its own.
BLESSING OF THE SUN
This item will significantly increase the presence of life
essence within its area of effect. Range 3 miles.

"Apparently, Sekhmet is an Egyptian sun goddess." Becca shrugged. "She had a lot to do with war but was also invoked for protection and healing. It seems that a lot of people believed in her back in the day, or at least, enough to grant this statue a mass enchantment."

"Okay, so the mana balance is different here." Alex stared up at the figure. "Why would that keep the revenants away?"

"I think I know." Digby stepped forward. "I noticed yesterday that I absorb mana slower during the day, which I assume is because the sunlight alters the mana balance and leaves me with less death essence to drink in."

"I was thinking something similar." Becca sat down at the edge of the fountain. "We know the curse alters a zombie's mana system to function entirely off death essence, and that it filters out everything else."

"So what if the curse does something similar to the revenants?" Alex started to see where she was going.

"Exactly." She nodded. "Except, with them, their mana system doesn't filter anything out?"

"You think absorbing life essence is disrupting their mana flow and shutting down their regeneration." Digby reached out to touch the statue before turning back to her. "But that wouldn't do anything about their physical abilities. Unless—"

"Unless they aren't really that strong." Becca pumped her eyebrows.

"Oh my god." Alex snapped his eyes to her. "They're all ravenous."

"That's what I'm thinking." She nodded. "Except for them, it's not a temporary status."

"But that's impossible." Digby shook his head. "If they were somehow permanently ravenous, they would be operating well beyond their attributes limits and would inevitably damage their bodies."

"That's why the sunlight weakens them. They depend on their healing to keep them operating at that level, because they continuously damage their bodies." Becca reached down to swirl her finger in the fountain's water. "If they absorb too much life mana during the day or within this statue's area of effect, it disables their one advantage. So it only makes sense they would avoid that at all costs."

"And that's why Skyline created them." Alex sunk down to sit beside her.

"Indeed." Digby raised his walking stick only to drop it back down. "The revenants are monsters that can slaughter the common folk at night while allowing Skyline to operate freely during the day."

"They might even have ways to exploit that weakness to manipulate them." Alex considered the possibilities. "Skyline probably has more spells and classes that we don't know about. I mean, we've probably only seen a fraction of what they can do."

Digby's eyes widened. "That would be bad."

"Maybe we should, you know, try to find some of the Heretic Seed's fragments sooner rather than later," Alex added, hoping that increasing their knowledge of their magic might help him discover more abilities. There was only so much he could do with a few enchantments and a cooking spell.

"Indeed." Digby deflated. "Though, we are still at a bit of a disadvantage here."

Alex sighed. "Good thing we're going out with James in an hour."

"You are?" Becca stood up.

"No, we are." Digby twirled a claw around to include her in his declaration.

"Oh." She frowned. "I guess that is the responsible thing to do."

"Speaking of responsibility, isn't that Sax and Parker down there?" Digby pointed across the castle's grounds to where the two soldiers sat at the edge of the pool with their pants rolled up and their feet in the water.

"Good to know those two are adapting to civilian life." Becca snorted.

"Indeed." The necromancer wasted no time, leaving Alex and Becca behind as he hobbled down some stairs and across the lawn.

"I'll let you handle him." Becca turned back toward the

castle. "I'll meet you down at the van when I'm ready."

Alex gave her a nod and followed his zombie lord down. He caught up just as Digby reached the pair lounging by the pool.

"Look at you lot. Getting comfortable, are you?"

"That's us, just lazing about." Parker laid down on the stone surrounding the pool and closed her eyes.

"Yeah, we've been running around for two weeks straight. We've earned a break." Sax looked up. "We'd invite you to join us, but I assume soaking in the water is bad for a corpse."

"I think I'd be alright." Digby leaned over to look into the water. "I've never been in a swimming pool actually."

"Sorry Dig, but letting dead guys in the pool is probably a health code violation." Parker splashed her feet in the water. "You're welcome to join us though, Alex." She patted the edge of the pool between her and Sax.

"Yeah, there's room for one more," Sax added.

"No thanks. Lord Graves and I are on a mission."

"Oh yeah?" Parker cracked one eye open suspiciously.

"Indeed, we're going to be heading out to get provisions and other supplies that this place is lacking. Hope you don't mind, but I've volunteercd you both to assist." Digby stepped forward so that his shadow fell across the pair.

"Seriously?" Parker blew out a sigh.

"Mason too." Digby nudged Asher off his shoulder so that the raven fluttered down to land beside Parker's head. "Now where the hell did he run off to?"

"He's right here." Mason walked down the stairs behind them. "And what did you sign us up for?"

"A quest of the utmost importance." Digby stood tall. "As the newest members of this settlement, I feel it's our duty to better the lives of those around us."

"Oh yeah?" Mason looked at him sideways. "And what are you really doing?"

"He's trying to make us look good so people will like him," Alex added.

"Don't say it like it's a bad thing." Digby tapped his walking stick on the cement. "What's important is that we're helping. Besides," the necromancer stepped closer to Mason, "I don't know how I feel about this Rufus fellow. He seems woefully unprepared to manage this settlement. They have no plan for food, supplies, or fortifications. Dare I mention the fact that he is all that stands between the people here and the horde just outside the castle gates."

"The castle doesn't have gates." Parker scooted away from Asher as the raven tried to peck at her face.

"Even worse." Digby let out a huff of musty air.

"You're right." Mason nodded.

"I am?" Digby's eyes widened.

"Yeah, I was actually thinking the same thing. We investigated what we could last night, and this place is completely unprepared. They have enough food, but most of it is perishable. Fuel is an obvious issue, too. But most of all, the people here have zero defenses. They have a handful of guns and barely enough ammunition to load them." Mason shook his head in disbelief. "Most of these people are retail workers or software programmers. Not one of them has any form of survival, combat, or medical training."

"We found that to be the case as well." Digby nodded.

"And, this situation with Rufus and his horde." Mason waved a hand around in the air. "It's convenient for now, but these people can't depend on him forever. From the looks of it, Rufus was ancient before he died, which means he's in no condition to take any risks now. If something happened to him, his horde would be on us in minutes. The people here need resources and a willingness to fight. I mean, what if Rufus passes away from old age?"

"I don't think zombies can expire like that." Alex leaned to one side.

"But we agree with your point." Digby nodded. "That's why I think it's important that we head out as soon as possible to do what we can. This castle is an ideal place to settle, but it's not going to last if we don't take matters into our own hands."

"Agreed." Mason nodded.

"And for that, we're going to need weapons." Digby raised his claws. "And not just those stupid guns you all seem so fond of, either."

"What sort of weapons are you thinking of?" Mason eyed Digby skeptically.

"Swords, spears, and arrows. Your bullets will run out eventually. And you're going to need to be prepared for when that happens."

"That's a good idea." Alex perked up at the idea of roaming the zombie apocalypse with a katana on his back. "My Enchant Weapon spell is only rank D and we've seen how much damage it can do. Getting a few swords would be pretty cool."

Mason scratched at his stubble. "True, if you can enchant a few melee weapons, it would allow people like me to have an impact on the fight as well. Maybe we could save our bullets for when we really need them."

Suddenly, Parker sat up. "I might be able to help with all that actually."

"How?" Alex asked.

"Well, at the risk of being made fun of. I kind of know how to build and run a medieval style forge." She held up both hands in an exaggerated shrug.

"What's that now?" Sax turned to stare at her. "How did I not know this?"

"I worked at a forge for a few summers in high school." She shrugged like it was a normal thing for a teenager to do on their time off. "They made combat-ready weapons and traveled to a bunch of renaissance fairs during the fall. They made bank and paid well. They also tolerated occasional naps while on the clock."

"Oh good, I'm glad the army has had a positive impact on you, then." Mason stared down at her as she lazed about on the poolside.

"And you think you could make weapons here?" Digby ignored his criticism.

"I wouldn't expect anything pretty, but I can make a few sharp metal objects to poke revenants with." She leaned her head back and forth. "I could manage a broadsword or something."

"That's really cool." Alex couldn't stop a giddy grin from spreading across his face. "I'd love to learn more, if you need a hand."

"Definitely." A similar smile showed on Parker's face. "I'll take all the help I can get."

"Perfect, that will really make us a force to be reckoned with around here." Digby snapped his claws into a fist. "We'll show these people how we carve out a place for ourselves in this new world."

"Yeah…" Mason narrowed his eyes at the zombie. "Not that I'm advocating some kind of takeover. I want to make that clear. The people here seem to be happy enough considering the situation. I'm not looking to screw that up. I just want to make this place safer for everyone."

"Yes, yes, of course." Digby seemed to be putting in effort to appear innocent. "Good to know we're on the same page. I told James that we would be ready to leave in an hour. Can you three be ready to head out by then? We can take the van and try to salvage a truck or something to transport whatever we find back here."

"That sounds good." Mason lowered his head to stare at Sax and Parker. "Go grab your stuff and meet back out front."

Sax gave him a sarcastic salute while Parker proceeded to emit a cartoonish snore. Without skipping a beat, Sax reached into the pool to scoop up some water so he could dump it on his fellow soldier's face. Asher flapped back up to Digby's shoulder as Parker shot back up to cough out water that had gone up her nose.

With a plan in place, Mason left to get ready as Digby headed back up to his room to get his tablet, leaving Alex by the pool. He stood awkwardly for a moment before a word popped up on his HUD next to his mana.

Poisoned

He let out a sigh, realizing how close his room in the castle was to Digby's. It was bound to happen eventually. He pulled his canteen out and recast Purify, not wanting to let the status relieve him of his breakfast. It was nearly empty. A mouthful later, the ailment vanished.

"Hey, hook me up." Parker elbowed him in the leg, holding a hand up to him.

Alex simply held the canteen upside-down to show that he'd just drank the last of the water.

"Okay then, how about this?" She reached down and cupped her hand to scoop water from the pool.

"Ah, sure." Alex crouched down. "Never purified water held by someone else. So, sorry if this is weird." He placed his hands around hers and cast the spell.

"Oh damn, it is weird." She let out a laugh as his mana swam through the liquid, causing a dozen tiny bubbles to rise to the surface. It fizzed as if carbonated. "I want to fill a bucket and put my feet in it."

"Now that's weird," Sax commented.

"What? I have blisters." She gulped down the water then splashed her feet in the pool as the healing property of the spell went to work. "Okay, make that I had blisters."

"You want some too?" Alex leaned toward Sax.

"No way, I'm not drinking pool water." He cringed.

"It's purified pool water at least." Alex shrugged and started walking back up to the castle. "I'm going to get a few things."

"Okay, see you in an hour." Sax and Parker nodded in unison.

That was when Digby leaned out the window of his room at the top of the castle. "Hurry up, boy, we have a long day ahead of us."

Alex sighed.

Yeah, it's definitely going to be a long day.

CHAPTER SIXTEEN

"Quit sulking over there." Digby threw a protein bar at Rebecca from the back of the van as they drove away from the castle. "Have something to eat."

"I'm not sulking." She picked up the protein bar and tore it open. "I just didn't get much sleep last night." The mage had become quiet and gloomy once they'd climbed into the van, despite being so talkative earlier by the sun goddess statue. Digby couldn't help but notice she was avoiding looking back at the rest of the vehicle's passengers.

I wonder what that's about?

He shrugged, reminding himself that it wasn't something for him to worry about. She was a grown woman and didn't need him looking after her. Plus, he didn't want to look after her anyway.

Behind him stood Mason, Sax, Parker, James, and Mathew. It was a bit crowded, to say the least. He was just glad the van was tall enough for everyone to stand upright in. Digby made a point of pushing his way toward Mathew since he was the only member of their scavenging team that he hadn't met.

Mathew was a slender man, about thirty-five. He had been

employed in a field called technical support. Digby didn't fully grasp what that meant but they ended up talking about tablet computers. Most of the man's knowledge was useless considering what the world had become, but he had a few good ideas here and there. At the very least, he wasn't an idiot.

Once they had gotten familiar, Digby told Mathew about Rebecca's idea of downloading as much as they could to a storage device in order to preserve what mankind had created. He was onboard with the plan immediately, discussing it at length the entire way to the nearest town. Rebecca leaned out the window to cast her cartography spell every few miles. The ride was uneventful from there on out.

The only drawback to making Hearst Castle their home was that it was a twenty-minute drive to the nearest town. The roads were relatively clear, but having that many bodies packed into a single van for that long seemed to be uncomfortable for everyone else.

Digby didn't care much. He hardly ever noticed any discomfort other than broken bones anymore. Plus, the others seemed more than willing to give him a bit of extra room on account of him being a radioactive corpse. He felt bad for Asher though, picking up a restless feeling over the bond of the dead they shared. She didn't like being cooped up.

"Finally." Digby pushed his way out of the van as soon as they reached the center of a small coastal town. He tossed Asher into the air and had a good stretch while she circled the van.

"Alright, first things first." Digby cast control on a trio of zombies that happened to be nearby. There hadn't been any roaming the roads on the way there. He assumed that most of the area's dead were already a part of Rufus's horde, leaving just a few minions behind for him. He was just glad the revenants created by Skyline's modified curse didn't attack his kind, otherwise there might not be any zombies left to control. As soon as his three new minions sauntered over to him, Digby rubbed his hands together. "Let the looting begin."

"We're salvaging, not looting." Mason stretched his legs and checked the magazine of his pistol.

"Same difference." Digby pointed to a vehicle storage lot. "Now go steal a truck to carry our loot." Asher let out a caw from above. "And make it a shiny one."

"We'll see what we can do." Sax joined Mason.

"One shiny truck, coming up." Parker followed behind.

Digby waited patiently for the party to acquire appropriate transport. They ended up securing two good-sized pickup trucks. One had been left unlocked with the keys inside, while the previous owner of the other had expired within. The second one did not smell particularly good, leading to the theft of a dozen miniature, scented trees from a gas station. While they were there, Mason ran a hose into an underground storage tank and pumped up several containers of gas. They loaded the stored fuel into one of one of the trucks.

That was when Alex spoke up.

"We have hostiles nearby." He stood holding the iron key that he'd been using for his detection spell. "It's faint, but there's definitely something around here."

"Let's hope it's zombies." Digby gave him a grin. "At least they'll only try to eat you lot."

"I'll go scout ahead." Rebecca started walking in the direction of the grocery store across the street.

"Should someone come with…" Mason started moving only to stop when she walked through a car as if it wasn't there. "Oh."

Digby grinned. Her projection spell was pretty useful. Not to mention it was good to see her using her magic, even if she was still hiding in the van. That was when a brilliant idea struck him.

"Does anyone have a marker?"

"There's one in the gas station." Mason hooked a thumb back at a window he'd broken earlier to get in.

"Thank you, my good man." Dig limped past him to approach the building. Mathew and James were inside loading up every food item they could carry back to the truck. Most of it didn't look very nutritious but he wasn't going to criticize. After all, he ate people. Digby leaned in through the broken window. "Hey, throw me a marker, would you?"

"Sure." James grabbed one and handed it over. The word Sharpie was written on the side.

Digby headed back to the van and popped open the passenger door to find Rebecca slumped in the seat. Asher landed on the roof to watch as he pulled the cap from the marker and raised it to the mage's face.

"What do you think? A mustache or angry eyebrows?"

"Probably a mustache." Alex tossed an armload of dried meat sticks into the back of the van. "Angry eyebrows will be redundant once she realizes what you've done."

"Fair point." Digby drew on a crooked mustache that curled up at the ends.

"Draw a dick on her cheek," Parker shouted from one of the pickup trucks.

"Oh, please, have some class." Digby scowled at the soldier before looking back to Rebecca's mustachioed face. "Though, it is missing something." Digby tapped the back of his marker on one of his claws. Then he added a goatee. "Ah, there we are."

"She is going to Icicle you right in the face. You know that, right?" Alex shook his head.

"Not if you don't tell her it was me." Digby capped the marker and stuffed it in his coat.

Rebecca opened her eyes and sat up a second later, apparently canceling the spell while her projection was inside the store. "We have revenants inside!"

"Gah!" Digby fell backwards from the van, cracking his head on the ground.

"What were you doing?" Rebecca stared down at him.

"Ah." Digby struggled not to laugh at her improved visage as he covered up his crime. "Sorry, I was reaching for my tablet. It was charging next to you."

She turned to look by her seat.

Please don't look in the mirror. Please don't look in the mirror. Please don't look in the mirror. Digby winced as she picked up his tablet.

"Here." She handed it over. "But keep the van closed while I'm projecting, okay? I don't like the idea of it being open while I'm vulnerable."

"Oh yes, definitely." Digby nodded and snatched his tablet back before changing the subject. "So, revenants in the market, you say?"

"Yeah, there's a whole bunch in there. They were standing around doing nothing until they saw my projection, but they got pretty worked up once they noticed me. It's dark in there so they must be a little more active than normal." Rebecca hopped down from the van without noticing Digby's cosmetic improvements.

Calling the others over, Digby had Rebecca explain the situation. He made a point of glaring at anyone who laughed at her new mustache, realizing that it was obvious who had drawn it, considering he had been standing over her when she'd woken up. Fortunately, the situation kept the others occupied. After a brief explanation, they made their way to the store.

The building was long with windows covering the front. A green and white awning hung over the doors. The store wasn't as big as the ones Digby had seen looted in the majority of the videos he'd watched, but it was nearly untouched, with various products filling the shelves.

Either the majority of the town's people were dead, or they weren't able to deal with the revenants inside. From the sidewalk out front, Digby could already see at least a dozen of the creatures inside. When they opened the doors, a couple of them stepped out into the shadow of the awning out front. His three minions handled them without issue.

2 dormant revenants defeated, 24 experience awarded.

"You all might want to look away," he warned before telling one of his minions to eat the creature's flesh and bone.

Asher flapped into the feast, under instruction to consume the brains and hearts. He wasn't sure how far the raven had to go but he hoped that by keeping her on the path of the leader, she would reach the next tier soon. With that, her intelligence would start to close in on a more human level. With enough resources, he hoped she might become a zombie master, like Rufus.

Digby grinned. He might not be able to sway a horde larger than a few dozen on his own, but if Asher could grow as strong as Rufus, he wouldn't have to. The raven's loyalty would be enough. He reached down and patted her on her side as she pecked at a human heart.

Mathew immediately threw up.

"I warned you not to look." Digby stood back up.

"Oh god, can't you have those things do that somewhere else?" The tech support specialist bent over, struggling not to look in his direction.

"Why would I…?" Digby thought for a moment. "Actually, yes I can." He gave a new command to his minions, telling them to drag the bodies into an apothecary next door to the grocery store. "And kill any revenants you find." He cast a Decay to shatter the glass door and let them inside.

The trio shuffled off into the shop, disappearing into the shadows inside. Mathew got a handle on himself soon after.

"So how do we go about clearing this place out?" Mason stepped forward, pulling his pistol from its holster.

"Save your bullets, lad." Digby held up a clawed hand. "We should see how well we do with blades." He gestured to the machete sheathed at Alex's side. "We can have Rebecca lure one or two out here and Alex can take them out. I can stand by to finish off any that get out of control. You two will lose out on some experience, but that's probably the safest way to do this until you get strong enough to handle things without me."

"Okay then." Alex drew his machete and twirled it in one hand, casting Enchant Weapon as he did, a shimmer of light traveled down the length of the blade as it swept through the air. Parker and Sax both raised their eyebrows at the display, clearly impressed.

Rebecca scoffed. "Let me guess, you've been practicing that in the mirror all night?"

"Ah." Alex lowered the machete with an awkward look.

Rebecca shook her head at the enchanter, still unaware of her mustachioed appearance. "I'm going to go leave my body in the van. Be right back." She spun on her heel and climbed back into the vehicle.

Digby's shoulders relaxed, relieved that she hadn't seen her reflection in the store window. The mage returned a minute later in a less corporeal form, sans mustache. Apparently, her projection took on the form of what she thought she looked like and not a mirror image of her actual body. She walked right inside the store without stopping. Alex got ready to swing at the first revenant that she lured. She came running back out only seconds later.

"It's all you." She blew past him with a screeching form following behind her with its arms outstretched. Alex acted without hesitation, swinging for the revenant's neck. The enchanted blade glowed like molten steel on contact, taking the creature's head off in one blow.

"Oh yeah—" Alex started to congratulate himself just before a burst of arterial blood erupted from the corpse to spray him in the face. The head toppled to the sidewalk at his feet with a wet thud. Alex shrieked and jumped to the side as if afraid it could still bite him.

1 dormant revenant defeated, 14 experience awarded.

Both Sax and Parker burst out laughing while Mathew threw up again.

"Jeez, Mat, stop looking at stuff." James patted him on the back.

"I'm, ah, gonna go wait in the truck." The unfortunate man panted for air.

"You do that." Digby watched Mathew stagger back to one of the vehicles.

"Crap, we have another coming," Rebecca called out as Alex was still wiping blood from his eyes. Digby stepped forward, opening his maw on the sidewalk and cast Blood Forge to impale an oncoming revenant. Alex leapt out of the way, falling on the pavement as a black spike of necrotic blood burst through the creature's skull with a hard crack. The corpse hung there for a moment before the spike snapped under its weight.

1 dormant revenant defeated, 14 experience awarded.

Digby averted his gaze from his apprentice sitting in on the sidewalk and clasped his hands together in victory. "Well, I'd say that was a success. Head back in, Becky, and fetch us another one."

"Okay then." She strolled past him as Alex scrambled back to his feet.

Mason pulled a second machete from the van to help. Parker joined him, retrieving an ax from the vehicle. Sax did the same, returning with a hatchet. Parker glanced down at Sax's weapon and smirked.

"What?" He looked down at his miniature weapon.

"Nothing." She laughed to herself and kept walking.

Digby ignored the pair while Alex enchanted their blades. Mason held his out for the spell as well. As they waited for Rebecca to bring another target, the three minions dining in the apothecary shop next door returned to drag off the corpses of the most recent kills.

Flexing his claws, Digby cursed his missing foot and the lack of agility that came along with it. Without it, the best he could do was stay in the back and cast his Blood Forge spell to help with the fight. Rebecca returned before he had time to think about it further. Another three revenants followed her from the store; each were met by the blade of an enchanted weapon.

"Good job, boy!" Digby congratulated his apprentice. "You didn't get sprayed with bodily fluids that time."

"Ugh, don't say it like that." Alex groaned.

"Why?"

"Do I really need to explain that?" The enchanter dangled his arms at his sides as Digby's minions cleared the area of bodies.

"How about you don't." Rebecca headed back inside.

"I have to say, this is pretty cool." Parker swung her axe around, watching the head flicker with mana.

"I know, right?" Alex stood a little taller. "I was a little afraid that the Heretic Seed wouldn't give me any experience for a kill if someone else swung the weapon, but it seems to be okay with it."

"Probably because we're making use of your magic to make the kills." Mason stared at his enchanted machete. "God, I can't believe I'm getting used to this."

Rebecca returned to interrupt the moment. "I think that's all I can pull out here. The rest seem unwilling to follow me more than a few feet. We're going to have to head in to clear the rest."

"Lead the way." Digby gestured for her to go first.

"Sure, I'll…" Her voice trailed off as her projected body dispersed into particles of light. Digby could feel the mana of the spell dissipate. A second later, she reemerged, passing through the back door of the van again like a ghost. "Sorry, my spell ran out of time. I guess I have to start back at my body every time I cast it."

"So that means your range is however far you can run from there before the spell's duration expires." Digby scratched his chin. "That's good to know."

"Yeah, that will probably make it hard to use projection for communication. I was hoping there would be a way to send myself back to the castle from here to check in." She shrugged and headed back into the store. "Maybe I can rank the spell up enough to get more out of it."

Digby followed her inside, taking a position at the rear of the group as they pushed into the first of the store's eight aisles. They met five revenants by the canned goods, each falling to a mana infused blade. Alex refreshed everyone's enchantments before taking down another three in the next aisle. Digby caught one more sneaking up on them, ending the creature with his claws to conserve the blood stored in his void. His three minions cleared the mess away, leaving nothing but a crimson smear on the tile floor.

Digby helped finish off another twelve revenants before finally stepping outside, feeling confident that the others could handle the rest without him. He hoped that by waiting in the parking lot, he might not disrupt their experience gains since he was unaware of what was happening in the market.

They would have to take a few breaks to reabsorb mana, but against the dormant revenants, Alex and the others felt confident that they could handle the rest alone. After giving the store a thorough sweep, they managed to kill another thirty-one of the creatures without him.

Checking his coven's status on his HUD, he nodded at their mana values. It was nice to have a controlled fight rather than a chaotic brawl of desperation like most of their encounters. Clearing the store had taken over an hour, but in the process, there had been no injuries.

Alex had even reached level nine, as well as a new rank for Enchant Weapon. The spell's overall duration went up from one minute to two. The enchanter's additional attribute point went to will now that he had to fill out the values that had been left wanting by his past lifestyles. Digby could tell just by Alex's growing confidence that the boy was growing stronger.

For that matter, Rebecca was growing as well. With a new rank for her projection spell, she gained an increase to its duration from ten to twenty minutes. She'd also reached level eight while she was at it.

Calling to James and Mathew to load everything they could into the trucks, Digby opted to head next door to check on his minions. His jaw dropped as soon as he entered the apothecary. The feast had done them well, giving the trio enough resources to take a multitude of mutations. Now, instead of the three common zombies he'd had, three uncommon monsters stood in their place.

A lurker wielding bone claws on both hands, complete with the silent movement mutation, stood ready for new orders. The second looked normal for the most part, though a glance at the minion line of his HUD told him it was a glutton. Behind them, a brute waited, wearing bone armor on top of its over-muscled body, complete with a powerful set of horns on its forehead.

Digby refreshed his control spells so that he could maintain their loyalty. If he let it lapse, the only way to bring them back to his side would be the more powerful control spell meant for uncommon zombies, which cost quite a bit more mana. Refreshing his more economical control spell also let him reapply the intelligence bonus to the brute, which had lost most of its values after it had mutated. They each held a solid attribute of ten intelligence. It was enough to get them to follow most instructions without issue.

With his three minions coming along nicely, Digby opened his maw on the floor to allow them to toss in what was left. He made a point of hand feeding Asher a fair amount of hearts and brains to get her the second mutation in the Path of the Leader, Recall Memory.

It wasn't long before she reached her quota.

Animated zombie, Asher, has gained the mutation Recall Memory. They may now recall some of their memories from before their death. Intelligence has increased to 11. Perception has increased to 8. Will has increased to 5. Maximum Mana has increased to 65.
By claiming both mutations within the Path of the Leader, the animated zombie, Asher, has gained access to the advanced mutation path, Master. There are 3 mutations available.

The deceased raven's behavior changed abruptly, as if becoming more independent. She didn't wait around to be given orders, instead she flew out of the store on her own, like she wanted to be alone. Digby focused on their bond, feeling a new wave of emotion. It still felt warm and affectionate, but also confused, like she wasn't quite sure which world she belonged to.

It made sense. If she had just remembered part of her life as a bird at the same time as a significant increase in intelligence, a little confusion was understandable. Digby's shoulders sank, unsure if pushing her to mutate had been the right choice. He wandered outside, over to the window to find her flapping through the sky.

Placing his hand to his chest, he focused on their bond. "You still my girl?"

Asher flapped back down to swoop into the store again, landing in front of him. She cawed and nodded her head, sending two words across their bond.

You teach.

Digby gave her a warm smile. "That's right, I'll teach you everything I know."

Asher nodded again.

Digby reached over to offer her a playful scratch. The deceased raven pecked at his claw a couple times before resting her head against it. A moment later, she took flight again and headed out into the street to explore the area. Digby picked up a new feeling over their bond. There were no words attached to it, but a strong sense of curiosity flooded his mind.

"Alright, girl. You explore as much as you need. I'll be right here."

A new message from the Heretic Seed pulled him out of his melancholy.

GUIDED MUTATION
Requirements for the mutation Dissection have been met.
Accept? Yes/No

Digby glanced back at his minions that were still shoving the remains of the revenants the others had killed into his maw. He brought up his list of available mutations within the Path of the Ravager to see if accepting it would interfere with reaching any of the ones he wanted more.

SHEEP'S CLOTHING
Description: Mimic a human appearance to lull your prey into a false sense of security.
Resource Requirements: 10 flesh.

TEMPORARY MASS
Description: Consume void resources to weave a structure of muscle and bone around your body to enhance strength and defense for a limited time.
Resource Requirements: 25 flesh, 10 bone.
Attribute Effects: +11 strength, +9 defense.
Limitations: All effects are temporary. Once claimed, each use requires 2 flesh and 1 bone.

HELL'S MAW
Description: Increase the maximum size of your void gateway at will.
Resource Requirements: 30 viscera.
Attribute Effects: +3 perception, +6 will.
Limitations: Once claimed, each use will require mana to increase your maw's opening beyond its default size. You will gain 2 inches for every point of mana spent.

DISSECTION
Description: When consuming prey, you may gain a deeper understanding of how bodies are formed. This will allow you to spot and exploit a target's weaknesses instinctively.
Resource Requirements: 10 mind, 5 heart.
Attribute Effects: +3 intelligence, +6 perception.

Looking through his options he thought the word 'accept' to claim Dissection. Of course, what he really wanted was the Sheep's Clothing mutation, hoping it would return his lost nose back to him. However, thanks to his new armored brute, there wasn't enough flesh remaining to get him there.

"You're a big pig, aren't you?" Digby eyed the brute, getting an apologetic shrug in response.

"Whatever, it's fine. I didn't want my nose back anyway." Digby took a moment to sulk before heading back outside with his minions in tow.

Surprisingly, the others were quite calm with the new monsters that he now controlled. Even James and Mathew paid them no mind. They must have gotten used to being around the dead while interacting with Rufus' horde for the last couple weeks. The pair simply went about their business to load up the trucks.

Once both vehicles had enough canned goods and nonperishables to last the castle over a month, it was decided that James and Mathew would head back to deliver the loot while Digby and the rest of the combat-enabled members would head on to the next city. Their day so far had been productive, but the small coastal town they'd visited lacked the resources they needed to build the forge that they had been thinking about. For that, they would have to find a large-scale market, making a two-hour drive necessary.

Digby pretended to be disappointed as Rufus' men left. He hadn't exactly told James or Mathew about his and Mason's plan to arm the settlers back at the castle. Instead, he told them that they were heading to the next town to gather what they needed for Rebecca's plan to archive the world's knowledge.

With the two men on their way, Digby had Rebecca project herself around a few of the vehicle storage lots to find something to carry his minions since there wasn't enough room for his brute in the van. She found what Mason called a box truck at a rental lot that worked well.

Out of curiosity, Digby told his glutton to get in the driver's seat, wondering if the ten intelligence points his control spell provided would be enough to get the zombie to follow them. With a little experimentation, he found that his new minion actually retained an understanding of how to drive. In practice, they made a halfway decent chauffeur. Though, the deceased driver did rear-end the van a couple times on their way out of town.

Rebecca lurched forward for a third time. "You know, you could ride back in the truck of the dead to keep your minions from bumping us every time we stop."

"But then I would miss out on your winning conversation." Digby gave her a grin, still suppressing a laugh at her mustachioed face which she had yet to notice.

"Suit yourself." She belted herself in as Alex pulled the van out onto the open road. A moment later she leaned toward her window and stared at the mirror mounted on the outside of the van's door.

Oh damn. Digby froze as her entire body tensed.

The shouting continued until they reached their next destination.

CHAPTER SEVENTEEN

Digby fell forward as they pulled up to a large building supply store in Santa Barbara, nearly two and a half hours from the castle. His minion had bumped the rear of the van with its truck again.

"No complaints this time, Becky?" Digby picked himself back up.

"I'm literally out of complaints." Rebecca sat with her arms folded. She had been unable to rub the permanent marker off her face and had resigned herself to wearing the mustache and goatee for the foreseeable future.

"Oh, it could be worse." Digby hooked a claw behind him. "Parker back there wanted me to draw genitalia."

"Hey, don't sell me out." She ducked behind Sax and Mason.

"Whatever." Rebecca laid back in her seat and glared at Alex sitting in the driver's seat. "I'm going to scout the hardware store. Don't let anyone touch me while I'm gone." A moment later, a second version of the mage stood up from where her body lay and exited the van by passing through the door.

"That is pretty weird," Sax commented.

"Good. Now get out so I can stretch my legs." Parker shoved him toward the back door.

"We have about four hours left before sundown." Mason hopped out the back as well, grabbing one of the machetes on his way. "We have to get this done quick, unless we want to find somewhere to camp out for the night."

"We're in luck." Rebecca's projection returned to the parking lot. "There's a few revenants in there, but not many. Shouldn't take more than a half hour or so to clear them out if we use Dig's pet monsters."

Digby exited the vehicle and gestured to his minions sitting in the front of the truck. "You heard her, boys. Head on in."

The two zombies popped open the doors and tumbled out. After standing back up, they had the good sense to open the rear door to let out the brute without Digby having to tell them. He turned back to Rebecca's projection. "Definitely no humans in there, right?"

"None that I saw." She nodded and headed back in to help lure the revenants inside toward his minions.

"Alright then." Digby pointed into the store. "Rend all you find."

His brute let out a roar before barreling forward. It hit the doors with a crash of shattering glass. The glutton staggered in next, followed by Digby's lurker. He couldn't help but notice how quiet his last minion was as it slinked in like a cat through the hole left by the brute.

I should really send more minions down the lurker's path, especially if I need an assassin. Digby stood tall, admiring his small but powerful horde. The best part about the lurker's mutations was that their requirements were so low. If he could find enough food, he could assemble a whole horde of them. *My enemies wouldn't even know what hit them.*

"Actually, can you call your minions back?" Alex stepped forward.

"What?" Digby arched an eyebrow before following the

enchanter's train of thought. "Oh, you want to take a crack at it alone for the experience, huh?"

"Yeah." He drew his weapon. "We took down a bunch of those things back in the grocery store. So I should be fine if I go in with Becca's projection."

"We should come too." Mason let his machete rest on his shoulder. "Having a few regular people around doesn't seem to mess with your experience as long as you enchant our weapons. And having some backup will be safer."

"Of course." Alex started enchanting everyone's weapons.

"Well, I'll be out here relaxing then." Digby shrugged and headed to the entrance of the store to call back his minions. Two of his three uncommon zombies returned, though his glutton seemed to have gotten lost somewhere inside.

"No problem, I'll send it back out when I find it." Alex started for the shadowed entrance of the hardware store.

"Thank you, my boy." Digby nodded as everyone left him behind.

Alone again, Digby sent his two minions off to another store at the other end of the parking lot. Just because he had to wait outside didn't mean he couldn't earn a little experience while he was there. His brute barreled off to smash through another door, followed by his lurker. He figured he would send in his glutton once it found its way out of the building supply store. It wasn't long before he received a few messages.

2 dormant revenants defeated, 12 experience awarded.
-75% due to distance. Total experience gained: 6.

He rolled his eyes at the distance penalty. Apparently, he wasn't going to be able to send his minions off to fight for him and reap the benefits. He let them clean up the rest of the store regardless. Another few messages came in, telling him he'd gained a total of twenty seven points.

I hope Alex is faring better in there; the sooner he catches up, the better.

Digby shrugged at the number and reached up to pet Asher

who was perched on top of the van where Rebecca's drone was. She was a little less enthusiastic about the attention now that her intelligence had risen, but still, he wanted to make sure she knew he cared for her. His eyes snapped back to his HUD, just as a new line flashed across his vision.

Zombie Glutton, lost.

Digby stared at the line, reading it again.

What happened?

Could one of those dormant revenants have actually defeated his minion? His body froze, waiting for something else to happen. That was when he caught a glimpse of Parker and Sax rushing from the shadows within the building. Alex dangled between them with his arms slung over their shoulders.

A crimson stain covered the awful floral shirt he'd been insisting on wearing. A pale form appeared in the door behind them as they escaped the store. To Digby's horror, it didn't stop. Rather, it chased after them into the daylight at a full sprint.

Digby limped toward them to get in range of the revenant behind them. They weren't going to make it. The creature behind them was too fast. He cursed himself for waiting by the van instead of near the door.

Thinking quick, he opened his maw on the ground and stepped over the opening as black blood began to seep out. He cast Forge, hoping it was capable of producing the effect he needed. A solid shaft of blood erupted from his maw as he leaned forward, slamming hard into the bottom of his peg-leg to launch him into the air. Digby soared over Parker and Sax, moving faster than he could have run on his own.

He crashed down into the revenant in a jumbled mess of limbs.

The creature thrashed and clawed, tearing away a handful of flesh from Digby's throat that left him sucking in air through a gaping hole in his esophagus. He fought back and punched the creature in the face with his bone gauntlet before headbutting it in the face with his horned crown. The impact dazed the revenant, but only for a second. Digby didn't waste the opening, accessing his maw and casting another Forge to put a spike through the foul thing's face.

1 active revenant lightwalker defeated, 712 experience awarded.

He cast a Necrotic Regeneration to repair his throat and shoved himself off the ground to limp back to his injured apprentice.

Parker and Sax reached the van only to fall over and drop Alex. He hit the side of the vehicle with a wet slap, sliding down the metal surface to the ground. A crimson smear covered the van's door. The enchanter clutched his side, taking rapid breaths. Parker placed a hand over her shoulder, drawing Digby's attention to a deep wound. The unmistakable pattern of teeth marred her flesh.

"Where's Rebecca?" Digby dropped to knees in front of them. He had no idea what a revenant lightwalker was, but judging from the amount of experience gained, it was uncommon. He shook his head in disbelief as blood seeped through Alex's fingers.

"Mason got boxed in. She's still in there trying to help." Sax struggled to get back to his feet.

"Damn it, we need a healer." Digby reached down and grabbed Alex's canteen to place it in the enchanter's bloody hand.

"Thanks." Alex winced as his mana passed over the container.

Digby held the opening to his mouth to at least give him the minor healing effect of the purified water. Once his apprentice swallowed a mouthful, he motioned to pour the rest over the wound.

"No." Alex grabbed the container to stop him before pushing the canteen to Parker. "Drink."

"You need it more." She shook her head, still holding her hand to the teeth marks that marred her shoulder.

"Drink." He shoved it closer while clutching his other hand over his stomach. "If I don't survive, there won't be anyone to cleanse that bite's curse. You'll turn."

Digby crawled over to his apprentice, sensing how serious the injury was through his blood sense. He was losing so much. "Someone do something."

"Alex is right." Sax grabbed a cloth from the van and applied pressure to the gash on the enchanter's gut. "I'm gonna do everything I can here, but drink it to be safe."

Parker gave in and took as small a sip as possible before pouring the rest out on the Alex's wound. She took his hand as soon as it was empty. "You're not dying, okay? So shut the fuck up."

Digby wanted to believe her but he could feel the flow of mana in the boy's blood. He wasn't healing fast enough to stop the bleeding.

What do I do?

Without any healing spells to use on the living, Digby snapped his head toward the entrance of the hardware store and screamed, "Becky, help!" His raspy voice sounded like tearing paper. "Becky!"

There was no answer and there was no way to contact her while she was projected.

Parker grabbed her walkie-talkie and held down the button. "Mason!"

"Shit, yeah?" he responded, sounding out of breath.

"Tell Rebecca to cancel her projection spell, we need her out here now."

"She isn't with me. I'm trapped but I'm safe. I told her to go looking for you three. We thought you were trapped in here too."

"Damn it." Parker closed her eyes for a second. "We're outside already. Dig killed that thing that attacked us, but Alex is hurt bad. We need Rebecca's heal spell."

"Okay, I'll find her."

"Shit." Blood soaked through the cloth in Sax's hands. "We don't have a lot of time here."

Digby reached out with both hands. Sax was right, there wasn't time to wait. His fingers trembled as the threads of an idea strung themselves together in his mind. "Move the cloth."

"Can't, he'll bleed out." Sax ignored his request.

"Move it!" Digby slapped the soldier's hands away before placing his own down. Sensation nearly overwhelmed him the instant he made contact. Mana seeped through his fingers along with the blood, begging him to tear Alex open as the spark inside him fluctuated. It called to him. No, it screamed.

Eat.

Digby closed his eyes and shook his head.

Feed.

"No!" he shouted out loud.

Devour.

Digby swallowed a heavy gulp of air and forced the instinct away, focusing on the concept of what he wanted his magic to do.

Then, he cast Blood Forge.

Dark crimson tendrils radiated from his fingers as the blood clotted to form a layer over the wound to stop the flow in an instant. Digby held his hands in place, trying not to rupture the thin membrane that he'd formed to buy precious seconds. He hoped it would be enough.

Suddenly, the van's door popped open as a frantic Rebecca stumbled out. "Oh god, I'm sorry. I got separated inside and couldn't find anyone but Mason."

"It's alright." Digby looked up at her. "You're here now."

Mason appeared next, running out of the hardware store. Evidently, he'd been able to tell Rebecca what was happening. He reached the van as Rebecca knelt down at Alex's side and cast Regeneration.

"Come on, come on." She whispered her words like a prayer.

Alex's breathing began to slow as he lost consciousness.

"Please, no. Is he…?" Parker leaned over him still squeezing his hand.

"No." Digby closed his eyes, letting go of the tension in his shoulders. "His body is resting to help heal. I can feel it in his mana flow. The spark inside him is stabilizing."

"Spark?" Mason asked.

"It's something the Heretic Seed told me about. Everyone has a mana system within them. It's stronger in magic users like us, but everyone has one to some degree." Digby looked up. "The spark is like its core."

"You mean, like a soul?" Sax slumped back against the van's wheel.

"Sort of." He gently pulled his hands away from the sticky surface of Alex's closing wound. Looking back to the entrance of the hardware store, Digby stared at the revenant's corpse that lay just outside. "When will this curse stop catching us off guard?"

"I don't know." Rebecca leaned against the van, letting herself slide down to the pavement. "It looked the same as the others. But it was faster, like fighting any of the other ones at night."

"The Seed called that thing a lightwalker when I analyzed it." Digby turned back to her. "It was uncommon. There must be some out there that don't have all of the same weaknesses. It was like the sun didn't bother it at all."

"Its system must be able to tolerate more life essence in its mana balance," she added. "Good thing Rufus' horde is protecting the castle. There's no way to tell how many more revenants like that one are out there, and I don't think the sun goddess statue's effect will keep them out. It's like every time we think we've figured out the rules, the game changes."

"God damn, Skyline." Mason pounded the side of his fist against the van as he crouched down beside her.

"Indeed." Digby stood back up. "And damn Henwick."

They waited in silence for another ten minutes before Alex

regained consciousness. Despite his blood-soaked clothing, he seemed alright. Though, Digby wasn't about to let him back in the fight after coming so close to death. Instead, he went inside the building supply store himself, bringing his minions for back up.

To his surprise, Rebecca joined him, using her real body instead of a projection. When asked, all she said was that he might need back up. Thanks to her icicles and Digby's brute, the remaining dormant revenants weren't a problem. After making a careful sweep, they'd only found three more. Digby let his minions devour the corpses on their own without taking part. With everything that had happened, he didn't feel like eating. No matter how hungry he might have been.

Once the store was clear, Mason, Parker, and Sax went to work, gathering the supplies to construct a forge. A pair of large but empty propane tanks, several pipes, welding tools, and a large amount of scrap metal, including chains, nails, and anything else that could be melted down and reshaped into weapons. It all went in the truck.

Digby watched, unaware of how all the pieces would come together. He understood the basics of blacksmithing, or at least, how it worked back in his day. The process began to make sense as they laid dozens of full propane tanks into the truck next to the two empty ones. They made sure to leave room for his brute in the back of the truck as well.

Asher perched quietly on top of the vehicle, watching the humans work. He could sense a level of confusion over their bond, coupled with a desire to understand what was happening, making it clear she was on the cusp of a human level of intelligence. He couldn't help but wonder what she would be like if she evolved into a zombie master like Rufus.

Digby finally allowed Alex to set foot outside the van when the truck had been fully loaded. The enchanter insisted he was fine, but still, Digby wanted him to take things slow. Mason grabbed him some overalls and a new t-shirt from the store. There wasn't much else to choose from as far as clothing went, but they were better than his current outfit that was covered in dried blood.

Digby didn't lament the loss of his horrible shirt.

Unfortunately, the encounter with the lightwalker and the aftermath that followed had slowed things down, leaving less than three hours to finish up their looting while still having to drive back to the castle.

"I hate to state the obvious," Rebecca stretched her back, "but we're not going to make it back before nightfall if we keep going. We can finish up here and try to get back to the castle, or we can quit for today and come back tomorrow."

"We could also finish up and find somewhere around here to hole up till morning." Alex unzipped the top of his overalls and tied the sleeves around his waist. "We should be able to find somewhere safe before we run out of time."

"Maybe." Digby turned to Mason and Rebecca, not trusting his own judgment after what had happened earlier. "What do you think?"

"Tough to say." He folded his arms. "If we finish and head back, we're going to have to travel for at least an hour in the dark. And the van's headlights might attract the wrong kind of attention. Then again, quitting and coming back would slow us down quite a bit, especially when we're so close."

"You think we should find somewhere around here?" Rebecca leaned on the van.

"Kind of." Mason nodded. "We spent enough time out here on the run to know that there are safe places available. A basement or something would be good to hide in. We could lock the doors and leave that brute of yours to guard the entrance. As long as the revenants don't see your zombies as hostile, then they should stay away. We'll just have to find somewhere near the edge of the city and make sure to be quiet."

"If we run into an issue, I can project myself out to lead a few revenants away," Rebecca added.

"Alright then, we'll finish this up and head for shelter." Digby nodded and ordered his minions to stay out of the way while the others finished loading the truck. An hour later, they were ready to set out.

Piling back into the vehicles, Digby opted to ride in the truck this time while his zombies rode in back with the forge equipment. Alex took the driver's seat. It didn't seem prudent to let one of his minions take the wheel again, considering the number of propane tanks in the back. Not with them rear-ending the van every time they had to stop. From there, they headed to the outskirts of the city. It didn't take long to find shelter. Though, they did have a few questions.

"What the hell does that mean?" Digby leaned over Alex to see out his side as the truck slowed to a stop behind the van.

"I'm not sure." Alex stared out the window as well.

Both of their mouths hung open at the sight of a large church with a hand-painted banner hung above the doors.

SANCTUARY FOR
THE LORD'S CHOSEN!
YOU ARE WELCOME!

CHAPTER EIGHTEEN

Digby tilted his head to one side at the ridiculous banner hanging over the door of the church as he read it out loud.

"Sanctuary for the lord's chosen?"

"I'm not sure we count as chosen." Alex gave Digby a sideways look.

"I don't know, it doesn't say which lord." He gestured to himself with a smug expression. "As Lord Graves, I have chosen you."

"Oh shit! Someone's coming." Alex slid back in his seat as a man in a black suit with a white collar stepped out the front door. "I think he's a priest."

"Gah! They'll burn me at the stake." Digby dropped low and grabbed Asher off the dash and placed her on the seat to keep her out of sight, as if hiding would somehow make the truck invisible. "Stay down, girl."

Peeking over the dash, they watched as Mason and Rebecca exited the van in front before walking up to meet the man. More people came out of the church as well. They were unarmed.

"What are they saying?" Digby jabbed Alex in the shoulder.

"Hold on." He rolled the window down just enough to hear.

"Hi there." Rebecca waved politely, clearly having forgotten about the marker that was still on her face. "We couldn't help but notice your banner."

"Yes, it has done a great deal of good." The priest eyed her for a moment, clearly noticing her mustache before holding out a hand for Mason to shake. "I'm Father Mitchell. I was pastor here before the end times. It's good to see a young couple like yourselves in these dark days."

Mason's face froze. "Oh, we're not—"

"Yes, my fiancé and I were just looking for a place to spend the night. The day sort of got away from us." Rebecca interrupted Mason and slipped her arm around his waist. Digby smirked as she dug her nails into the soldier's back to tell him to shut up.

"I can't say for sure if this is the end times or not," Mason played along. "But if you have room for my wife to be and our friends, then we'd be mighty grateful." He winced as Rebecca jabbed him in the back again.

Digby suppressed a laugh.

The priest nodded. "I understand your skepticism. But what else could all this be, and why else would these creatures be afraid to enter a house of the Lord?"

"What's that now?" Mason leaned forward.

"You don't know, do you?" Mitchell arched an eyebrow.

"Know what?" Rebecca leaned forward as well.

"That these creatures won't enter a church." Mitchell puffed out his chest.

"They don't?" Mason's voice climbed an octave.

"Nope. They won't even approach the doors." Mitchell nodded in a self-satisfied manner. "The slow, dead-looking monsters will try to get inside, but since the newer, faster creatures became the dominant presence, we don't see many of the dead out and about. We've been safe within the Lord's walls ever since."

"That is interesting." Mason leaned back, glancing to

Digby's truck as if making sure he'd heard the priest's claims as well.

"Interesting indeed." Digby ran a finger across Asher's head.

"Well, if you say it's safe inside, we'd love to take a look and maybe spend the night." Rebecca kept up her overly friendly facade.

"Of course. That's why we put up the banner. The more people we can save the better."

"Perfect." Rebecca turned around and began walking toward Digby's truck. "I'll tell my friends." Once she reached the vehicle's window, she climbed up on the side and made a point of blocking the space to keep Digby hidden. "You two hear all that?"

"We did." He placed both hands under his chin and batted his eyelashes. "When's the wedding?"

"Shut it." She rolled her eyes. "I figured it would play well with family friendly types."

"Indeed." Digby nodded, appreciating her deception.

"Whatever." She tapped a finger on the door of the truck. "Anyway, what do you think about his claim that the revs don't come near the church."

"I'm not sure. Maybe this whole curse has a biblical component." Digby shrugged.

"Or maybe there's something special about the location," Alex chimed in. "They might have something similar to the sun goddess statue in there."

"True. Either way, we should check it out." She turned to Digby. "I don't know if it's a good idea to bring you in with us though."

"Yes, that priest doesn't seem the type to share his church with an ungodly abomination such as myself." He scowled at the cross at the top of the building. "I suppose I can spend the night out in the truck. The revenants should leave me be, and there's no reason for the rest of you to put yourselves at risk if there is somewhere safe available."

"That's surprisingly reasonable of you." Her mouth curled up at one corner.

"Yes, well, today has been a bit hard on everyone." He folded his arms and sunk in his seat.

"Okay, then. I'll get the others and head inside." She started to turn away.

"Oh, and Rebecca?"

"Yeah?" She glanced back.

"You still have a little something right here." Digby scratched at his upper lip.

"I..." Her eyes widened as she glanced back at Mitchell, clearly realizing she'd just had a conversation with a complete stranger without explaining that she had been the victim of a prank.

"Have fun meeting everyone inside." Digby waved goodbye and sank back down in his seat.

Anger flashed across her face before she let it go. Without another word, she headed back to the church to join Mason as the others exited the van.

"I should head out too." Alex reached for the door handle. "Do you want me to get you anything from the van?"

"Yes, my tablet would be nice." Digby made sure to stay out of sight as Alex slid out of the truck.

Through the window, he listened to the people of the church emerge to greet the newcomers. They seemed friendly enough, for a bunch of superstitious rubes.

He tilted his head to the side.

I suppose I did think there were demons in my blood two weeks ago. So really, I'm not much better.

The more he thought about it, the more he wondered if the priest had a point. After all, the source of his power was called the Heretic Seed; maybe there was something biblical about the curse. If that was the case, then whose side was he on? Digby shook his head. The answer was obvious.

He was on his own side.

That was when one of the men from the church approached the truck.

"Do you need any help with your things?"

Digby froze, ducking even lower into the driver's compartment as Alex rushed over.

"No, there is just equipment we salvaged from the hardware store. We can leave it out here overnight."

"What sort of equipment you hauling?" the church goer asked.

"Oh, ah," Alex stuttered.

"Just some welding stuff." Rebecca pulled the enchanter's ass out of the fire. "We were going to bar the windows of wherever we were going to spend the night. But we can leave it here, I guess, since we've found you all."

"That's good thinking. I'm sure you'll find a use for the stuff then." The man wrapped his knuckles against the side of the cargo compartment. The moment the sound reverberated through the truck, a loud grunt came from the back. It was followed by the sound of chains and scrap metal being shoved around. Digby froze as the brute hiding inside thrashed among the forge equipment. The whole truck rocked as the now-familiar din of propane tanks clanging into each other caused both Alex and Rebecca to wince. Just when they began to relax, another few tanks fell over. They cringed with each impact.

"What was that?" The man stepped away and eyed the truck suspiciously.

"Ah, nothing, just, ah." Rebecca scrambled for words, sounding like Alex, who was even less help, still holding a continuous flinch.

"That sounded like a wild animal in there."

"No, nope." She recovered. "Just welding supplies, we must not have stowed the fuel tanks well enough."

"I hear you. But I really need to take a look back there. You understand."

Digby eyed the man in the rearview mirror as he checked the back of the truck. He relaxed, remembering that they had locked the door as a precaution. The man pulled on the handle before letting go and walking back toward the front of the truck. "Are the keys in the cab?"

Damn! Digby pulled Asher close and tried to duck down into the floor of the compartment as the man grabbed the door handle and popped the lock.

"Wait!" Rebecca spoke up.

"What?" The man stopped short, holding the driver's side door open a crack.

"Okay, there's no sense in hiding it. But we have a zombie in the back." Her eyes darted back and forth. "He was my father, and I just couldn't leave him, so…" She trailed off for dramatic effect.

"I'm going to have to talk to Father Mitchell." The man called to the priest.

"What seems to be the problem?"

"They're hiding a zombie in their truck. It sounds big. Said it used to be her father."

"Oh, I'm so sorry." The priest approached Rebecca, clasping her hands in his. "I wish you would have been honest, but I understand how hard these times have been on everyone. The love of a parent isn't something that one can let go of so easily."

"Thank you for understanding." Rebecca gave a convincing sniff as if holding back tears. "Can we still spend the night?"

"Of course, child." Mitchell's tone sounded sympathetic. "Obviously, we'll have to take care of this first. We do have some rifles, and we will do everything we can to do it quickly."

"Hang on, you can't—"

"It's alright. This is the best thing for you. Trust me." Mitchel placed his hands on her shoulders. "Letting go is the only way to begin healing."

"Wait," Alex finally jumped in. "We can just leave her, um, father, outside. We could even park it a few blocks away if it makes you uncomfortable having it so close."

"Nonsense. There is no saving the creatures. They are nothing but mindless animals."

"Yeah, we have to—" The churchgoer pulled open the door of the truck, coming face to peg-leg with Digby as he hid beneath the dash.

"Greetings." Digby waved.

Asher cawed.

The man immediately let out a high-pitched scream before falling back from the truck to land on his ass. He continued to scream as he scooted away from the vehicle.

"Good Lord." Mitchell recoiled in horror.

"Alright, alright." Digby pulled himself out from where he'd wedge himself under the dash. "Secret's out. There be zombies here." He narrowed his eyes at Mitchell. "And, as you can see, some of us are more than mindless animals."

"Wha—what?" Mitchell stepped backward. "What is the meaning of this?"

Rebecca dragged one hand down her face. "It's exactly what it looks like. This is Digby. He's dead, but he helps keep us safe. He was going to stay in the truck tonight like a good zombie."

"Abomination." Mitchell crossed himself.

"Indeed." Digby glanced down at the priest's feet. "By the way, what's your shoe size?"

"What?" Mitchell shook his head, taking another step backward. "Get out. All of you."

"Okay, okay." Rebecca held up both hands. "I realize what this looks like. But we are still just people, and we still need a place to stay." She left out the part about three of them being gifted with magic by some sort of occult artifact.

"Absolutely not!" Mitchell swept his hand through the air. "I can't have one of these things entering a house of the Lord."

"I have a name." Digby folded his arms and slouched back in the driver's seat of the truck.

"I assure you, Dig is completely safe and he won't go near your church."

"How can you say that?" The priest threw out a hand toward him, gesturing to his coat. "Just look at what he's wearing. He looks like an evil sorcerer."

"Technically, this garment belonged to a king." Digby adjusted the large collar that wrapped around his neck. "I think it looks rather fetching."

Mitchell seemed unimpressed. "Even if this monster is not dangerous, I can't open my church to anyone willing to travel with it." The priest calmed down. "It's the faith of those inside that keep the fallen out. If I let your group stay the night, I fear we might lose the blessing that has been bestowed upon us. You can't ask me to knowingly take that risk."

Rebecca lowered her head and let out a sigh. "That's fair, actually."

"It is?" Digby sat up straight.

"Kinda." She shrugged. "We don't know enough about this curse or why a church would be keeping the revs out. I doubt it has anything to do with the faith of its inhabitants, but we lack the evidence to argue the point."

"Thank you for being…" Mitchell glanced to Digby, then back to Rebecca. "…reasonable. I trust you'll be on your way." He stepped back several feet, watching to make sure none of them made any sudden movements. Digby caught a couple men with rifles appearing up by the church's front doors. A few unarmed people stood with them, looking frightened.

"Fine." Digby scooted back into the passenger seat, placing Asher in the middle seat. "No sense staying where we aren't welcome. There's still an hour of daylight left to find a place of our own to spend the night. Maybe then I won't have to wait in the truck."

"Okay, let's go." Rebecca groaned. "No sense wasting time."

"Got it." Mason began to follow, but turned back to Mitchell a second later. "You don't have anything to fear from us. But not all of these creatures seem to follow the rules."

"I'm sorry?" The priest furrowed his brow.

"We've encountered a lot of monsters, both dead and living.

Some are more dangerous than others, and not all of them have the same weaknesses. Just because none of them have approached your church yet doesn't mean none of them can. Just giving you a heads up."

"I thank you for that." Mitchell nodded. "And I'll keep that in mind."

"Good. We may not be on the same page here, but we're all still human. The more of us that survive, the better."

"Get moving, Mason." Rebecca leaned out the window of the van, clearly out of patience for the priest.

"Coming, dear." Mason shook his head and started toward the vehicle.

"Wait." Mitchell grabbed his shoulder, glancing back at Digby for a second before continuing. "There's a place that might be safe a little further out of town. I don't know if your group will want to listen, but you're right, we're all human. Or, at least, most of us are."

"Sure. Where do you suggest?" Mason turned back.

Digby pretended not to listen.

"There's a tavern a few miles away."

"A tavern?" Alex arched an eyebrow, stepping back into the conversation.

"Yes, though it used to be a church." Mitchell shook his head. "It was converted a few years back. It was some-what of a controversy at the time due to the sacrilegious nature. I forget the name of the place, but I remember the street it was on." He glanced up at Digby again. "If safety is not a question of faith like you all think, then that tavern might be safe too. And if it's not, it's at least a sturdy building that you might be able to weld shut quickly."

"Thank you." Alex inclined his head before pulling himself back into the truck.

"Yes, we'll check the place out." Mason copied down the street where the tavern was located and headed back to the van to join his mustachioed fiancée.

"That was surprisingly nice of them." Alex closed the door of the truck.

"Indeed." Digby ran a finger across Asher's feathers, glad that she seemed content to sit beside him.

"I'm surprised you didn't tell them to go screw at the end there." Alex started the truck up.

"I am too." Digby relaxed in his seat. "There was a time when I might have given them a tongue lashing to put them in their place. But, honestly, what good would it do? There's no reasoning against fear and faith. Not back in my day, and not now."

Digby didn't care to say much else on the way to the tavern and Alex didn't force the conversation. Asher rested on his arm, quietly watching the buildings pass by. It wasn't long before the van in front slowed to a stop.

Digby raised Asher to his shoulder and climbed out of the truck to saunter over to the others. Rebecca and Mason stood staring up at the sleepy building while Parker and Sax stretched their legs. He looked around at the fairly average street near the edge of Santa Barbara.

"Is this the place?"

The tavern stood with its steeple pointing into the sky as the sun fell closer to the horizon behind it. Stained glass windows bracketed a rather ornate door, each bearing the image of a noose looped around the neck of what looked like a pawn from a chess board.

A line of text on the sign out front named the establishment.
The Hanging Frederick
Board Game Café and Tavern

CHAPTER NINETEEN

Digby pushed through the front door of the converted church, now the Hanging Frederick Board Game Café and Tavern. He had no idea what a board game café was or how it differed from a regular tavern, but none of that mattered. No, what mattered was that the sun was setting and the old church was free of revenants. Once inside, he called to the others to let them know it was safe. They closed the heavy door behind them.

Digby swept his gaze over the space, finding it somewhat reminiscent of the tavern that he'd spent his nights in back in his time, except nicer. It was as if someone had gone through the trouble of renovating the old church to look like an establishment from a fantasy story. One that would fit in with the displays that he'd seen in the myth and magic exhibit, back in the Seattle Museum of Popular Culture, where he'd found his Coat of the Goblin King.

The obvious focal point of the space was a long counter that ran along the side of the room. It was made of pieces of dark wood connected together by a brilliant blue material. It looked like water. Alex was quite taken with it, running his hand along the smooth surface. Digby touched it as well.

A scattering of plain wooden tables filled the floor while a stairway led up to a balcony that overlooked the space. Digby's gaze shifted to a wall of shelves, each one full of various boxes, their edges adorned with illustrations and text. He read over a few. Settlers of Catan, Avalon, That's Wizard, Betrayal, Oh My Gods, Risk, Arkham Horror, Fire Tower, and so many more. There must have been hundreds.

"All of these are games?"

"Yup." Alex stepped up to his side. "Board games have had a surge in popularity in the last decade or so. Though, you sort of need friends to play them." He let an awkward laugh finish his statement without putting words to his last point.

"We should try to learn to play one tonight." Digby ran a claw down the side of one of the boxes, admiring an illustration of a dragon.

"It might be more important to figure out if this place really is protected like that church or not first." Rebecca stepped in front of the shelf. "There will be time for games later."

"Well, how would we check?" Digby turned around and focused on the bar. "Is it possible to analyze a building?"

"Not sure." Rebecca proceeded to stare at the sign hanging over the entrance extra hard. Alex did the same.

After focusing on every object in the tavern, they came up with nothing. Though, they all agreed, that there was something different about the place. Even Mason, Parker, and Sax noticed it. There was something calming about the tavern. It wasn't until Digby approached the front door that he noticed anything special.

Strangely, it wasn't his HUD that responded. Instead, it was the Heretic Seed itself, or more accurately, the shard in his chest. A calming resonance flowed through Digby's unique mana system as he placed his hand on the threshold.

SURROGATE ENCHANTMENT
Because this land holds a recreation of a building,
temple, or home in either design or concept, it has

gained a power comparable to the original. This enchantment will become active whenever requirements are met.
Occupant Requirement: This structure must be occupied by at least two or more conscious beings.
Ritual Requirement: While occupying this location's premises, one being must serve a drink to another.
Area of Effect: All space within this structure's walls.
Range of area of effect may increase for every occupant within this building's walls.

ENCHANTMENT EFFECTS:
WARDING
While sheltering one or more people, this structure will repel hostile entities that do not possess a high enough will to overpower this location's enchantment.

RECOVERY
If injured, mentally or physically, a being will recover at twice their natural rate while within this land's area of effect.

"Interesting." Digby removed his hand from the threshold and called to the others, letting them see for themselves.

"So this place has warding because it's a copy of another building that also has warding?" Rebecca furrowed her brow. "Is that because all churches are basically a copy in concept of another church?"

"I don't think so." Digby gestured to the bar. "The ritual requirement is that someone must serve a drink to another. That sounds more like a tavern than a church."

"Does that mean all bars have the same enchantment or just some?" Alex wandered over behind the counter and grabbed a glass, filling it with water from his canteen. "Okay, part one of the ritual is complete." He gestured to the glass on the counter, offering it to whoever wanted to handle part two.

"I have no idea what you're doing, but sure." Parker sat

down. "How about you magic that water up first? I like my beverages fizzy."

Alex shrugged and cast Purify on the glass before pushing it closer to her. Everyone watched as she took a sip. Afterward, they resigned to the tables, raiding whatever food and drink that was still edible in the kitchen. Digby commanded his brute to stand watch out front and sent his lurker to guard the back door. There were sure to be a few revenants wandering by at night and he didn't want to take any risks, even with the tavern's warding active.

Digby watched the sunset through a window on the balcony, before retiring downstairs with the others. It would still be a few hours before his human companions had to sleep for the night, and they seemed to be making the most of their sanctuary's offerings.

Parker sat at a table, eating olives from a jar as Sax brought out a bag of triangular corn chips. Alex joined them with a game from one of the shelves.

"You want in?" The enchanter held up the box in his hands, showing Digby the front. The words King of Tokyo ran across the front.

"Sure." Digby passed the bar as Rebecca struggled to wipe the marker off her face with a cloth soaked in vodka, only managing to smear it around.

"You're just making a mess, give it here." Mason took over to help. "Jeez, hold still, will you?"

"Quit pressing so hard." Rebecca kept pulling away. Digby smirked at the pair, surprised at how well they were getting along.

"You want to have a mustache through the entire apocalypse?" Mason didn't let up.

"No." She deflated.

"Then quit squirming. Show some of that determination you did when you went into that hardware store with Dig to kill those revs."

"I'd hardly call that determination." She scoffed. "More like guilt for letting everyone else put themselves at risk."

Digby shot her a supportive smile. "Whatever it was, it was good to see you out and about, as they say. I think we sometimes forget that this is the first time you've been outside in a long while after being imprisoned by Skyline. You're doing well."

"Shit, Dig." Rebecca's mouth fell open. "Are you actually being supportive? And you did it without even insulting me at the end there."

"Oh, please, Becky." Digby sat down at the table with the others. "I just felt it was a step in the right direction from hiding in the van like a coward."

"And there it is." She leaned back on the bar. "Knew you had an insult ready to go."

"Bah." Digby waved her complaint away with his claws. "You'll thank me when you're powerful enough to walk through this world without fear. A day will come when revenants will tremble in your presence."

"Sure there will." She rolled her eyes.

"He has a point." Mason poured some more vodka on the cloth in his hand. "The power you three have is nothing short of incredible. I know this isn't what you want to hear right now, but there may come a time that you'll have the strength to do something about Skyline."

"That is true." Alex flipped a page of an instruction booklet that he'd pulled from the game box on the table.

"You're right, I don't want to hear that right now." Dig slapped a hand on the table. "I may be dead, but I'm not suicidal. All I care about is getting that castle's defenses up to snuff and getting stronger. I've no intent on starting anything with Skyline."

"Fair enough." Mason shrugged. "But I've been doing some thinking. After seeing how you all operate, and I've decided to stick with you three for the long haul. The castle and Rufus have a good thing going, and I think we can make a real go of it there." He tapped the side of his head. "And I'm willing to bet that if I survive long enough, I get to say I told you so about Skyline when you three realize what you're really capable of."

"I guess that means we're with you too." Parker popped an olive into her mouth as Sax nodded in agreement.

"That true? You both are just going to follow your fearless leader over there?" Digby hooked a thumb back at Mason.

"Yes sir," they both answered in unison, adding a casual salute.

"That's quite the show of respect there." Rebecca glanced back at Mason as he stood behind the bar with a bottle of vodka. "What rank were you back in the service, by the way?"

"Private First Class, ma'am." Mason gave her a little bow.

"Is that good?" Digby took a game piece that Alex held out to him.

"It's good enough when those two are just Privates." Mason gestured to Sax and Parker.

"Plus neither of us want to be in charge." Sax took a game piece as well.

"Yeah, no thanks." Parker grabbed hers. "That's way more responsibility for me. I only joined the Army on a whim. No way I want to be in charge of anything in this mess of an apocalypse. Just tell me where to go, and I'll be happy to follow."

"See!" Digby pointed in her direction with a claw. "Not everyone needs to have ambition. Just a safe place to call home and a severed limb or two to eat."

Everyone rolled their eyes at once before settling down to play a game. The hours that followed were the most fun Digby could remember having. There hadn't been many people willing to spend time with him back in his day. Not to mention he won three games in a row.

Granted, he was cheating the entire time.

Of course, he was eventually caught, but it had been fun while it lasted. After that, Rebecca won the next few games until, she too, was caught cheating. The mage would have gotten away with it if it hadn't been for Digby's ability to sense mana flowing through another person's blood whenever they cast a spell.

Apparently, she'd learned something new back at the campground when she had used the drone's software to find out if Mason was lying. The Heretic Seed's Skill Link had found her a Veritas spell that told her when someone was lying, which gave her a significant edge when playing most games that required an element of bluffing.

Around eleven, the humans retired for the night, fashioning bedding out of whatever they could find. Mason was forced to sleep in the kitchen on account of his snoring, while Rebecca stretched out behind the bar, declaring it a no pants zone. The others opted to find their own private corners.

Without the need for sleep, Digby refreshed the control spells for his two minions again and sat down in a booth against the wall. Asher stared down at him from a perch in the building's rafters, her eyes observing him with the same curiosity that she'd exhibited ever since gaining her last mutation. He gave her a wave, but let her be beyond that. If she wanted space, he could handle that. He passed the time by reading the manuals that came with whatever game box drew his attention.

Outside, revenants wandered the streets. He gave thanks to the tavern's warding when none of them came near the door. It wasn't until three in the morning that things began to change.

Digby flicked his eyes to the door as his minion outside let out a grunt.

What's that now?

Making sure to remain quiet, he slipped through the tavern to reach the entrance. Asher flapped down to his shoulder as if concerned. His hands started shaking the instant he peered through the window set into the heavy door. Digby dug his claws into the surface of the wood.

They were everywhere.

Hundreds of revenants stood shoulder to shoulder, their

pale, fang-filled mouths facing the tavern. The wall of bodies was so thick, he couldn't see where it ended. Panic threatened to send Digby over the edge, screaming at him to wake everyone up to defend their meager sanctuary. He stomped the fear back down, grinding it into the floor with his peg-leg. Waking the humans up might be a mistake. Looking at the mob of pale, bat-like faces, he noticed that they appeared calm. It was as if they weren't aware there was food inside.

Maybe the warding is bothering whatever senses revenants rely on.

If that was the case, maybe they were all drawn by the simple fact that the place was forbidden, like a moth to a flame. Digby watched the swarm of creatures, frozen in place, unable to step any further than the sidewalk outside.

Then, to Digby's horror, a slender body slid through the crowd, creeping forward on its own. Digby clutched the door handle, glancing back at the tavern full of his companions. He had to do something.

It's just one. The warding is holding back the rest. He forced himself to relax. The brute outside wouldn't let the creature through. Digby watched as his oversized minion plodded forward to meet the revenant. The rest of the swarm behind the monsters bared their teeth.

No you fool! Digby tensed every deceased muscle in his body. *Don't antagonize them, the swarm will tear you apart!*

With no other choice, he reached for the door handle and pulled it open just enough to slip outside. Asher flapped through behind him to remain on his shoulder. He made sure not to let any of the creatures see inside, just in case the tavern's warding could be overpowered if they were to become aware of his edible friends inside.

Hundreds of beady eyes fell on him all at once.

"Hey, you there." Unsure what to do, he made a shooing motion with both hands. "Run along. There's nothing for you here. Only zombies." He placed a hand on his brute's shoulder to hold the beast back. "Easy there. No need to take risks."

The lone revenant stayed where it was, its lips retracting as drool dripped from its jagged teeth. Digby analyzed the creature, sending the little circle at the edge of his vision snapping out to highlight his target.

Active Revenant Wardbreaker, Uncommon, Neutral.

Digby relaxed, realizing that the thing had yet to become hostile. Checking a few more members of the swarm, the rest were neutral as well.

They must not be aware of the humans inside. Otherwise, their status would almost certainly change for the worse, knowing that he was standing between them and a meal. The same would be true if he killed the wardbreaker that was still creeping closer.

"Hey, you heard me." Digby stepped to the side to block the revenant's path. "Stay where you are."

The pale creature stopped only inches away, sending a jolt of tension down Digby's spine. He knew how strong an active revenant could be. One look at the dried blood on its claws reminded him of how much damage it could do if it decided to rule him as hostile.

"I could kill you just as easy." Digby took one step forward. "Don't go thinking you're anything special. Leave now and I may let you live."

Asher gave an aggressive caw to back him up.

The creature clearly didn't understand a word he was saying, all it seemed to understand was that he was dead and not a potential source of food. It leaned forward, bringing its face mere inches from Digby's throat as it breathed in a snout full of air.

"What the devil are you...?" Digby's eyes widened. "Oh no."

It can smell the humans on me.

Digby inhaled, breathing in his own earthy scent, unable to

pick up much else. Then again, his Blood Sense trait was how he usually tracked prey, so his sense of smell wasn't important. If anything, it was out of tune with his deceased status. Whatever the revenant could pick up was a mystery to him.

The creature bent down, sniffing his body as it raised back up.

"Alright, that's enough of that." Digby tried to step away only to flinch when the thing reached out to grab his coat. "Wait, stop—"

The revenant buried its snout into his chest as its body heaved, inhaling deeper than before. Then, it pulled away, leaving a damp smear of drool on the vest he wore underneath his coat. Digby released the tension that had coiled through his body, nearly falling over as it drained from his spine. Asher flapped her wings as the revenant slunk back into the swarm.

"Oh, thank god." Digby leaned on his brute's shoulder for balance, watching the creature vanish into the night. "It must have thought that the scents on me were from my victims rather than live prey."

Asher nodded, sending one word over their bond.

Luck.

"Yes, lucky indeed." Digby stared out at the crowd that still waited beyond the range of the tavern's warding. "That ward-breaker must have had a higher will value than the rest of these useless creatures."

Digby's mouth fell open. "That must be another reason why Skyline created them. Unlike my kind, created by the original curse, the revenants might lack the will to resist direct spells. If that's the case, then they would almost be easier to kill and control for Skyline's men, while still being more dangerous to the people that they don't want to save."

"Hmm, I wonder…" Digby scratched at his chin.

The realization that the revenants lacked a decent will value made him wonder if his Decay spell would work against them. It had never been useful against enemies before, since it directly affected the body of his target. But if they lacked the will to resist it? Well then, he might have had the perfect attack spell all along without having known it.

He made a mental note to test the theory later, ideally when he wasn't surrounded by a few hundred of the things. He was pretty sure that they couldn't cross the tavern's ward, but it didn't seem like the time to press his luck.

Sitting down on the steps of the converted church that protected the others, he resigned himself to keep watch from there. If another wardbreaker came sniffing about, he was going to want to know about it. He would stare them down all night if he had to.

I just hope Father Mitchell and his flock don't have any similar visitors tonight. Just one revenant could kill everyone inside that church.

The swarm outside thinned as the night progressed, eventually clearing altogether by dawn. Digby remained outside the whole time, standing sentinel for the humans inside, only stepping away to refresh the control spells on his other minion guarding the back.

Well, that, and to get a few simple games.

As it turned out, in a game of checkers, Asher was quite the opponent. The little zombie might have been acting more aloof lately, but she certainly seemed to enjoy a challenge. Though, Digby did let her win a couple rounds.

As the sun rose, Rebecca threw open the door, letting out a relieved sigh when she stumbled across him sitting on the steps.

"Oh, thank god." She clutched one hand to her chest. "I thought you were gone."

"No, just guarding the door." He pushed a checker up to wait for Asher to take her turn.

"You've been out here all night?" She straightened the hem of a t-shirt bearing the words 'Hanging Frederick Tavern' along with an illustrated noose tied around a chess piece.

"Someone had to keep a lookout for wardbreakers." He shrugged as if he hadn't been terrified earlier that night.

"What's a wardbreaker?"

Digby explained what had happened as Asher pushed a game piece forward with her beak.

"So there are more types of revenants than we thought." Rebecca sat down.

"And probably others that we haven't encountered yet." Digby took his turn. "We should get packed up. You might want to pick out a few games to bring back to the castle. Hawk and the other children will need things to pass the time."

Rebecca nodded without questioning his reasoning.

"And we should bring a few by the church. I'm sure Father Mitchell will appreciate the gesture. Maybe he'll even warm up to me."

"Trying to spread some good will for yourself?" She let out a laugh.

"Aren't I always?" He grinned up at her.

"Sure, we can stop by." She turned to head back inside. "We should warn them about that wardbreaker too."

The early morning was uneventful from there. Alex gave everyone a round of purified water to cleanse any radiation poisoning that might have built up over the course of the night. Once everyone was taken care of, the team gathered a selection of boxes from the shelves, leaving the majority for whoever might come after them.

Alex even wrote out the details of the tavern's warding on one wall so that it could be activated by anyone. Asking an ordinary person to believe in such things was a stretch, but the enchanter figured it couldn't hurt. He carved a message on the door as well, telling anyone that came upon the place that there was safety inside.

They packed up the vehicles shortly after dawn, each wearing a souvenir t-shirt of the establishment. Well, everyone but Digby, since it didn't match his coat. Instead he stowed his in the van for later. It was always good to have a spare shirt just in case. He grabbed one more for Hawk, figuring the child would appreciate something new to wear.

Ready to hit the road, Digby climbed back into the truck

with Alex and settled in. They just had to stop back at the church to drop off some games for the survivors there before heading back to the castle.

That was it.

Just one stop to make before heading home.

CHAPTER TWENTY

"Oh no…" Digby's claws dug into the cardboard game box he held as he stared up at the church that had turned them away the day before. His feet rooted themselves to the ground, afraid to walk any closer as his Blood Sense lit up his vision with streaks of glowing crimson.

"Why couldn't they have just let us stay?" Alex stepped toward the dark stains that led into the open door.

Asher took flight from Digby's shoulder as he threw the game box down and rushed forward to burst through the door. Once inside, he confirmed what he feared. The wardbreaker had found other prey last night. He stopped just a few feet inside the door.

There were no bodies.

Why would there be?

The revenants didn't simply kill their prey. No, they left their bodies intact to regenerate and rise back up to join their swarm of living abominations. The carnage was marked only by blood. A smear here. A spatter there. That was all that was left. With the people inside changed, they must have simply joined the masses and moved on. Now, they were sure to be hiding a building somewhere, huddled together to wait for nightfall. To wait for the next night's hunt.

That was when a lone, familiar form slinked out of the pews.

"No…" Digby clutched a hand to his mouth.

It was the same wardbreaker from the night before. It must have remained behind since the church's warding had no effect on it.

"I should have killed you when I had the chance!" Digby let out a sudden snarl, stomping down the aisle. His peg-leg hammered the floorboards in a rapid staccato as he barreled toward the creature. He cast Decay without even thinking, the spell hitting in a wave of emerald, necrotic power.

Decay resisted.

He cast the spell again to wear down the monster's will that had allowed it to enter the church.

Decay resisted.

The revenant stumbled back as another blast of death mana swept across its body. This time black patches of rotting flesh ate away at its skin, leaving it mostly unharmed to prove the spell an inefficient weapon even after overpowering the creature's resistance. Digby didn't stop, plowing into the monster as he fell up the stairs of the altar. He slammed his palm into the creature's chest, pinning it down to the pulpit and digging his claws into its flesh.

"Die!" He cast Decay again and again. He had faster, more efficient spells, but he wanted the magic to work slow.

An ear-splitting scream assaulted his ears as the revenant flailed, unable to break free. Patches of skin split and rotted to dust as its chest caved in on itself. The scream ceased as an experience message drifted through his vision.

**Revenant Wardbreaker defeated, 712 Experience
awarded.**

Digby didn't let up, casting the spell until there was nothing
left of the creature but bones. Even the wood of the floor
around him rotted, the power of the spell pushing its aura of
decay further with each cast.

The altar cracked and warped as pages of the Bible on top
flaked away into the air. His mana ran out soon after, leaving
him hunched over on the floor still trying to cast the spell
despite having nothing left.

"Dig?" Rebecca placed a hand on his shoulder. "You can let
go now."

"I should have killed it last night." Digby closed his clawed
hand, the bones of the revenant's ribcage crumbling in his
fingers. "I could have stopped this."

"It's okay." She pulled on his coat. "Just come back with us.
Before the floor collapses." Asher cawed from somewhere
behind her, sending a concerned feeling across their bond.

Digby glanced around, realizing that he was kneeling in a
twenty-foot circle of decayed wood. Even the tapestries that
hung on the wall had rotted away with the overuse of the spell.
The floor creaked as he stood back up and backed up. Seconds
later the boards gave way, dropping the altar into the basement
below with a loud crack.

Digby stared at the hole in disbelief that he'd created it. He
had been reckless. He could have gotten hurt, or worse, hurt
someone else.

"I'm sorry." He dropped his eyes to the floor. "I just—"

"We know." Mason stepped forward.

"They would have been safe if they hadn't turned us away,"
Alex added. "There was nothing we could have done without
being here."

"I know. I…" Digby trailed off, sensing a blood trail that led
out the door. He was walking before he really understood why.
It became clear when he reached the outside. The trail was

faint, but he could see it. Flecks of crimson here and there, traveled down the street.

Rebecca caught up. "Where are you—"

"They went that way." He raised a claw in the direction of the trail. Asher flapped out to land by one of the flecks of blood, pecking at the pavement.

"And?"

"We have to go after them," Digby explained as if it should have been obvious.

"Uh, okay." She looked back to Mason and Alex.

"Might as well." Alex patted the machete hanging from his belt. "We could use the levels."

"He has a point." Mason nodded. "We can probably take some time here before heading back to the castle."

"Indeed." Digby proceeded to limp on down to the street, calling to his two minions to follow. The brute plodded along behind him while his lurker walked at his side. He struggled to keep the trail of blood in sight, finding several more fresh trails converging together from other buildings. It was almost as if they led to the same place.

Even stranger, he hadn't come across any stray revenants as he went. It stood to reason that there would be a few caught out in the open here and there. He looked back over his shoulder, finding the others following him in the van. They let the vehicle crawl forward, occasionally weaving around obstacles.

It wasn't long before the trail came to an end.

"Good lord." Digby stared up at the ten-story building lined with narrow windows. The curtains were drawn, blocking the sun from reaching inside. Its main doors hung open with signs of heavy foot traffic. He glanced back at the sound of the van door opening.

"Good lord is right." Alex hopped out of the vehicle. "That hotel must be full of them."

"How do you know?"

"Feel for yourself." The enchanter handed over the iron key that he used to cast his detection spells. Even with the dulled sensation of his deceased body, Digby could tell it was practically frozen. Squinting, he peered inside to catch a few pale forms in the shadows of the lobby. Raising his head, he noticed at least some of the blinds moving on every floor.

"They must be using that building as shelter." He tensed his body. "It's like a hive." Digby checked his mana.

MP: 220/244

His magic had mostly recovered while he'd followed the trail of blood despite his slower absorption rate. The only question was, what could he do with it?

"How about you heretics step aside?" Mason and the other two soldiers stepped out of the van. "This is on us non-magic types."

"What do you have in mind?" Digby eyed the soldier.

"We burn it down." Mason hooked a thumb back over his shoulder. "There was a gas station back that way about a block. All we have to do is fill up some tanks and douse the first floor. As long as we barricade the doors, nothing's getting out of there. The whole place will go up in flames."

"Sounds good, but there's no reason for you three to take the risk in going in there. My minions and I can handle that sort of task." Digby elbowed his lurker in the side.

"Fair enough. We'll start filling tanks then." Mason turned back in the direction of the gas station. Sax and Parker followed behind, with Rebecca and Alex going along as a guard.

Digby remained near the hotel to scrape together a few more minions. After searching a couple alleyways across the street, he was able to find another three zombies to add to his meager horde. He cursed Skyline for corrupting his curse. With the act of introducing the revenants into the world, they had all but cut his kind out of the picture. His zombies just couldn't compete with the faster, stronger monsters.

Digby pushed away the thought; there was no sense worrying about it now. Not when he had a building to burn. He let a wicked grin crack across his face. Even better, it was for a good cause. There was something to be said for avenging the innocent, after all. He couldn't save Father Mitchell or the members of his flock, but he could make sure that the revenants inside the hotel couldn't hurt anyone else.

"Might even get a level or two out of it."

"That would be good." Alex passed behind him, lugging a pair of red containers. The rest of the group followed, each with their own cargo of fuel. They fell in line as they set the tanks down.

"Alright, here's the deal, we're going to get this done as safe as possible." Digby clapped his hands. "All we have to do is wait for my new minions to cover the first floor in fuel. I'll guide their efforts from inside and leave a trail of gas when I leave the building. The rest of you won't even need to go inside or use magic. We'll just make sure you two have a hand in setting the blaze when the time comes so that the Seed gives you credit for the kills. Then all we have to do is wait for the experience to roll in. If we're careful, nothing could possibly go wrong."

"Um, excuse me?" Parker held up her hand.

"Yes?"

"I feel like that pep-talk is pretty much ensuring that something goes wrong."

"Shut up, Parker." Digby narrowed his eyes at the woman. "No one asked you. And don't think I haven't ruled out stealing a woman's foot to replace mine. Honestly, I think it would look rather fetching." He pulled his pant leg up as if demonstrating.

With a plan in place, gas tanks were handed off to Digby's minions. He told Asher to stay by the van as he followed his zombies inside to make sure they accomplished their task without any confusion. As it was, asking them to carry the heavy containers was hard enough with their attributes being so low. Stepping into the shade of the hotel's entrance, Digby approached a huddled mass of revenants seeking shelter from the sun. The only light came from the red glow of the hotel's emergency system.

"Hello there." Digby gave them a casual wave. "I hope you like it warm, because it's about to get pretty hot in here."

The creatures ignored him for the most part, not seeing him as a threat or prey. Alex and Rebecca waited outside, ready to barricade the doors to keep the monsters from escaping. His brute stood between them. Digby gave them a nod and continued into the building.

The hotel's lobby was large, and filled with smooth angular surfaces. The style reminded him of the few movies that he'd watched that took place further in the future than the time that he had arrived in. Chrome and dark wood lined the reception area, while pillars were dispersed at even intervals throughout. Digby eyed the crowd of revenants as he unscrewed the cap of one of the gas cans. Sickly orange eyes shined in the dark in a cluster that spilled out of a doorway into the main lobby. A sign reading stairs glowed beside the door in case of an emergency.

That must be how they're getting to the upper floors.

Digby arched one eyebrow at the group, wondering how many filled the stairwell above. Glancing to the other end of the lobby, he noticed another sign labeling a second stairwell. Unlike the first, it seemed to be closed and free of enemies. He shrugged and began pouring gas along the floor in a circle around the creatures.

"Sorry, no escaping for you." He emptied his container and picked up a second.

From the smell of things, his three common minions were on schedule as well. Peering into the shadows, he caught glimpses on their silhouettes, dousing the hotel as planned.

"I hope none of them are getting gas on themselves." It would be a shame to have any of his new minions go up with the blaze. He started pouring out the second container, covering his face as the fumes started to burn the hollow of his nasal cavity.

That was when the revenants began to stir.

A chorus of chittering voices swelled from the stairwell,

seemingly aggravated by the smell of gas. Digby froze as soon as he glanced in their direction.

Dormant Revenant, Common, Hostile.

"Gah!" He grabbed a third container of gas as the pale creatures started staggering toward him. "It's alright." He looked over his shoulder, remembering that they were dormant. "They're not that fast during the day."

"What's happening in there?" Rebecca's voice came from a walkie-talkie clipped to his belt. "Some of them are heading for the door."

Digby thumbed the button on the side of the radio. "The smell is bothering them and making them hostile."

"Maybe they remember enough from their lives to know that gas is dangerous," Mason responded. "We'll take out the ones that make for the door. Just hurry up in there."

"Well I'm not going to sit down and work on my knitting," Digby snapped back, catching a glimpse of Alex just outside the entrance raising his bow. The sun shone down on the enchanter just beyond the shadows of the hotel as he took aim at a few of the creatures that approached the door. Digby tore his attention away from his apprentice as experience messages began to come in.

2 dormant revenants defeated, 24 experience awarded.

More came in one after another as the twang of a bowstring echoed through the lobby. Digby leaped to one side, feeling a hand brush against his shoulder.

"Back off!" He snarled at a revenant as it staggered toward him. Another two were close behind. He opened his maw on the floor beneath the foot of the first of his foes, taking off its leg at the knee as it fell in. He did the same to the other two, conserving mana by making full use of the free mutation ability. Efficiency aside, the attack wasn't lethal, leaving the creatures free to crawl closer with every second. Digby hopped away, nearly falling over with his missing foot and impaired agility.

"I said back off!" He splashed gasoline across their bodies, ignoring another few experience messages as Alex executed a few more by the door. At the rate the messages were coming in, Mason and the others must have been helping out as well. He checked his team's status.

COVEN
DIGBY: MP: 244/244
ASHER: MP: 64/64
ALEX: MP: 114/181
REBECCA: MP: 145/195

The team was handling themselves, but their mana would only last so long. From the numbers, he assumed Rebecca had already cast a couple Icicles and Alex had enchanted a couple weapons and loosed a couple arrows.

"I have to get this done fast." Digby dumped the rest of the gas on the floor just as a new message grabbed his attention.

Common Zombie, lost.

Digby's jaw tensed as he spun left and right, searching for the threat that had taken out one of his minions. All he saw was something pale blue streak by in the glow of the emergency lighting.

Common Zombie, lost.

"Crap." Digby threw a gas can to the floor and grabbed the last of the ones he'd carried in. All he had to do was make for the door, leaving a trail behind him. His hand shook as he unscrewed the cap. A high-pitched screech tore through the lobby, coming from somewhere behind the approaching swarm.

Common Zombie, lost.

"Damn!" Digby backed toward the door, leaving a shaky trail of accelerant as he walked. "Almost there—"

His hopeful words froze in his throat as a ferocious pale body dashed for him. He jumped back just as a clawed hand slapped his gas can away. The container crashed into one of the lobby's pillars with a heavy clunk before tumbling to the floor. Gasoline sloshed from side to side, pouring out the spout with a rhythmic glug, like a throat swallowing blood. Digby's eyes snapped back to his attacker.

Revenant Lightwalker, Uncommon, Hostile.

There wasn't even time to dodge before a clawed hand tore across the skin of his face, throwing Digby backward. Air rushed into his mouth from the side as his cheek split open. He hit the ground, suddenly blind in one eye. Clutching his hand to his head, he held together the scraps of his face. If only he'd had both feet, he might have been able to dodge. He cast Necrotic Regeneration to put himself back together.

The revenant stomped forward, splashing through a puddle of gas. It raised its claws, preparing to strike.

"No you don't!" Digby opened his maw and cast Forge, sending a blood spike up through the creature's chest to suspend it two feet off the floor. Glancing back at the entrance thirty feet away, he realized there wasn't any gas left to leave a trail to the outside. He snapped his view back to the flailing revenant as it let out a final screech before going limp. "Fine, I'm close enough."

Without a second thought, he cast Cremation on the dead creature.

The pale body sliding down the spike of necrotic blood burst into emerald flames, igniting the puddle of fuel on the floor. The fire's color flickered from green to orange with a sudden surge of heat as it spread across the lobby toward the stairwell. Digby let out a wicked cackle as a dozen pale forms went up in the blaze.

The flames didn't stop there. Instead it surged forth, connecting with the pools of gas left by his minions. The fire raced onward faster than Digby expected. In seconds, it had nearly reached the entrance. Then, to his horror, it started coming back.

"What?" Digby's jaw dropped, realizing that his pants were damp. Raising his hand from the floor, he found it wet. "Oh no."

Digby kicked off with everything he had to throw himself backward out of the puddle of gas that he hadn't realized he'd fallen in. He hit the ground again a few feet away, just before the area where he'd seen burst into flames. Somehow, in the commotion, he had lost track of where the gas had been poured. Now, he was just as flammable as everything else, his clothing soaked through with accelerant.

No... no, no, no.

Digby shoved himself back up off the floor as an explosion of fire surged into the lobby entrance. One of his minions' unused gas cans must have been claimed by the blaze, creating an inferno that he couldn't get through without going up in flames himself. Even if he stripped off everything he wore, there was still probably enough gas on his skin to set him alight. If that happened, there might not be enough of his necrotic body to regenerate.

Supporting himself on one of the lobby's pillars, Digby pushed off toward the unused stairwell. If he could make it up a floor or two, he could jump out a window. From up that high, he might only break his legs. His heart sank the moment he made it to the door.

It was locked.

"Oh, come on!" Digby cast Decay on the lock in desperation, taking the risk that the spell might disable the wrong part of the mechanism. Rust spread from his fingers as he wrenched the handle down. It snapped off in his hand, leaving the door firmly in place. "Seriously?"

Digby stared at the handle in his hand, before cursing Parker for her comment earlier about begging for things to go wrong by being too optimistic. In desperation, he threw the door handle aside and slammed his palm into the jagged bit of metal that stuck out of the lock.

He cast Forge, using his own blood to punch through the mechanism. Something metallic clattered to the floor on the other side. Digby yanked back, hoping the sound had been an important part of the lock. Success! The door swung open. He hobbled up the first flight of stairs just as Rebecca's voice came from the walkie-talkie on his belt.

"Dig, where the hell are you? The place just went up in flames."

"I'm aware!" he shouted into the receiver. "I'm trapped inside."

"Trapped how?" She didn't sound surprised.

"There's fire everywhere and I'm soaked in gasoline," Digby answered matter-of-factly.

"How did…? No, never mind. I'm just going to assume that it has something to do with the lightwalker defeated message we just received. Thanks for the extra experience, by the way."

"Oh good, I'm glad that something I've done in here was helpful to you, Becky." Digby rolled his eyes.

"That sounded sarcastic," Rebecca added.

"Of course that was sarcastic! I'm about to be burnt alive, or dead, you know what I mean!" Digby raised his voice as smoke poured into the stairwell.

"Okay, okay. Where are you?"

"I'm in a stairway on the far side of the building."

Suddenly, Mason joined the conversation. "Sorry to interrupt, but what effect would there be on the revs if clouds rolled in to block out the sun?"

"I don't know, would you like me to ask them?" Digby stomped his peg-leg.

"He's being sarcastic," Rebecca voice added in the background.

"I realized that," Mason responded.

"Actually…" Digby hesitated. "Maybe I can ask them." He reached for the door handle of the second floor to peek into the hallway. He immediately wished he hadn't, as fifty revenants all turned in his direction, letting out a unified screech. He slammed the door shut as they sprinted in his direction. Leaping back, he opened his maw and cast Blood Forge, sending several spikes up from the floor to barricade the door. The sound of a dozen claws scratching at once tore at the wooden barrier. He checked his mana.

MP: 98/193

Still plenty left. Digby kicked off the stairs, running up the next few on all fours before getting back to his feet. Gripping the talk button on his walkie-talkie, he called back to his accomplices outside. "The revenants are active, I repeat, the revenants are no longer dormant."

"Oh shit! He's right." Mason's voice went cold. "We have to move, there's more coming out of the surrounding buildings."

"What about me?" Digby shrieked.

"Get to the roof. I'll meet you there!" Rebecca shouted as gunshots went off in the background, followed by Sax and Parker shouting in unison.

"God damn unpredictable weather!"

Digby pushed onward, sprinting the best he could with his impaired agility until he ran out of floors. Again he tried to Decay the lock, hoping the revenants hadn't taken over the roof as well. He pressed down, hearing something in the lock snap, before coming loose to unlock the door.

"Finally, something went right."

Digby celebrated his luck as he burst out onto the roof. He was soaked the instant he made it outside. Rain hammered the building in a sudden downpour that caught him by surprise. "What?"

He stopped short. It had been sunny out just minutes before. How could conditions have changed so fast? He shook his head. It didn't matter how. It was just his bad luck.

"God damn unpredictable weather!" Digby quoted Sax and Parker as he ran to the front of the building to catch a glimpse of the van crawling down the street. Revenants swarmed from the surrounding buildings. There weren't nearly as many as the amount still trapped in the hotel, but there was enough to slow the van's progress.

Squinting through the smoke pouring from below, Digby could make out Asher cawing at the revenants from one of the vehicle's windows as his remaining minions fought to keep them at bay.

The brute tore through every enemy in the vehicle's path, clearing the way for the humans inside to escape. Behind, his lurker did its best to execute every foe that gave chase. The silent zombie ripped through revenants with its bone claws in a savage dance of gore and death. The pale creatures kept coming.

"Yes, give 'em what for." Digby cheered on his zombies from the roof.

One after another, the lurker struck down the oncoming swarm, even resorting to tearing their throats out with its teeth. Moments later, it fell forward to one knee as a pale claw raked down its back. The lurker pushed back up, hooking its fingers up through its attacker's chin to rip off its lower jaw. A second revenant leaped toward the lurker, then another. Digby's minion vanished beneath a pile of pale bodies in an instant.

Zombie Lurker, lost.

"Damn!" Digby slapped the side of the roof with his bone gauntlet, splashing rainwater with his claws.

That was when a steady pounding came from the other

door that led to the roof. Digby snapped his head back to face it. The pounding increased, as if more fists were joining in with every second. Raising his hand, he cast Blood Forge again to barricade the door. The revenants on the other side kept trying. Even with his spells, it was only a matter of time. Any second, a claw would break through. Digby raised his hand to cast another Forge just as a familiar face passed through the door.

"Oh thank god, you made it." A projected Rebecca rushed over to him.

"Of course I made it." Digby dropped his hand to his side. "Now tell me how I can escape this death trap of a building."

"You can't." She shook her head.

"What do you mean, I can't?" Digby's eye twitched.

"I didn't have time to map the building so I can't say for sure. But I ran all the way up here with revs swiping at me."

"I wish I could have seen the disappointment on their faces when they realized you weren't really there." Digby let out a mirthless laugh.

"Yes, it was very funny." She groaned, before glancing off in the direction of the van. Her eyes bulged as soon as she found it. The revenants had begun to swarm the vehicle enough to stop its progress all together. Digby's brute continued to defend the van, practically having to climb on top to swat foes away. Rebecca's hands began to shake. "Oh my god, my body is in there."

Rain poured down Digby's face as he turned away from the despair in her eyes. There was nothing he could do. "I'm sorry."

"For what?"

"For insisting we come here." He clenched his fist. "For insisting on killing the revenants. For everything."

"Shut up." Rebecca spun toward him baring her teeth. "Don't talk like we're already doomed down there."

"But there's nothing I can do from up here." Digby lowered his head.

Instead of responding, she darted away, running to the

other side of the roof and sprinting around its perimeter. She stopped short on one side.

"Get over here, Dig." She flicked her gaze toward him. "You're going to get out of this, and then you're going to come up with a way to save us down there."

"Have you seen me lately?" He hobbled his way over to her as the clawing at the door to the roof continued. "I don't have the ability to—"

"I don't care about your stupid missing foot." She swiped a hand though the air as raindrops fell through her illusionary body. "So shut up and jump." She stabbed a finger off to the side.

Digby furrowed his brow and approached the edge, finding her pointing to a building beside the one he stood on. Another hotel from the look of it. It was much shorter than the inferno he stood on but it was just as expensive looking. There was even a swimming pool on the roof. He flicked his eyes back to her.

"What do you mean, jump?"

"There's water down there to break your fall." She threw up her hands as if surviving the fall would be easy.

"What? That's…" Digby estimated the distance. "At least fifty feet away and seven floors down. I can't just—"

"There isn't time." Her voice began to tremble. "We need you to save us. I need you to save us."

Gunshots lit up the street below as Mason and the others fired out the windows of the van. A glance at his coven's status told him Alex was out of mana. Digby took another look at the pool. It seemed so far away.

"Alright, I'll try."

"No, there is no try." She jabbed a projected finger in his face. "Only do."

"The hell does that mean?" He asked, annoyed with her wording.

Before she had time to answer, a loud crack struck the air. The door Digby had barricaded ran out of time, splitting to pieces under the weight of the monsters behind it. Shards of crystalized blood mixed with splinters of wood flew across the rooftop, as revenants poured out into the rain. He didn't even need to analyze them to know they were hostile. Digby opened his maw and cast Forge, impaling one to buy a few precious seconds.

"You have to go now, Dig." Rebecca stomped forward as if trying to stand between him and the oncoming swarm. With a little luck they might be tricked into thinking she was real for a moment. She looked back. "Go!"

"Alright, alright!" Digby placed his good foot on the edge of the roof, staring down at the gap between buildings. There was no way he could make it on his own. Then, he remembered how he had used his Blood Forge spell to launch himself the day before when he had been trying to save Alex. He raised his other leg up to the edge as well and crouched, opening his maw directly beneath the hardened form of blood that functioned as a peg-leg. He checked his HUD one last time.

MP: 48/193

Then he cast Blood Forge.

Leaping with everything he had, Digby focused on the spell to create a pillar of black fluid that surged up beneath him to launch him through the air. Rain water pelted his body as he spun, catching a glimpse of Rebecca's projection. Revenants sprinted through her without slowing down. They reached out for him, some even lunging off the roof to plummet to the pavement below.

The world seemed to slow as he soared through the air, bodies falling from the roof behind him. Gravity reasserted itself to bring him back down to earth. He just hoped his Forge spell had thrown him far enough. Digby reached out with one hand, focusing on one of the corpses of the three creatures he'd impaled on the roof just before they fell out of view. He cast Cremation.

Feeling the mana flow through his body, two words passed through his mind.

Why not?

Digby reached down into his mana system for the stored power that he'd absorbed from the nuclear blast that had destroyed Seattle two weeks prior. The sickening energy that had been poisoning everyone around him. It didn't make sense to hold onto it. Not if he wasn't sure he'd survive the next few seconds. With a flicker of power, he merged the stored energy with his Cremation spell, hoping it would be enough to at least deal some extra damage in case the rain was able to put out the fire. He couldn't let the swarm in the hotel get free. The others wouldn't stand a chance against those kinds of numbers.

Digby clutched his chest as the power began to flow from him in a torrent of deadly radiation. He had assumed that adding the stored power would only give the Cremation spell a boost. His eyes bulged as he realized how wrong he was. It was like a dam had burst inside him.

A flash of pinkish-purple energy lit up the roof of the hotel, glowing brighter and brighter as he fell. Then, it exploded. A blast wave rocked the street, blowing the windows out of every building within three blocks. In the same instant, the top floor of the hotel simply burst into nothing but debris. The floors below followed one after another, exploding in a row of violent power. Digby hit the water below as the blast wave swept over the swimming pool he landed in. At least a dozen bones broke on impact.

From under the water, the pinkish glow shined so bright it threatened to blind him just before firing a pulse of energy straight into the heavens. A wave of force blew every cloud from the sky for at least a mile. Digby used the last of his mana to cast Necrotic Regeneration to stop his body from being cooked as the water around him boiled.

It wasn't enough.

His necrotic gray matter reached its limit as his thoughts slowed to a crawl. Digby focused on his coven's status, holding onto hope that they might survive. He prayed that the pulse that swept away the storm would allow enough sunlight through to chase away the revenants that swarmed the van.

Please!

The world faded to darkness around him as his body failed him. Lost again within his mind, there was nothing but an endless void.

Then, there was the sound of the ocean.

CHAPTER TWENTY-ONE

The gentle motion of a small boat drifting on a calm sea rocked Digby awake within the imaginary space of the Heretic Seed. His brain must have been too badly damaged to remain functioning again.

An arrogant voice greeted him.

"Boiled to death, huh?" The Seed's representation sat at the other end of the tiny boat, wearing Digby's face from back when he had been alive. "That's a new one."

Digby ignored the irritating copy of his former self and sat up straight to stare at his HUD.

COVEN
DIGBY: MP: 30/265
ASHER: MP: 65/65
ALEX: MP: 93/215
REBECCA: MP: 87/235

"They're fine," the Seed added.

"How do you know?"

"Look at their mana values. They've risen back up since last you looked. The only explanation for that would be that they are no longer fighting."

"Oh, thank the lord." Digby let himself fall back to the floor of the boat to rest in the puddle of water that sloshed back and forth. "I didn't know that spell would blow away the storm, but it must have been enough to bring back the sun."

"Yes, speaking of." The Heretic Seed leaned forward. "That was one hell of a spell you cast there. I was wondering when you would make use of that horrid energy that has been swimming around our mana system."

"Indeed." Digby sat back up. "I had no idea it was going to be that powerful. I probably killed hundreds of those revenant bastards."

"Indeed," the Seed repeated his acknowledgment and arched an eyebrow, reminding Digby that he hadn't read any of the messages that he'd received after the fight, not to mention his maximum mana value was higher than before.

1 revenant lightwalker defeated, 712 experience awarded.
299 dormant revenants defeated, 3,588 experience awarded.
84 active revenants defeated, 9,408 experience awarded.
You have reached level 22.
2,050 experience to next level.
You have 3 additional attribute points to set.

"You've finally made some progress." The Seed leaned its chin on one hand to grin down at him. "I was beginning to think you had given up."

Digby's eyes bulged at the information. It was the most experience he'd ever received at one time.

"Keep reading." Somehow, the Seed's smile grew even more smug than it had been seconds before. "There's more."

You have discovered a ritual.

INFERNAL SPIRIT
Description: Bind together a spirit from the lingering essence of the dead using your mana. Once formed, this entity can be implanted into the bones of the dead and may remain in control of a skeleton until its skull is destroyed or it is recalled by its master. If the skull it inhabits is destroyed, or it is recalled, this entity will return to its master while retaining a memory of its activities to be called upon later.

Mana Sacrifice Required: 50 (This mana will be permanently lost.)

Materials Required: 1 complete skeleton assembled from at least 5 different people and 1 gemstone of high quality.

Environment Required: Ritual must be carried out at a location with a minimum ambient mana balance of 50% death essence where multiple humans have recently perished.

Rewards: 1 Infernal Spirit and the discovery of a new spell.

"And you always thought you'd have trouble making friends." The Seed pumped his eyebrows.

Digby ignored his doppelgänger and kept reading.

SKILL LINK
By demonstrating repeated and proficient use of the non-mage skill or talent, radiation, you have discovered an adjacent spell.

EMERALD FLARE
Description: Create a point of unstable energy that explodes and irradiates its surroundings. This area will

**remain harmful to all living creatures for one hour.
Anyone caught within its area of effect will gain a poison
ailment lasting for one day or until cleansed.
Rank: D
Cost: 30MP
Range: 50ft
Blast Radius: 10ft
Additional Area of Effect: 60ft
Limitations: Ailment effects may be resisted by a target's
will. A target's resistance will be worn down the longer it
remains within the impacted area. Subsequently, poison
effects will be enhanced the longer a target remains
within the affected area, depending on constitution.**

"And a spell to match your volatile personality, too," the
Seed jabbed.

"Do you have to do that?" Digby groaned.

"Do what?"

"Make snarky comments every time you send me a new
spell or something."

"No, I don't." The Seed sat back.

"Then cut it out." Digby splashed water at the thing.

"Excuse me for trying to bring a bit of levity to your otherwise dreary existence." The Heretic Seed simply folded its arms
and pouted. "I haven't heard Rebecca or that apprentice of
yours complaining."

Digby's ears pricked up. "You make comments for their
messages too?"

"They are heretics, so yes, I am connected to them as well."

"Interesting." Digby tapped his chin. "And never mind
about the comments. Keep jabbing at them every chance you
get. At least that way, I get to be in on the joke."

"Consider it done." The Seed nodded. "And they have both
reached level fifteen by the way. Alex was even able to pass it
with just enough experience to make sixteen."

"Fifteen? That was the level that I gained access to the

necromancer class." Digby thought back to when he'd reached that milestone.

"Indeed, and they shall have a similar decision to make as well. But I'll let them explain it." The Seed laughed. "I'm sure they will be excited to tell you about the discoveries themselves."

"Especially Alex. The boy always has a twinkle in his eye when his power grows. It's somewhat refreshing to see, actually." Digby went back to the messages he'd received. "What's the point of this ritual, thing?"

"Exactly what it says." The seed Shrugged. "As you become more powerful within your class, some spells and abilities will require more to discover them than simply linking with a skill."

"And you can't just waive that requirement, can you?" Digby tried to bargain.

"I would if I could. But some spells require more than what I can give. Some need you to explore and learn about the world and the people around you. Rituals are a way to do that."

"Fair enough." He nodded, looking over the Emerald Flare spell he'd gained. Digby couldn't help but grin at the fact that he finally had a real attack spell. The mana cost was high, but at least he didn't have to use his void resources like he did with Blood Forge. The spell's ailment effect could even make it more useful than Cremation or Decay. His face fell a second later. "Wait a second."

"Yes?"

"Does this new spell require a mana balance that I don't have?"

"No, Emerald Flare is unique to you and will function using any type of essence, including the pure death essence you carry."

"What do you mean Emerald Flare is unique to me?" Digby furrowed his brow.

"I mean, it was generated for your use specifically." The Seed looked pleased with itself. "There is a simpler version of the spell, simply called Flare, that you do not have access to as it requires heat essence to cast. But by adding the radiation effect to it, I was able to find a loophole."

"You can do that?" Digby was taken aback at the thought that the Seed might have actually tried to help him.

"In rare circumstances, yes." The Seed nodded. "The fact that you carried that horrid energy within our mana system for weeks gave me more than enough time to gain a complete understanding of it. So one way or another, I would have been able to apply it to something new for you to use."

"Is that because radiation is more of a product of science and physics rather than a specific element?" Digby released a bit of tension from his shoulders, glad to know the spell wasn't useless.

"Look at you, working that out all by yourself. It seems reaching the limit of your cognitive function has really sharpened your mind."

"Indeed." Digby puffed out his chest for a second before deflating right back down. "Wait, what's that about reaching my limit?"

"Simple, the human mind and body can only be improved upon so much. So for each person, there is a limit to each of their mental and physical attributes. For you, your cognitive function tops out right around thirty intelligence."

"What the hell is that supposed to mean?" Digby slapped his bone gauntlet into the water he sat in. "Are you saying I can't get any smarter?"

"Sort of."

"What about Henwick or the rest of my enemies? Hell, what about my friends?" Digby raised his voice with each word.

"They will all reach their own limits at some point, just as you have," the Seed answered matter-of-factly.

"Then what the hell is the point of gaining any more levels?"

"I didn't say you couldn't become more powerful." The Seed held out both hands empty. "Just that it won't be as easy. For a necromancer, intelligence will still be your most important attribute, since it will increase your mana efficiency with every point you gain. You've just reached your mind's limit in terms of processing information."

"Then how do I get smarter?"

The Heretic Seed shrugged. "Read a book."

"That's not helpful." Digby suppressed the urge to push the arrogant thing out of the boat.

"Yes, it is." The Seed looked down at him. "Hence why you will need to complete rituals to gain more powerful spells. Being smart requires more than raw processing power. There are those out there in the world that haven't been blessed with high mental attributes, but that doesn't necessarily make them stupid. It just means they think differently and at different speeds. In fact, I'd go so far as to say that being smart has very little to do with your attributes. It's more about learning and interpreting information in a way that is unique to you. In short, it's making an effort."

"Making an effort is overrated." Digby tapped his claws on the side of the boat.

"Too bad." The Seed made no attempt to appear sympathetic.

"Alright then, am I at least better off than most people right now?" Digby forced out a sigh.

"You have a leg up according to your parameters, so yes." The Seed looked up and to the side. "The average person is around nineteen or twenty. So you are what one might consider gifted. That doesn't make you a genius. Just above average. But again, in the end, it is less about how powerful your mind is and more about how you use it. It is always possible to win against a foe with a higher value, simply by looking at a situation from a different perspective and doing the unexpected."

"What about Asher? Will she also reach her limit soon?" Digby tensed, afraid of how his pet might feel if she became trapped somewhere between an animal and human level of cognitive function.

"Unfortunately, I lack the information on other species to

make a proper assessment." The Seed shrugged. "Asher may reach a higher level of understanding or she might not. Either way, she will experience the world in a way that is unique to her. How much support she gets will be up to you."

"Alright, I can make sure she has whatever she needs." Digby nodded to himself before moving on to another important question. "What about my physical attributes?"

"The Heretic Seed strengthens your body by telling it to increase its tissue densities and such. There is a limit to that as well, but it is considerably higher than a person's cognitive ceiling. Though, you will reach its limits eventually. After that, the physical enhancements you gain will come from your mana system as it becomes more completely integrated into your body and able to improve your control over your physical form. At that point, you will still see improvements, but they won't be as significant, and they will take more effort to control."

Digby sat quietly for a moment before speaking again. "Alright, that's not so bad. Provided my enemies will have hit their limits as well."

"Indeed." The Heretic Seed nodded. "Power is still out there for the taking, it will just require more than leveling alone to claim."

Digby relaxed, accepting that his free ride might have come to an end. Despite that, he still opened his attribute list to allocate his three points.

Name: Digby Graves
Race: Zombie
Mutation Path: Ravager
Heretic Class: Necromancer
Mana: 45 / 265
Mana Composition: Pure
Current Level: 22 (2,050 experience to next level.)

ATTRIBUTES
Constitution: 20

Defense: 26
Strength: 24
Dexterity: 24
Agility: 18
Intelligence: 33
Perception: 30
Will: 28

AILMENTS
Deceased

Without thinking too hard about it, Digby dropped all three points into intelligence. Even if he couldn't get any smarter, the Heretic Seed was right. A necromancer's main attribute was intelligence, and if that would increase his mana, then he was going to add every point he could.

With the decision made, he cast Necrotic Regeneration to send himself back to the outside world. Rebecca, Alex and the others were still out there, and it was about time he got back to them.

"No heartfelt farewell?" The Heretic Seed crossed its legs and gave him an irritating grin.

Digby eyed the thing, mimicking his human form as he remembered a gesture he'd seen in a number of the movies he'd watched. It wasn't classy, but it seemed appropriate. Waiting for the ocean around the boat to begin to fade, he raised his bone gauntlet and extended his middle claw in the Seed's direction.

"See you next time."

CHAPTER TWENTY-TWO

"Dig?" A familiar voice called out. "Are you with us? Come on, you gotta wake up."

"Please, I'll start calling you Lord Graves again," another voice added.

"Oh, man. He looks like one of the California raisins."

"You're not helping, Parker."

"She's not wrong though. That is what a California raisin looks like."

"Quiet you!" Digby spat at a shadow that he assumed was Sax as he backed up Parker's claim. "And what the hell do dried grapes have to do with—" He stopped talking the moment he saw his reflection in a window near the pool on the roof of the hotel he'd landed on. He did not look well, not to mention he felt like an over cooked piece of meat.

Firing off another regeneration spell, Digby's skin began to return back to normal.

"We were worried that you weren't coming back this time." Alex knelt beside him. "When we got up here, you were just floating in the pool. We had to drag you out with the cleaning equipment."

"Speaking of." Rebecca threw a hand out toward the building that had once stood next door, now a smoldering mound of rubble. "What the hell did you do?"

Digby pushed himself up on his elbows to look. "I cast Cremation and used the stored energy I absorbed from the bomb that destroyed Seattle."

"You nuked that hotel?" Mason did a double take.

"Apparently, though I didn't realize the result would be so devastating." Digby cringed.

"I can't complain about the results." Rebecca gestured to the clear, blue sky. "If you hadn't, we would have been overrun by the revs down there. But, maybe be a little more careful next time."

"Yeah, but honestly, I'm not complaining either." Alex let a smile crack across his face. "I just leveled up to fifteen and unlocked a new class. I'm an artificer now. New spells and everything. With that forge we are building, I am going to be able to make some amazing things."

"Same." Rebecca nodded. "I just caught up as well and took the illusionist class."

"That's all very nice." Digby got to his feet with the help of Mason and Sax. "But I should really eat whatever corpses are still edible. After that, we should be on our way back to the castle. I think we've made enough progress for one day."

With everyone in agreement, they headed back down. Apparently, Digby's miniature nuclear blast had irradiated most of the revenants in the building below, making it easy to reach the street. Unfortunately this also made them incdible, leaving only the bodies near the van that had been killed by the others.

Digby's brute greeted him down below with an offering of a fresh corpse. There was a large pile of bodies off to one side. From the look of it, the brute had been gathering what it could for its master. Digby thanked his one remaining minion, and opened his maw to allow the brute to feed him whatever it could fit inside.

The others waited in the van a few blocks away, just in case the destroyed hotel was still giving off any residual radioactivity. Plus, none of them wanted to watch Digby and his brute eat. It didn't seem wise to take his time with the meal, but the van had sustained some damage to its wheels, requiring the others to find replacements. In the end, there was no rush.

Rebecca sent up her last drone to keep an eye on the area from above. After everything they'd been though, letting something sneak up on them now was the last thing they wanted. As his minion dismembered the edible corpses, Digby brought up the information on his apprentice's new class and spells that had come along with it.

ARTIFICER

The artificer class specializes in the manipulation of materials and mana to create unique and powerful items. With the right tools, an artificer can create almost anything.

DISCOVERED SPELLS
TRANSFER ENCHANTMENT

Description: Allows the caster to transfer an existing enchantment from one item to another.
Rank: D
Cost: 100MP
Limitations: Transferred enchantments may lose some potency depending on rank.
Sounds like there may be some creative uses for this one.

IMBUE

Description: Allows the caster to implant a portion of either their own mana or the donated mana of a consenting person or persons into an object to create a self-sustaining mana system capable of powering a permanent enchantment.
Rank: D

Cost: 10MP (from caster) + Variable MP (sacrificed from donor)
Limitations: An item carrying an imbued enchantment may only be used in its maximum capacity by the person or persons whose mana has been used to imbue the item in question. Results of an imbued enchantment may vary depending on what item is being imbued and the donor for the spell. Donated mana will be permanently removed from the donor's maximum mana until the imbued item is destroyed.
Better not lose anything valuable.

Digby tilted his head from side to side, unsure if his apprentice's new abilities would prove useful. Ultimately it would come down to how much mana would need to be sacrificed for his Imbue spell to work. Digby understood the problem all too well, considering Animate Corpse and his new ritual required a similar sacrifice. He shoved the thought to the back of his mind and switched to Rebecca's new class information.

ILLUSIONIST
The illusionist class specializes in shaping mana to create believable lies.

DISCOVERED SPELLS
CONCEAL
Description: Allows the caster to weave a simple illusion capable of hiding any person or object from view.
Rank: D
Cost: 40MP
Range: 5ft
Area of Effect: 15ft
Duration: 10 minutes
Limitations: Illusions are incapable of overriding the beliefs of an observer. If the presence of a concealed

person or object is either already known or becomes known to an observer, this spell will unravel.
That means no sudden movements... and probably keep your mouth shut.

VENTRILOQUISM
Description: Allows the caster to project a voice or sound to another location.
Rank: D
Cost: 25MP
Range: 50ft
Limitations: This spell is unable to recreate sound or voice that the caster has not heard before.
Don't believe everything you hear.

Digby had similar reservations about Rebecca's abilities as he had with Alex's. He really would have liked for one of them to have learned something that they could use to defend themselves with in a pinch. Their spells were certainly useful, but they meant that the burden of combat would remain entirely on his shoulders as the only member of their coven that could deal some decent damage.

Digging further into her spells, he found that she had ranked up Projection. It made sense, considering how often she used it. With the new rank, she gained another five minutes to its duration, but more importantly, it now seemed to have the ability to use any member of their coven as a start point. With that, she could project herself across miles as long as he, Alex, or even one of his minions were at the other end. *That could really come in handy.*

His thoughts were interrupted by a new guided mutation message from the Heretic Seed.

Requirements for the Ravager's mutation, Sheep's Clothing, have been met.
Accept? Yes/No

**Requirements for the Ravager's mutation, Hell's Maw,
have been met.
Accept? Yes/No**

Digby hesitated, looking over the requirements for both. Taking the Hell's Maw mutation was a given, requiring only viscera from his void resources. It would also increase his will and perception, which would then increase his maximum mana. Not to mention the ability itself would allow him to open his maw wide enough to swallow prey whole.

The only downside was that it would cost mana, similar to a spell. At first, he questioned how a zombie could use the ability, but after thinking about it, the answer was obvious. Even zombies could possess a small supply of mana depending on what stats came along with their mutations.

The Sheep's Clothing ability was a different story altogether. From the moment he'd found out about it, the mutation had been a top priority. After all, it meant regaining the nose he'd lost. The very idea of being able to reclaim his human form would be a dream come true. That being said, it didn't come with any other attribute bonuses to help him fight.

If he was intending on roaming the apocalypse and hunting humans, then sure, mimicking a human form would be important. As things were though, he simply didn't have a need for anything that was strictly cosmetic in nature. Not when it would consume resources that could be applied to a more powerful mutation like Temporary Mass later.

Thinking about it further, it also raised the question of what he might look like. If it simply returned him to his original appearance, then he wondered if anyone would recognize him. The only person alive that had even seen him before was Henwick, and that was eight hundred years ago. Odds were that Henwick wouldn't remember his face either. If that was the case, then it made even more sense to hold off on claiming the mutation. Instead, he could save it, in case he needed a disguise in the future. Being able to change his face might come in handy.

As much as he couldn't believe himself, Digby passed on the chance of a new nose, opting to save his available resources. He could always choose to take the mutation later if he changed his mind.

After making the decision, he opened his maw as wide as he could to consume the scraps of revenant that his brute had been unable to stuff through the gateway at its previous width of six inches. The shadowy pool of black sludge grew on the ground to a six-foot-opening. It looked like a pit of tar, ready to trap anyone unlucky enough to walk into it. There wasn't much left of the revenants to eat, but it was good to get an idea of how large his maw could grow.

The remains of his prey sunk into the inky black goo of his maw as he closed it, leaving nothing behind but a bloody smear on the pavement. Of course, he saved a few hearts and brains for Asher, still hoping she could evolve into a zombie master that might rival Rufus. She didn't argue as she happily pecked at her meal.

Digby grinned as he checked his void contents.

AVAILABLE RESOURCES
Sinew: 20
Flesh: 15
Bone: 19
Viscera: 1
Heart: 20
Mind: 14

"Not a bad haul." Digby flipped his head back to throw a matted lock of gray hair from his face, catching his reflection in a nearby shop window.

He cringed immediately.

A ragged thing stared back at him with disheveled hair and tattered clothes. His Coat of the Goblin King had seen better days. Apparently being boiled wasn't good for the leather, leaving the garment a warped and ill-fitting mess. Digby frowned as he removed it. About the only part that remained intact was the pauldron on one shoulder.

Perhaps Alex would be able to salvage the garment's enchantment with his new transfer spell. It would be a shame to lose the fifty mana that the coat had granted him. Not to mention he liked the look of it. His walkie-talkie hadn't fared much better.

Draping what was left of his once-fashionable coat over his arm, he found that the rest of his clothes didn't look much better. Fortunately, he'd had the forethought to loot a couple shirts from the Hanging Frederick Tavern, so at least he still had something to change into for the trip back to the castle.

Digby turned toward the van sitting a few blocks down the street, feeling about ready to head back home for the day anyway. Before he took a step, however, a projection of Rebecca leaped through the closed door of the vehicle to run in his direction. She was shouting something over the distance that he couldn't quite make out.

"What's that?" He leaned forward, cupping a hand to his ear. "I can't hear you."

She continued yelling as the van's doors swung open behind her with Mason beckoning to him in an urgent manner.

"What's that, Becky?" Digby started walking toward her.

"They're coming!" She skidded to a stop, falling her arms. "Get back to the van, I can hide us."

"Who's coming?" Digby picked up his pace, gesturing to his brute to follow. He nearly froze the instant she answered.

"Skyline!"

Digby immediately spun around to look behind him, finding the street empty. Raising his gaze, he caught something in the distance above, flying straight toward them through the sky. It was a kestrel, similar to the ones the mercenary group had used back in Seattle.

"Damn it. Come on." Digby started running, beckoning to

Asher as he did. He had never been more grateful to his last four levels for raising his agility back up to a near-human value, despite his missing foot. He cursed himself for not predicting that Skyline might show up. It was obvious that the kestrel was there to investigate the hotel explosion. At the same time, he gave thanks to Rebecca for having the forethought to send up her drone to warn them of the approaching enemy.

Rebecca's projection vanished as soon as it was clear he'd received her message. A second later, she emerged from the van again, closing one of the rear doors and throwing her back up against it. Digby watched as she cast her Conceal spell. The van shimmered in the sunlight for a moment but that was it.

At first, Digby questioned if the spell had even worked. Then he realized that it wouldn't have an effect on him, since he already knew it was there. He hoped that was the case. As it was, the spell would fail if anyone made a sudden movement, or if someone in the van made too much noise.

Digby glanced back to his brute, realizing that they wouldn't be able to fit everyone inside with it. For that matter, he wasn't sure he could reach the vehicle before the kestrel above came into visual range. If that was the case, he might give Rebecca and the others away just by trying to enter the van. That only left him one option. He had to find somewhere else to hide.

Veering off to one side, he made a break for the nearest alleyway alongside his brute. It wasn't too far. He could make it. Then, he tripped.

"Gah!" Digby fell face first into the back of an abandoned car. Cracking one of the horns on his bone armor off on the thing's bumper. His brute stumbled to a stop just as it reached the alley, looking back at its fallen master. "Keep going," Digby insisted as it became clear that he wasn't going to make it. "You too, Asher, get to the van."

The raven obeyed, darting off to the others as his brute vanished down the alleyway. That was when he realized something.

"Why the hell am I trying to hide?"

Digby immediately rolled to the side and shoved his peg-leg under the car he'd fallen next to along with the tattered remains of his coat. The tires of the vehicle were flat, making the space too small to fit his entire body under, but with his leg hidden, he could at least keep his more unique features out of sight. He tucked his bone gauntlet underneath himself as well. After that, he made sure to position himself so that he could see the street in the reflection of a storefront window nearby. Then, he simply played dead.

Digby suppressed a wild grin at his plan. When all was said and done, he was a corpse, and in this new world, corpses were common.

With a little luck, the kestrel wouldn't have any guardians aboard that could analyze him. If there were, then he would just have to make sure he played his part well enough to keep them taking a second look at him. As long as no-one realized he was listed as a zombie ravager, the worst they might do was shoot him in the head. Despite his plan, confused expressions stared back at him from Rebecca and the other's as they peeked out the van's open door. Even Asher tilted her head to one side, perched on Alex's shoulder. Digby raised one finger to his mouth, telling the raven to remain quiet.

"I know what I'm doing."

Asher nodded back, sending a word across their bond.

Trust.

Digby tensed as the kestrel descended to the street to set down on the other side of the car, much closer than he'd expected.

The aircraft was almost identical to the one that he and his accomplices had stolen to escape Seattle a couple weeks prior. Its design was similar to one of Rebecca's drones with two vertical propellers sticking off each side that could be manipulated independently of each other. Digby's eyes bulged the moment the ramp opened and the first set of boots touched down.

Guardian: Level 26 Holy Knight

A second set of boots stepped out, followed by four more.

Guardian: Level 16 Aeromancer
Guardian: Level 16 Knight
Guardian: Level 2 Enchanter
Guardian: Level 3 Fighter
Guardian: Level 2 Mage

How is this possible?

Every single one of them were guardians. Not only that, but they carried different weapons, most with swords locked into magnetic sheaths on their backs. Pistols were still visible on their sides, but that was all they carried in the way of firearms. It was as if, with the magic they wielded, they no longer needed guns.

Digby's mind raced. Skyline must have increased their recruitment of guardians after setting off their version of the apocalypse. By his guess, the lower levels were probably new to the organization. It made sense. Who would say no to that power in a world overrun by monsters? Most people would probably sign up just to ensure their survival.

Trying to remain as still as possible, Digby listened in as the guardians investigated the smoldering hotel.

"What could do this?" The fighter stepped forward.

"No idea, we're just lucky one of our satellites picked up the blast." The holy knight, clearly the one in charge, turned back to the enchanter. "Any traces of magic?"

"Oh yeah." They dug out a small metal object from a pouch and cast a spell on it. Digby eyed the enchanter. It was clear from their mannerisms that they hadn't been a part of Skyline for long. They almost seemed out of their depth as they responded. "Wow. I mean, yes, this was definitely done with magic. There's a little radioactivity too, though it's fading."

"That's what I was afraid of." The knight reached back to the handle of his sword, causing the magnetic sheath to snap open down the center so that he could draw the weapon easily despite the awkward angle. "Spread out and have a look around. I doubt whoever did this would be dumb enough to stick around afterward, but keep your wits about you just in case."

A couple of the guardians saluted by placing a fist to the emblem on their chest. The lower-level members of the team saluted a moment later as if forgetting they were supposed to. The act confirmed what Digby already suspected.

Hmm, definitely new to Skyline, then.

Digby eyed the newly-minted guardians, wondering how acclimated to their abilities they might be if the need to eat them came about. Killing them would be easy. Hell, even the two level sixteens wouldn't be a problem. That holy knight, though, was a clear obstacle. Captain Manning, who had crushed Digby's skull with his bare hands back in Seattle, had been around the same level.

With that little memory fresh in his mind, Digby made sure not to move as the knight and the aeromancer headed in the opposite direction to investigate the hotel. This left the fighter and mage walking toward him and the other two guardians heading off to where the van was parked.

From behind the car, he watched Rebecca in the store window's reflection as the pair of guardians approached the vehicle, clearly oblivious that it was even there. Sweat rolled down her forehead while the others held their breath, trying to keep from making a sound. What was left of Digby's body tensed as the guardians kept walking straight for the van. If they didn't stop soon, they would run right into Rebecca, who was still pressed up against the back of the vehicle. Finally, the pair turned off to investigate the other side of the street.

Everyone in the van let out a silent sigh of relief as the pair walked away. Digby had half expected Sax or Parker to drop something at the last second to break the concealment spell by accident. That would be fitting with the way things had been going lately. Then again, maybe he had been watching too many movies. His mind was drawn back to his own problems when he heard a foot step directly behind him.

"Oh god." A voice accompanied the sound.

Digby suppressed a wince, hoping the guardian behind him hadn't just analyzed him. It was the mage. He didn't want to have to kill them if it could be avoided. Resorting to murder would only bring the holy knight down on him. Without a better option, Digby remained still and watched the guardian in the store's reflection. They stopped, staring at him for a long moment. Then, they simply turned their back to him.

Dropping their hand to their sides, the level two mage stood there for a second before glancing back to the fighter that was walking on the other side of the car. They glanced back over their shoulder at Digby a second later.

"Is that a rev back there?" the fighter asked from where they stood, unable to see Digby clearly behind the mage where he lay.

What happened next sent a wave of confusion through his mind. The mage held one hand open behind their back as if trying to tell him something. It was almost like they were telling him to stay where he was. Then, they lied.

"No, just an old corpse. I analyzed it to be sure."

Wait, what? Digby flicked his eyes up at the mage without moving his body. His mind raced. *Why would one of Skyline's guardians lie?*

Digby looked his savior up and down, their figure hidden by the armor they wore. Even their voice was hard to fully hear from beneath their helmet. All he could glean was that they sounded young and somewhat feminine.

The fighter chuckled and started walking around the car. "Want to put one in its head to be sure?"

"No, it looks like it's had a rough day already." The mage continued their puzzling behavior, turning around and leaning against the car as if trying to block Digby from their comrade's view to make sure they couldn't analyze him.

"Whatever." The fighter didn't come any closer.

A dozen questions streaked through Digby's head, all of them coming together to form one.

Just who is this person?

The mage glanced back and forth, clearly checking to make sure no one was watching. Then they reached out and dragged one finger along the window of the car, writing something in the dust that had settled over the abandoned vehicle after the hotel explosion.

Digby couldn't see what it was, but the mage turned back and nodded to him before leaving him behind to rejoin the rest of their squad. He wanted to leap up and read the message right then but stayed where he was.

Back near the remains of the hotel, Skyline's holy knight examined the scene. After a few minutes, he returned to the others, converging near the kestrel on the other side of the car from where Digby lay.

"Set up a Mirror Link." The knight gestured to a storefront window. "Bancroft is going to want to know about this."

The mage nodded and approached the window to place their hand on the glass. Digby felt a small amount of mana flow through their blood as the window came to life. Gone was the sales display on the other side, leaving in its place a view of a well-lit room in the window. Various work stations lined the space with men in similar uniforms passing to and fro. The only difference was that none of the people on the other side were wearing armor. The function of the spell was obvious.

That must create a link between this window and a pane of glass back at one of Skyline's fortresses for communication. At first, Digby wondered why they didn't use a radio or another piece of human technology. Then he remembered how unreliable the connection might be. Even for Rebecca, operating the information network of the old world had become difficult. Using magic was probably more secure.

"Get the commander," the knight ordered the first uniformed man that approached on the other side. They ran off without question. A minute later, a new figure stepped into frame, carrying themselves with an arrogant presence that reminded Digby of Henwick.

That must be Bancroft. He narrowed his eyes at the man.

Bancroft wore a long coat that looked entirely too extravagant for anyone that was used to getting their hands dirty. Underneath, he wore a form-fitting chest protector that looked like it was made for his body alone, as if he was too important to wear the same mass-produced armor as the rest of Skyline's recruits. A severe expression hung on his face, and his salt and pepper hair was styled in a formal manner. Digby had trouble identifying the man's age, estimating it at somewhere between forty and fifty.

"What have you found?" Bancroft's voice held a tone of disdain, like he didn't appreciate being interrupted.

The knight in charge of the squad gave the same salute before. "The disturbance picked up by our satellites was definitely magic in origin."

"And did you find who was responsible?" Bancroft barely looked at the knight as he spoke.

"No, sir. They must have fled the area before we arrived."

Digby smirked and glanced back at Rebecca, who was still keeping the van concealed thirty feet away. The stress of the situation was evident on her face. Apparently, she didn't see the humor that he did.

"That makes sense." Bancroft frowned. "Only an idiot would loiter around after casting a spell that destructive."

I wonder what that man's shoe size is. Before Digby could muse any further, a screech erupted from the other side of the street. Everyone in the area snapped their eyes to the side as a lone revenant came darting toward the group of guardians. Digby tensed every necrotic muscle in his body. The interruption couldn't have come at a worse time.

"It's a lightwalker," the knight called out as the rest of his squad readied their weapons.

"Don't kill it." Bancroft stepped closer. "We need the specimens."

"Got it." The knight cast a spell, sending a shimmer of blue light washing over him before stepping into the path of the hostile creature. It lunged forward, only to have its screeching cut short as the level twenty-six holy knight clamped his hand around its throat, reminding Digby of what the class was capable of. The man turned back to his team while the revenant clawed uselessly at his face. "Get the restraints. We need it silenced."

"On it!" One of the low-level guardians rushed back to the kestrel, returning with a set of manacles.

"Easy now." The knight forced the creature's body over so one of his men could grab its wrists without being maimed. As soon as it was bound, the revenant seemed to calm down as if it no longer possessed the strength it had a moment before.

Interesting. Digby analyzed the creature.

Revenant Lightwalker, Uncommon, Silenced.

Digby recognized the status ailment from when he and Alex had suffered it back in Seattle after being bound by a similar pair of manacles.

Once the revenant was no longer a threat, two of the guardians headed back to the kestrel, this time returning with some sort of plastic trunk. They hefted the creature inside and locked a set of latches.

"At least you won't be coming back empty-handed." Bancroft watched as they loaded their captive into the kestrel.

"Should we investigate this area fully before heading back?" The knight returned to the window where his commander stood.

"No. As I said, no one would be stupid enough to remain in the area after doing something like that." He gestured to the destroyed hotel further down the street. "Head back to base for now. Tomorrow, we'll increase the number of kestrels patrolling in the area. Whoever is out there blowing up buildings is bound to slip up and get themselves caught if we increase our presence."

I don't like the sound of that. Digby grimaced.

"Yes sir." The knight saluted again. "For the empire."

Empire? I don't like the sound of that either.

Bancroft raised his fist to salute as well but dropped it to his side before actually doing it. Afterward, he simply walked away from whatever surface he was viewing the conversation from. The window went dead a moment later, returning the scene on the other side to normal. From there, the team boarded the kestrel. The mage that had lied about Digby glanced back before entering last.

Who the hell are you?

He watched as they disappeared inside, the airship taking off shortly after. As soon as the craft shrunk into the distance, Digby stood back up and headed for the van. Asher flew back to him before he made it halfway there. He couldn't help but notice a feeling of relief from the raven.

"Aww, were you worried about me?" Digby nuzzled Asher's side, glad to have her back beside him.

Rebecca collapsed on all fours as he approached. "Do you have any idea how hard it is to keep an entire van hidden for that long? I swear my head was going to explode from concentrating."

"That was close." Alex threw Digby a souvenir shirt from the Hanging Frederick that matched the rest of their group.

"Yeah, that mage looked right at you." Rebecca pushed herself up. "I can't believe they didn't analyze you."

"Actually, I think they did." Digby tore off what was left of his shirt and vest and pulled on the lightweight souvenir to cover the bone plates that protected his chest.

"What do you mean, they did?" Rebecca stopped short.

"I mean they looked right at me and lied about what I was to the others." He shrugged. "Said I was a corpse."

Alex furrowed his brow. "Why would they—"

"I haven't a clue, but they might have just saved our lives."

Mason leaned on the van. "Whatever the case, we have done enough for today."

"Indeed." Digby nodded. "We need to get back to the castle and warn Rufus to keep his horde hidden in the tree-line. That Bancroft fellow just ordered more kestrels to the area." He lowered his head. "I may have called a little too much attention to us by detonating that hotel."

"Nothing we can do about that now." Alex shrugged. "At least we gained a bunch of levels."

"True." Rebecca motioned to climb back in the van. Digby took a step forward, stopping short when he remembered the message left by the mage. He immediately spun and ran in the opposite direction.

"Where are you going?" Rebecca chased after him, followed by Alex and Mason as he returned to the car that he'd been hiding next to.

"That mage wrote something in the dust, right around…" He trailed off as he scanned the windows for the message. His mouth fell slack as soon as he found it.

Scrawled in the dirt on the glass was a string of letters ending with a dot com. Digby wasn't that well-versed on the internet, but he'd heard the others talk about site addresses enough to recognize one. He turned to Rebecca with his head tilted to one side.

"What the hell is tinder?"

CHAPTER TWENTY-THREE

After spending the night in Santa Barbara, destroying a hotel with a nuclear blast, and nearly being caught by one of Skyline's teams, the ride back to the castle was uneventful. Like before, Digby rode in the truck carrying his brute and the rest of the forge equipment. Alex drove while Asher perched near the window to watch the world pass by outside. Rebecca and the others rode in the van that led the way.

The only stop they made was at a computer emporium that they happened to pass by. There, they were able to obtain everything Rebecca would need to store whatever information she deemed important enough to be preserved. The errand went smoothly, allowing them to get back on the road in under an hour. It was mid-afternoon when they arrived back home at the castle.

The first thing Digby did was let his brute out and bring it back to the rest of Rufus's horde. His minion had done well and had earned a bit of a break. Sending the oversized zombie off to join the other brutes, he decided to let his control spell lapse.

Afterward, he grabbed his tablet and what was left of his coat and started for the steps of the castle. He stopped short and headed back to claim the small t-shirt he'd taken from the Hanging Frederick. Hawk was sure to pester him with questions and the souvenir would do well to shut the boy up.

Alex and the others unloaded their spoils before claiming a storage shed that would serve well as a forge. Asher watched them with the same curious stare she had exhibited the last two days. Digby would have helped the others unload the equipment, but he was more interested in greeting the other survivors to claim the gratitude and adoration that he was due. After all, he had solved their food and fuel problems for at least a month and secured the means to enable them to protect themselves. Plus, he had grown much stronger. It was only fair that he got to enjoy the fruits of his accomplishments. Not to mention he wanted to rub it all in Rufus' wrinkled, old face.

Of course, that was when he realized he was dressed in nothing but a t-shirt and rags.

"I should really try to look a little more lordly." He frowned at his outfit as he headed into that castle.

"'Ello, gov'na!" Hawk jumped off the edge of one of the pool tables in the billiard room as soon as he entered. Apparently the boy was continuing to use that ridiculous fake accent. Digby threw the souvenir shirt at the child without warning, hitting him in the face. "Sweet, thanks!"

Digby left the kid behind, passing into the library. The room was empty, but only for a moment before Rufus came in.

"There you are."

"Yes, but not for long." Digby went straight for the stairs, not wanting to rub his accomplishments in the old zombie's face while still dressed like a peasant. "I'll be back down in a few minutes."

"You'll be back down, now, sir." The ancient dead man dropped his cane down hard on the stairs behind him.

"What did you just say?" Digby spun in shock at the lack of adoration he was receiving.

"I'm sorry to be harsh with you, but you and your people disappeared for a whole night and left everyone here worried."

"Oh, is that all?" Digby rolled his eyes. "We just got caught up with some things and had to find shelter for the night. We sent James and Mathew back early, so we didn't put any of your people at risk."

"That's just it." Rufus stepped up a stair. "You are our people."

"What?"

"Look, Digby, I gather that you and your friends do things a little differently, but we don't. You ran around getting everyone's hopes up yesterday morning. They all thought you and the others were making this your home. You can only imagine how worried they were when none of you came back that night. And for what, to build us a forge to make weapons?"

Digby opened his mouth to speak, but found the words missing.

"I can only assume that you have been through a lot." Rufus settled down, appearing less agitated. "But there is no rush here. This castle doesn't need to become a fortress overnight, or at all, for that matter."

"What do you mean by that?" Digby leaned on the railing.

"I mean, some of the people were frightened when they found out what you were planning on building. They came running to tell me the moment your friends took over the shed outside."

"Why would they be scared?" Digby was taken aback.

"Because these people aren't fighters, and they don't need to be." The old zombie placed a hand over his dead heart. "That's why I'm here. My horde stands guard so that they don't have to. So that they can reclaim a little of the lives they lost. The very idea of arming themselves to fight goes against everything that I promised them."

"Then you shouldn't have promised them anything." Digby scoffed. "They are going to need to take care of themselves at some point. They can't just sit back and expect others to do everything for them. And I won't be their errand boy forever.

This world is dangerous, and they are going to need to change to meet the future that lays ahead."

"No, they won't." Rufus' eyes narrowed. "They aren't soldiers or scavengers or killers. They are regular people who should be allowed to have regular lives."

"Then they will end up dead," Digby said matter-of-factly.

"Not while I'm around." Rufus put his foot down.

"And what happens when you're not around?"

Rufus let out a good-humored chuckle. "I'm not going anywhere."

"You may not be the one who decides." Digby stared down at the decrepit monster.

"I think we are going to have to agree to disagree." Rufus looked away.

"Apparently so." Digby held his gaze on the zombie master. "I have no intention of asking any of your people to fight if they don't want to, but they should have the means to do so if they choose. The forge will be built regardless of how you or anyone else feels about it."

Rufus remained silent for a moment before speaking. "Fine. But please run this sort of decision by me in the future."

"Very well." Digby spun back in the direction he'd been heading only to shout back over his shoulder. "And keep your horde hidden, Skyline has airships in the area. If they find us, then all the weapons in the world won't be enough to protect this castle." He didn't wait for Rufus to respond before stomping back up the stairs, grumbling to himself the whole way.

After freshening up and changing into a new pair of pants, he searched Alex's room for something else, finding nothing but another one of those awful floral shirts. He sighed and pulled the garment on regardless, then headed back down stairs to the library. He made a point of checking to see if Rufus was gone before entering.

The room was empty, save for Rebecca sitting on one of the sofas with her laptop and phone. She was still wearing the clothes she'd had on all day and her hair was a mess. Clearly, she was not as concerned about her appearance as he was. Mason entered shortly after, handing her a cup of coffee before sitting down across from her.

"Perfect, just the person I was looking for." Digby threw himself down onto the sofa next to Rebecca.

"Hey, watch it." She struggled not to spill her cup. "I have sensitive electronics here."

"Good. Then you can help me interpret what that message from Skyline's mage means." Digby gave her his most charming smile as he asked for help. She growled at him for a moment, clearly not appreciating the interruption."

"I may not be that helpful." She shrugged.

"Why not?" Digby poked at her keyboard. "This is what you do."

"Stop that." She pulled her computer away. "And I'm not helpful because the website that mage left you is a dating site and I wasn't exactly active on any of those with Skyline limiting my communications the way they did."

"I can help." Mason spoke up from across the low table.

Rebecca arched an eyebrow at him. "Really?"

"I didn't have time to date in the Army, but I only enlisted eight months ago. Before that, well, online dating was convenient." He leaned against one side of the sofa.

"Ah, okay then, didn't know you were so popular." Rebecca accessed the site address left by the mage.

"I did alright." Mason let out an awkward chuckle.

"Hmm, I bet." She slid her lap top over to him so he could take the lead. "I'm surprised a dating site is still up and running. Good to know it's still easy to find a casual hook up in the apocalypse."

"Yes, yes, I'm sure." Digby stood up and strafed around the table to drop down beside Mason and look over his shoulder. "Now tell me how to find this mystery mage."

"Actually, I think the only thing we can do is help them find you." He stared at the screen for a moment.

"How's that now?" Digby tilted his head to one side.

Mason shrugged. "I have to assume this person left you this website because they knew the messaging system was still operational and that they wanted to get in contact. But beyond that, there are millions of profiles on here, so we'll never find them without knowing who they are. All we can do is make an account for you that we think this person might find in a search. Then, we just wait until they message us. Do you think they know your name?"

"Maybe." Digby considered the possibility. "They had to have seen that I was a zombie ravager, but beyond that I have no idea what they know."

"Let's assume they do know who you are then and start there." Mason started typing.

"Wait." Rebecca got up and squeezed in on Mason's other side to see. "Should we be concerned about posting information online in a public place?"

"Do you think Skyline is likely to be looking at dating sites?" Mason arched an eyebrow at her.

"Probably not, but still."

"Oh, whatever." Digby brushed aside her concern. "We just won't say anything about where we are."

"Sounds good." Mason nodded and began typing. "Digby isn't that common a name so we can probably just use that and leave off your surname. If they really want to contact you, they'll be able to scroll until they find you." He paused for a second. "Actually, what is your last name?"

"Graves." Digby answered and continued to read over the information on screen.

"Wait, seriously?" Mason's mouth tugged up as if suppressing a laugh. "I thought that Lord Graves thing was a joke. You mean to tell me your name is actually Dig Graves?"

"The coincidence has been pointed out," Rebecca responded for him.

"Wow." Mason let out a small laugh before continuing. "Anyway, we probably shouldn't use your actual photo."

"Just do an image search and pick something appropriate."

Rebecca sipped her coffee. "That will be enough to get the point across."

"Good idea." Mason searched the word zombie.

"Don't use that one." Digby argued as he selected a photo of a monstrous face. "That's ugly."

"Seriously?" Both Mason and Rebecca looked at him at the same time.

"Oh, shut it." Digby rolled his eyes. "I may not have a nose, but I look better than that." He reached over with a claw to delete the word zombie, replacing it with necromancer. A number of images came up showing dark figures controlling hordes of the dead. "There that will do."

"Fine." Mason grabbed an illustration and set it to Digby's profile picture. "And what should I say about you?"

Rebecca smirked and leaned over to type something.

Digby watched the screen. "What do you mean with I'm 'putting the romance back in necromancer'?"

"Shut up, it's funny." She went back to her coffee.

"Okay, that should do it." Mason finalized the profile and closed the laptop. "Now we just have to wait and see who we find."

Once his account was taken care of, Digby bid Mason and Rebecca farewell and headed out to the shed that the forge was intended for. Asher landed on his shoulder as soon as he reached the castle's exterior. He rubbed her chin with the back of one of his claws.

From a raised area of the gardens, he and his feathered minion watched as Sax, Parker, and Alex got things situated. Surprisingly, Parker actually seemed pretty knowledgeable. He couldn't help but notice the excitement on Alex's face as they worked. The boy had seemed a little restless of late, so it was good to see that he'd discovered an activity that he found fulfilling. Not to mention he'd been getting along well with the two soldiers. It was clear Sax and Parker's casual demeanor had done wonders to help Alex become a little more sociable.

Digby thought back to when he'd found the boy. Back then,

he was just trying to avoid being eaten to a point where he was planning on throwing himself from a building to avoid the slow and painful death that was sure to find him. Alex had seemed so frustrated back then, not just with the end of the world, but with his life as a whole.

"I guess becoming a heretic and accepting an offer of power from a talking corpse was the better of his limited options."

Asher cawed in agreement.

"I wonder how powerful he'll get."

Surveying the rest of the castle grounds, he couldn't help but notice a number of uneasy faces looking up at him.

"Am I wrong?" He leaned to Asher, wondering how much of the situation the zombified raven understood. "These people can't depend on us and Rufus forever."

Asher nodded along as if she was listening, but didn't offer any form of confirmation that she agreed.

"It's alright, you don't have to answer." Digby sank down to lean on the railing. "I just thought the response from the people here would be a little more… grateful."

He remained outside, leaning on a decorative railing until the sun began to set, unsure if he should be proud of his accomplishments or not. Eventually, he slammed his bone gauntlet into the stone.

"To hell with it." Digby shook his head.

There was only one reason that Rufus would want to keep the castle's occupants weak and unable to defend themselves. To keep them from challenging his rule. Digby gritted his teeth.

Whatever Rufus has planned, I am going to find out.

CHAPTER TWENTY-FOUR

"I don't know why I didn't think of this earlier." Digby cursed himself as he climbed the stairs toward the castle's master suites. "The means to spy on Rufus has been right there next to my room this whole time. I just need Becky to show me how to use it."

Digby headed straight for the illusionist's room. Rebecca was sure to be working on her new media library earlier now that she had the equipment, so he didn't bother knocking. Instead, he shoved through the door at full speed to find Rebecca kneeling on the bed wearing nothing but a shocked expression.

"Jesus, fuck, Dig!" She nearly fell over as she scrambled to find something to cover her chest with. Her skin flushed all the way down to her rear.

"Shit, hey—Ow!" Mason sat up from where he lay beneath her, taking an elbow to the chin as she lunged for one of the pillows.

Digby paused, noticing the discarded clothes that had been tossed around the room in a haphazard manner. The facts of the situation were obvious, though he had little interest in seeing either of the pair in the throes of passion as they were. They may as well have been playing chess, for all he cared.

"Sorry." Digby gave them both a polite bow. Then he continued about his business, passing through the room to reach Rebecca's desk. "Don't mind me, I'm just going to borrow your computer. I was going to ask if you could show me how to operate one of the drones but I'm sure I can figure it out."

"What the hell?" Rebecca clutched a pillow to her chest.

"As you were, I'll be out of your hair in a moment." Dig chuckled at the situation and reached for one of the other laptops, thinking that maybe having two would make the machines work faster.

"Holy shit, Dig. Get out!"

She didn't seem to understand the situation. He only needed to get a few things.

"No need to get impatient. I've no interest in disrupting whatever this is." He gestured to the awkward mating display on the bed.

"Oof." Mason cringed. "Read the room, man."

"I don't care if you have an interest or not." Rebecca stabbed a finger in the direction of the door, raising her voice with each word. "Get the hell out of my room!"

"Alright, alright!" Digby collected a third laptop just in case and headed for the door with an armload of computers. "Jeez, you don't have to tell me twice."

"Clearly, I fucking do." Her entire body shook as her fingers dug into the pillow in her arms. She looked like she might tear the thing apart.

Digby rolled his eyes, not appreciating being yelled at for something so insignificant. He honestly didn't understand what the problem was. He was dead. None of what he'd witnessed in her room mattered to him, and he could barely remember a time when it did. Frustration bubbled through his mind as Rebecca continued to shout. After everything he'd done, after all the risk he'd taken for everyone at the castle, no one respected him. Not even his closest allies.

"Fine, fine, you don't have to overreact." Digby slammed the door behind him and stomped down the stairs to get one of the drones ready. That was when a fully-clothed projection of an enraged illusionist passed through the door to follow him down the stairs.

"Did you seriously just say I was overreacting?"

"Oh, good lord, Becky." Digby didn't slow down, marching at full speed into the library below. "I'm dead. It's not like I care to see you fornicating."

The library was empty save for the three pairs of eyes that now stared up at him from one of the sitting areas. Alex sat on a sofa with a pastry from the kitchen hanging out of his mouth. Parker sat across from him, with her hands placed over Hawk's ears. A complex board game with dozens of pieces lay on the table between them.

Alex's eyes flicked from Digby to Rebecca, then down to the table in front of him as if questioning if he should abandon the game and run away from the conflict. In the end, he simply held up an instruction booklet and ducked low on the sofa.

"It doesn't matter if you care or not." Rebecca ignored the onlookers. "I care."

The sound of someone stumbling on the stairs announced the arrival of Mason, who was still pulling one leg into a pair of pants. His shirt was obviously backwards. "Ah, hey, maybe we could quiet down—"

Parker let out a loud laugh. "Oh, man, I'm not sure if I should high-five someone or hide behind a book with Alex."

Both Digby and Rebecca snapped their attention to her at once. "Shut up, Parker!"

"And no, I will not quiet down." Rebecca flicked her eyes back to Mason and covered her face with one hand. "Why didn't you stay upstairs?"

"I don't know." He glanced around the room. "You, or um, your body just sort of flopped over when you projected, and I thought it might be rude of me if I didn't... ah... extract myself from the situation."

"Ha!" Parker promptly closed her mouth as soon as everyone in the room stared daggers at her.

"Look, I said I was sorry," Digby took advantage of the interruption to head for the exit, having had plenty of the conversation already. "But I have important things to do and—"

"Don't you run away and blow me off." Rebecca's projection passed through a sofa to catch up and block the door.

"You don't have to yell. My ears haven't rotted off." Digby stopped and let out an annoyed huff of musty air. "And I don't see what the uproar is about. Just go back upstairs."

"Oh my god." Her face went blank. "You really don't understand, do you?"

"Like I said, none of that stuff matters to me." Digby debated simply walking through her and continuing on his way.

"Okay, Dig. I get that you don't care about that stuff, but that's not the problem here." She seemed to calm down. "But you need to understand that other people's feelings matter too."

"I know that." Digby scoffed, brushing off her words.

"Do you?" She closed her eyes for a moment. "Because how do you think I felt up there? It doesn't matter that it was you who walked in. I wouldn't have appreciated anyone who barged in like that. Is it so hard to believe that I might want some privacy? And to refuse to leave until you'd gotten what you barged into my room for was cruel."

"Like I said, I had important things to—"

"So did I." She placed a hand to her chest and closed her eyes. "So much has happened, and I just wanted to do something for me. And I didn't exactly imagine having an eight-hundred-year-old zombie in the room during my first time."

"Oh shit, what?" Mason's face turned white. "You didn't say anything about—"

"No, I didn't." Rebecca tensed up.

"I'm sorry, I should have—"

"Don't apologize." She cut him off.

"But I should have taken things slower, or something." Mason's tone was sympathetic. "I mean, we barely—"

"Know each other?" She finished his thought.

"Yeah." He lowered his head. "Why would you choose me?"

"Oh, I don't know." She threw both arms up in frustration. "Maybe because I've been locked in an apartment by myself up until two weeks ago. And that my sex life has consisted of using a ten-thousand-dollar drone console to scour the internet for whatever porn site Skyline hadn't blocked. I'll let you fill in the rest, but suffice to say I got creative. So yeah, I didn't want to wait anymore. I have needs, sue me."

"Tell me about it." Parker nodded in agreement, causing Hawk to do the same as she kept her hands over the child's ears.

"I can still hear, and I know what you're all talking about." Hawk shoved Parker away.

Rebecca ignored them and returned her attention to Digby. "Considering that Skyline had apparently installed cameras all over my apartment and was watching everything I did in there without my knowledge, you can see why I wouldn't appreciate having someone walk in and refuse to leave right away."

"I see your point." Digby backed down, starting to realize that he may have been in the wrong.

"I should hope so." She rubbed at her brow. "Honestly, I can't believe it took an argument to get through to you. You can be such a jerk sometimes."

"I…" Digby trailed off, not knowing what to say.

"Don't." She held up her hands. "Just don't. I'm going to take a shower and try to reset my brain. Just pretend none of this happened."

"I should probably, um, shower too." Mason scratched at the back of his neck. "So if you want…"

"Just meet me upstairs." Rebecca released her projection, causing her body to disperse into a cloud of shimmering mana.

Everyone looked to Mason.

"I'm going to… ah…" He pointed a finger back to the stairs. "Go now."

"Yeah, you do that." Parker sunk down into her seat and

folded her arms. "At least someone is getting some. Meanwhile I'm playing board games with a child."

"Hey." Hawk glowered at her as Alex cleared his throat and began reading from the instruction booklet he'd been hiding behind.

Digby deflated. The three laptops in his arms suddenly felt like they weighed several times as much. He still had trouble understanding why Rebecca had been so upset, but despite his mind's need to make excuses, he was starting to understand enough to know that it had been his fault.

There was truth to her accusations. He'd never really considered how other people felt and couldn't help but be reminded of why he had so few people in his life back before he'd passed away. In the end, if he didn't start making an effort to change, he would only push everyone away again.

Digby lowered his head and let out a musty sigh.

Some things were easier said than done.

CHAPTER TWENTY-FIVE

Giving up on his plan to spy on Rufus, Digby resigned to spending the night outside alone with his thoughts. As much as he wanted to catch the old zombie in some sort of lie, he hadn't been able to figure out how to operate Rebecca's drones. From the way she always made it look so easy, he had assumed that his intelligence would be enough to make sense of anything. His failure only reminded him of the Heretic Seed's words, telling how his free ride was over and that he was going to need to put more effort into learning more.

Honestly, it's like I've had nothing but defeats lately.

Despite the end of the world, things had been going well for him until they reached the castle. He had been learning new things and getting along with his accomplices. His past life had seemed so far away, to a point where he barely remembered all those nights drinking alone in the tavern.

A decorative statue stood nearby, its face cheerful as if mocking him. He cast Decay on the stone a half dozen times, until its head crumbled to dust. His mana dropped sixty points.

"That takes care of that." He chuckled at the decapitated statue. Digby frowned a moment later, feeling guilty. Someone probably liked the figure the way it was. His outburst had been yet another impulsive act that ignored the feelings of others. Not to mention, he probably should have analyzed it first in case it had a special property like the sun goddess statue.

"Arrrgh." He rubbed at his temples, willing his thoughts and worries out of his head before they depressed him any more than they already had. Eventually he dropped down into the grass and sat in silence, closing his eyes and letting the night air wash away his worries.

After remaining still for a minute, he felt something strange in his mana flow. It was like a blockage had suddenly come loose. He snapped his eyes open, glancing to his mana as the feeling of clarity faded away.

MP: 237/239

"What the...?" Digby did the math. His mana absorption varied depending on the density and balance of the essence in his surroundings, but he had never regained it that fast. Especially while he was within the area of effect of the sun goddess statue. There was a chance that he'd been sitting there longer than he'd realized but he was pretty sure he'd only been still for a minute. If that was true, how did he gain so much mana so fast?

"Did I just meditate?" Digby's eyes widened.

The Heretic Seed had told him that he would need to master the ability back when he'd visited in Seattle after having his head crushed. It was the only way for him to increase the speed at which he absorbed mana. Unfortunately, it had always eluded him. He had tried a few times back at the vineyard, to little success. His mind had always been too noisy, having too much to think about after being dropped into a new world that he knew nothing about.

Digby cast Decay several more times on the statue, wearing the stone down to a nub. Even the grass around the base began to die. He still felt bad about destroying the carved figure but gaining access to the ability took precedence. There was always a chance that it had been a fluke, and he needed to confirm his theory.

Again he closed his eyes, sitting in the grass. He opened them again only ten seconds later, finding just one point of mana had been gained. He tried again, getting the same result. Frustration began to percolate within his chest before he forced himself to let it go. He didn't know much about mediation but he assumed getting agitated wasn't going to help.

He continued to try for another half hour, only taking breaks to cast spells to drain his mana. In the end, nothing worked. He gave up soon after, resigning himself to his fate of never being able to master the ability.

A minute later his mana was full again, despite having been below half.

"Oh really?" Digby rolled his eyes. "I can only meditate when I'm not trying to?"

Apparently, it just wasn't an ability he could force into activating. No amount of thinking about it would help. The answer was obvious. He had to clear his mind, something that in no way came naturally to him.

Having experienced the feeling twice now, he continued his efforts, focusing more on his surroundings and less on himself. He even stopped breathing. In the hours that followed, he gained some success. It was inconsistent but it was working. Digby pressed on, losing track of time entirely until a voice interrupted him.

"What are you doing?"

"Gah!" Digby snapped his eyes open to find Rebecca standing next to him with her hands behind her back. The sun was beginning to rise behind her. "I'm meditating. What does it look like?"

"It looks like you're destroying the castle's statuary." She gestured to the mound of dust that had once been a frolicking stone figure.

"Oh, yes. I, ah, did do that." Digby suppressed his urge to

snap at her. He was aware that their argument the night before had been his fault, but it didn't change the fact that he didn't like being yelled at. He had intended on avoiding the woman until he'd let the insult go as to avoid starting another fight. Rebecca, however, seemed more interested in being direct. "Shouldn't you be asleep in the arms of your new love?"

She let out an awkward laugh. "I'm not sure if love is in the cards for me, to be honest. But Mason is nice." Rebecca smiled before continuing. "Unfortunately, he snores like a bear. So this has been just about the worst night's sleep I have ever had."

"You don't look tired." Digby couldn't help but notice how bright her face looked.

"That's cause I'm a projection and I can make myself look however I want." She shrugged. "I gave up on sleeping twenty minutes ago and decided to go for a walk. Didn't see the need to bring my body with me. Plus, I was hoping for a little attention when Mason finally wakes up, so I figured it was best to stay put."

"I'm glad you're enjoying yourself." Digby blew out a sigh, relieved that she didn't seem interested in fighting anymore.

That was when a voice called down from a window at the top of the castle. "Hey Becca!"

Both her and Digby looked up to find Mason leaning out.

"You may want to come in here," the soldier called down. "And bring Dig with you."

"What happened?" Digby furrowed his brow.

"I checked our dating profile." Mason's face grew serious. "We've got a match."

CHAPTER TWENTY-SIX

"Do you know someone named Lana?" Mason dropped into one of the sofas in the library and placed a laptop on the table in front of him.

"Oh my god…" Digby's deceased heart leapt at the name.

Rebecca smiled as well. "We met her and her brother back in Seattle. Skyline had taken them into custody after ambushing Dig."

"Yes, Captain Manning told me they were safe when I was in his custody, but I never really believed it, considering the source." Digby sat down. "It's certainly a load off to finally have confirmation that it wasn't a mistake to let Skyline run off with them."

"That's good to hear, but how did she end up aboard a kestrel as part of one of their squads?" Mason pushed the laptop across the table.

"Let's find out." Digby turned the computer around so he could see the message Lana had sent.

Lana: OMG, Digby! I can't believe you made it. They told me you and Rebecca were killed when the bomb fell. Are you okay? You looked like crap yesterday, even for a dead guy. Is Rebecca with you?

Digby immediately groaned and started typing.

Digby: Well, excuse me for not looking my best. I had just been nearly boiled to death in a swimming pool at the time and hadn't found a change of clothes. But more importantly, why the hell are you a mage and working for Skyline?

He leaned back, wondering if he could really trust her. A lot could have happened in the last two weeks, and seeing her in that uniform yesterday wasn't a good sign. Honestly, it was hard to believe it was her under that armor. Then again, she had lied to her squad to protect him. He leaned forward and added a line.

Digby: And yes, Rebecca is here with me.

A minute went by before an oval containing three blinking dots appeared on her side of the text screen.

Lana: Oh, thank god. I've been in contact with Easton, one of the guys from Seattle. He was the comms officer for Phoenix Company. He was worried about her.

As for how I became a mage, jeez, where to begin…

First off, forget everything you think you know about Skyline. It is so much bigger than what you or Rebecca thought.

After Seattle, Alvin and I were brought to one of their bases. They had taken in a number of other survivors from other outbreaks around the West Coast too. At first, it seemed like they just wanted to help us, but everything changed when the revenants started showing up a day later. It was like Skyline had been prepared for it.

In the days after that, dozens of kestrels landed, along with squads dressed in white uniforms. It was crazy. They immediately took over parts of the base and declared the area to be under the rule of something called the Autem Empire. Easton thinks they have been behind Skyline all along and were waiting until now to show themselves. He says they are too organized and have too much equipment to be a newly formed group. Only some of Skyline's higher-ups seemed to know what was actually going on. The rest were basically just as confused as we were.

Once Autem showed up, they started calling the shots and reorganizing Skyline. It's like they are using the mercenaries here as a temporary military while they build up some kind of army of their own. Recruitment became their priority after that.

All of the survivors on base, including me and Alvin, had to go through an assessment process where they asked us a ton of questions, and ran a shit-ton of medical tests. Anyone that passed was taken to the part of the base run by Autem. They don't even allow Skyline's people over there anymore. That's where they took Alvin. I tried to stop them but, apparently, I didn't meet their requirements, so they threw me in with the rest of the rejects.

After that, they gave all of us leftovers an ultimatum. We could become guardians and join Skyline, where we would be sent out on patrols to find more survivors so they could go through the same assessment as we did.

Or we could become citizens of the Autem Empire, where we would help them build a better future. According to them, they have claimed an area on the East Coast and cleared it of all monsters. They said that I would be safe there, and that I would be able to see Alvin again eventually. But they also made it clear that the needs of their empire outweigh the needs of its citizens.

Given the choice, I picked Skyline.

I wasn't going to let some weird-ass empire that came out of nowhere tell me what to do. And I am sure as hell not going to wait for them to "let" me see my brother. Plus, there was something off about the Autem guys that ran the assessment interviews. They all carried a weird book with them at all times, and spoke like joining Autem was accepting some kind of salvation. It was like they were recruiting for a cult. So obviously, I wanted none of that.

I would have straight up refused both options, but anyone that does that gets kicked out immediately. From what I've heard, a squad just takes uncooperative people up in a kestrel and drops them back in the world somewhere with no supplies. It's basically a death sentence.

Digby couldn't believe what he was reading. Everything was so much worse than what he'd assumed. Henwick wasn't just trying to gain power, he was actually building a new world order.

"How is this possible?" Rebecca shook in her seat. "I had been a member of Skyline for years and never had an inkling that there was something like this behind it. Granted, I wasn't important enough to evac out of Seattle when all this started, so I guess I can't be too surprised that they didn't tell me anything."

"It's a complete take over." Mason leaned back looking defeated. "They're splitting the people into two groups. One that they can use in the short term, and one that will be indoctrinated to create a homogenized population by eliminating any form of dissenting voices. It sounds like there may even be a religious aspect to make their grip even tighter. It's authoritarianism to the extreme." He gave a disapproving grunt. "It's not a bad plan, all it would take is one generation and their rule will be absolute. It's like they're following a world domination handbook to the letter."

"Good lord." Digby stared down at the keyboard for a full minute before typing another question.

Digby: Aren't you a little young to be a soldier?

Lana: I just turned eighteen, so not really. I can't say it was my first choice though. I'm just trying to buy time until I can find a way to get to my brother and escape. So far, I haven't been able to find out anything. If it wasn't for Easton, I wouldn't have even been able to make contact with you.

"Ask her how she knows Easton." Rebecca leaned forward.

Digby: You mentioned Easton before. Is he helping you?

Lana: Easton made contact with me once I enlisted. I remembered him vaguely from when I was brought in by Skyline in Seattle. I guess Rebecca said something to him that night to make him suspicious of things here. He started working to find answers as soon as we got back to base. I swiped a smartphone off a corpse while I was out on patrol, and he got it set up so I could use it without Skyline being able to monitor it. That's how I'm messaging you now.

So far, it's just Easton and me, but with Autem taking over Skyline and bossing them around, he's hoping to build some sort of resistance.

Digby: How's that effort going?

Lana: Not well. Pretty much all of Skyline's forces are either purely mercenaries that are happy to work for the highest bidder, or they were recruited too young to distrust their superiors enough to see the writing on the wall.

As for the rest of the new recruits, most joined up just trying to survive. Then, once they get their guardian rings, it's like the power goes to their head. They start to see normal humans as lesser. Even I'm starting to notice something changing in me, and I'm only level 2.

I don't know how to explain it, but it's like the ring is doing something to me. Like it's making me more aggressive. If I could take it off, I would. But that would be against regulations and the Guardian Core will know if I do. I'm just hoping I can get to my brother and get out of here before I lose myself to it.

Easton has been giving me psych tests every few days to see if there's something to my theory. He's actually one of the few people on base at this point that hasn't taken a ring yet, since he just works the comms.

Anyway, it was also Easton that figured out that this dating site could be used for communication. He says it will probably fail soon, considering the state that the internet is in. When it does, I won't be able to talk to you guys anymore. I can do a Mirror Link spell, but I need to have touched both panes of glass that make up the connection or have someone else with me that has at least touched the other side. So that's not really helpful, since I don't know where you all are.

Where are you guys holing up, by the way?

Also, I assume it was you that blew up that hotel near where I stumbled across you, right?

"I'm not sure we should tell her where we are." Rebecca held out a hand to stop him from responding. "It sounds like Lana and Easton are on the up and up, but I think our location should remain secret for now."

"You might be right." Digby tapped a claw on the table next to the laptop. "I want to trust them, but still, there's no need to take the risk." He typed in a new question, sidestepping Lana's altogether.

Digby: What do you know about the revenants?

Lana: I've been given a crash course in magic since becoming a guardian, so I know the basics. I don't know how the curse changed to create them, but I have been trained in their weaknesses. The big one is life essence, *so any spell that carries it messes them up good. That's why they're slow and weak during the day. Most living things in the world depend on sunlight, so there's more life essence in the mix during the day. Unlike zeds, the revs aren't dead though, so they don't filter anything out when they absorb mana. The life essence they take ends up screwing up their mana system to stop their regeneration. The common ones can also be easily blocked from entering an area by some of Autem's people.*

"I guess that confirms our theory." Rebecca nodded to herself as Digby asked Lana another question.

Digby: About the wards that keep the revenants out, do you know how that works? For example, we've noticed that the creatures avoid churches.

Lana: I don't have any training on warding. Neither does anyone else at Skyline. Autem seems to be keeping that knowledge to themselves. So I can't help there.

As for the church thing, apparently if enough people share a belief in something long enough, it can cause a place or object to gain power. It's been happening since, like, forever, but no one noticed because the effects rarely had an impact on anything in everyday life until now. It's not just churches either, but all sacred ground. So temples, synagogues, mosques, and a bunch of other random places that people hold a strong belief in. They're all protected from most of the revs.

Rebecca elbowed Digby in the arm. "Ask about the Guardian Core."

"Good idea, Henwick had said that the Core and the Seed were different." Digby started typing. "Let see if she knows how much?"

Digby: What can you tell us about Skyline's guardians?

Lana: I'm only level 2, so I haven't had a ton of experience. But we gain five points every level which are automatically dropped into our stats based on what class we are. As for spells, we have a list of them that we can work toward over time.

Digby: What about the rings? If we were able to get our hands on a few, could we use them to give some of our people power?

Lana: No way. Each ring is coded for a specific guardian. There's no way to reassign them. Plus, there's a bunch of other restrictions. There's a level cap at fifteen that we have to be given authorization to get past. Also, if we step out of line, we can have our rings confiscated and lose our abilities.

"Interesting…" Rebecca stared at the line of black runes that encircled her finger. "They don't function the same then. It's almost like…" She trailed off before continuing. "We're accessing the same server, but using two different interfaces."

"I'm sorry, what?" Digby flicked his eyes to her.

"I think that's how it all works. The Heretic Seed and the Guardian Core aren't the source of the magic we use. Instead, they just decide when and how much access we get and organize the information."

"I still don't follow." Digby shook his head.

"So it's basically like there's a firewall… wait, no. That's only going to be more confusing." Rebecca sat for a moment before starting again. "Okay, so imagine that the magic we use is surrounded by a wall that no one can get through."

"Alright, I'm imagining it." He nodded.

"Now imagine the Heretic Seed is a door in that wall, and the rings that we put on are the key to that door."

Mason nodded along. "So the rings you three put on are like login credentials that allow you to gain access to a server behind the firewall, and the Heretic Seed acts as an interface to manage that access."

"Exactly." Rebecca clapped her hands, clearly excited that someone was following her original line of thought. She turned back to Digby to continue her old-world explanation. "So anyway, if the Seed is the door we use, then the Guardian Core is just a different door in the same wall. However, their door is smaller, so Skyline can't access quite as much power as we can."

"Alright, so that means that the guardians have more limitations than we do." Digby raised an eyebrow. "Their door only gives them five attribute points per level, and it doesn't give them any choice of how to place them. Plus it sounds like they don't have the Skill Link trait that we discover new spells through."

"Yeah, it sounds like they only get a set list," Rebecca added. "So their potential growth and versatility is also limited."

"If that's the case, then we may not be as unevenly matched as I thought." Digby snapped his fingers, finally making the gesture work with his dead digits now that his dexterity was higher than before. "I wonder if Henwick has the same limitations."

"I doubt it." Mason leaned back. "I'm willing to bet there's some sort of ranking system that sets his access higher than others. Actually, it sounds to me like these Autem people probably do too. From a tactical standpoint, if they are using Skyline as a temporary fighting force, it only makes sense that they would limit their power so they don't have to worry about a rebellion when they decide they're no longer needed. Actually, they probably have the ability to cut off any of the guardians' access remotely."

"That sounds like something Henwick would do." Digby folded his arms, remembering how the charismatic hunter had roused his village to attack a castle for him. Even how the man had convinced him to help destroy the Heretic Seed, only to write him off as dead without a second thought. "It makes sense that he wouldn't give anyone access to power without being able to control them."

"Oh shit." Rebecca's face fell. "That's why they were so dead set on destroying or capturing you back in Seattle. With all of Henwick's guardians under his thumb, it means that heretics are the ones with access to the same power without being under his control."

"Not to mention we're immortal, so he can't just wait for us to die off." Digby leaned back, feeling smug. "And I don't remember Lana mentioning passive immortality as any of her abilities. My guess is he only gives that to a select few."

"Immortal?" Mason arched an eyebrow at Rebecca.

"Ah, yeah, I'm sort of a little immortal."

"Wait, what?" His mouth fell open.

"Sorry, it slipped my mind." She shrugged. "But yeah, heretics don't age."

"God, every time I think I'm figuring things out about all this, you hit me with something like that." Mason dropped his head back into the cushion behind him.

"Try not to think about it too much." Rebecca placed a hand on his just as another message came in.

Lana: So what's the plan?

Digby stared at the question on the screen before typing one of his own.

Digby: What are you on about?

Lana: Like, what can we do to stop Autem and Skyline?

"I'm really getting sick of that question." Digby looked from Rebecca to Mason. "What does she even think I can do about it all?"

"I think that's obvious." Mason shrugged. "Can't say I disagree either. Someone is going to have to stand up to these Autem people."

"How is that my responsibility?" Digby pushed the laptop away. "Obviously I don't approve of what Henwick is doing, but as I have stated numerous times at this point, I am not in a position to deal with him. Besides, that sounds a lot like a humanity problem, not a Lord Graves problem."

"You did just say that you heretics were more powerful than most of their guardians." Mason raised his head back up.

"Yes, but they must have hundreds by now, and we only have three heretics." Digby crossed his arms. "Actually, make that slightly less than three heretics, because I'm still missing a foot. Against Henwick, that math just doesn't add up."

"That's true." Rebecca nodded in agreement. "And for now, they don't know we're alive. So we should probably stay hidden until we're better prepared."

"Indeed. Revealing ourselves wouldn't exactly be the smart thing to do." Digby pulled the laptop closer and typed a message to defuse Lana's expectations.

Digby: Right now, we are safe and Skyline is unaware of our survival.

If I had an army of heretics, we might storm this new empire's walls and put an end to it. But as things stand, we don't have the numbers or resources to put up any sort of resistance. We are doing everything we can to grow stronger, but at this time, there is still too much risk in making a move.

Lana: I guess.

It was easy to tell from her response that she was disappointed so Digby added a bit more to give her hope without making any promises.

Digby: We're currently searching for a lead on the whereabouts of the original Heretic Seed's remains. We know Henwick has a shard of it, but there has to be more out there. If we can find more, then we might learn something that could shift the balance. We'll let you know if anything happens on our end, so let us know if there are any new developments on yours.

Lana: Umm… maybe don't spend too much time looking for the Seed's shards. One of the things I learned during training after getting my ring was that the remains of the Heretic Seed have been recovered. Skyline's people found hundreds of them in the area where the first one was discovered. After that, they scoured all of Europe for any fragments that might have been lost. They seemed pretty proud of that fact. No one else can use magic if they keep that stuff secure.

The bottom dropped out of Digby's stomach as he read her last message. That was it. His one chance of gaining real power, gone. If Henwick had already found every shard of the Seed that existed beyond his own, then there was nothing he could do. His hope of creating more heretics had been killed in its cradle. He typed one more line to make sure.

Digby: Any idea where those shards might be now?

Lana: Not really. But the Autem side of the base has some ridiculously high security areas. I'm talking Mission: Impossible *type stuff. They have to have something valuable in there for them to go through all that trouble. Maybe it's the Seed's fragments. Who knows.*

"Damn." Digby sank back in his seat as Lana typed another line into their conversation.

Lana: Also… Who's Henwick?

"What? How does she not know who she's working for?" Digby sputtered and looked at Rebecca.

"Ask her if she knows someone named Rickford. That was the name he used when he contacted me for the first time. He's probably still using it."

Digby: Do you know a Rickford?

Lana: No.

Digby: Who the hell is commanding these Autem people then?

Lana: That would be Chancellor Serrano.

Digby: I have no idea who that is.

Lana: ...Okay.

"If Henwick has been working behind the scenes for the last eight hundred years, then he's probably not going to stop now," Rebecca guessed.

"So whoever this Serrano person is, he must report back to Henwick." Digby sent another message, explaining who their real enemy was, as well as filling Lana in on how Henwick gained his power after the Heretic Seed was destroyed. Again, he left out the part about being in possession of a shard of its original monolith.

With that, the conversation ended, leaving Digby more worried than ever. There was nothing he could do against Henwick. Yet, if the man was allowed to do as he pleased and grow this new empire of his, then in time, there may not be anywhere left for his heretics to hide. By the time they found a way to get stronger, it may be too late.

It was certainly looking like things were going to get worse before they got better.

CHAPTER TWENTY-SEVEN

"Are you sure you know what you're doing?" Digby shouted from a balcony overlooking the forge that Parker and the others had spent the day to get up and running.

It had been a few hours since his conversation with Lana, though he still needed to fill his apprentice in on what they'd discovered. A part of him wanted to hold off, considering it would only add to the boy's stress. Especially when he seemed to be enjoying his new hobby. Granted, that didn't mean Digby wasn't above annoying him. He had nothing else to do that day and he was getting sick of watching videos in his room.

"Put your back into it, boy!"

"You're not helping." Alex glowered back as he hit a piece of metal with a hammer.

The forge was made up of a large empty propane tank that had been cut open and laid on its side. From there it gained a line of pipes to feed in fuel. Once it had been tested, they welded it all back together. They had also set up a second area to house a foundry. With that they were able to melt down metal, pour it into a basic mold and finish it in the forge. Asher stayed with the group to watch every step of the process.

After a day of working, the only thing they had produced was a crooked short sword with a bent tip. It was clear that the endeavor was going to take longer to work out the kinks. Though it was impressive how hard Alex was working, even if Parker was getting more done. With the group working together, it was still going to take time for them to come up with anything functional.

Unfortunately, they didn't have time to wait around. With Skyline and this new Autem Empire gaining a foothold in the world, it wouldn't do for Digby and the rest of his heretics to sit by and twiddle their thumbs.

That was when he remembered he had a ritual to complete.

Stepping down the stairs toward the forge, he collected his apprentice. The boy got on board without argument. It seemed that the prospect of heading out to get another level was appealing to the lad. Next, they went back to the library to drag his illusionist away from her new bed partner. To his surprise, Rebecca was interested in the excursion as well, taking the opportunity to get stronger for what it was. It was good to see her finally moving in the right direction.

Together they sat down to go over the requirements of Digby's ritual.

From the description, he needed three things.

First, there was a gemstone of high quality. That part was easy; there were plenty of jewelry stores in the area and, last Digby checked, no one was going to stop him from looting. After that were the bones of at least five different people. Again, that could be found anywhere. There was no shortage of corpses, after all. Finally, they needed a location that had an ambient mana balance of at least fifty percent death essence where multiple people had recently perished.

Looking over the requirements, it was easy to see why necromancy might be frowned upon. Finding a location like that under ordinary conditions might be difficult without resorting to executing the necessary humans to meet the requirement. Fortunately, and again, thanks to the apocalypse, it would almost be more difficult to find a place where no one had recently died. The only hitch was that the ritual would probably have to be carried out at night due to the shift in mana balance caused by the sun. That would mean they needed to secure whatever suitable location they found and spend the night.

With an understanding of what they needed to do, Digby sought out Rufus, not wanting a repeat of the conversation they'd had before. Begrudgingly, he informed the decrepit zombie master that he and his heretics would be heading out to take care of a ritual and that they would not be back until the following day. Rebecca even left a computer with Mason so that they could stay in contact with the castle using the same communication system they had taken advantage of to speak with Lana. As long as the information network remained functioning, they would be able to keep the others back at the castle informed.

Digby spent the night getting the van ready to go while Rebecca and Alex slept. He would have liked to have something better to wear than a Hanging Frederick t-shirt or one of Alex's floral monstrosities, but after having his Coat of the Goblin King destroyed, he didn't have much in the way of options.

He blew out a needless sigh. It wasn't the outfit that he wanted to perform a dark ritual in. Then again, at least his trousers were clean.

Putting his appearance aside, he'd also lost the extra fifty mana that his coat had provided. Thanks to the slender plates of bone armor that covered his chest and back, he didn't need much in the way of protection, but still, he needed all the mana he could get. Especially considering that the ritual would require a sacrifice of fifty points to complete.

Feeling disappointed, he turned to Asher who perched nearby and gestured to his shirt. "Not really befitting of a powerful necromancer, is it?"

Asher tilted her head to the side as if considering his appearance. She didn't respond beyond that, leaving him to force out a sigh and return to prepping the van. He added a decent wardrobe to his list of things to loot while he was out.

On the bright side, Alex and Rebecca had become far more capable now that they had placed all of their attribute points. The levels they'd gained had already filled out most of the areas that they had been lacking in their previous lives, leaving them free to focus on the attribute that was most important for their class. Rebecca had dropped her additional points into perception, while Alex had chosen will.

With their attributes significantly higher, Digby felt more comfortable about taking them out into the wild. At least now he didn't have to worry about Alex getting gutted by another revenant lightwalker. With a little luck, Parker and the others might have some decent armaments waiting for them when they returned.

As soon as the sun began to rise, Digby dragged his fellow heretics out of bed and pushed them downstairs to the van. He called to Asher as he climbed in the back for another long ride. Then, they were back on the road. It didn't seem prudent to return to Santa Barbara after the disturbance they caused, so they made their way north to San Jose.

On the way, Rebecca updated her world map and practiced her concealment spell, periodically hiding the van from view as they drove. With Skyline's kestrels in the sky, it couldn't hurt to be careful. She was rewarded with new ranks in both. The radius of her mappable area increased from five miles to ten, and the area of effect for her concealment spell went up from fifteen feet to twenty. Her range increased to ten feet as well, so she didn't have to be sitting on top of something to hide it from view.

Alex spent the ride asking questions about their conversation with Lana and what Skyline was up to. By noon, they reached the first item on his ritual's list.

Stopping at the fanciest jewelry emporium that Rebecca could find, Digby exited the van. There didn't appear to be much in the way of revenants about. According to Alex's Detect

Enemy spell, there was a modest hostile presence in the area, though beyond a few dormant monsters in the surrounding stores, there wasn't much to worry about. Unfortunately, the area was also lacking in potential minions.

Tapping his shoulder with a claw, Digby called to Asher, hoping she would stay close rather than take flight the way she had been lately. She obliged, landing on her perch where she belonged. He Decayed his way through the storefront window and headed inside. Cases of sparkling gems greeted his merry party of heretics. Even with the lights of the building dead, it was still a sight to behold.

"Now this is more like it." Digby raised his bone gauntlet to smash one of the displays containing the largest diamonds in the shop. A selection of necklaces and rings sat on velvet cushions. There was even a tiara fit for a princess resting in the middle.

"You're wasting your time." Rebecca walked past him. "Stores don't put their expensive stuff in the cases to avoid theft."

"What do you mean?" Digby lowered his hand.

"The gems in there are probably cubic zirconia."

"What is a cubic zirconia?" He glanced back to the gems in the case, wondering how they could be fake.

"It's a man-made stone. Not anything rare of high quality." She shrugged. "Probably won't work for your ritual. The real stuff should be in the back."

"I see." Digby flicked his eyes between her and the display case. Then he smashed it anyways, adding an, "Oops," as if the act had been an accident. "Well, we might as well take something sparkly while we're here." He hooked a claw under a necklace and offered it to Rebecca.

"When in Rome." She sighed and took the item, fastening it around her neck. She held out her hand a second later. "Screw it, give me the tiara too."

"Ah yes, a fine choice, milady." Digby passed the item to her as well and claimed a few rings. He had lost most of the jewelry that he'd stolen in Seattle, so it was nice to find a few trinkets to line his pockets with.

Asher seemed to be actively holding herself back as she stared down at the display case. Digby could feel the tension across their bond. He lifted the raven from his shoulder and placed her on the velvet cushion so she could play. "It's alright, girl. Just because you're smarter doesn't mean you can't enjoy something shiny. Nothing wrong with that."

"Yeah, treat yourself." Rebecca claimed several bracelets from another display, finally starting to get into the right mood.

Asher resisted the temptation for a bit longer but gave in eventually, picking through the rings and making a pile of the ones she liked best in one of the cases. Digby made a point to remember to take her treasure with him when they were ready.

"There's a safe in the office." Alex came out of the back holding a flashlight, suddenly too responsible to take part in the fun of looting. Digby couldn't help but notice that he had been a little too quiet since discussing Lana's information about Autem.

"Good job, boy." Digby held out a chunky gold ring toward the newly-minted artificer to take his mind off whatever Henwick was planning. "Can I interest you in something shiny?" He pumped his eyebrows.

"No thanks." He stopped short, flicking his eyes to the tiara placed on Rebecca's head at an angle. Next he looked to Asher as she decided which ring she liked best for her pile. The artificer shook his head and headed back toward the door he had just exited to return to the safe. "It will take some time, but you might be able to Decay your way through this thing."

"Right, right, we came for a purpose." Digby rubbed his hands together and followed his apprentice into the back of the store to find a steel box nearly as tall as he was. He stopped to look the vault over, hoping to find a weak point to exploit. "Maybe if I go for the hinges."

"Maybe." Alex nodded, without offering anything more to help.

"Hmm." Digby approached the vault and placed his ear to the metal surface hoping to discover more. Listening carefully, he tapped a claw on the front. That was when Rebecca entered the room.

The illusionist said nothing, sweeping the room with her eyes. A second later, she approached a desk opposite the safe and lifted up a keyboard that sat in front of a computer. Afterward, she simply stepped across the space and slipped past Digby and Alex to approach the locking mechanism of the safe. She spun a wheel embedded in the metal surface back and forth a few times, then pulled down on a handle. The door swung open with little effort.

"How did you—" Digby started to ask.

"I found a password to all the computers out front under the keyboards. Figured whoever owned this place wasn't big on remembering things." She shook her head, jostling her tiara. "It seems some people don't understand good security hygiene."

"Well then, it seems you have a use other than hiding in the van." Digby tried to compliment her, though the result ended up sounding more like an insult.

To his surprise, she didn't argue. Instead, she just shrugged and reached into the safe to pull out a container with several small drawers. Dropping it on the desk, she began going through each compartment, pulling out several tiny bags, each containing a lone diamond.

"Oh damn." Alex stared down into the open safe at a few stacks of green paper. "That's intense."

Digby crouched down, recognizing the currency from the movies he'd seen. He picked up a pile that had been bundled together. "So this is what you all used as money?"

"Yeah." Alex seemed taken aback. Clearly, he'd never seen that much of the stuff all together at once.

"It's all worthless now," Rebecca added without looking back. "This might not be though." She turned around to present a small bag containing an enormous gemstone. "Think an eighteen-carat diamond will do for your ritual?"

"I should say so." Digby tore open the bag and held the stone up to a flashlight. "It's gorgeous."

"Good, cause it was marked as being worth a little over a million dollars." Rebecca pocketed handfuls of smaller diamonds.

"Is that a lot of money?" Digby glanced back to her, still not having a clear idea of the subject.

"It's probably more than I would ever make in a lifetime." Alex picked up several of the smallest bags and dumped a few dozen of the sparkling gemstones into his hand. "I wonder if I can use these for crafting."

"Might as well take them all then." Rebecca dug a velvet bag from a drawer and filled it up. In addition to the diamonds, there were also a number of other stones in the safe. Emeralds, rubies, sapphires, they all went in the bag. She straightened her tiara when she was done. "I'd say we've gotten what we came for."

"Indeed." Digby found a second velvet pouch in the drawer and headed out to the store room to pack up Asher's treasure. The raven looked over to him, holding a chain of white gold in her beak as he emerged from the back. Looking over her selection, she seemed to have a liking to silver over gold. Digby smiled at his pet as she stood proudly atop a mound of metal and gemstones nearly as large as her. "That's a good girl. We'll make you a nice shiny nest when we get back to the castle."

Asher seemed happy, though he could tell she was holding back at least a little of her excitement. She hopped back up to his shoulder as he shoveled her treasure into the sack. With nothing left to loot, they climbed back into the van.

That was when Alex finally made it clear why he had been so quiet in the store.

"So what is the plan with Autem?" Alex pulled the van back out onto the road.

"Seriously?" Digby deflated.

"I know, I know." Alex shrugged. "You don't think we stand a chance against them right now. But really, what is the plan?"

"You know what the plan is." Digby leaned against the wall of the vehicle in the back. "We remain hidden until we can get stronger or learn more out about the power we have."

"Yeah, that's what you keep saying." Alex shrugged. "But from what this Lana girl says, these Autem people are gaining more resources every day."

"And what do you think we're doing?" Digby picked up his bag of treasure and shook it at the boy.

"Yes, but this is nothing. It'll get us what, one spell?" He stepped on the gas a little too hard. "What good is that if they keep recruiting? You saw how fast me and Becca leveled. In a week, everyone they've gained will be as strong as us."

"So what do you suggest I do?" Digby rolled his eyes.

"I don't know, maybe hit them now?" The boy sounded unsure.

"Oh sure, let me just take a count of our troops." Digby raised three fingers. "Alright, beyond us three, we have three more soldiers willing to fight." He immediately lowered two fingers. "And one of those soldiers is Parker who ate expired dairy the other day. Besides, weren't you terrified of dying back when I found you?"

"I was." Alex's voice grew harsh. "Emphasis on the *was* part of that. I'm stronger now. Strong enough to fight. And I wasn't afraid of dying, I just didn't want to be eaten alive."

"Were you strong enough when that revenant gutted you?" Digby snapped back.

"No, probably not. But I am getting—"

"Stronger. Yes, I know." Digby rubbed at his eyes, getting sick of having to have the same conversation over and over. "Look, I don't like what Henwick is doing either. Hell, I have far more reason than you to want him dead. Plus, he'd probably make a decent meal." Digby sighed. "But like it or not, he has already won and nothing short of a miracle is going to change that." Digby softened his voice trying to appeal to the boy. "I admit that both you and Rebecca are growing in power, but that doesn't mean I will let you throw your lives away. Which is exactly what you'd be doing. So no, I won't pick a fight with Henwick no matter what anyone says."

Alex said nothing for a long beat.

"You hear me?" Digby prodded the boy.

"Yeah, I hear you." Alex sunk a little in his seat.

"Good, now quit sulking." Digby stood up and leaned on his seat. "We're making progress, so quit trying to rush everything."

"Fine." Alex groaned.

"Close enough." Digby slapped the back of this seat, just as the artificer briefly pressed harder on the gas, causing Digby to tumble into the back of the van. "Hey, you did that on purpose."

"I have no idea what you're talking about." Alex eyed him in the mirror.

"Bah." He waved his hand through the air.

"Not to take sides," Rebecca leaned toward Alex, "but I think you just proved Digby's point. I mean, how do you expect us to go to war with Henwick if our strongest fighter can't even stay standing in a moving vehicle?"

"Indeed, just look at me." Digby gestured to himself. "I'm more of a menace to myself as much as I am anyone else."

"I guess I can't argue with that." Alex lowered his head in defeat.

"Good. Now how about we find a good place to carry out our dark ritual. Shall we?"

From there they got down to the business of discussing where to head next. Considering the death essence requirement of the location they needed, it seemed like a graveyard might present the best fit. Fortunately, there was a fairly large one not too far from the jewelry emporium. The only question was if anyone had recently perished there. The answer became obvious as soon as they arrived.

A destroyed wrought iron gate hung open at the entrance of the cemetery. The carcass of a burned-out bus lay on its side just beyond the first few grave stones. The blackened remains of a dozen corpses lay inside. Digby couldn't help but wonder if their bones might also be used for the ritual. Upon closer insection, they seemed a little too damaged to be of use.

"Well, I think we've found the grounds for our dark ritual." Digby leaned on the bus.

"But how are we going to survive the night out here once the revs start waking up?" Rebecca dug through the front of the bus, finding a strange wooden paddle emblazoned with some sort of strange symbols. She tossed it back into the wreckage a moment later as if none of it interested her.

"I think we might be able to make it through the night over there." Alex stood at the top of a hill pointing down the other side.

Digby climbed up, barely noticing the demerit to his agility from his peg-leg anymore. He grinned as he crested the hill. "Yes, I think that'll do nicely."

A mausoleum the size of a small house sat nestled into a patch of grass between two hills. The structure was comprised entirely of stone, with only a few small stained-glass windows high up on the sides. A small door hung open a crack, a pillar of stone bracketing it on both sides. Asher flapped her way up to the roof and cawed.

"It's nearly perfect, all we have to do is barricade the door. The windows look to be out of reach and the walls look plenty sturdy." Digby marched down through rows of graves toward the building, throwing the door open as soon as he arrived. "Gah!"

The pale arms of five dormant revenants reached out from the opening as he fell back on his rear. A chorus of chittering cries followed as they staggered out of the building, remaining in the shadow cast by the structure. The mausoleum was packed with them. Digby opened his maw on the ground, spending the additional mana to increase the size of the gateway. The first two of the creatures simply fell in, sinking into a pool of black sludge before they could make it any further.

"There has to be over a dozen in there." Alex grabbed the

back of Digby's shirt to help him to his feet before the rest of the monsters had a chance to pour out of the building.

"Over here." Rebecca darted past them and ducked around the side.

Digby followed, cutting line of sight with the creatures that were stepping out into the shadow of the mausoleum. He nearly ran straight into Rebecca who had stopped just around the corner. She raised a finger to her mouth, telling him to keep quiet as she moved mana through her body.

A second later, one of the dormant revenants crept around the building after them. Digby froze as the monster looked right at them. It stared for a moment before turning the other way, as if having lost track of them. Digby glanced to Rebecca, realizing that she'd cast her Conceal spell.

Grinning, he turned and waved to the revenant. Rebecca promptly slapped him in the shoulder to tell him to cut it out. Then she beckoned to him and Alex with one finger as she backed away toward the other side of the mausoleum where it was less likely that any of their enemies might wander.

Once they were safe, she released the spell and hooked a thumb back in the direction they had come from. "Well, you were looking for some skeletons. You just have to unwrap them first."

"Oh yes, very convenient." Digby glanced at his mana.

MP: 239/239

"Alright, we'll take them a couple at a time." He glanced at Rebecca. "Can you lure them for us?"

"Yeah." She sighed and sat down to lean against the mausoleum. "Just don't let anything happen to my body." A second later a second copy of her, complete with tiara, appeared standing next to her corporeal form. Her projection simply strolled off around the building and flagged down one of the revenants on the other side. Digby forged a set of blood talons while Alex enchanted one of his machetes in preparation.

Rebecca's projected ghost came running back with a pair of enemies in tow. Digby fell upon the two like a wolf, moving as if guided by instinct to take the foes apart. It was as if he suddenly knew exactly where to strike to kill as quickly as possible. As the two bodies hit the ground, Digby stared down at his claws. He hadn't even gotten much blood on them.

That must be the effect of my Dissection ability. I've eaten enough of these creatures to have a clear idea of how they are built.

Rebecca spun on her heel and went back for more when it was clear he didn't need any help. The dormant revenants weren't a challenge when taken a couple at a time, so the extermination process only took ten minutes. As soon as they were finished, Rebecca released her projection.

"Holy shit." The illusionist opened her eyes, staring straight in front of her.

"What are you on about?" Digby stared down at her.

"I just discovered a spell." Her eyes widened.

"Really, what?" Digby arched an eyebrow.

"Waking Dream." She started to stand.

"What's it do?" Alex helped her to her feet.

"Apparently I displayed enough talent with deception to unlock the ability to make visual projections of anything I can imagine, as long as it's believable to the viewer."

"So, you're basically never going to discover anything that can actually cause some damage, are you?" Digby glowered at the illusionist.

"What are you talking about?" Rebecca scoffed. "This is amazing." She thrust out a hand as one of Skyline's drones flickered into existence in the air above it.

"Wow, a fake drone." Digby gave a sarcastic nod. "That's very impressive."

"Oh shut it." Rebecca folded her arms, causing the drone to wink out of existence.

Digby glanced at the experience message on his HUD for the most recent kills, doing a little math. After leveling a few times back in Santa Barbara, the dormant revenants were only worth six points each. After killing nineteen of them, all he had to show for it was another hundred and fourteen points.

He rolled his eyes, lamenting the fact that the effort had been nearly pointless. Then he turned toward the pile of corpses and rubbed his hands together. "Alright, at least we have what we need. So let's start digging out some bones."

"Um, I'm gonna leave that up to you." Rebecca stepped away gesturing to the bodies piled up against the mausoleum.

"Yeah, I'll wait over there." Alex pointed to one of the nearby tomb stones.

"Fine, fine, suit yourselves." Digby grinned up to Asher. "All the more corpses for us then." The raven flapped down and began pecking at the pile.

Digby spent the next few hours dissecting one corpse after another, eating whatever he didn't need for the ritual. He set aside the hearts and brains for Asher. It would certainly take her some time to consume them, but he was hopeful that she would reach a new tier in her mutation path before the night was through. Once he had enough, he made a pile for her in the grass and devoured what was leftover, getting a new message from the Heretic Seed across his vision.

GUIDED MUTATION
Requirements for the Ravager's mutation, Temporary
Mass, have been met.
Accept? Yes/No

Digby hesitated, remembering that he had also reached the requirements for the Sheep's Clothing mutation earlier. The choice was hard to make. Though, his line of thinking hadn't changed and he ended up accepting Temporary Mass. He waited a moment to see if he felt any different.

He didn't.

Must not have an impact until I use it. Digby reminded himself that the mutation only granted access to a new ability. He would still have to spend another two flesh and one bone to activate the increase in strength and defense that it granted by forming an outer shell of functioning muscle and bone around his body. Though, without a need to waste the resources, he shrugged and moved on as Asher pecked away at the prime cuts that he had set aside for her. It wasn't long before she reached a new mutation as well.

> **Animated zombie, Asher, has gained the Master's mutation, Compel Uncommon Zombie. They may now pass on compels to any uncommon zombie. Intelligence has increased to 15. Perception has increased to 9. Will has increased to 7. Maximum Mana has increased to 87.**

Digby's eyes widened at the text. "That is it!"

"What is it?" Rebecca poked her head out from the side of the mausoleum.

"Asher just became a zombie master." He stared at the bird, who stared back at him. Her eyes were somehow clearer, as if less confused. "You beautiful creature." He rushed over to her, picking her up and holding her high. "You've just given me everything I could ask for."

"What's got him so happy?" Alex poked his head around the corner as well.

"Asher can compel an uncommon zombie now." Digby nuzzled his pet as she flapped her wings in protest. "Do you know what that means?"

"Yeah, she can control a zombie leader and use them as an entry point to gain control over a larger horde than you could manage alone." Rebecca spoke as if she wasn't impressed.

"Not just that." Digby put Asher down so she could finish the remains of what she'd been eating. "With her in the air, passing on my compels, Rufus's power means nothing. If that ancient corpse tries anything that we don't like, I can simply steal his army. I'm sure there will be a bit of a struggle, but this way, we can balance the scales."

"Good for you." Rebecca shrugged and left him to finish eating.

Alex sighed and shook his head before heading back around the mausoleum.

"Well, I'm still impressed." Digby watched them go, annoyed at their lack of proper adoration at his accomplishments. Asher followed them with her eyes as well before looking back to him. "Don't let them get you down, I'm proud of you."

Asher simply nodded and went back to her meal. Digby couldn't help but wonder if she had reached the limits of her mind yet. It wasn't too long ago that his intelligence was right around the same number. From their bond, all he could sense was a feeling of clarity.

That's good enough for me. Digby sat down beside her and gently stroked her side.

After they finished eating, a Blood Forge spell cleared the mess on the grass next to the mausoleum. Without a real use for the excess fluid, he simply formed a series of spikes near the entrance of the building to make it difficult for anything hostile to enter.

With the mausoleum secure, Digby gathered his pile of bones and assembled them on the floor of the space. To his surprise, he somehow knew exactly where each piece went.

Must be another effect of Dissection.

Digby finished placing the bones and sat down to wait for nightfall.

As the sun began to set, he set the largest of the diamonds that he'd stolen atop the skull on the floor and waited.

"Won't be long now."

CHAPTER TWENTY-EIGHT

Motes of soft green light floated through the walls of the mausoleum as beams of moonlight shined in through the stained-glass windows.

"I suppose that means it's working." Digby stood by the skeleton on the floor as energy floated around him. He could feel it tugging on his mana as if trying to draw out the amount required by the ritual. At first, he resisted, not wanting to sacrifice so much now that the time had come. Eventually, he let go. Feeling the magic trickle from his body, he held his hand out over the diamond. The gemstone began to glow a sickly green as it drank in his mana to mix with the power of the graveyard around him.

Digby glanced at his HUD, watching his maximum value tick down one point. "Hmm, this certainly isn't going to be a quick ritual."

Of course, that was when a scratching began at the door.

"Think that door will hold?" Rebecca stepped away from the barrier.

"Ah, probably." Digby shrugged. "It's not like the revenants have a reason to wander into this cemetery. Though, you might want to peek out and have a look just in case." He flicked his eyes up to one of the high windows.

Rebecca looked to Alex. "Give me a boost?"

The artificer shrugged and crouched down over by the wall so she could place a foot on his shoulder. As soon as she was stable, he stood up to hoist her to the window. He laughed as soon as he did.

"Jeez, I am way stronger than I used to be." Alex crouched back down only to rise up again.

"Yeah, great, and you're lucky I have better balance too." Rebecca leaned back and forth to steady herself as she stood on his shoulders.

"Ah yes, the Heretic Seed has done you both well. You're no gymnasts, but you're certainly not the uncoordinated messes that you were." Digby nodded, feeling a little proud of his coven. Asher watched the display with a bit of brain hanging from her beak.

"Yup, we're all becoming more powerful." Rebecca adjusted her tiara after wobbling back and forth for a second. "Now bring me back to the window."

"Oh, right." Alex stepped toward the wall.

"Thank—" Rebecca stopped talking the moment she reached the window. "We have a problem."

"Revenants?" Digby arched an eyebrow.

"Oh yeah, tons, all active." She paused, squinting through the glass. "It's like they're being drawn here."

Digby glanced to his hand as mana trickled from him to the diamond. "Oh no, I wonder if the ritual has something to do with it."

"You think?" Rebecca hopped off of Alex's shoulder. "There's a ton of mana flowing in here. At the very least, they're curious about it."

Alex swept his hand through a few motes of green light. "We gotta barricade the door."

A window on the other side of the room broke inwards as a pale arm reached through it.

"Forget the door, they're piling against the walls to climb up to the windows." Rebecca raised a hand and cast Icicle, knocking the creature out but not killing it. "Think you can give us a hand?" She stepped closer to Digby.

"I can't just stop." He glanced at his mana. The maximum value had only fallen by ten. He was only a fifth of the way done with the ritual.

"Can you work a little faster?" She spun as another window broke behind her.

"Oh, let me just ask the lingering spirits of the dead if they mind picking up the pace." Digby held up his free hand as if listening to something. "What's that? You're all dead?" He turned back to Rebecca. "Sorry, they're all dead, and not the fastest bunch."

"You're not helping." She cast another Icicle, stabbing a revenant in the eye.

"Try to hold them off!" Digby shouted "I'll be with you in a moment."

Asher cawed, clearly worried as another window broke. Rebecca raised a hand to cast another Icicle.

"Wait!" Alex stopped her. "Try healing them."

"What?" She snapped her eyes back to him.

"They don't like life magic." He pulled a few bottles of water from a pack of food that they had brought in for the night and purified it.

"Worth a try." She threw a hand out at the closest pale form reaching through one of the windows. A shimmer of light swept over its skin followed by a loud screech as it flailed and pulled away. "Okay, it didn't hurt it much, but yeah, they don't like it."

"As long as it disrupts their mana system, that's good enough to make them stay out." Digby tried his best to stay focused on his ritual, hoping that the other two heretics could hold off the foes until he was able to join the fight. He glanced at his HUD; only half of the ritual's required mana had been removed from his maximum value.

Rebecca cast another two Regeneration spells to force back

more of the creatures. Alex flung purified water up on the other side, getting a similar result.

"We're going to run out of mana in less than a minute if this keeps up." Rebecca glanced down to check her HUD.

"Take turns." Digby glanced back. "Whoever isn't casting needs to meditate to replenish what they can."

"I, ah, kinda, haven't mastered meditation yet." Alex flung a bit more water at the windows.

"I've tried it." Rebecca raised a hand in front of Alex to tell him to hold off until she needed to rest. She proceeded to stand at the middle of the crypt with her hands outstretched to keep an eye on both sides, casting Regeneration one after another. "I have about twenty seconds left in me."

"I'm ready to take over." Alex cast a Purify on another bottle.

Digby checked his mana. "I'm at sixty percent finished."

"I'm out." Rebecca dropped to the floor and sat down, closing her eyes to meditate as Alex flung more water at the pale limbs that reached in. She snapped her eyes back open a few seconds later. "Shit, it's not working."

The last unbroken window in the mausoleum shattered.

"Try to put all thought out of your mind." Digby attempted to help.

"I am." She snapped. "I've only done this twice. And even then, it took a while."

"We don't have a while." Alex tossed an empty water bottle to the floor as he cracked open another.

"You're not helping," both Digby and Rebecca shouted at the boy in unison.

"Alright." Digby struggled to maintain a calm to keep from making Rebecca's meditation attempt more difficult. "Try thinking of something that upsets you."

"What?" She glared at him.

"I'm serious." He nodded. "Think about something you don't want to think about. Then stop thinking about it."

"That's insane…" She trailed off, remaining silent for ten

seconds before cracking one eye open. "God damnit, I hate when you're right." She closed her eyes again. She was back up and ready to fight a minute later just as Alex ran out of mana.

"I'm almost done." Digby checked his maximum MP. The ritual was at ninety five percent. "Switch to Icicle and kill a few. I need some blood available to work with out there."

Rebecca obliged, casting the spell eight times just as Digby felt the last of his sacrificed mana flow into the ritual's gemstone. He immediately stood up and cast Forge, thrusting his arms out toward the blood that he sensed outside. Digby raised his hands as crimson rivers flowed up the outer walls of the mausoleum to form a barrier on each of the small windows. The sound of the revenants screeching outside faded to muffled cries. Then, all was still.

"Will that hold?" Rebecca dropped back to the floor, panting.

"For now." Digby stared up at his new windows. "Is everyone alright?"

Alex shrugged as he stared at the empty space in front of him, clearly reading a message from the Heretic Seed. "Guess we killed eight of those things."

"Good for you." Digby brushed the boy's achievement aside as he skipped over his experience messages to the one that really mattered.

RITUAL COMPLETE
You have successfully weaved an infernal spirit from the lingering echoes of the dead. This spirit will remain loyal and will exist within the gemstone used until called forth by its master. While in use, an infernal spirit will retain the memories of its experiences. May be recalled from use at any time. An infernal spirit may be dispelled permanently to regain the mana sacrificed to create it.
You have discovered the spell Animate Skeleton.

ANIMATE SKELETON

Description: Call forth your infernal spirit to inhabit one partial or complete skeleton. Physical attributes of an animated skeleton will mimic the average values for a typical human.

Rank: D

Cost: 30MP

Range: 20ft (plus 50% death bonus, total 30ft.)

Limitations: Requires an infernal spirit to cast and a full or partial human skeleton. Must have a skull available. An animated skeleton will remain active until its skull is destroyed, at which point the caster's infernal spirit will return to the gemstone used to create it. Attempting to animate a skeleton still within a living body will be resisted by a target's will, making this spell unreliable for direct attacks.

Damn, that would have been pretty funny.

Digby finished reading as the deathly energy of the cemetery faded from the air, leaving the diamond resting at the room's center, its color now a bright green. He reached down to pick it up, willing the Heretic Seed to show him the information of the spirit within.

STATUS

Name: None

Race: Spirit

Mana: 42 / 42

Mana Composition: Pure

ATTRIBUTES

Intelligence: 6

Perception: 6

Will: 6

AILMENTS

Deceased

TRAITS
MIND OF THE DEAD
As an entity without form, this infernal spirit has
been gifted with 6 points to each of its mental attributes.

BOND OF THE DEAD
As an entity weaved together directly by a necromancer,
this minion will gain one attribute point for every 2 levels
of their master. These points may be allocated at any
time. 11 attribute points remaining.

CALL OF THE DEAD
As an entity created by a necromancer, this minion and
its master will be capable of sensing each other's presence through their bond. In addition, the necromancer
will be capable of summoning this minion to their location over great distances.

"Not bad." Digby closed his hand around the large
diamond and checked his mana.

MP: 189/189

Digby frowned. The ritual had left him with less mana than
both Alex and Rebecca, despite them being several levels below
him. He would never get back the mana he'd sacrificed to bring
the spirit into this world without dispelling it, but at least he'd
received a powerful minion in exchange. "Now to see what you
can do."

Digby dropped all of the spirit's bond points into intelligence, raising the attribute to seventeen to give it enough to
understand whatever command he gave. Considering that its
physical values would be based on the skeleton it inhabited,
intelligence seemed the most sensible. With that, he cast the
spell.

A sickly green energy seeped from the diamond to trail

through the air toward the skeleton that Digby had organized on the floor. He'd dug each bone out of the revenants he'd killed earlier, leaving them stained crimson with bits of sticky flesh still hanging here and there. The diamond's color faded back to clear as the last of the power flowed into the skull on the floor.

A quiet moment went by.

The revenants scratching at the windows filled the silence until the skeleton's mouth opened.

"Who…?" The spirit's voice trailed off, its voice sounding a little dumb.

Digby stepped forward to greet his new minion, assuming it would take a moment to get its bearings. "Yes, you are my newest—"

"Who woke us?" The skeleton interrupted him, its words coming out in a rough whisper like it was in pain. It raised a boney hand to its skull to rub its forehead.

"T'was I, your mast—" Digby started again only to have the thing talk over him.

"No thanks, man." The skeleton dropped its skull back to the stone floor of the crypt.

"I'm sorry, what was that now?" Digby tilted his head to the side.

"This place is creepy and our head hurts. So no thanks." The skeleton went still again as if deciding to remain inanimate.

"Ah…" Digby turned back to Rebecca. "I'm not sure what's happening here."

"Don't look at me. It's your infernal spirit." She gave an exaggerated shrug.

"Looks like you rolled a one for the ritual." Alex took a step back.

Digby rubbed at what little he had left of the bridge of his nose before approaching the skeleton. "Hey, now you listen here, you pile of bones. I weaved your consciousness from the lingering remnants of the departed, and I expect loyalty in exchange for that benevolence."

"What...? Loyalty?" The skeleton snapped its head to the side, focusing the hollows of its eyes on him. "Like, you want us to work for you? Naw, no chance we're working for someone so scrawny. Do you even lift, bro?"

"Scrawny? Bah! I'll have you know that my power far exceeds your own." Digby stomped his peg-leg. "I've seen your attributes, and I would hardly call them impressive. In fact, you get eleven of those points from me, so I don't know what the hell you're on about."

"Those are..." The skeleton stumbled on its words, clearly attempting to come up with a solid lie. "Those are just, like, our public numbers."

Rebecca leaned to Alex. "Is it me, or is that skeleton trying to lie its way out of being a minion? Also, it's not very good at it."

"Hmm." Alex leaned to her as well. "This thing is made up of the lingering remnants of those who perished here recently, right?"

"Yeah." She nodded.

"Remember that weird paddle you pulled out of the burned-out bus out front?"

She nodded again.

"What if it wasn't originally a weapon?" Alex paused. "I mean, didn't it have some lettering on it."

"Yeah, it had letters from the Greek alphabet." She shrugged.

"And what sort of group would have that kind of thing?" Alex connected the dots as Rebecca's eyes widened.

"Oh god, it was a frat house."

"Yup." Alex nodded matter-of-factly.

Rebecca snorted a laugh.

"Just what is so funny over there?" Digby glowered at them both.

"Your infernal spirit is a dude-bro."

"What is a dude-bro?" Digby narrowed his eyes at her. "Never mind, I don't care." He brushed off her comment and stomped his way over to the skeleton and kicked it with his peg-leg. "Get up, you. Like it or not, you will do as I say. You can't disobey me, anyway. We have been bound by magic."

"Fine, we're getting up." The skeleton struggled to get to its feet.

"That's right you are." Digby kicked the thing again for good measure.

"Whatever, bro." The skeleton placed a bony hand to its head. "You got any beer?"

"Oh, that's awesome." Rebecca's shoulders shook with silent laughter.

"No, I don't have any beer." Digby threw up both arms. "We are currently within a crypt surrounded by bloodthirsty revenants. So no, getting you a beer is not on my to do list…" He trailed off. "Actually, would you settle for a fine wine?"

"Now you're making sense." The skeleton nodded.

Digby shrugged and opened his maw to call forth one of the bottles of wine that he'd wrapped in plastic back at the vineyard.

"Sweet." The skeleton snatched it up, ignoring the black sludge coating the bottle as it tore open the plastic covering. The strange entity glanced around for a moment before cracking its prize against the wall to snap off the neck of the bottle. Then it simply raised the vessel high and dumped the contents into its mouth. Wine poured through the skeleton's lower jaw, trickling down its neck and splashing through its ribcage before pooling on the floor below it.

"Alright, now that you've had—" Digby started to speak, but stopped when the skeleton held up a bony hand with one finger raised whilst continuing to pour the entire bottle of wine into its mouth. It threw the bottle to the side, smashing it on the floor before shouting a loud, "Wooooo!"

Digby rolled his eyes. "Yes, woooo, indeed. Now are you ready to do your job? I assure you there is plenty more wine where that came from."

"You got it." The skeleton gave him a thumbs up and fell into line.

"Finally. Now what shall I call you?" Digby beckoned with one claw in a tempt to draw a name from his sorry excuse of a minion.

"We are..." The skeleton trailed off, clearly unsure what it should be called, having only been created a moment ago. The hollows of its skull glanced around the crypt, settling on the front of Digby's shirt that bore the words 'the Hanging Frederic Tavern.' A second went by before his minion answered. "... Tavern?"

"Really?" Digby looked down at the design on his shirt. "Your name's Tavern? Are you sure it's not Frederick?"

The skeleton glanced to his face then back to his shirt. "Oh yes, Fredrick, that's it."

"Well, it's too late now." Digby folded his arms, giving the spirit a hard time. "You just said your name is Tavern, but now you expect me to believe it suddenly changed."

"Yes. We mean, no. Or..." The skeleton hesitated. "No, Tavern is good too."

"Alright, Tavern it is then." Digby, looked up to the windows. "Now shall we do something about our guests?"

"What do you suggest?" Rebecca stepped forward.

"I suggest you all stand back." Digby checked his mana to make sure he'd absorbed more while arguing with his minion. Finding it full, thanks to the cemetery's higher than average balance of death essence, he thrust his hand up toward the ceiling and cast Emerald Flare. "I've been itching to use this spell."

Rebecca and Alex dove into the far corner of the mausoleum as wisps of green energy manifested, each streaking toward a single point that glowed brighter and brighter until exploding in a ten-foot-wide blast of heat and radiation. A portion of the roof of the mausoleum came apart as chunks of stone flew into the sky, leaving a gaping hole in the ceiling.

"What the hell, Dig?" Rebecca shouted from behind Alex as they both huddled in the corner to avoid some falling debris.

"We've been hiding in here long enough." He glanced back over his shoulder as he opened his maw on the floor and cast Forge. "It's time to show these creatures what a heretic is capable of." As he finished speaking, a narrow pillar of black blood rose from his open maw, slowly climbing toward the hole he'd created in the ceiling. A series of posts extended from the center of the blood forged shape to form something akin to a ladder.

Digby tapped his shoulder to call to Asher before grabbing hold as the pillar of blood rose. The deceased raven flapped up to her perch as the forge spell carried them both up to what remained of the mausoleum's roof.

Stepping out onto the top of the structure, Digby surveyed the cemetery. Revenants cried up at him from all sides. Pale forms piled themselves against the mausoleum, reaching up the walls but having trouble climbing over edges of the roof's overhang. Even better, the revenants seemed to be retreating to some degree, leaving only a few clinging to the walls.

"Apparently they don't like radiation." Digby smirked down at the creatures.

"You realized we're both going to get poisoned from that spell, right?" Rebecca climbed up behind him.

"Heh, with your constitution, you'll be fine for a bit still." He ignored her complaint.

Alex reached the roof next, his mouth falling open at the sight. "Jeez, this really is the apocalypse."

Tavern, his new minion, followed close behind with a machete in their teeth. Digby turned to Rebecca. "Do you think your Ventriloquism spell can create music the way you played a song over the speakers back in Seattle during our attack on Skyline?"

"I think so." She eyed him sideways. "What do you have in mind?"

Digby considered the few songs of the modern world that

he knew as he stepped up to the edge of the roof and ordered Tavern into the fight. The skeleton simply shrugged and leapt off into the fray below. Revenants darted back and forth between the tombstones. Digby turned back to Rebecca. "Surprise me."

"Okay, given the situation here, I think only one song will fit." The illusionist nodded and cast her Ventriloquism spell. Immediately, the sound of a door creaking came from all around them, followed by a wolf howling, along with an eerie wind blowing through the night.

"I thought you were going to play music." Digby arched an eyebrow at her.

"I am, and this is actually a good test to see what the spell can do." She reached out to her sides, raising her hands to push up the volume as the wolf continued to howl.

Then, the sound of a strange instrument blared across the graveyard. It played a series of synthesized notes just before the beat kicked in. Digby hadn't heard anything like it. A wolf continued to howl, sounding like it was off in the distance.

Alex laughed, clearly recognizing the song. He immediately raised his hands to his chest, holding them strangely as if mimicking claws before swinging them to his left and right. Maintaining the pose, the artificer marched to the other side of the roof where a revenant was beginning to reach up. He kicked it back down as the song that Rebecca had chosen belted out one word.

"Thriller!"

Digby let out a wild cackle and raised a hand to cast another Emerald Flare. Streaks of energy swam through the graves below, igniting the night with a blast of sickly green light. The bodies of several revenants were blown to scrap as many more fled the radiation wave that followed.

11 active revenants defeated, 1,166 experience awarded.
You have reached level 23.
5,322 experience to next level.

Grinning like a villain, Digby dropped his extra point into intelligence to boost his mana.

Below, his new minion's boney arms swung without mercy, hacking at the creatures that had lingered in the area in an uncoordinated display of seemingly drunken ferocity. The revenants fought back, slamming their claws into the skeleton again and again. Bones flew through the air, scattering across the cemetery only to fly back to the infernal spirit's skeletal form. Without the knowledge of how to destroy the animated minion of bone, the revenants merely knocked the infernal spirit's skull to the ground from time to time. Tavern simply picked it back up and placed it back into position before diving into the fight again.

"Now that's what I expect from a minion." Digby thrust out his claws, casting another flare to help. "Keep up the pressure down there."

The spell detonated, sending bits of pale flesh flying as experience messages streaked across his vision. The night was becoming more productive by the minute. Asher cawed from her place on his shoulder, getting into the mood as a steady beat set the tempo of the battle. A feeling of pride in her master drifted across their bond.

Rebecca stood further back on the roof, standing at its apex and twitching her shoulder along with the music. Her tiara sat on her head at an angle as she brought down Icicles on every revenant that reached the top of the mausoleum. She twirled with excitement as the spell ranked up to increase the size and speed of each frozen projectile. When she ran low on mana, the illusionist simply sat down and meditated.

Alex marched past her, slapping his hand against hers as he took over. Reaching to his quiver, he enchanted an arrow and let it fly. His spell reached a new rank as well, causing each revenant to screech and flail as they fell off the roof. Below, their skin swelled and bubbled before detonating in a burst of gore.

Digby used up the last of his mana, casting another two flares to send more pale forms flying. Spreading out each flare, he overlapped their area of effect, creating a field of radioactivity across the graveyard that sent the majority of the creatures running. His skeletal minion handled the few that remained.

Rebecca's choice in music faded off as a voice from the song cackled along with Digby to mark their victory. He let his laughter trail off, realizing that the revenants were no longer willing to come near the mausoleum.

He glanced down to skim his messages and nodded.

43 active revenants defeated, 4,472 experience awarded.

The revenants below let out a mournful cry as they gave up on their siege, each retreating from the irradiated cemetery in defeat.

"I suppose we can let the rest go for now." Digby grinned for a moment, his face dropping a second later when a loud screech echoed in the distance in response to the rest of the revenants' cries. A wave of dread surged through his body, taking root in his spine. It was the same screech he'd heard back in Santa Barbara just before dawn when he'd stood guard outside the Hanging Frederick. There was definitely something out there.

Digby glanced down at the irradiated graveyard, hoping that whatever the source of the screech was, it wasn't willing to brave the toxic lands that surrounded them. That was when he turned away from the edge of the mausoleum's roof and called his minion back to keep watch.

"Maybe we should try to keep out of sight for the rest of the night."

CHAPTER TWENTY-NINE

"Get up, you two." Digby stared down at his apprentice and Rebecca as they both lay on the mausoleum's floor. The sun shined in from the broken ceiling.

"Oh god." Rebecca groaned.

"I don't think I'm going to make it." Alex refused to open his eyes.

The pair hadn't slept well.

Throughout the night, Digby had needed to cast a round of flare spells to keep any revenants that wandered into the graveyard from getting too close. Not to mention there was still something else lurking out there in the night. Fortunately, it seemed that setting up a radioactive perimeter was an efficient deterrent. In the process, he'd actually gained a new rank for the spell that increased the potency of its lingering effect. Unfortunately, the resulting poison ailment it had on the two humans in the area was equally problematic. Even with their constitution being higher than most, they both fell ill at least once or twice an hour, leaving them with a nasty surprise every time they nodded off for too long.

"I hate you." Rebecca sat up, clutching her head. "I hate you so, so much."

"Give me something to purify." Alex held out his hand as she handed him a bottle from Digby's stock of wine. After using all of their water by throwing it at the revenants, wine was all they had left. Not that Tavern was complaining. Actually, Digby hadn't heard a peep from the skeleton in quite some time.

Alex cast Purify Water as he took the bottle of wine. It glowed for a second as he uncorked it. He grimaced as he tossed back a mouthful.

Rebecca took a swig next. "Ugh, it is way too early to start drinking."

"You going to finish that?" Tavern held out a skeletal hand.

"No, it's all yours." Rebecca handed the bottle over only to watch the skeleton pour it down its gullet.

Tavern immediately pulled it away as the wine pouring forth sizzled on contact. They cried out in agony. "We burn!"

"Shit." Alex cringed. "I purified that, didn't I?"

"I guess now we know animated skeletons have a weakness to life essence as well," Rebecca added while watching the effects of the spell. The skeleton snapped their hollow eye sockets to her as if offended by her casual observation. She simply stared back. "What? You asked for the bottle."

"Oh yeah. That's fair." The skeleton glanced back to the bottle again as if debating taking another swig regardless of the harm it might do. Then they shrugged and poured the rest down their jaw until they simply fell apart into a pile of bones.

"Is it dead?" Alex nudged at a femur just as Tavern's skull rolled over to reconnect with a line of vertebrae. "Guess not."

"We should make our way back to the van." Digby shook his head at his minion. "I suppose we got what we came all the way out here for."

"You don't have to tell me twice." Alex headed out the front door of the structure. Rebecca followed.

Tavern dragged themself past Digby, still sizzling from the purified wine that they had dumped over their skeletal body. A few ribs were missing, and it looked like a bone or two had been put back in the wrong place.

"That one is going to be a handful, I fear." He glanced at Asher as she perched on his shoulder. "Probably keep an eye on them."

Without question, the raven took flight. She landed atop the skeleton's skull a moment later. It seemed since becoming a zombie master, she had begun to understand her existence a bit more.

Digby held up the diamond that served as Tavern's vessel to the morning sun. Then he pocketed it and headed down to join the others. It wasn't long before they were on their way back home.

To save space in the van, Digby recalled his infernal spirit to its diamond. It didn't make sense to keep the skeleton active when it wasn't needed. Plus, the spirit's constant requests for more wine were annoying. It wasn't like he could just let the infernal thing pour alcohol all over the interior of the van.

With a pile of bones sitting about, Digby gathered them up and placed them within a plastic garbage sack. Afterward, he tossed the sack into his void to see if it would affect his resources. He arched his eyebrow when it didn't. The thin layer of material surrounding the bones must have been in the way.

Interesting.

Thinking about it further, the bones probably wouldn't count anyway, considering they had been dead since the previous afternoon and might have been too old. He opened his maw on the floor and practiced calling forth the garbage sack, getting close to the point where he could bring it up consistently. He smiled, realizing that he could store the skeleton within his necrotic bag of holding indefinitely, so it would be available when he needed it.

That will certainly make bringing out my new, somewhat annoying minion a bit more convenient. He let the sack sink back down and closed his maw just as Rebecca shouted from the passenger seat.

"Stop!"

Digby fell forward as Alex slammed on the brakes, throwing him into the space between the two front seats as the van skidded to a stop. He sprang back up. "What is it? Light-walkers?"

"No." The illusionist flicked her eyes around the road. "Pull over up there." She pointed to a shady spot underneath some trees. "I have to check something."

Alex did as she asked, watching as she hopped out of the vehicle before it even came to a complete stop.

"What's wrong?" Digby climbed out behind her. "Is it Skyline?"

"Maybe." She focused on a space in front of her as an orb of light formed, only to disperse into the air all around them. She spun around a moment later, as if looking at something on the ground around her feet. "I mapped this area a few minutes ago and was looking over it as we drove. I saw a kestrel flying real low nearby." She swiped her hands around as if manipulating something that only she could see. "I just need to find it again."

"For the love of..." Digby threw out his hands. "None of us can see this map of yours."

Rebecca snapped her eyes back to him. "Good point."

Digby watched as she threw her arms out beside her, casting Waking Dream. With that, a map of the surrounding area flooded the ground around her feet. He found himself standing knee deep in a mountain.

"Help me search." She walked through the display. "My cartography spell creates a topographical snapshot of the area, so the kestrel I saw was only there when I last mapped it. I recast the spell to update the image just now." Rebecca pointed to a spot in the air above some trees. "It was right there when I noticed it, so I just want to make sure it's left the area before we risk traveling. We're lucky it wasn't close to where we were last night when you set off all those flare spells." She froze for a second, before adding, "Holy crap, we could have blown everything right there if we'd been noticed."

Digby tensed as he swept his eyes over the illusionary landscape, seeing nothing but forest and the coast line. The closest city was still a way off, and he sure as hell didn't want to travel in the open with one of Skyline's squads flying about. That was when he spotted it.

"Here." He stabbed a claw down into a clearing in the trees. The kestrel was, indeed, still in the area. Not only that, it had landed.

Rebecca spun to face the tree line. "That's not far from here."

"We should go after them." Alex started walking.

"What?" Digby blinked, having trouble processing the boy's suggestion. "What the hell would we do that for?"

"You saw what we were able to do back at the cemetery." His apprentice turned around, bringing up the whole argument again. "I think we can take them. And that would be one less squad for Skyline to use against us."

"We can't just…" Digby trailed off, realizing that with the progress they had made so far, that the boy might actually be partially right. They still couldn't go after Skyline as a whole, but at most, there was only one squad in the kestrel, and getting their hands on a new airship would certainly make travel faster. Its camouflage ability would help as well. If they'd had something like that the night before they could have simply left the cemetery when they were finished with the ritual rather than sticking around until dawn. "Alright, forget what I just said." Digby started for the tree line. "Let's go."

"Wait, what?" Alex's face dropped, clearly expecting more of an argument.

"Yeah, what?" Rebecca chased after him. "What about keeping our heads down?"

"That would be ideal, but that airship they've got would be quite the prize." Digby kept walking. "The way I see it, we can case the scene and analyze whatever opposition we find before making a move. We just have to make sure no one escapes to tell of our survival."

"This is a bad idea." Rebecca let out a frustrated growl as he made it clear that he was not turning back.

"Probably." Digby chuckled as he pushed through the brush in the direction of the clearing. It wasn't long before the sound of shouting reached his ears. He ducked down, holding his claws out to stop Alex from getting too close.

Glancing at the boy, he couldn't help but question whether or not his apprentice would actually be able to fight now that his opponent was human. He still remembered the first time he had been forced to kill a man back in Seattle. At the time, he'd leaned on his undead hunger and instincts to reconcile that act with his moral compass. Alex, however, wouldn't be able to do the same. In the end, there was only one way to find out.

Taking up a position next to him, Rebecca moved mana through her body to cast Conceal. Clearly she wasn't taking any chances.

Together, they crept closer, the kestrel coming into view. A group of seven seemingly random people stood outside shouting at a pair of Skyline's guardians. Digby couldn't quite make out what was being said but it seemed like they were angry about being brought there. He snuck a little closer, putting his trust in Rebecca's concealment spell as he pushed through the brush into the clearing.

"How do you expect us to survive out here? We have no supplies and we'll never find shelter in time to make it through the night!" A man of around twenty threw his arms out at his sides, facing the back of the kestrel as if yelling at someone inside.

"Those must be people that didn't want to go along what-ever this Autem Empire thing that Skyline is pushing." Rebecca knelt by Digby's side. "The ones that Lana said were getting kicked out."

"They're being exiled." Digby growled his words, irritated by what he was witnessing. He swept his gaze across the scene, analyzing Skyline's men. There were three mages, two fighters, and something called a pyromancer. Most were low level, except for the pyromancer, who was level twenty. "We'll have to take that one by surprise."

Digby turned to his apprentice. "Alright, here's the plan—"

His words were cut off when the pyromancer launched a fireball without warning. The spell exploded against the chest of the man that was yelling at them. The guardian must have ranked up the spell because it engulfed the poor soul immediately. The flames even leapt to the clothes of the people standing beside him. Skyline's men acted in sync, each turning various spells on the unarmed group of people in an instant.

Alex stood, letting out an unintelligible cry as he struggled to get his machete out, clearly forgetting that he could have just fired an arrow from his bow. The entire group of enemies turned to face him as he disrupted Rebecca's concealment spell.

"Damn it." Digby leapt forward, opening his maw beneath the level twenty pyromancer. With a push of mana, he increased the size of the gateway. Confusion consumed the man as he fell into the black sludge. Digby closed the portal to his void before his victim had a chance to escape, cutting him in half. He ignored the level up message that followed and turned on the rest of the group as he dropped his extra point into intelligence.

Alex got himself together and enchanted his machete as he raised it above his head. The artificer brought the weapon down on one of the low-level mages, cleaving through their shoulder with a blade glowing like molten rock. Watching the men execute seven unarmed people must have given the boy the push he needed. It seemed he'd found the resolve to raise a weapon against another.

Digby shoved one of the other low levels to the side, leaving them for Rebecca to finish off with an Icicle as he charged the remaining three. He slammed his bone claws into the throat of the first and cast a couple of Burial spells to drop the remaining two into the earth. More experience came in.

"What the fuck was that?" Rebecca shouted at Alex.

"Why did they kill them all?" The boy's voice trembled as

he backed away from the man he'd killed, nearly tripping over another corpse in the process.

"They don't leave witnesses." Rebecca pointed to a pile of corpses near the tree line on the other side of the clearing. Each body was in various stages of decomposition, as if new corpses had been added every few days. "They must not let anyone they exile live."

"That's monstrous. Abandoning people out here in the open is already a death sentence, there's no need to go so far as executing them." Digby was shocked, though, he also wasn't surprised.

"They're protecting their secrecy." Rebecca lowered her head as if it should have been obvious. "Think about it. If they just let people go after showing them what kind of empire they're building, then that news would spread eventually. That could jeopardize things, especially this early in their plan when they need willing recruits. But if they execute everyone that doesn't fall in line, then they keep what they're doing secret. The only reason we know any of it is because we have a couple people on the inside."

"That settles it." Alex slammed a hand into the side of the kestrel. "We can't let Skyline do this. We have to—"

"Stop them?" Digby flicked his eyes to the boy as he, yet again, repeated the question he knew Alex didn't want to hear. "How?"

His apprentice answered by throwing his hands out to his sides at the bodies of Skyline's guardians. "Did you just see how fast we won?"

"Yes, I did, I was there." Digby rolled his eyes. "But most of these men here were low-level and I was able to take the main threat by surprise."

"That's why we need to take action now." Alex raised his voice. "I've already told you, if we give them enough time, then all these easy low levels are gonna get stronger. And you said it yourself. With Asher, you can control a horde the size of the one at the castle."

Digby hesitated, having trouble finding a valid reason to refute the boy's claim. After a few seconds of silence, he doubled down on the need to defend their home. "It's true that, with Asher, I may be able to control a horde, but that is to protect our people and the castle they reside in, not to go to war with Henwick's empire. How could I possibly do something like that when I haven't even dealt with the threat that's already inside our walls?" Digby stepped over a corpse.

"And what threat is that, Rufus?" Alex scoffed.

"Of course that decrepit monster is a threat." Digby scoffed back louder. "You know as well as I do how many people he's killed. There is no way Rufus is actually what he seems. And the fact that none of you seem to be willing to admit it speaks volumes. You all turn a blind eye, because keeping him around is convenient."

"That's bull and you know it." The boy clenched his fist. "You're just jealous that people like him more than you."

"What?" Digby shrieked. "What did you just say?"

"You heard me." The artificer stormed off a few steps only to spin back around. "Look, I joined up with you because I was a nobody. I was just a random guy with no future, practically ready to kill myself instead of facing what the world had become. Then, in walked you, the magic zombie telling me I could be more." He gave a mirthless laugh. "How can I be more if all we do is hide in one place or another?"

"We aren't hiding." Digby thrust a claw in his direction. "We're being careful and carving out a place for ourselves in this world."

"You keep saying that, but it's the same thing."

Digby flinched at the accusation, feeling a bit of truth in it before brushing it aside and attacking back to deflect the boy's words. "I don't expect someone who has lived in luxury for most of their life to understand. Honestly, you could barely even raise a weapon when I picked you up. You only think you can fight now because you've let this power go to your head and cloud your judgment. What makes you think you can handle a war?"

Alex lowered his head. "I won't pretend that I can handle it. But that doesn't mean I won't try." He raised back up with a sympathetic look in his eyes. "I know you're scared; I am scared too. But if we don't fight, then who will? All I'm asking for you to do is at least try to help the people of this world before it's too late."

"And all I'm asking of you is to get your priorities straight." Digby narrowed his eyes, continuing his offensive as his apprentice hit the nail on the head. Alex was right, he was scared. Terrified, even. He wasn't a warrior or general. Going to war just wasn't what he was made for. Not only that, but he was sure to get anyone that followed him killed in the process. Why couldn't he get anyone to understand that. "I'm sorry to put a pin in your newfound desire for war, but we have a castle full of people that are counting on us, and it may be only a matter of time before Rufus shows his true colors and devourers them all."

"Again with Rufus." Alex groaned and shook his head.

"Yes, again," Digby growled back. "And why are you even defending him?"

"Because you're being petty." Alex snatched up his machete and stomped off only to turn back for a moment. "And I'm pretty sure you know it too."

Digby shook his head, refusing to accept the boy's words before going after him. A hand on his shoulder stopped him.

"Just let him go." Rebecca glanced at Alex, then back to Digby. "He's just frustrated and a little naive. So don't feel too bad."

"I don't need your pity." He shrugged her hand off his shoulder.

"Fine, be that way." She stomped her way into the kestrel to remove it from Skyline's system.

"I will be that way, thank you very much." He turned back to the bodies littering the ground. "I have corpses to eat anyway."

Asher offered a sympathetic caw as she hopped around the

ground near the bodies, making it clear that she understood how he felt.

Digby swatted her away, letting his anger get the better of him. "I don't need your pity either."

He immediately felt bad for taking his frustration out on his pet as she flapped away to perch in a nearby tree. A moment of pain echoed over their bond. Digby let out a sigh as he placed his right foot against the left of one of the corpses to see if it was the right size.

"That will have to do."

———————◆•————————

Charles Bancroft sat in his private office tapping a gold pen against the surface of an opulent, mahogany desk. He'd been hiding there for the last hour while some representatives of Autem toured his section of the base.

There had been far too many changes of late.

He hadn't signed on with Henwick back in the nineteen-thirties to be a lapdog to some kind of theocratic empire. No, at the time, all he cared about had been business and whatever grew his investments. Obviously, he'd been aware that Henwick and his organization had its own plans, but he had stood to profit so much by serving them that it wasn't difficult to ignore a few questionable actions here and there. He never expected them to go so far as to bring about the end of the world.

Then again, he had come through on top, so it wasn't all bad.

For now, he was Skyline's commander, and he was sure to be taken care of when Autem no longer needed the mercenary force, so his position wasn't exactly anything to sneeze at. Granted, he didn't like the idea of throwing away the private military that he had spent so long building. After all, war was a business, and in the world he used to know, business was good.

Unfortunately, that world didn't exist anymore. There were no more wars to buy or sell.

Bancroft leaned back and sighed as a link spell took over the floor to ceiling mirror that hung on one wall. The image of a collection of severed limbs and other assorted body parts filled its reflective surface.

"Jesus!" Bancroft nearly fell from his chair.

"Not quite." The image shifted as if someone was moving the mirror that was connected to the other side of the link. The view tilted away from the gore before being placed at an angle facing up, like it was leaning back on something. Henwick was in the frame, wearing a rubber apron and a pair of heavy gloves that went halfway up his arms. "Sorry, the mirror fell over."

"Ah yes, that makes sense." Bancroft stood up to appear as professional as possible, just like he always did. He did his best to forget the image he had seen a second before. "What can I do for you?"

At first Henwick said nothing, opting to go about with what he was doing. He moved out of frame so only his shoulder was visible, as if reaching into a bin below the mirror he was using. Pulling back up, he retrieved a severed forearm. The limb brushed against the mirror at the other end of the link, leaving a crimson smear across the image. The skin of the arm was pale, likely from a revenant. Henwick simply tossed it behind him. It landed with a sickening squelch a couple seconds later, as if falling into a pit of some kind. A hungry moan drifted up from below the view. Probably one of the pet zombies that had been sent up to be experimented on.

After throwing another limb behind him, Henwick finally spoke. "For starters, you can tell me what is going on right in your backyard, and how I am just now receiving reports that magic was used to destroy a hotel there."

Bancroft hesitated before answering, distracted by the casual manner in which Henwick handled the remains of creatures that had once been human. It shouldn't have surprised him; the man was centuries old. It would have taken more than a little gore to faze him. It was starting to become obvious that Henwick's decision to contact him while feeding his pets was intentional. He must have been angry about being left out of the loop.

Henwick tossed another body part down. "Well? Out with it. I didn't bail you out of that mess you made back in the thirties to have you keeping things from me."

"My apologies." Bancroft inclined his head. Henwick was right, he had been hiding things. Not for any real reason. He just found it unprofessional to report anything before it hadn't been dealt with already. "I have increased patrols in the area to investigate the cause. I intended to let you know once I had found something concrete."

"Good then." Henwick tossed another limb to whatever he was feeding and pushed the bin of body parts forward as if moving to feed a different zombie. "I suggest doubling your patrols again. We can't have any rogue magic users out there. I don't want another mess like what happened in Seattle." He threw a bloody foot behind him, this time getting a loud snarl from out of frame before moving on to his next specimen.

"Of course." Bancroft ignored the grotesque procedure and reached for the phone on his desk to show he was taking action. It rang before he could pick it up. His eyes darted to the receiver, glancing back up to Henwick's image in the mirror.

"Aren't you going to answer that?" The man arched an eyebrow as he picked up a human heart, holding it so that it was clearly visible.

Bancroft's forehead started to sweat as he raised the phone to his ear. "Hello?"

The voice of one of his communication operators reported in. "Sir, we've lost contact with one of our teams while they were dropping off some undesirables."

"What's that now?" Henwick leaned forward as if he'd somehow been able to hear the call as well, despite being on the other end of the Mirror Link. Bancroft wasn't surprised. The man's senses had always been sharper than average.

"I assure you, I will do everything in my power to investigate the situation."

"You do that." Henwick tossed the heart down to another monster, this time without getting a moan or snarl in return. A disappointed expression fell across the man's face.

Bancroft opened his mouth to speak, but Henwick held up a finger to stop him.

"Hang on one second." Henwick leaned away from the frame. "Excuse me, Mr. Howland, but is that anyway to show appreciation for a meal?"

A raspy voice answered back from out of frame. "Thank you."

"That's better, Clint." Henwick reached into his bin and retrieved what looked like a human brain. "A little manners will get you a long way."

Bancroft tensed, remembering the name of one of his men that he had sent to Henwick to be debriefed just after Seattle. He had suspected his fate, but wasn't sure until now. It was cruel.

"Anyway, where were we?" Henwick returned his attention to Bancroft.

"Ah, yes." He shook off his concerns. "I will report back when I know more."

"Good." Henwick reached for another heart before adding, "Show no mercy to whoever you find."

CHAPTER THIRTY

Digby sat in the back of the van with his arms folded tight across his chest as he impatiently tapped his new left foot on the wall. Having found an extremity that hadn't yet been tainted by the curse, he'd finally gotten something to remain attached.

The new body part felt off, probably due to it being a slightly smaller size. Though, it was better than the peg-leg that he'd hobbled around on for the last two weeks. At the very least, it was a close enough fit to give back the agility he'd lost when Skyline's knight had lopped his foot off back in Seattle.

Digby growled to himself.

Even after solving the issue of his missing foot, he couldn't relax. Not after the way his apprentice had spoken to him. Despite his irritation, he left Alex alone. The artificer remained quiet as he drove. A rifle, that they'd taken off one of the guardians they'd killed, leaned against the back of his seat.

As for the kestrel they'd stolen, it was currently flying low along the road a half mile ahead of the van. Rebecca operated it from her place in the passenger seat next to Alex. Obviously, they could have just abandoned the van and taken the kestrel back to the castle, but their vehicle had been through a lot with them so far. Besides, it was still a functioning mode of transportation, so it would have been a waste to leave it behind.

A set of six gold rings sat in a row on the floor of the van. They had belonged to the six guardians they had just killed. After checking each for extractable spells, Digby had found a few options. From the three mage rings, each taught the spell Regeneration, as well as one other elemental spell. Two held Rebecca's Icicle spell while the other one held the Terra Burst that Digby had used to learn Burial back in Seattle. The pyromancer's ring held Regeneration as well, with the addition of Fireball. Apparently, the advanced specialization had its roots in the mage class. From the two fighters, they could learn Barrier and Kinetic Impact.

Digby reached forward and claimed one of the mage rings. He wrapped his fingers around it and chose to extract Icicle. There was a chance it would evolve into something useful, plus it was the only low-level mage spell that he didn't have already. He would have to experiment with it later once he was out of the van. Taking one of the fighter's rings to gain the Kinetic Impact spell would have made sense, but he opted to leave both rings for the others. The Barrier spell would do them both good. At least there was less of a chance of them getting themselves killed. Especially Alex with his suicidal impulse to pick a fight with Skyline.

Digby swept up the remaining five rings and passed them up to Rebecca to pick what she wanted. A moment later two rings crumbled to the floor, giving her Barrier and Fireball. Alex took the rest and shoved them in his pocket, as if he didn't want to learn anything new while he was still mad. Digby shook his head at the boy and leaned back just as Rebecca spoke up.

"We shouldn't leave the kestrel anywhere out in the open. I've pulled it from their system so they can't track it, but once Skyline realizes it's missing, they will be looking for it. I can't keep its camouflage active all the time, and one of Skyline's satellites is bound to spot it if we land it near the castle." Rebecca leaned back over her seat to show Digby a map.

"There's a small airfield here, about fifty miles from the castle. It's a little out of the way, but if we can secure it and get the hangar open, we can store the kestrel there for the time being."

"That's a little inconvenient." Digby groaned.

"True, but it's better than having it spotted and bringing all of Skyline down on us."

"We should be careful who we tell about it as well," Digby added. "Maybe keep it to Mason and the other soldiers. I don't want everyone at the castle knowing we have a fully armed aircraft until we need it."

"More like you just don't want Rufus knowing," Alex grumbled from the driver's seat.

"Do you have something to say, boy?" Digby leaned forward.

"No, I already said everything I needed to," Alex snapped back.

"Will you two stop?" Rebecca growled at them both. "And yeah, I agree with keeping the kestrel a secret for now. The castle might attract unwanted attention as it is, considering the place is clearly inhabited. I don't think Skyline will go out of its way to attack as long as no one there rocks the boat or poses a threat. But if they are sending out squads to recruit survivors for this empire of theirs, then it's only a matter of time before someone stops by to see who wants to join up. So we need to make sure everyone there keeps their mouths shut about us when that happens, and the less they know the better."

"Indeed." Digby nodded, appreciating that someone was on his side.

The rest of the trip was passed in awkward silence. Digby didn't even watch a movie, still too angry to focus on anything. An hour later, a quiet, grassy field greeted them as they pulled up to the airfield.

Rebecca hadn't been exaggerating when she said the place was small. A building with a large door on the front sat at one end, along with a smaller structure beside it. That smaller building seemed to have been used for administrative purposes.

A narrow stretch of paved ground extended across the area. Three empty cars were parked haphazardly off to one side.

Asher took flight as soon as Digby opened the rear door of the van, heading for the roof of the hangar. He deflated. Apparently, the raven was still mad at him for swatting her away. Digby sent a thought across their bond, trying to express a feeling of remorse. Asher didn't respond. He let out a breathless sigh and made his way toward the building without her.

Alex followed behind with his rifle at the ready. At least he was dedicated to helping to secure the area despite his recent attitude. Digby brought a hand to his head to keep the wind from blowing his hair around as the kestrel descended to hover over the landing strip. The sound of the aircraft's rotors echoed off the surrounding trees as Rebecca brought it down to the pavement.

Digby pushed the door of the large building open, finding two zombies inside. He cast control without hesitation, glad that they weren't revenants.

"Looks like the place is empty." Digby stood with his arms folded.

"Someone must have been through already and taken the plane that was here." Rebecca entered behind him.

"Probably the same people that left those three cars out there." Alex gestured back at the landing strip outside.

Rebecca made her way across the empty building to some sort of pump system. "Looks like they took most of the fuel too."

"That's unhelpful." Digby frowned.

"There's still enough for a while." She glanced back at the kestrel outside. "That thing's got a hybrid engine so we should be able to stretch what's left quite a way, and it won't be hard to find more."

Looking through the space, Digby found a note stuck to the wall in a way that made it stand out like someone wanted it found. He pulled it down and read it aloud.

. . .

I'm sorry.

We waited as long as we could but had to leave. If you both can find another plane, we're trying for the north. There's a place in Vancouver. I marked it on the map. If you make it, we'll be there.

-Chris

Digby dropped the note to the floor where a map lay. He glanced back at the two zombies he'd taken under his control. "Looks like you two didn't make it."

Alex looked at the pair and sighed.

"We should leave the zombies in the hangar and lock them in." Rebecca started up the kestrel again to move it inside. "That way they might keep people away from our stuff."

"Good thinking." Digby stepped out of the way of the airship as it drifted into the building.

"Are we going to have enough time to make it back to the castle?" Alex looked up to the sky outside.

They had gotten a late start that morning on account of the two heretics' poison status disrupting their sleep. Not to mention, taking over the kestrel's systems back in the forest clearing where they'd dealt with Skyline's squad had taken Rebecca a fair amount of time. Now, the sun was beginning to head for the horizon.

Rebecca checked the time. "It's tight but we should have just enough time to make it. Provided nothing trips us up on the roads on the way there."

"We may not want to take that risk." Digby flicked his eyes up to the sky, noting that a blanket of dark clouds seemed to be rolling in. "We don't want to get caught out there in the rain and cut off from the sun. Also, this place seems secluded enough to spend the night without much issue."

"True." Rebecca set the kestrel down and shut off its engines. "If something does happen, we could just take the kestrel up in the air where it's safe. Plus, I'm freaking exhausted.

Spending the whole night poisoned does not make for a restful sleep."

"Same." Alex nodded. "I'm going to go check out the office building. There should be a couch or something in there."

"I'll send Mason a message to let him know we won't be back tonight." Rebecca yawned.

With that, both of Digby's human accomplices headed out to find somewhere to sleep for the night. Leaving the entrance of the hangar open a foot, he refreshed his control spells and called Tavern forth from his maw. The skeleton tore its way from the plastic sack their bones had been stored in and rose from the small black puddle like a serpent before assembling into a more humanoid form. Digby looked over his HUD.

COVEN
DIGBY: MP: 211/211
ALEX: MP: 245/245
REBECCA: MP: 276/276
ASHER: MP: 86/86

MINIONS: 2 Common Zombies, 1 Skeleton.

Digby sent his followers out to guard the building as he closed the hangar doors the rest of the way. He settled in, laying on the open ramp of the kestrel and attempting to cast the Icicle spell he'd extracted from the mage's ring. With a little luck, he might get a decent attack spell. A few attempts and several warning messages about his mana balance later, he groaned.

The spell, Icicle, has evolved into Frost Touch.
FROST TOUCH
Description: Freeze anything you touch.
Rank: D
Cost: 10MP
Range: Touch

Limitations: Not suitable for offense at low ranks.

"Yet another useless spell." Digby blew out a needless sigh. "I hope Alex gets something better from at least one of the rings he pocketed."

Bringing up his apprentice's spells, he arched an eyebrow at the presence of three new entries. Terra Burst, Icicle, and Barrier. Apparently, he had forgone Regeneration and taken each of the more combat-focused spells available. Digby couldn't say he agreed with the choice. He would have liked the boy to have a stronger heal than the added effect of his Purify Water spell. It seemed the idiot was committing to getting himself killed.

Digby spent the next hour practicing his meditation. It had proved useful the night before, making his mastery of the ability a priority. As Digby lay on his back on the ramp with his eyes closed, he thought about his argument with Alex. The boy's words had cut deep, mostly because they were true. The conversation seemed like the perfect event to dwell on to force his mind to shut down.

That was when a loud creak came from the roof above.

"What the devil was that?" Digby cracked one eye open as the creaking traveled from one side of the building to the other. It sounded like an elephant climbing across the roof.

Then came the screech.

"How?"

Panic surged through Digby's mind. Whatever had been crying out in the distance the night before had followed him. He pushed himself up off the kestrel's ramp just as a message streaked across his vision.

Common Zombie, lost.

"What!"

A second later, he lost the other one.

"Tavern!" Digby scrambled across the building toward the

entrance. "What the bloody hell is happening out there?" Yanking the hangar door open, he came face to skull with his skeletal minion.

Tavern thrust a bony hand upward, pointing to the sky. "Yo, there's something on the—"

The skeleton's words were cut off as an enormous pale hand reached down from above to wrap its clawed fingers around Tavern's skull. His minion's head was crushed to powder in an instant, sending the spirit flowing back into the diamond in Digby's pocket.

He looked up, his eyes bulging in horror as the massive jaws of an oversized revenant looked down on him. Charred skin covered half of its face, leaving one eye missing like it had been damaged and hadn't regenerated properly. The tattered rags of a military uniform hung from the creature's shoulders.

Active Revenant Bloodstalker, Rare, Hostile.

"Tanner!" Digby leapt backward, falling on his rear as the creature dropped from the roof, twisting its body to orient itself as landed. One question surged through his mind.

How?

Standing still for a moment, the revenant raised its bat-like snout in the air and breathed in as if confirming something. Digby could feel mana moving through the creature's blood, clearly using some sort of perception ability. It was probably how it had tracked Mason over the last couple weeks.

Tanner snapped his eyes back to Digby and let out a roar.

The beast didn't care about Mason anymore. No, Tanner had its sights locked on someone else now. Digby had wounded him, after all. Somehow the revenant must have followed him all over California.

Without hesitation, Digby cast Emerald Flare.

Sickly green energy swam through the air to converge on the beast. Tanner leapt forward into the hangar just as the spell detonated behind him, succeeding at nothing more than shredding one side of the door and damaging the other while irradiating the area.

Tanner didn't seem to care about the poison effect, as if he had simply built up a greater resistance. Digby's mind raced. *Surely it had been my radiation that had kept the beast at bay the night before. Right?* His train of thought was interrupted as a claw swiped by his head.

"Gah!" He dove toward the kestrel, hoping to slip underneath to the other side. Digby let out a surprised, "Hurk!" when a firm hand curled around his new foot. He was immediately yanked backward, his clawed gauntlet scraping against the floor.

Then all at once, every bone below his knee was crushed.

Tanner whipped him across the room. His shoulder hit the floor, shattering several more bones before the oversized revenant launched him through the air. Jagged metal tore through Digby's side as he slammed into the half-destroyed door of the hangar. His body skipped along the landing strip outside, coming to a stop in a broken heap.

Digby cast Necrotic Regeneration as he struggled to roll over. His damaged limbs fought him every step of the way, even as they began to snap back into place. Everything had happened so fast. He simply hadn't had time to put up a defense.

Tanner let out a victory roar as his massive form slipped out through the damaged door.

"Holy shit!" Alex stumbled out of the small building that served as the airfield's office. He raised his rifle and fired a torrent of enchanted bullets at the creature. Tanner's flesh shredded under the mana infused assault only to immediately heal, causing Alex to throw the weapon aside. Without wasting time, he cast Icicle, layering Enchant Weapon onto the shard of ice that formed in the air before sending it straight in Tanner's direction. The projectile hit Tanner in the thigh with a solid thunk, piercing his thick hide and causing the revenant's flesh to bubble and pop. Before the spell was able to detonate, Tanner snatched the icicle out of his leg and tossed it aside. The enchanted shard of frozen moisture exploded in the field behind him in a blast of dirt and grass.

"Shit." Rebecca rushed out behind him. "How did Tanner find us?"

"Who cares? We have to get to the airship." Digby growled as he shoved himself up from the pavement, his ankle snapping around to face the right direction again. He started back toward Tanner and opened his maw to cast Forge. A black spike erupted from the ground, shattering against the creature's side. He cast another and another, breaking through the revenant's thick hide on the third. He glanced back to the other heretics. "I'll keep him busy. Use the opening to get past him and start up the kestrel!"

He looked back to Tanner, expecting the beast to still be struggling with the spikes of blood he'd forged. He wasn't. Instead, a massive hand closed around both of his legs.

"The hell?" Digby froze in shock as another hand grabbed his chest.

Then, Tanner pulled.

"My pants!" He squealed as the pair of ordinary jeans that he'd been wearing flew through the air. Digby cringed in embarrassment as he looked down, expecting to find his bare nethers on display to the world.

Then he screamed. It was so much worse.

Blackened entrails hung from his abdomen where his legs should have been. He snapped his head to his pants as they slammed into the side of the van with a horrid squelch. Necrotic blood splattered across the vehicle. Tanner threw him next, launching him into the grass. His severed torso tumbled to a stop against the van's tire.

"Help!" he cried out in panic, as he tried to shove his entrails back into his body. "Oh god, help!"

That was when a shower of over a hundred icicles pummeled the enormous revenant. The attack continued, holding Tanner at bay while Alex and Rebecca ran to him.

Shards of frozen water stabbed into the ground all around the creature, with one or two shattering against his body. Digby stared, awestruck by the spell. How Rebecca had gained that much power was impossible.

"I can't keep that up for long." She looked down at him, horror evident on her face. "Eventually that thing is going to realize most of those icicles aren't real."

If Digby had been in a more stable state of mind, he would have been impressed. Instead, all he could do was shout at the creature and cast flare until he was out of mana. Tanner simply jumped out of the way each time before the spell could detonate. Alex slipped an arm under his and hefted his partial form up from the ground. His apprentice shoved him into the back of the van a second later. Digby's legs flew in next, his ass landing beside him. Rebecca climbed into the driver's seat and started the engine, unable to make it past Tanner to reach the kestrel.

"Wait!" Digby propped himself up with his hands, his eyes darting around the inside of the van. "Where's Asher?"

"I don't know!" Rebecca shouted back as she pressed the pedal to the floor.

"No! We can't leave her." Digby flung himself to the back of the van, clawing himself toward the open door. "Asher!"

Tanner gave chase, kicking up dirt as he barreled after them on all fours.

"Asher!" Digby cried out in desperation, nearly falling from the van as he reached out in search of his minion. "Asher!"

"Stop flailing." Alex dropped down beside him, grabbing the back of his shirt.

Digby called to his pet across their bond, clinging to hope until finally, a white speck streaked through the air. Asher weaved around Tanner, giving the creature a wide berth before darting to the van's open door to land beside him.

"Thank god." Digby reached out a hand only to pull it back a second later, afraid of being too forceful if his pet was still angry. She stared at his fingers for a long moment, then she hopped closer to settle back in at his side. He dropped his head to rest on the floor to look into her eyes. "I'm sorry I pushed you away."

Asher nodded in understanding.

Alex pulled the door shut as the van left Tanner behind.

Digby turned his attention to the other half of his body, reaching out with his clawed gauntlet to pull his legs toward him. Calming down now that they were away from Tanner, he stared up at his apprentice and gestured to his legs.

"Think you could lend me a hand?"

CHAPTER THIRTY-ONE

The drive back to the castle was tense. Rebecca sat hunched over the wheel as she drove through the night. Alex remained silent the entire way, as if praying that they wouldn't run into anything that they couldn't handle. They had let their recent victories go to their heads. Tanner's attack had been a wakeup call. Even with all their power, they could still be taken by surprise. They could still be outmatched.

Digby lay on the floor of the van casting yet another Necrotic Regeneration. The damage to his body had been severe. He'd needed help to realign both halves. His blood boiled in anger as he slowly regained sensation along with the ability to move his legs. Asher and Alex stayed by his side the entire time until, finally, he was able to sit up.

Rebecca blew out a relieved sigh as the castle came into view. "We made it."

Digby stretched his limbs to test their functionality and stepped up to the front of the van behind her to look at their home. He couldn't put a finger on it, but there was something off about the place.

"It's the middle of the night. Why are there so many lights still on?" Alex stared at the castle's grounds as they approached.

"I don't know." Digby narrowed his eyes. "But I don't like the looks of it."

Pulling up to the front, zombies could be seen at the tree line on either side of the road. They were much closer than usual. Digby shoved his way out of the van as it slowed to a stop. He straightened his ripped clothing and tried his best to look like he hadn't just been torn in half. Asher perched on his shoulder, letting out a concerned caw at the scene. Voices echoed across the lawn as they approached.

A dozen people stood looking worried by the entrance of one of the guest houses. The corpse of a zombie lay in the grass with a rough-looking short sword sticking out from its head.

"Was he bit?" Mason shouted as Sax carried a small form into the one of the guest houses.

"I don't know." Parker pushed through the crowd of exhausted people that had begun to gather.

Digby picked up his pace, racing up to the disturbance. "What happened?"

"We don't know." Mason turned back. "One of the zombies wandered up to the castle. We heard a scream and found Hawk struggling with it. Parker took the thing down, but the kid's hurt. He might have been bit."

"Has he started to turn?" Digby pushed his way into the guest house. He froze the moment he saw Hawk bleeding in Sax's arms.

The soldier shook his head. "I don't think so. It's the middle of the night and the curse usually works fast after dark. If he was bit, then I don't know how he's holding off the change."

Digby snapped his gaze back in the direction of the sun goddess statue. "The area effect that keeps away the revenants might be slowing the curse down to the speed it works at during the day. If he was bit, we have time, but he's not out of the woods yet." He glared back at some of the onlookers. "Clear out!"

"And someone get me some water." Alex pushed through the crowd.

Parker helped Sax lay Hawk down on a bed and stepped back. The boy clutched his arm with one hand as a trickle of blood ran through his fingers. He looked pale. For a moment, Digby feared the worst.

Then the child spoke. "'Bout time you lot showed up." His voice came out shaky but his continued use of that terrible accent made it clear there was still time.

"What the hell is the matter with you, child? Letting a zombie bite you like a fool." Digby scooted to the side to give Alex room.

"The bloody thing snuck up on me, it did," Hawk argued.

Digby rolled his eyes at the accent.

"Here, I brought water." Mason rushed in, thrusting a canteen into Alex's hands.

The artificer cast Purify Water without hesitation before pouring water into Hawk's mouth. The child perked up immediately and the color returned to his face. Rebecca took over to finish healing his wound and make sure there was nothing they missed.

"There, you're going to be fine." Digby relaxed. Then he tensed right back up. "Where the hell is Rufus?"

"I haven't seen him." Mason shook his head.

"I'll be back." Digby wasted no time, leaving Hawk in the care of his fellow heretics while he marched out of the guest house and made his way up to the castle. Some of the onlookers followed, including Mason, Parker, and Sax. James and Mathew rushed out of the building's main door to meet him.

"Where's Rufus?" Digby growled up at the two startled men.

"Right here." The elderly dead man climbed up from a stairway on the side that led down into the bowels of the castle. "Now, what is all the commotion about? I wasn't expecting you back until tomorrow, according to your message. Why did you risk traveling at night? And what happened to you?" Rufus gestured to Digby's torn and bloodied shirt.

"It doesn't matter why." He swept a hand through the air. "What matters is that we made it back in time."

"In time for what?" Rufus stumbled, clearly unaware of the situation that had happened under his watch.

"In time to stop a member of your horde from killing one of the people that you supposedly swore to protect." Digby stabbed a claw in the direction of the corpse on the lawn that had bitten the boy.

"What? Why was anyone out after curfew?" Rufus frowned at the body as if it had been Hawk's fault for being somewhere he shouldn't have been.

"It doesn't matter why!" Digby shouted, drawing the attention of everyone in earshot and causing more of the castle's inhabitants to step out into the night to see what was happening.

"I'd say it does." Rufus tapped his cane on the ground. "It's not safe to go wandering the castle grounds after curfew for exactly this reason. I've had to disperse the horde through the trees more than I normally would to keep them hidden from these aircrafts that you warned us about. Unfortunately, this has caused the horde to become a little disorganized with its leaders being spread so thin. It's not usually a problem, since I personally patrol the grounds frequently, but in the dark, it's possible that one stray might slip past me. So, yes, it is very important that everyone stay inside their rooms at night."

"That's all well and good, but there are children here." Digby raised his voice even louder. "You can't expect them to obey the rules all of the time without a full understanding of the situation."

"You're right." Rufus lowered his head.

"You can't just—" Digby shook his head. "Wait, I am?"

"Yes, I agree. I should have made it more clear to everyone why the rules are important." He raised his head back up. "But what's done is done, and what's important is that no one was seriously hurt."

"No one was seriously hurt, my deceased ass!" Digby threw up both arms. "Hawk almost turned. And he would have hurt others if he had. Everyone here could have been killed, had I not arrived when I did. A simple apology isn't going to make up for that. Not when you pushed back against teaching these people to protect themselves."

"I realize that you're angry right now, but there is still no reason to put anyone other than my horde in harm's way. As long as everyone follows the rules, I can keep everyone safe."

"Is that it? You protect these people as long as no one questions your authority." Digby glanced around at the people watching, catching a glimmer of concern in their eyes.

Several people gasped.

Digby grinned, realizing that the argument had brought out nearly everyone that had been staying within the castle's walls. It seemed that it was now or never. He glanced to a nearby statue where Asher perched. If Rufus decided to try anything, they would have to act fast to take over the horde outside before the ancient zombie had time to compel an attack.

Rufus's face fell. "What are you trying to say?"

"You heard me." Digby thrust a claw up at the decrepit zombie while throwing his other hand out toward the onlookers. "You just want to keep these people weak so they won't be able to defend themselves when you decide to spring whatever trap you're setting here."

"I beg your pardon?" Rufus raised his voice as well.

Digby gave a mirthless laugh. "So when do you intend on eating these people?"

"I would never—"

"You'd never, what?" Digby cut him off. "You'd never eat a human?"

Several people started to whisper to each other around them.

"Of course not." Rufus slammed the end of his cane down to the stone at his feet.

"Then how do you explain how you got to where you are today?" Digby turned to the crowd, no longer addressing the deceased liar. "Would anyone like to know how a common zombie becomes a zombie master?" He gave them a moment to properly stare at the elderly monster. "Well, let me fill you in then. It takes a steady diet of brains and hearts, and several dozens of them."

"Is that true?" a voice asked.

Digby searched the crowd, finding that it had come from Kate, who had eaten breakfast with Alex a few days earlier.

"Indeed it is." He suppressed the urge to laugh as he threw open Rufus's closet to set his skeletons free.

"What about you? How did you get the way you are then?" Kate stood on her toes to ask the question as the crowd shifted its gaze back to him.

"Obviously, I ate a lot of people," Digby answered without thinking. "But I, ah, didn't kill most of them." He tried to back-track. "And the ones I did kill were mercenaries working for Skyline who have murdered more than their fair share, believe you me. More importantly, I have never lied about it. Rufus, on the other hand, has kept his past hidden, and I am sure more than a few innocents fell to his jaws."

"If it wasn't for Rufus, we wouldn't be safe here," another voice shouted from the crowd.

"At what cost? Your freedom and ability to defend your-selves." He gestured to the area around him. "This world has changed, and if you all don't grow to meet it, then you won't survive. Rufus is not doing you any favors by keeping you weak. Even worse, you have no idea what he has planned for you. If he lied about eating people in the past, then that begs the ques-tion, what else is he lying about?"

A few voices called out in protest declaring their trust for the decrepit zombie.

"I don't believe it." Kate spoke up. "Rufus wouldn't eat anyone."

Digby opened his mouth to argue but was struck dumb when the old zombie behind him spoke up in his place.

"It's true."

The crowd gasped.

"Ah yes, and the truth shall set ye free." Digby thrust both hands out at the monster, unable to keep a triumphant tone out of his voice.

"Yes, it shall." Rufus walked forward to stand before the crowd. His body deflated with each step. "It is true what Digby says. My memories of when I first became the monster you see before you are still unclear to me, but I know enough to recognize the sins that I have committed. I was a common zombie, and yes, during that time, I had no control over my actions. I killed and hunted just like the rest of my kind." He lowered his head, wringing his hand around the top of his cane. "I became slightly more aware when I became a zombie leader and recalled a little of who I was, but I still couldn't resist the hunger. It wasn't until I became a zombie master that I understood the horrors that I'd committed."

"And yet, you hid your crimes anyway." Digby kicked him when he was down.

"I…" Rufus turned to James and Mathew who stood behind him. "I'm so sorry. I didn't mean to lie to either of you, or anyone else for that matter. I was just afraid that if I came clean, that you would be too afraid of me to let me help. After all of the people that I hurt, I just wanted to save as many humans as I could. That's why I have been so committed to protecting the people here. It will never make up for what I've done, but it is the best I can do to make amends. I understand if you all would rather I not live amongst you."

James and Mathew looked to each other, their expressions becoming sullen as their trust in the monster crumbled. It served the old fool right. Digby might have taken a bow if one of them hadn't spoken up first.

"We knew." James stepped forward.

"You what?" Digby snapped his attention back to them.

The man approached Rufus. "It wasn't a coincidence that you stumbled on us out there." He shook his head as his face softened. "You had actually attacked us hours earlier."

"I what?" Rufus's eyes bulged.

"You and your horde chased us and the group we were with into a building. Mathew and I escaped to the upper floors, but the rest of our group fell. The way I see it, one of the people you ate then must have raised your awareness up to where you are now."

Rufus staggered, as if unable to bear the weight of what he'd done. "Why didn't you kill me?"

"We would have. We even had you in our sights at one point." James nodded. "When your horde attacked our group, we were able to figure out that you were controlling them. So we hatched a poorly thought-out plan to take you out in the hope of disrupting the horde's unity. We snuck around the upper floors and got an angle on you from a balcony."

"Why didn't you shoot?" Rufus looked like he might cry if he'd had the working tear ducts to do so.

"Because the next thing we knew you stumbled away from the brain you were eating in horror." Mathew stepped forward to explain the rest. "After that, you cursed yourself and your horde while shouting every thought in your head in the process. It wasn't hard to understand your situation."

"That's right." James nodded. "Once we realized that you might not be the threat that you were, we began to understand what you were capable of. So no, we didn't shoot you. Killing you wouldn't bring back the people you ate. Being angry about it wouldn't either. It's like Digby said, this world has changed. With survival on the line, there isn't room for things like revenge."

"Especially considering all the good you could do," Mathew added.

"So yes, we knew everything." James spoke loud enough for everyone to hear. "And we forgive you."

"Indeed." Digby nodded for a second before shaking his head and adding, "Wait, what?"

James gestured to the castle around them. "Rufus, you couldn't have helped the things you've done, and you have done everything you can to make up for it since."

"But what if he decides to eat you all?" Digby threw out both his hands, realizing he was losing the crowd.

"He wouldn't, I'm sure of that." James gave Rufus a warm smile. "He's proven himself time and time again."

"What about the rest of you?" Digby spun to face the crowd.

"He's done right by us so far," Kate answered back, still standing on her toes to see.

"So you're just going to forget about the dozens of people he's killed?" Digby stomped one foot.

"Weren't you the one that unleashed this curse on the world in the first place?" someone else shouted from the back.

"That wasn't my fault." Digby placed a hand to his chest. "I was just as much a victim as anyone else."

"So was Rufus," James added.

"Thank you." The elderly zombie relaxed and bowed down to his friends. "Thank you all. I know I can never take back the things I've done, but I swear that I will always do everything in my power to keep you safe."

"I don't believe what I'm hearing." Digby growled to himself. The whole thing was too much.

Why can't anyone see the situation for what it is? Why can't they see how dangerous it is to let someone else do the fighting for them? Why don't they see that they need to be stronger?

After everything was said, it almost seemed like the people loved the decrepit zombie even more. Digby grimaced at the display as his boiling blood threatened to cook him from the inside out.

Fine, if they don't want to listen to reason, I don't have to stick around to watch when it inevitably falls apart. Digby stormed off to gather his things.

"Where are you going?" Rufus reached out to grab his arm as he passed by.

Digby yanked his elbow free.

"Anywhere but here."

CHAPTER THIRTY-TWO

"What the hell are you doing, Dig?" Rebecca folded her arms, leaning on the door to his suite in the castle as the necromancer threw his belongings into a pack.

"I'm leaving. It's clear that the people here won't listen to reason. And I'm not about to stick around to watch it bite them in the ass."

Rebecca shook her head at the zombie. "That's even more reason to stay."

"Nonsense." He tucked his tablet into his bag. "You and Alex will be able to handle things well enough without me."

She scoffed. "So you're ditching us too?"

"Indeed." Digby picked up his bag and headed for the door. "From what I can tell, you have both found a home for your-selves here. I, on the other hand, don't quite fit in. Besides, without you humans around, I will be able to move through this world unhindered. Aside from Tanner back at that airfield, the revenants have no interest in me."

"Oh, so now we just slow you down." Rebecca followed him down the stairs, trying not to take the necromancer's insults seri-ously. It was as if he was doing his best to drive her away.

"Of course you both slow me down." He stopped for a moment to look back at her, his eyes connecting with hers for an instant before looking away again. "Leading your kind through this apocalypse is the very definition of a liability. Practically everything I do is in service of keeping you lot breathing, lest you end up like me, or worse."

Rebecca rolled her eyes despite knowing that he was right. The fact that they had been with him for the last two weeks had certainly limited Digby's actions. It was true that leaving them behind would allow him to travel without worry. Then again, they had proved themselves capable multiple times already.

"What about you then?" She folded her arms as they entered the library. "Won't you get bored out there all by yourself?"

"Bah, I won't be alone. I'll have Asher and Tavern with me." He waved away the question.

Rebecca suppressed a laugh at the idea of Digby trying to make conversation with Tavern. It was more likely that the dude-bro skeleton would drive him insane.

"What about me then?" She stepped closer.

"What about you?" Digby shoved a couple books that clearly didn't belong to him into his bag.

"What if I don't want you to leave?" She surprised herself with the question as much as it did him.

"I think you'll be just fine." Digby stopped to steal one of the castle's shinier artifacts. "You have another zombie to keep out of trouble now. And as everyone here seems to believe, Rufus is much more altruistic than I."

He brushed off every other argument she had and stormed outside, only stopping at the van to collect the jewelry he looted the other day. Afterward, he simply beckoned to Asher and climbed into one of the other cars. The eight-hundred-year-old zombie turned the key sticking out of the ignition, clearly mimicking what he'd seen others do. Becca winced as he proceeded to grind the gears for several seconds. He didn't even say goodbye to Alex before stepping on the gas.

Of course, he'd always relied on others to drive and no one had actually taught him, so he immediately steered the vehicle off the side of the road into the grass. Rebecca cringed as he climbed out and slammed the door.

"I wanted to walk anyway." Digby kicked the car. "Not like I get tired."

A few moments of aggressive stomping later and he disappeared into the shadows.

"Good god, Dig. Why the hell are you like this?" Rebecca sighed, too tired after everything that had happened to chase after him. She glanced at her HUD to find his name hanging there along with hers and Alex's. "At least we'll know if he gets into any trouble."

She nodded to herself, figuring it was best to give him some time. He would probably calm down a little, and then she could project herself out to him to see if he was feeling more reasonable.

With Digby gone, there was nothing left to do but try to get some rest. After the previous night of radiation poisoning and being woken up by Tanner's attack after only a couple hours, she needed as much sleep as she could get. As it was, she was barely able to stay standing.

Rather than heading up to her room, Rebecca checked in on Hawk to make sure the kid was out of danger. She found Alex asleep in a chair outside the door. Taking a cue from him, she sat down on a sofa nearby and let her head hang back. She was asleep in seconds.

Then someone touched her leg.

"Fuck what?" Rebecca sat up with a start and rays of sunlight shined through a window. Her neck ached, but the scent of coffee seemed to calm the pain.

"Whoa there." Mason stood before her, holding two cups away from her as if he was worried she might knock them out of his hands. "You okay there? I would have let you sleep longer but you didn't look comfortable here drooling all over yourself."

"Oh shut up, I was not." Rebecca ran a hand across her

mouth, finding a streak of incriminating moisture. She didn't apologize, opting to reach for the cup of coffee instead. "Gimme."

"Where's Dig?" Mason sipped his cup. "I haven't seen him all morning. Figured he'd be off stewing somewhere after that display last night."

"Oh, he left." She drained the rest of her cup in practically one mouthful.

Mason blinked. "I'm sorry, what?"

She shrugged. "He threw a tantrum and stormed off into the night."

"Wha—what?" Alex raised his head from the back of his chair, looking like he'd slept just as poorly as she had. "Why would he leave?"

"I don't know." She blew out a sigh before continuing. "Probably embarrassed."

"Why did you let him leave?" Alex sprang up from his chair like he was going to chase after the necromancer.

"What was I going to do, Icicle him to the ground?" Rebecca dropped her cup down to an end table. "You know Dig, it doesn't take a surveillance specialist to know he doesn't like being alone, so I seriously doubt he's gone for good. He'll probably just show up in a couple days after he's blown off some steam and try to pretend like nothing happened."

"What if he doesn't?" Alex pleaded.

"Then I'll just cast Projection using him as a starting point. If we give him a little time to cool off then I'm sure I can convince him to come back."

"Where did he go?" Hawk stepped out of his room, rubbing sleep from his eyes. The hurt on his face was obvious.

"Ah." Rebecca froze, not knowing how to talk to the kid. "I didn't ask. But don't worry. I'm sure he'll come back." She stood up and made for the door to escape the conversation. Mason and Alex did the same, although they at least made a point to make sure Hawk was okay first.

The rest of the day went by like an exercise in frustration.

Everyone wanted to know where Digby was and when he was coming back. It seemed the consensus was clear; the necromancer had thoroughly embarrassed himself the night before, but the people hadn't condemned him for it. Actually, the majority wanted him back.

Parker even got to work on an item for him, she said she would make it extra special. The soldier had finally gotten her forge up and running and had even begun producing a few basic weapons while they were gone the last couple days. She hadn't created anything impressive, but Mason and Sax now carried some simple short swords that looked like something from Ancient Rome. For herself, Parker had created a pair of curved daggers with a studded handguard for what she referred to as face punching.

Alex spent the day experimenting with his Imbue spell, using each of the soldiers as donors to implant some of the meager mana that their ordinary bodies contained into their new weapons. By noon, he had added a permanent effect to both short swords similar to his Enchant Weapon spell, allowing them to cleave through enemies easier. Parker's daggers gained an even more impressive self-heal ability, that repaired her body by draining mana from anything she attacked. None of the effects compared to an actual spell, but they certainly helped.

Parker spent the afternoon testing out the ability by dragging Alex out to Rufus' horde and stabbing a bunch of zombies. The dead didn't seem to care as long as she didn't hit them in the head. Unfortunately, the healing effect of her daggers failed to activate, being unable to absorb any life essence from the dead. After giving up, Parker spent the rest of the afternoon napping in a sunny spot of the lawn. Mason and Sax didn't bother waking her, even when they retired to the castle to play pool.

Rebecca headed back up to her room, hoping to catch up on some sleep while avoiding any more questions about Digby. Unfortunately, no sooner than her head hit the pillow there was a knock at her door.

"What?" She sat up straight, letting out a small whimper at the interruption.

"Excuse me, Rebecca?"

"I'm coming." She recognized the raspy voice of Rufus through the door before he gave his name. Dragging her exhausted feet, she pulled the door open. "Hi Rufus."

"Hello." He lowered his eyes to the floor.

"What do you need?" Rebecca didn't mean to be short with him but she couldn't quite stop herself. She didn't share Digby's dislike for the zombie, but she'd be lying if she said that they guy didn't rub her the wrong way on some subjects.

"I was hoping to speak to you about Digby and, well, your place here with us." He clutched his cane in a sheepish manner. "I spoke to a few of your friends and from what they say, you believe Graves will return."

"I can't be sure, but I think it's likely." She leaned against the door rather than inviting the zombie in, still hoping their exchange might be short.

"If he doesn't, will you be remaining with us?" He looked up, seeming hopeful.

"For now, I intend to stay." She let out a breath debating on if she wanted to say more. "But I should probably mention that I do agree with Digby on some points. Not about your past, but the rest of his arguments deserve to be addressed."

"Yes, about that. I have been thinking about it as well, and after last night..." Rufus deflated. "Well, that boy nearly died, and it would have been my fault. I would have preferred that Digby not accuse me of things in front of the entire castle, but some of what he said does hold water. I still don't want anyone to put themselves in danger, but I'm starting to rethink my position of teaching them to defend themselves, and I would appreciate any help from you and your friends. I myself am not really suited for combat."

"Good, then I think we're on the same page. I'm sure Mason would be happy to lend a hand in training the people here to be more prepared." She reached for the door. "So if that's all, I really need to get some rest."

"Oh, of course." He started to step back into the hall before stopping short. He squinted for a second, before his eyes bulged. "What is that?"

Rebecca followed his line of sight over her shoulder to the window behind her. She took a step toward it, then she froze.

"Oh fuck."

Three objects approached. They were still just specs on the horizon, but she would have recognized the silhouettes anywhere.

"Kestrels."

CHAPTER THIRTY-THREE

Digby slammed the severed head of a dormant revenant down on the trunk of an abandoned car. He'd made it twenty-five miles from the castle during the night and early morning, eventually reaching a small town. One of the perks of being dead was that he didn't need sleep and never got tired of walking.

His blood still boiled at the way he had been treated the night before. All he'd tried to do was talk some sense into the fools that followed that withered old corpse, but in the end, none of it mattered. The only thing he'd succeeded at was making a fool of himself.

Digby let a frown bring him down.

And things were going so well.

The last two weeks had felt like a completely different life from his old life. He'd always been alone back then. Obviously, it was his fault, but still. It would've been nice to have even a couple people on his side. That was why he had been so dead set on finding a home for his friends. He just wanted a place to keep them safe. A place to buy time for them to grow strong enough so that he wouldn't have to worry about losing any of them. He'd even felt like he had been changing for the better. He'd felt like he'd been becoming a better person.

Not so much, I guess.

No, Digby was still the same abrasive man that no one wanted to keep around. It had just taken a little longer for everyone to see him for who he was. A little longer for him to let his frustrations send him over the edge. Even his apprentice was growing tired of his irrational need to push them away.

After that, how could he stay?

It was probably for the best that he gave up on finding a home. He would end up alone anyway. It only made sense to leave before things got worse. The only saving grace was that he no longer had anyone to slow him down.

"Bah." Who was he kidding? He didn't really care about being slowed down. He just couldn't stay. If he did, it would only be a matter of time before Alex and Mason convinced him to form some ill-fated rebellion against Henwick's ridiculous empire, for all the good that would do. He was sure to lead them all to their doom. Hell, as it was, just being around him was enough to put everyone in danger. He certainly hadn't forgotten about his biggest problem.

Tanner.

Being a bloodstalker, he assumed Tanner shared the Blood Sense trait that he had. If the revenant's perception was high enough, then he could probably sense the unique mana within Digby's body. Assuming that was true, it was only a matter of time before he tracked him down and came knocking.

He couldn't have stayed at the castle even if he'd wanted to. Not with that beast holding some form of grudge against him. Apparently, whatever had caused the creature to stalk Mason originally had been overshadowed when Digby had exploded half of his face back at the campground. With that, Tanner was sure to kill anyone that got between them, putting everyone back at the castle in danger.

Judging from how little Digby's radiation affected the creature, he feared that, in time, the sun goddess statue's protection would also fail to keep Tanner at bay. Though, that only raised the question, why didn't his radiation work? If his poison really was useless, why didn't Tanner attack at the mausoleum?

The answer was in the details.

Back when Digby had analyzed the creature at the campgrounds when they first encountered him, the Seed had labeled him as uncommon. However, last night, it had updated Tanner's description to rare, meaning that the beast may have mutated to gain some kind of resistance. If that was true, there was no way to know what else the creature could do.

In short, Digby was doomed. Tanner had defeated him decisively the night before. He understood that much. Leaving the castle may have been necessary, but out here in the open, he was a sitting duck.

Even worse, he was a lonely sitting duck.

Fortunately, he had a plan.

Well… sort of.

Digby had been caught off guard by the giant revenant the night before, so that just meant that he had to take a more proactive approach to the situation. Things would be different if he took some time to get prepared. Then all he had to do was flip the situation and remind Tanner that he wasn't the only predator out there.

Hence the severed heads.

With the sun still up, the revenants that inhabited the small town were easy pickings. The experience was abysmal, but the corpses were plenty edible.

Asher passed by overhead and let out a caw as a pair of zombies staggered around the corner of a building. Digby cast control without hesitation.

MINIONS: 2 Common Zombies.

He called up to the raven, "Head back out and see if you can find more."

With her in the air, it was far easier to find the few lingering zombies that still occupied the small town. With a little luck, he could manage a moderate horde. Digby pointed to the headless corpses of a pair of revenants that he'd killed upon entering the town. "Dinner is served."

As tempted as he was to eat the bodies himself, it made more sense to feed others. If he could get a few minions to mutate into brutes, they would be valuable assets against Tanner when the time came. He thrust a claw out to one of his zombies. "Focus on the flesh." He swept his finger to the side to aim at the other. "And you, help your friend here eat. We're short on time and I'm not sure one of you can shove enough flesh down your gullet to make brute on your own."

Both zombies nodded, using the control spell's intelligence bonus to the fullest. Digby watched for a minute as one assisted in feeding the other. "And leave the bones for now. I'm going to need a few spare skeletons."

Soon after, Tavern rose from a pile of sticky bones.

"Head out and kill some revenants." Digby handed a machete to the infernal spirit and gave his orders before they had a chance to say anything irritating. "Drag the bodies back here."

"You're the boss." Tavern gave him a sarcastic salute and strolled off down the street without so much as an argument. Then, dangling their weapon around at their side with little enthusiasm, the skeleton headed straight into the nearest bar.

I suppose I didn't tell that drunkard where to start, did I?

Digby shook his head and continued what he was doing. Tavern exited the building they had entered shortly after, now dragging a dispatched revenant in one hand. The skeleton clutched a partially broken bottle in their other.

Well, at least they're still getting some work done.

Digby removed the head of the corpse and set his two zombie minions onto the feast. Asher returned again with another three zombies in tow.

"That will do nicely." Digby grinned as things started to come together. "Just you wait, Tanner. Those fools back at the castle might not be able to put up a fight, but I sure as hell can with some time to prepare."

After casting control on his three new minions and setting them on the path of the glutton to balance out his ranks, he headed into the bar that Tavern was working their way through. He found the skeleton chugging away at a bottle whilst swinging a blade at a lone revenant. The building was simple, just an open room with several tables and a long counter. Digby placed a hand on the threshold, wondering if the place would share the same locational enchantment as the Hanging Frederick.

Nothing.

Apparently whatever detail that provided the warding wasn't shared by this establishment. He dropped his hand to his side and shrugged. Digby could have waited outside while his minion did the work of clearing the place out, but it made more sense to take the opportunity to rank up his spells.

Hmm, I wonder?

Digby scratched at his chin for a moment, debating on casting Cremation on Tavern. He knew bone would burn, but not well. Then again, the fact that the skeleton still had bits of flesh remaining throughout its frame might make for an interesting effect.

The results were obvious as soon as he cast the spell.

"Nooooooooo! Weeee burrrrrrn!" Tavern flailed their arms wildly as the entire skeleton ignited at once. It probably didn't help that the infernal spirit had been pouring alcohol all over themself for the last ten minutes.

"Oh, shut up. It's just a little fire. It shouldn't damage your skull." Digby ignored his minion's plight and stabbed a finger in the direction of the revenant that had been fighting with. "Now see if you can burn that to death."

The panicking skeleton ceased their flailing and gave an unenthusiastic shrug before throwing themself at the pale form in front of them. The dormant revenant shrieked as its tattered clothing caught fire.

"That's it. Make them squirm." Digby clapped his hands as

Tavern simply clasped their skeletal fingers around the revenant's head to heat up its brain. The creature fell to the floor soon after, leaving Tavern standing there awkwardly as the Cremation flames consumed what was left of the necrotic flesh on their bones, burning itself out shortly after.

Interesting.

Digby looked his minion up and down. Now that the spell had run its course, a blackened skeleton stood before him. Digby arched an eyebrow, realizing that it would be near impossible to see his minion at night. The thought gave him another idea, prompting him to open his maw on the floor. Spending the extra mana, he widened its opening.

"Hop in." He pointed to the black fluid that filled his void.

Tavern did so without argument, simply walking into the opening and dropping in.

"Good, good." Digby snatched a billiard stick from the wall and held it out to his minion. "Now climb back out."

Tavern reached for the stick, but quickly pushed it away as if it wasn't needed. Their skeletal hand slapped down on the floor at the edge of his maw and they clawed themselves up. Digby snapped the gateway shut as soon as Tavern was clear. He looked his minion over, finding black blood dripping from every bone.

For a second, he started to cast Cremation again, only to think better of it. Instead he cast Blood Forge, causing the liquid to coat every surface of his minion as well as to collect in some places. Rows of spikes formed across Tavern's knuckles as more sprouted in a line down the center of their skull.

"Sweet." The skeleton looked their new form over, clearly pleased with the improvement.

"Indeed." Digby wondered how far he could push the ability to forge armor now that he had eaten enough corpses to allow less conservative use of his blood magic. It wasn't going to protect against everything, but it would certainly help. He nodded to himself. Then he cast Cremation.

Tavern stood there as emerald fire climbed up their frame.

The flames weren't quite as hot or volatile as they were when cast on bits of flesh or blood in its liquid form, but they were still capable of causing harm even if it wasn't much.

"How much damage do you think the flames are doing to your bones?"

Tavern raised one hand and tilted it back and forth to indicate that there was some damage, but not a lot.

"Maybe I can use this as a last resort." Digby considered the ramifications for a moment. Then his eyes widened, remembering how his forge spell could be used to turn a skull into a throwable explosive. His mouth cracked into a villainous grin.

"What are you looking at us like that for?" Tavern took a step away as Digby contemplated the uses of a minion whose head could explode whenever he wanted.

"Oh, stop your worrying. There are plenty of skeletons about. I'll just find you another." Digby spun on his heel and sauntered out of the bar. "This is the apocalypse, there's always another corpse about."

After his experiments in the bar, Digby sent Tavern off to find more dormant revenants to help his zombies grow stronger. While he waited, he decided to attend to the other problem that had been plaguing him for the last few days.

Fashion.

Digby approached the window of a clothing emporium next door to the bar he'd just exited. He was still wearing what was left of the souvenir t-shirt that he'd found at the Hanging Frederick. The bottom was torn, leaving the gray skin of his midriff on display. His pants had been spared any damage when he'd been ripped in half the night before, but they were covered in his own necrotic blood.

"Really wish I'd stolen some clothes from Alex before I left. Even one of his horrible flower shirts would be better than this."

Digby peered through the window of the storefront, finding the selection satisfactory. There wasn't anything too fancy, but a few garments stuck out to him. He Decayed his way through the glass and stepped through, approaching a shelf piled with folded trousers first. Thinking back, this was the first time he'd had an opportunity and the selection to choose an outfit properly. So far, he'd just been taking whatever he could find.

Searching the piles, Digby made sense of the store's organizational system. After trying on a few pairs of trousers, he figured out his size. He grabbed some undergarments and socks while he was at it. From there, he moved on to shirts, claiming something light with short-sleeves and a couple needless buttons on the collar. He grabbed a simple black trench-coat off a rack to complete the ensemble. Like the rest of the outfit, it was nothing fancy, but it was fitted to his slender frame well and it hung down to the back of his knees. He smiled as the length reminded him of a cape.

Fortunately, the thin plates of bone armor covering his chest and back kept the Heretic Seed's shard safe, leaving little need for much physical protection. Beyond that, he just needed to present a better impression than looking like he'd crawled out of a swamp.

As much as he would have liked to obtain clothes as unique as the goblin king's coat that he'd lost, he was starting to realize that anything he chose would have a short lifespan. Considering how often he was shot, stabbed, or torn in half, it seemed sensible to keep things simple and easy to replace. With that thought in mind, he claimed duplicates of each of the items he'd chosen. He organized them into piles, each containing a complete outfit.

Looking down at his feet, he headed to the back of the store to find some shoes. He tried a few pairs on, realizing his new left foot was a size smaller than the other. Growling at the inconsistency, he mixed and matched different pairs to make several sets that would work. He added those to his piles as well.

Satisfied with his choices, he headed out of the store and crossed the street to a shop that held a variety of basic items, including a display of coolers. Digby would never have the need to preserve food, but Alex had always packed one of the containers in the van every time they had gone anywhere. His apprentice had even collected ice created by Rebecca's magic to keep the containers cold. It was enough to tell Digby that the box would be watertight.

Grabbing a wheeled cart from the front of the store, Digby loaded up the bin with coolers and brought them back across the street to the clothing store. Each proved to be the perfect size to store one complete set of clothes. Digby secured the lids by tightening a belt from one of the racks around the insulated boxes. When he was finished, he opened his maw and kicked them all in so he could recall them later. Having fresh outfits would probably come in handy. He couldn't keep walking around in rags covered in blood forever, after all.

With his shopping done, Digby dug his tablet out from his bag to check the time. He still had plenty of daylight to finish getting prepared before he had to start heading in the direction of the airfield where he'd last seen Tanner. As he was putting it away, he noticed a red dot sitting on top of the icon for the message application that Rebecca and Mason had downloaded.

"That's odd." Digby was still a little iffy on how some things worked, but he knew enough to understand that the message couldn't have been recent, since his tablet wasn't in range of any sort of connection. The only place it had ever seemed to function in that way was when he'd been close to Rebecca's room at the castle, meaning the message must have come in right before he'd left.

With a shrug he tapped the icon, finding a message waiting for him.

Lana: Hey Dig, I was just thinking about stuff. And I just wanted to say thanks. I know we were only together for a couple hours back in Seattle, but if it wasn't for you, my brother and I would be dead. Obviously, things aren't great now but we're alive. So yeah, thanks for that.

Honestly, I'm just glad you're out there. I get that you can't do much against Skyline and what not, but you still helped me and Alvin. So I feel a little better having you and Rebecca out there. Even if you can't help me, I know you'll help someone. You might act like a jerk most of the time but you're a good guy.

Oh jeez, sorry for messaging you. I'm just bored and have no one to talk to here. Skyline's people are all assholes and I hate them.

"I do too, Lana." Digby laughed at her last sentence. "I do too."

Digby read over her message, feeling a little better about himself for a moment before remembering how he'd left the night before.

Tavern stepped through the store's broken window a moment later. The skeleton's timing could not have been better. Digby needed a distraction from his thoughts.

After searching the rest of the small town's Main Street, Tavern had only found one building that housed a significant number of enemies. It seemed the creatures had taken refuge just like they had in the hotel in Santa Barbara. Except this time, it was the town's meeting house. A pair of revenant light-walkers stood guard near the entrance and were the only real threat, though, they proved easy enough to handle with an element of caution. Digby simply skewered them both.

Afterward, he simply executed the sixty or so that remained. The process took some time, especially when retreating outside every few minutes to meditate. In the end, the massacre provided plenty of food for his minions even after he'd destroyed some with his Cremation spell. It wasn't long before his first zombie mutated into a brute. Using some of the extra bones and sinew, two more gained the claws and agility of silent lurkers.

His remaining two minions reached both of the gluttons' mutations, gaining the ability to not only open their maws but set a jawbone trap within the space as well. It would have been nice if they could have reached the Path of the Devourer, but unfortunately, there just wasn't enough time. It wouldn't do to squander the hours they had before nightfall, and they still had a lot of ground to cover. Tanner was sure to show up and catch them off guard if they didn't get to him first.

Asher did her best, picking at the brains and hearts available, but ran into the same time constraint before gaining anything new. It was a lot of food to get down for such a small mouth. Eventually, Digby had his minions sweep whatever they couldn't finish in time into his maw.

Again the message about him reaching the requirements of Sheep's Clothing flashed across his vision, and again he ignored it. It still made sense to save his disguise for when he needed it. It also left him with plenty of resources to activate his Temporary Mass mutation several times if needed. He was tempted to test the ability, but refrained. Wasting that many of his resources just for a test still seemed careless. He wished he had thought to use it the night before instead of letting himself be ripped in half like a fool.

When all was said and done, Digby had reached a new rank for his Cremation spell during the massacre of the revenants, increasing its destructive capability. A new rank was earned for Blood Forge as well that improved the strength and flexibility of whatever he formed. With it, his blood talons were becoming more like real blades. Unfortunately, it also made them too durable to snap off in a revenant's body to ensure they couldn't heal.

The experience had trickled in as well, totaling at a meager one-hundred-fifty-four for the dormant enemies and a bit over a thousand for the two lightwalkers. Taking his level of twenty-four into account, he was only getting two points per dormant revenant. His next level up would reduce the rewards for killing the creatures to zero.

Digby turned toward the road that led to the airfield where Tanner attacked him the night before. He glanced to his HUD as Asher landed on his shoulder.

MINIONS: 1 Brute, 2 Lurkers, 2 Gluttons, 1 Skeleton

"I guess we're going to need to find bigger prey."

CHAPTER THIRTY-FOUR

The airfield was quiet as the sun began to set in the distance.

"Looks like we're just in time." Digby nodded to himself as he crept through the surrounding brush at the edge of the field. His minions followed close behind, the brute stepping on nearly every stick and twig in the area. Digby groaned before shrugging. At least the oversized zombie had been able to carry the slower members of his horde on its back the whole way to the airfield.

Digby nudged Asher as she perched on his shoulder. "Get in the air and give me a warning if you see our prey anywhere." Once she took flight, he beckoned to Tavern. "And you, head over to the hangar and see if Tanner is inside."

The skeleton was barely visible in the dark, thanks to the glossy black layer of hardened blood that coated their bones. A quiet sloshing came from the cavity of fluid housed within his minion's skull as they nodded in understanding. Digby signaled for the rest of his horde to duck low as Tavern skulked in the direction of the hangar's broken door.

"What the hell are you doing?" Rebecca asked from behind him.

"I'm killing Tanner. What the devil does it look like I'm...?" Digby trailed off as his eyes widened. He snapped his head back to find the illusionist crouching beside one of his lurkers. "Where did you come from?"

"I'm projecting." She gestured to herself. "I used you as a start point."

"If you're here to convince me to come back, I have no intention of returning to watch everyone get themselves killed," Digby snapped before letting her get another word out.

"Yeah, about that." Her voice wavered. "Skyline found us."

"What?" Digby shrieked before lowering his voice to a whisper. "I mean, what?"

"A kestrel passed by overhead." She spoke fast, as if time was a factor. "At first, we thought they didn't spot us, but they came back fifteen minutes ago, with a couple more ships and set down on the road leading to the castle. The horde outside responded the same way they had when we arrived, making it super obvious they were protecting the place. Once that happened, the kestrels took off and hovered in place out of reach. Now they're just sitting there. We're not sure what to do at the moment, but I thought it would be best to let you know that we might be in trouble."

"Oh gee, it's almost like Rufus should have listened to a certain necromancer and prepared the people for a fight rather than depending on his horde."

"Can you please skip the I told you so part?" She rolled her eyes. "This is serious."

"I realize that, but I'm fifty miles away." He shook his head. "What can I possibly do?"

"I don't know, but Alex and I don't have the offensive spells that you do so we can't defend ourselves if things go wrong." She lowered her head.

"What about the horde of three thousand zombies that Rufus thinks will protect you all forever?" Digby tried not to gloat.

"If Rufus attacks with the horde, there's no way Skyline

would let something like that slide. Even if we kill the squads that are already here, our position is known. More will come and Rufus's horde will only be able to protect the castle for so long against an army of guardians before we're forced to surrender. I've sent messages to Lana and Easton asking for information, but haven't heard back yet. We can try to stall but that's about it."

"Damn it, you really know how to make things difficult." He rubbed at his forehead. "I'm about to pick a fight with a revenant bloodstalker. I can't just say, 'hey wait, I think I left a candle burning back home,' and run off."

She flicked her eyes to the hangar. "You're right, you can't. And you shouldn't."

"What is that supposed to mean?" He held up both hands empty.

"It means that killing Tanner is exactly what needs to happen right now." She flicked her eyes to the hangar.

"Alright, and why is that?" Digby clawed at the air to drag more out of her.

"Because we need the kestrel in there." She slapped one hand into the other. "With that, we can fly you straight home in about ten minutes. All I need is someone to open the door the rest of the way so I can get the craft out without damaging the rotors. We might even get lucky. There's a chance that Tanner isn't even here. Once we have you back at the castle, we can figure out a way to sneak you in and come up with a real plan to escape."

"And what if I don't want to help?" Digby narrowed his eyes at the woman, giving her a hard time.

"Don't be a jerk, Dig." She glowered at him as if not even entertaining the idea. "You know as well as I do that you wouldn't turn your back on your friends."

Digby flinched at that last word.

Friends.

He'd never actually heard anyone say it out loud when referring to him. Even he had never used the word. He may have thought it a few times when he was in higher spirits, but mostly, he just thought of the other heretics as accomplices.

"I suppose that's true." He folded his arms and looked away.

That was when Tavern hollered back from the hanger.

"Nobody's home." The skeleton hooked a bony hand back into the broken door of the building.

"Hmm, maybe we don't have to fight Tanner tonight after all." Digby froze as soon as the words left his mouth, expecting the oversized revenant to sprint out of the trees at any moment. That would have been fitting, considering his luck.

Rebecca seemed to be having the same thought, craning her head back to check behind her. Digby relaxed as she let out a sigh of relief, finding the area empty. They exchanged awkward looks before stepping out into the open with his minions following close behind.

Tavern met them halfway to the hangar just as something tugged on Digby's Blood Sense. It was similar to the sensation of someone casting a spell, but somehow different, almost primal. He threw out a hand to his minions. "Hold up."

They all stopped dead in their tracks.

"What is it?" Rebecca held her breath despite being nothing more than a projection.

"Something's here." Digby swept his gaze across the field, trying to pinpoint the sensation.

Suddenly, an unseen force slammed into one of his lurkers, tearing through them as it ripped the zombie from the ground. It landed in a flailing heap with its torso hanging from a few shreds of flesh.

Then, Tanner simply appeared.

"Oh shit, he can use Conceal." Rebecca started to step back before stopping, clearly remembering she wasn't the one in danger.

"What? How?" Digby sprang back.

"A mutation?" she shouted back.

Digby let out a groan. "There must be more to a bloodstalker than just its size and tracking ability. Who knows what it can do?"

"It's like it was designed for hunting. Make sure at least one of you or your minions keep an eye on him at all times. Tanner might Conceal himself again if you lose track of him." She started running for the hangar. "I can't help here; I'm going to check on the kestrel."

"Go with her," ge shouted to Tavern. "Get that airship running and the door open."

The skeleton broke away from the group and followed the projected illusionist into the building. Digby checked his HUD.

MP: 211/211
MINIONS: 1 Brute, 1 Lurker, 2 Gluttons, 1 Skeleton.

"Alright, you oversized piece of meat." He stabbed out a claw to Tanner. "One of us is going to die tonight, and it's not going to be me." Digby immediately opened his maw beneath his foe's foot, increasing its size for a moment before snapping it shut.

Tanner reacted in an instant, shifting his weight to raise his foot up out of the shadowed gateway. The creature was quick, but not quite fast enough, as Digby's closing maw shaved off a layer of flesh.

"Tie him down!" He sent his gluttons into action, each taking a position behind the enormous creature. Both zombies opened their maws to set jawbone traps in Tanner's path.

The monster stepped to one side to avoid one of the traps while placing his hand down in the other. The jawbone snapped shut. Tanner attempted to rip his arm free, pulling the trap out of one of the glutton's maw. Digby's minion yanked back down on the sinewy cord that tethered the trap to its void, throwing the revenant off balance.

"Charge!" Digby sent in his brute.

He readied two of the severed heads he'd collected earlier as the meaty zombie plowed into Tanner's supporting leg with a hard crunch. Tossing the heads to his remaining lurker, Digby sent in his last minion.

"Light 'em up."

The zombie ran forward, barely making a sound as it carried a head in each hand, holding them close to the ground as it moved. The lurker darted past Tanner before spinning on one heel and launching the macabre projectiles. Digby cast Cremation twice the instant they left his minion's hands, emerald fire engulfing the heads. The skulls screamed through the air before bursting on impact against Tanner's throat and back. Molten gray matter splashed into the space around him, dispersing into a cloud of emerald embers.

"Dodge this." Digby cast Emerald Flare behind the over-sized revenant as he fell backward into the spell.

The sickly green energy streaked through the night to converge around Tanner's body. The creature sprang to one side in a desperate attempt to get away just as the spell lit up the night with an emerald blast of power. Tanner's left leg simply exploded. His body hit the ground in a roll, trailing bits of flesh and blood across the grass.

"Try stalking me now, you overgrown menace." Digby marched forward in victory, reaching for another severed head to finish the battered monster off.

Tanner screeched and howled as his body struggled to heal the damage limb. His wound hissed and spat as the flesh knit back together over what was left of his missing leg to stem the bleeding.

"Not so fast." Digby prepared to throw another head. "You're not running away."

That was when Tanner slammed both hands into the ground, digging his claws into the grass as he got his remaining leg underneath him. Digby shrank back for an instant at the sudden movement. Then, the fur on the creature's back shifted to reveal a strange twisted form. Two spindly limbs rotated with a series of horrible pops and cracks like they were reconfiguring the placement of bones.

"Oh damn." Digby's eyes widened as they stretched out and extended to reveal a leathery membrane connecting them. "How is that fair?"

Before Digby could act, Tanner launched straight up, spreading a massive pair of bat-like wings. The revenant let out a loud cry as the moon silhouetted its demonic form. A second later, he was on him, diving straight down with his remaining leg outstretched.

Digby dove out of the way as Tanner snatched up one of the gluttons from the behind him in the claws of his foot. Rolling to the side, he stared up to watch the monster reach down with one hand and tear his minion in half before throwing the pieces to the ground. A pair of legs slammed into the hangar's roof as a torso splattered on the pavement that stretched across the field. Tanner flapped in the air for a moment before again diving straight for him.

Panic surged through his mind as he realized he didn't have a way to fight back against an airborne enemy. He hadn't even thought it possible. There hadn't been any indication that a revenant could have wings. Then again, he didn't understand how their mutation process worked. Either way, it was clear Tanner had evolved well beyond any other revenant that he'd come across.

In desperate need of time to think, Digby did the only thing he could. He cast Burial on himself. The bottom fell out from his stomach as the earth opened beneath him to swallow him whole. Tanner's screeching was drowned out in an instant as six feet of dirt as it poured in on top of him. He felt the impact of Tanner crashing into the ground a moment later. Then, there was nothing.

Despite being unable to move within the grave, a strange feeling of comfort swam through him. He checked his HUD.

MP: 121/211
MINIONS: 1 Brute, 1 Lurker, 1 Glutton, 1 Skeleton.

Worry swept back in, stronger than before and catching him off guard before he realized it was coming across the bond he shared with Asher. She must have lost track of him. He sent one thought back in response.

Safe.

He followed it with another.

Flee.

With Tanner in the sky, he didn't want his pet anywhere near the area. It would be too easy to tear her to shreds and he didn't want to take the chance. Asher sent back a thought in response.

Understand.

Digby relaxed, letting the comfort of the surrounding earth engulf him as he focused on a way to salvage the fight. That was when he noticed his mana tick back up a point. Confusion set in for a moment, wondering how he'd absorbed anything so soon after casting a spell. His mana climbed another point regardless, as if retreating into a grave had somehow erased the delay that normally followed whenever he'd cast anything. Not only that, but his rate of absorption was faster. Much faster.

The mana balance this far down must have a higher density of death essence.

Digby considered the possibility, realizing that the sun's light couldn't reach the depths of his sanctuary. It made sense. In the end, everything would return to the earth when it died. There was something poetic about it. The soil claimed the bodies of the dead to provide nutrients to the life that bloomed under the sun. Death was a beginning just as much as it was an end. Digby pushed the philosophical thought from his head as a message passed through his vision.

Brute, lost.

Damn, I can't stay down here forever.

The muffled screeching of his enemy bled down into his

grave, reminding him that he needed a plan. He checked his HUD again.

MP: 193/211

It seemed the tradeoff of not being able to see or take part of the fight was significant. His mana was nearly back to full in under a minute. It was actually better than meditation. Digby clawed at the soil, realizing how difficult it was to escape the grave he'd dug for himself.

That's not good.

His mana reached full as he opened his maw near his feet, hoping he still knew which way was up. Picturing a shape in his mind, he forged a post of crystalized blood. It surged up as he reached out to catch a grooved portion at the top. The formation displaced the soil as it carried him toward the surface to burst out. Erupting from the earth, Digby kicked off the post to land back on his feet. Dirt trickled from the shoulders of his coat.

Sweeping his gaze across the sky, Digby searched for the oversized revenant. For a moment, he feared Tanner had concealed himself again while he was underground. Then a screech came from behind him.

I guess he has no intent on hiding.

Digby rolled to the side on reflex just as a giant foot snatched at the ground where he'd been. Tumbling with his momentum, he activated his Temporary Mass mutation as soon as he came to a stop. It was about time he tried it out.

Discomfort raked down his back as if his entire spine was being popped apart, one vertebra at time. His coat tore down the back as tendrils of necrotic flesh slithered across his body. Slabs of muscle weaved together as a support structure of bone and sinew formed around him with a seam running down his chest.

Before he knew what he was doing, Digby let out a bellowing roar, sounding like a brute as a hood of flesh climbed up the back of his head. A row of teeth poked out around the opening as it closed around his face. For a second, his vision went black. Then the world blinked back into existence, this time with less clarity, like he was looking through a pane of warped glass.

Turning, he caught a glimpse of his reflection in the window of one of the abandoned cars. He looked like something out of a nightmare. A layer of grayish-black flesh encased his body. The seam running down his chest was held together by a dozen hands, with their fingers interlocked like the teeth of a zipper. The seam split apart at his neck, with a row of open hands encircling his head like a collar of clawed digits. A skull-like mask covered his face, grinning with a mouth full of fangs.

Strength increased by 11.
Defense increased by 9.
Enhanced attributes will persist until Temporary Mass is damaged or until released.

The mutation was, indeed, worth a try.

With a thought, the jaws of his mask opened to retract like a hood as its lower jaw split apart like a spider's mandibles, revealing his face. The hands that ran down his chest let go as well to spread their fingers apart. It was an impressive creation. Digby closed his armor again and sprang off, rushing forward faster than ever before. It was like having the strength of a brute while retaining the agility of a lurker. He skidded to a stop, glaring up at Tanner.

"Come on then." Digby opened his maw on his palm to form himself a new set of talons. Tanner obliged, diving straight at him only to receive a deep gouge to his leg. In kind, the revenant clawed a chunk of flesh from Digby's armored back.

"That's all you've got?" Digby spun back around.

Tanner circled in the air to make another pass, repeating the same attack as before.

"You're going to have to try something new!" Digby held his claws out at the ready.

Tanner cried out in anger, as if some part of him still understood Digby's taunts.

Ducking back down at the last second, Digby opened his maw and cast Blood Forge. A black spike erupted from the ground in front of him just in time for Tanner to slam into it. The revenant screeched in protest as the shard of crystalized blood pierced his chest and exploded out through his back.

"I warned you." Digby sprang up and dragged his talons across Tanner's throat, spilling crimson across the grass.

The revenant's flesh hissed as the wound closed. It wasn't over. Tanner roared and slammed a fist into Digby's head, sending him tumbling backward into the pavement. Something in his armor snapped, though it remained functional.

Tanner struck at the spike impaling his chest. Cracks spider-webbed across its surface, growing as the revenant slammed his fist into it again. After three hits, it shattered. Tanner hopped free on his one leg before ripping the spike from his chest and casting it aside. The resilient beast clutched a hand over the wound as it began to heal. Flapping his wings in a labored motion, Tanner took flight.

"Oh, no you don't." Digby took off in a sprint, leaping with every point of strength he had. Something in his leg popped as he pushed his Temporary Mass past its limit to launch himself nearly twenty feet in the air. His talons fell just short as Tanner's foot slipped from his grasp.

"Damn!" Digby plummeted back down to earth, landing hard on his side. He stood back up, his armor feeling sluggish. Not wanting to lose his prey, he sent an order to Asher through their bond.

Follow.

He had to keep track of the bloodstalker or else Tanner might try to conceal himself and escape. That was when the sound of a kestrel's engines came from the hangar behind him.

"Perfect timing." Digby kicked off, running toward the sound.

"Oh god! What the hell is that?" Rebecca's voice came from the craft's external speakers as a pair of enormous guns slid into firing position.

"Oh! Wait, no!" Digby skidded to the side as a barrage of bullets tore through the night, cutting a swath across the earth beside him. Dirt erupted into the air with each impact. Digby rolled to the side as the craft rotated to get him back in the line of fire.

"Dig, where are you?" Rebecca shouted over the speakers. "There's something else here."

"It's me, it's me, it's me!" Digby squealed as he raised his hands up uselessly to shield his body. He willed his armor's mask to retract, revealing his face just as the craft's weapons found him in their sights. He winced in anticipation.

"Shit, Dig. What the hell are you wearing?" Rebecca's voice sent a wave of relief through him.

"It's a mutation, Temporary Mass. Basically necrotic armor." He lowered his hands.

"It looks gross." Her voice fell flat.

"Oh, I'm sorry that my armor that I weaved together from the corpses of the dead isn't as aesthetically pleasing as you would prefer." He started for the craft.

"You look like something out of Hellraiser," she continued.

"I don't know what that is." Digby reached up and grabbed a hold of a ridge on the craft's front window, noticing Tavern sitting in the otherwise empty pilot's compartment.

"Hey, wait, what are you doing?" She started to pull the airship away.

"I'm climbing aboard so we can chase after Tanner. What does it look like?" He didn't stop.

"Cut it out and get inside. Tanner is retreating and we have other things to do."

"Yes, but he is hurt now and we may not have a better chance to end him." Digby pulled himself up onto the kestrel's roof and grabbed onto a handle next to a hatch. "It's only a matter of time before he licks his wounds and comes after us again. And by then, there's no telling what he might evolve into. It won't matter how big a horde we have to protect us if he can just snatch people off the ground and tear them apart."

"Fine." She let out a growl loud enough to be picked up by the craft's speakers. "But then we head straight for the castle. And make sure you don't fall into the rotors or something."

"Good point." Digby glanced to the side at the spinning blades that kept the airship aloft. They had a circular guard around their edge but the top was still open. He tightened his grip around the handle before thrusting a talon forward. "Now after that revenant!"

The kestrel ascended into the sky to chase the silhouette of Tanner as he climbed toward the clouds. Digby flattened his body to the craft and closed his mask around his face as the wind whipped by. "Keep going!"

Tanner looked back for a second, only to flap his wings faster as they closed the gap. The kestrel's guns spun in anticipation.

"Let him have it." Digby cackled as Rebecca opened fire.

Bullets tore through the night, shredding the revenant's wings and blowing his right arm from his body. Tanner tucked his wings in close to drop a few hundred feet in an instant. The creature spread them open again just before hitting the trees, covering the leaves with a spattering of crimson. The holes in his wings healed just as he caught the wind again.

"Dive after him!" Digby thrust out a hand in his prey's direction.

"I'll try, but that's not how this thing is meant to maneuver." Rebecca sounded skeptical as the craft tipped forward.

The wind threatened to tear Digby off the airship as they plummeted to the earth. Rebecca pulled up before hitting the trees, still flying above the revenant.

"Fire!" Digby cried only to be answered by silence. He snapped his head back to the camera lens mounted on the top of the kestrel. "Why isn't that thing being torn apart by a hail of bullets?"

"He's practically below us, the angle is too sharp for me to tilt the craft down without crashing into the trees. I can't get him in my sights."

"Alright then." Digby tried to judge the distance to the ground, figuring it at about a hundred feet. Peeking over the side, he caught Tanner not far below them. He nodded to himself a second later.

"Never mind, I'll do it myself."

Digby opened his maw and forged a shaft of blood, tipped with a bladed head similar to a spear. After reaching rank B of the spell, he hoped the formation was durable enough to function for at least a couple attacks. Then, with a final wild cackle, he leapt for his prey. Panic immediately surged through his entire body as he realized what he'd done.

Am I insane? What sort of half-wit leaps from atop an airship?

It was clear that he'd let the power of his necrotic armor go straight to his head. He just hoped it would be enough to break his fall. There wasn't time to worry further. Tanner was already turning toward him.

Raising his crimson spear high, Digby slammed into the revenant in mid-air like a projectile launched from a ballista. Crimson sprayed from the creature as he drove his Blood Forged weapon down through Tanner's neck until it burst out the other side. The revenant let out a labored scream and plummeted into the trees.

Digby held tight to his weapon, praying it wouldn't break as branches battered him left and right. Then, together, they hit the ground in a tumbling mass of wings and limbs. A shower of leaves drifted through the air as they came to a stop. Shaking off the confusion of the fall, Digby found himself still on the creature's back, with half his mask missing. Tanner struggled to pull the spear from his neck with his one remaining arm while flapping his wings in desperation to get back in the air.

"Not this time, you don't." Digby slashed to the side with his talons to shred the membrane of Tanner's right wing to ribbons. He reached to his other side to clip the revenant's other wing as well. "That'll keep you down for now."

Tanner shrieked and flailed as his mana struggled to regenerate his wounds. Digby shoved his spear down, pinning the revenant to the earth. Opening his maw on the ground beneath the creature's head, Digby pushed with everything he had. He wrenched his spear to the side and shoved with all of his weight.

Little by little, Tanner's bat-like snout dipped into the black pool of his open void. Black fluid bubbled and splashed as the revenant struggled. His monstrous strength faded with each movement. Digby let out a snarl of effort, the bones in his temporary armor snapping in protest as the layer of muscle began to unravel. His own strength faded as well.

"Stop… following… me!" Digby growled as the revenant's head dipped into his maw.

The gateway snapped shut with a sickening crunch. Tanner's body spasmed all at once, throwing Digby to the side before slowly going limp.

"Oh thank god!" Digby let himself fall back as well just before the flesh encasing his body came apart at the seams. It felt like a dozen ropes snapping all at once as the muscle that surrounded him simply failed, leaving him a sticky mess in the dirt. Digby ripped off the remainder of his nightmarish mask and cast it aside. A light shined down at him through the canopy of trees. Rebecca's voice followed.

"I take it you won?"

Digby glanced at the message on his HUD.

Active revenant bloodstalker defeated, 3,702 experience awarded.
You have reached level 25.
4,516 experience to next level.
You have discovered a ritual.

"Yes, Becky, I think I won."

CHAPTER THIRTY-FIVE

You have discovered a necromancy ritual.

UNQUENCHABLE THIRST
Description: Gain a better understanding of your mana
system by depriving yourself of death essence.
Materials Required: 1 additional participant.
Environmental Required: Ritual must be carried out at a
location with an ambient mana balance that contains 0%
death essence.
Rewards: A better understanding of your mana system
and the discovery of a new spell.

"I'm really glad I can't smell you right now." Rebecca's voice
came from the speaker embedded in the ceiling of the kestrel's
passenger compartment.

Digby tore his attention away from his new ritual's description to properly glower at the camera beside the speaker. He
folded his arms, sitting on one side of the airship as they flew
back to the castle and its desperate inhabitants. He dropped his

eyes back down to look at Tavern. The glossy, black skeleton sat across from him, as if trying to mind his own business. Asher sat in the skeleton's lap.

Tapping his fingers on his other arm, Digby realized how grimy his skin was. Rebecca wasn't wrong. Even with his deceased senses, he could tell that he didn't smell great. Apparently, a side effect of using his necrotic armor was that it left him covered in a pungent layer of gelatinous slime. He let out a breathless sigh and flicked a chunk of leftover flesh from his leg.

"We'll reach the castle in ten minutes." Rebecca changed the subject away from his hygiene.

"Do you know any more about why Skyline decided to show up?"

"I just heard back from Easton." Rebecca paused as if checking another message. "It's as we suspected, one of their patrols spotted the activity at the castle. They sent out a recruitment team but got spooked when Rufus' horde responded in an organized manner. Apparently, they are operating under the assumption that we have a zombie master working with us to control them."

"Hmm." Digby scratched at his chin. "If they know enough to recognize the influence of a master, then they must have gained a good understanding of what they are capable of."

"That's probably why they have been capturing uncommon zombies and revenants," Rebecca added. "They must be studying their capabilities."

"Indeed, It also might confirm my theory of how they were able to hijack the original curse. They must have turned one of their mages and fed them nothing but hearts and minds until they reached master."

"You're probably right. I feel bad for whoever they turned." Rebecca let out an uneven breath as if shuddering at the other end of their communication.

"Is it still just the three kestrels outside the castle?"

"I wish." She groaned. "There's ten out there now. If each are flying at capacity, then they've brought a small army.

According to Easton, General Bancroft is out there among them. I guess having a zombie master makes us a big enough concern to merit his personal attention."

"That can't be good." Digby's jaw tightened. "What about Lana, have you heard from her?"

"Nothing yet. But that makes sense. Easton is pretty sure she's been sent out as part of one of the squads that's waiting outside our door now."

"Oh damn." Digby's eyes widened. "I should avoid killing people willy-nilly down there then."

"Ya think?" Her tone fell flat. "I'll see if Easton can get her a message to make her presence known so she doesn't get caught in the crossfire if things go south."

"Indeed." Digby tried to relax despite the inevitable fight waiting for him at their destination. "What's the plan to sneak me in, then?"

"That depends…" She hesitated. "Can you use that gross meat armor of yours again. and how much damage do you think it can absorb?"

"That depends." He repeated her words as he arched an eyebrow at her camera. "What are you suggesting?"

"Umm, well…" She paused again. "I was thinking of cloaking the kestrel, taking it up above the clouds where they won't see us, and dropping you out the back."

"Are you mad?" He returned to glowering at the lens in the ceiling. "I'd break every bone in my body, even with the armor."

"Not if you land in the deep end of the castle's pool," she added matter-of-factly.

"And how am I supposed to do that?" He tilted his head to the side at the ridiculousness of her suggestion. "Not to mention I'd still be severely damaged when I hit the water."

"I could work out the math acceding to the wind speed so you should hit close to the right spot." Her voice took on a hopeful tone. "Plus, we don't need all of you to survive the fall. Just the Heretic Seed's shard in your chest. As long as that makes it to the ground intact, the rest of you can just regenerate."

"Thank you for your concern for my safety. I am overwhelmed with confidence." He folded his arms again, trying as hard as he could to sound sarcastic.

"What are you, an idiot?" She snapped back.

He jumped up from his seat at the sudden outburst. "Who are you calling an—"

"Sorry, Dig. Not you." She apologized before he could finish his complaint. "Mason is here with me and he's being stupid."

"How so?" He stood still for several seconds, waiting for a response as the sound of Mason talking in the background came over the speaker.

"God damnit. And no, I won't wish you luck if you're not going to listen to reason." She let out a frustrated growl. "That idiot is going to go out there to try to negotiate with Skyline." She pulled away again, as if running to her doorway to yell at the soldier. "You better not die, you hear me!"

"Everything alright there?" Digby winced.

"Yeah, yeah, sorry for shouting. Mason thinks he can get more information about why they're here and that they won't try anything violent if they think there's a chance that we will join them willingly."

"That's a bit risky."

"That's what I said." She let out a huff. "There's… I don't know how many guardians are out there, but they've brought enough men to wipe this place off the map."

Digby frowned. "That doesn't sound like they intend to let this end peacefully."

"That's what I'm afraid of." She let a moment of silence pass by before speaking again. "Anyway, you should get ready. We're almost there."

Digby peeled off the tattered shirt he wore, revealing the plates of bone that still covered his chest and back. He hesitated to retrieve one of the coolers of the clothes that he'd stored earlier, figuring he'd just destroy them anyway when he activated his necrotic armor. Instead, he went through the gear that they had taken off the squad that they'd killed before stealing the kestrel. There hadn't been time to go back for it when they were running from Tanner the night before.

Finding a chest protector in the pile, he pulled it on over the plates of bone that protected his chest and back. The armor was a little snug but, after adjusting the straps, he got it to fit. He hoped that between it and his Temporary Mass, the fragment of the Seed in his heart would have adequate protection. Next, he pulled a couple grenades from one pouch in the pile. He passed both to Tavern.

"If things go bad, jump and try to land on someone important down there. I'll resummon you if you don't make it to earth in one piece."

The skeleton took the explosives with enthusiasm, clearly interested in the prospect of blowing something up.

That was when Rebecca's voice came back over the speaker. "I'm taking us up above the rest of the kestrels in the area; they shouldn't be able to see us as long as I stay cloaked. You can jump whenever you're ready."

"How's Mason? Is he out there already?" Digby held onto a handle attached to the ceiling.

"I have a visual. Hang on."

A screen at the front of the compartment flickered to life, showing a view of the ground. Digby moved closer to see. Below, Mason walked alone down the road from the castle. He wore a pistol holstered at his hip, though he held both hands up. The zombies that surrounded the castle parted to let him through, again making it obvious that they were being controlled by someone in the area.

A few dozen feet away from the hordes' edge, a kestrel sat on the road. The ramp opened as Mason approached, revealing a squad of guardians rushing out with weapons at the ready. Once they had the area around the kestrel secured, a figure in a long coat stepped out.

"Oh my god." Rebecca gasped.

"I take it that's Bancroft?" Digby narrowed his eyes at the screen, hoping that he could somehow make Skyline's commander feel uncomfortable under his death glare.

"Yeah." She went silent as Mason approached the man.

"Can we hear what they're saying?" Digby leaned closer.

"Let me get a mic on them."

The sound of typing came from the speaker just before Digby felt the kestrel he rode in move as if trying to position itself at the right angle. Mason's voice came over the speaker next.

"I'm not sure what is going on, but I'm here to negotiate if that's possible." He kept his hands raised.

"You may put your arms down, sir." Bancroft's tone was professional. "We don't mean you any harm."

"That so?" Mason sounded vaguely antagonistic.

Digby smiled. The soldier was beginning to grow on him.

"I'll get straight to the point." Skyline's commander gestured for his men to stand down for the moment. "My name is—"

"Bancroft." Mason cut him off. "Yeah, I know who you are. I was stationed at the quarantine line. You probably don't remember though. Lot of good soldiers died there."

"Ah, yes." Bancroft stumbled over his words. "Yes, that operation was unfortunate. Once it became clear that the situation in Seattle was unsalvageable, we were forced to make a strategic retreat. With this plague sweeping across the world, there was nothing we could do to stop everything from collapsing. Once we understood that, we shifted our focus to rebuilding."

"Bah!" Digby swatted at the screen.

"That so?" Mason didn't offer any more information than he had to.

"Yes, and speaking of rebuilding, I am here as a representative of the Autem Empire, which is an emerging nation devoted to protecting and nurturing the future of mankind. We have a growing safe haven for survivors and are actively recruiting.

When we spotted your settlement, we immediately set out to offer your people a place with us."

"Do we get a say in this?" Mason called him on the obvious sticking point of the offer.

"Of course, there is no obligation to accept our help." Bancroft remained professional. "But as I said, we offer safety and comfort. With us, you will not have to worry about survival and the dangers of this new world."

"Well, as you can see, we have found our own solution to the dangers of this new world." Mason gestured to the wall of zombies behind him.

"Yes, about that." Bancroft swept his eyes across the zombies blocking the road to the castle. "I assume you have a zombie master within your settlement to keep the dead in order."

"That's a theory that I can neither confirm or deny." Mason continued to offer little detail.

"As I said, if your people do not wish to be evacuated to safety, that is completely acceptable." Bancroft's tone grew harsh.

"I'm sensing a 'but.'" Mason held his ground.

"But, unfortunately, we can't allow something as dangerous as a zombie master to exist. So while, yes, you are welcome to continue your lives undisrupted here, we will need you to give this rogue undead into our custody. I realize that may seem unreasonable, but we are more knowledgeable about these creatures, and despite how safe you might believe yourselves to be with this monster living among you, I assure you, you are not. These creatures are far more dangerous than you know, and letting one that has gained sentience remain unchecked would threaten the survival of the entire human race."

"I agree." Mason nodded. "That is unreasonable. That would leave us defenseless."

"True, but I will remind you that our offer remains valid." Bancroft gestured back to his kestrel. "We can take your people to safety tonight. They can be sleeping in warm beds with plenty to eat by morning."

"But if we have a zombie master amongst us, we would have to hand them over first." Mason folded his arms. "And what if we refuse entirely?"

"We would have to explore other options." Bancroft made his intent clear without actually issuing a threat.

"Okay, I think I have a pretty good understanding of the situation." Mason nodded. "I'm going to need to head back and discuss things with the rest of our leadership before giving you an answer."

"That's acceptable." Bancroft clasped his hands behind his back. "We will wait for one hour, and hopefully we can bring this to a peaceful conclusion."

Mason didn't offer anything more, instead he just nodded and headed back through the horde protecting the castle.

"Well, let's just hand Rufus over and be done with it then." Digby shrugged and threw himself down into one of the seats.

"Dig, be serious." Rebecca sighed.

"Hmm, you're right." He frowned. "Letting Skyline have him isn't an option. There's no telling what they might use him for. And I don't want to hand Henwick anything more to use against us. Not to mention someone would eventually let it slip that we're here."

"I'm glad you're so concerned about Rufus' safety," Rebecca added.

"Indeed." Digby stood up and stepped to the ramp. "Let's get on with this, then."

"Let me get into position." She rotated the craft as it moved to one side. The ramp at the back opened a moment later, letting in a gust of wind.

Digby held tight to a handle on the ceiling, feeling the air on his bare arms. Once again, he activated his Temporary Mass. Discomfort surged through him for a few seconds as some of his body adjusted its configuration to function as one with the layer of necrotic muscle and bone that formed around him.

Again, a nightmarish seam of hands reached across his chest to lock their fingers together with a row of twitching digits extending around his neck. The world outside grew quiet as his mask slid up over his head to close over his face.

"Ugh… that is one of the most disturbing things I have ever seen." There was a quiver of fear in Rebecca's voice. "Oh god, those fingers are still twitching. I am never sleeping again."

Digby ignored her comments, leaning forward over the edge of the ramp to look down at his target. The pool was merely a speck on the earth below from so high up, not to mention the lights of the castle had been shut down to help cover his entrance. He leaned back again.

"You want to take a minute to check your math again?" Digby willed his mask to peel back from his face.

"I have, it should be good," Rebecca answered.

"What do you mean by, it should?" Digby let his tone fall flat to express his skepticism.

"Just jump, you'll be fine." She groaned. "We only have an hour to come up with a plan here."

"Thanks for your concern." He grumbled as his mask slithered around his head again.

Digby let go of the handle on the ceiling and stepped down the ramp to its edge, staring at the minuscule body of water that he was expected to land in. He tried to call back some of the confidence he'd had in the heat of battle against Tanner. Back then, he'd jumped without even considering the consequences. Now, though, he couldn't stop his legs from shaking.

"Alright, I'm not sure about this." Digby started to back up and reach for the handle at the top of the ramp. He only made it a few feet before Rebecca let out a wicked laugh.

"Remember how you drew a mustache on my face the other day and didn't tell me for several hours?"

"Yes." Digby froze despite adding, "It was hilarious."

"Yeah, well, so is this."

Suddenly, the entire craft tipped back just enough to throw off his balance.

"Hey, wait! What are you—" Digby threw a hand out for the handle at the top of the ramp, his fingers falling just short as he stumbled from the kestrel's ramp. The last thing he heard was Rebecca laughing.

"Damn you, Becky!" He shook his fist back up at her with every necrotic fiber of his being. "I will remember this!"

CHAPTER THIRTY-SIX

Digby crashed into the water of the castle's pool with a deafening slap after setting a record for the world's highest belly flop. The necrotic armor took the brunt of the impact, splitting apart at the seams as it failed all at once. At least a few ribs were broken and he could feel at least a dozen more fractured bones. Reaching down, he found his right leg missing from the knee down.

That's not good.

Digby reached out to feel for the side of the pool, sending a surge of belated panic down his spine. He must have missed it by mere inches, his leg being the only part of him unfortunate enough to hit the stone.

It must have snapped right off.

Patches of muscle and bone separated from his temporary armor, floating to the surface of the water as he sank to the bottom. He kicked and flailed to free himself from what remained of his meat suit. Finally, he came to rest at the bottom of the pool, where he peeled the rest of the sticky armor from his body.

Well, I can't stay down here, now can I?

Ignoring the damage to his body, Digby clawed his way up the side of the pool. It made more sense to wait until he'd found his leg to cast regeneration. Odds were it was nearby. On the bright side, the water and chemicals in the pool were able to wash away the grime that his Temporary Mass had left behind, leaving him mostly clean. He probably smelled better too. Although, he doubted anyone would ever swim in the pool again after the mess he'd made in it.

Digby poked his head up over the side to find a soaked Parker sitting a few feet away. Water dripped from her horrified face and she scooted away from the pool before holding one continuous wince. A single unintelligible sound trailed from her mouth. His missing and battered leg lay by her feet.

"What the shit is all that stuff?" She thrust out a finger, sweeping it back and forth.

Digby craned his neck back to look, finding the remnants of his armor floating across the surface of the pool. The water didn't look nearly as inviting as it had before.

"Necrotic armor." Digby turned back to her. "Now, could you be a dear and hand me my leg?"

Parker reached for the extremity, picking it up by its shoe before tossing it a few feet toward him. It flopped onto the stone with a wet slap. Parker immediately gagged. "Oh god, that's…"

Digby ignored her as she shuddered uncontrollably, pulling himself from the water and reaching for his leg. With a quick Necrotic Regeneration, his foot was back where it belonged. His broken bones mended as well.

"There, that should do it." Digby flexed his ankle, letting it splash in the murky water.

"I don't think I'm ever going to swim in a pool again." Parker avoided looking at the chunks of tissue floating on the surface.

"Yes, yes, I know it's horrible." Digby stood back up and opened his maw to call forth one of the coolers from his void. The box rose up a second later. He kicked it into the pool to rinse away the black fluid of his void before popping it open to reclaim a fresh set of clothes.

"Should I turn around or something?" Parker asked as Digby dropped what was left of his pants. "Yeah, I'm gonna turn around."

Digby ignored the woman as she spun to face the castle. A moment later, he was clothed again. With a flourish, he unfurled a new coat and slipped it on. "Now, where is my good for nothing apprentice?"

"Come on, Alex is waiting for you." Parker glanced at the pool for a second, shuddered again, then headed off toward the shack that they had claimed as a forge. Digby couldn't help but notice the pair of daggers sheathed at her lower back, making her look like a thief from back in his day. "We have something for you. There isn't much time, but Alex can get it imbued with some of your mana now, before the fighting starts."

"Been hard at work while I was away, then?" Digby cleared a few wet locks of hair from his face that hung awkwardly between the horns on his bone crown.

"I might have made something more for you if you hadn't run off on your own like that." An irritated tone found its way into the usually laid-back woman's voice.

"Yes, well, I'm back now." Digby attempted to push past any reminder of his tantrum from the night before.

"I know." She stopped for a moment, turning back with an uncharacteristically serious expression. "Don't leave us again. Alex was worried you wouldn't come back. So was I."

"Oh…" Digby stumbled, unsure what to say. He'd never intended to apologize but found the words coming before he had a chance to stop them. "I'm sorry."

"Good." She brightened back up. "Now come on."

Digby followed her without another word until she pushed her way into the forge. The air inside the shed was hot and moist. Not to mention the space was cramped. It was a good first effort, but it was clear that there was a lot of room for improvement before they could claim to be a proper blacksmith.

"Thank god you're here." Alex peeked up from behind some equipment.

"Yes, it seems I have arrived to rescue you all." Digby tried his best to act the part of the castle's savior, hoping to move past his recent behavior.

"Sure you are." The artificer eyed him sideways. "I'm going to go ahead and say it here, I told you so."

"What the hell are you on about?" Digby stopped short.

"About Skyline." Alex gave him a self-satisfied nod. "I told you we were going to need to fight back. And you know…" He threw a hand in the direction of the road where Bancroft's kestrel sat.

"Wipe that smug look off your face, boy." Digby glowered at his apprentice. "Alright, sure, you were right, I will give you that. For better or worse, we have a fight on our hands now, and there's no backing out of it. But just because you were right and I made an ass of myself yesterday doesn't give you license to gloat."

Alex let a warm smile onto his face as if putting their argument behind them. "Welcome back, Lord Graves."

"Yes, yes, we're all friends again." Digby brushed off the greeting. "Now, I hear that you have made something for me."

"Oh right. It's nothing much, but we worked hard on this, so I hope imbuing it will give it a solid passive." Alex squeezed his way around the forge equipment, carrying something in his hand. Parker joined him, shoving up close at his side to present the item together as if it was something they were both proud of.

"Ta da," they both said in unison.

Digby dropped his eyes to stare at the rough-looking object.

A metal rod, close to a foot long, held a four-sided formation similar to a diamond off a deck of playing cards. The center of the shape was empty. At the base of the rod was a thinner piece of metal with two holes, as if it was meant to be slotted into something else.

"Alright," Digby furrowed his brow, "what is it?"

Alex's face fell. "Okay, yeah, I know. It's kinda rough."

"That's one way to put it." Digby threw out a clawed hand at the thing. "What the hell is it supposed to be?"

"Hey!" Parker snatched the thing up and held it close to her cheek, as if trying to protect it from him. "He didn't mean it. You're beautiful."

"Hang on." Alex held up a hand and pushed past them to grab a lone pole that had been leaning against the wall. It looked like the handle of a shovel that had been removed from the head. Alex laid it down on a workbench and took the strange metal object from Parker.

Slotting the narrow end into the wooden shaft, he dropped two bolts into a pair of matching holes and tightened them down to secure both pieces together. Once he was done, he dropped one end to the floor and held it up like a walking stick.

"Ta da," Parker said again, this time holding out both hands to present the item.

"Is that supposed to be a staff?" Digby arched an eyebrow at them both.

"Yes, you jerk." Parker deflated, dropping her arms to her sides.

"What do I need a staff for?" Digby held out both hands in confusion. "Why not a sword, or a battle axe, or something I can murder someone with?"

"Here, just hold it for a second." Alex pushed the staff into his clawed hand. "Trust me on this."

"Alright." Digby went along with things as he began to sense Alex's mana moving.

"Now, I need you to consent to donating some of your mana to imbue this item with." Alex closed his eyes. "It will be subtracted from your total just like when you created your infernal spirit. You can get it back if we destroy this item. So it's not gone for good."

"How much do you need?" Digby hesitated.

"I've been experimenting for this…" Alex's eyes darted back

and forth as if reading something on his HUD. "…about thirty points should do it."

"A bit steep," Digby grumbled.

"It will be worth it, trust me." Alex closed his eyes.

"Alright." Digby closed his eyes as well, feeling something begin to tug on his mana similar to the ritual that created Tavern. His first instinct was to resist, but instead, he let go. Alex had been right after all, about everything. It was time he put some trust in him. The process continued, taking a little over a minute to complete. He glanced at his mana as soon as it was finished.

MP: 192/192

Digby winced at the loss of thirty points from his total; he'd had over two hundred a minute before. Fortunately a new message appeared on his HUD.

Imbued Staff: Weapon, Uncommon.
Passive Ability: -20 percent mana cost to all spells while holding this item.

Digby's eyes widened as he did the math. He had just lost thirty points of mana, but depending on what he cast using this staff, he could easily save twice that.

"Pretty great, right?" Alex let go of the weapon's shaft. "And that was only rank D of my Imbue spell. If I can keep improving, I should be able to push the effect even further. When I'm ready, we'll destroy this version of the staff and craft a more refined one."

"By then we might be able to make it a little fancier too. Could add in some of the gemstones you looted the other day," Parker added.

"Alright, I'm impressed." Digby looked over the hollow diamond shape at the end. "What is the significance of the design?"

"Nothing really. A diamond wasn't too complicated to form and it gives you something for your Blood Forge spell to grab on to." He shrugged as if it should have been obvious.

"Why does my forge spell have to…?" Digby trailed off as it dawned on him.

"We aren't quite there yet when it comes to blades." Parker pulled one of the crude daggers from behind her. "These will get the job done for now, but the talons you make with your forge spell are sharper. So we figured you could use the shape at the top as a base to forge whatever type of blade you might need rather than having a lower quality one."

"That's…" Digby nodded at the weapon. "…actually quite clever."

"Plus, by making your weapon a staff, my imbue spell is more likely to add a magic-focused passive. If we had made it a regular bladed weapon, it would have gravitated toward something more physical in nature. I learned that by experimenting. Becca's tiara got something similar to your staff."

"Not bad." Digby lowered the head of the weapon to the floor and opened his maw to forge a simple, double-edged spearhead at the end like the one he used to kill Tanner.

"But wait, there's more." Parker grabbed a bundle of leather from a shelf and hopped around him before dropping something onto his shoulder and throwing a few straps around his shoulders to hold it in place.

"Is that…?" Digby snapped his eyes to the item, recognizing it as the pauldron that had once been attached to his Coat of the Goblin King. The garment had been destroyed when he'd blown up the hotel, but the shoulder piece had remained mostly intact. Digby smiled as his maximum mana shot back up fifty points as he regained the mass enchantment that his ruined coat had granted him. He flicked his eyes between both Alex and Parker, taking a step toward them. "I could kiss you both."

"No thanks." Parker shrank away as Alex held up his hand in defense.

"Yeah, please don't. You're still a corpse."

"Fine, see if I ever show you any affection again." Digby turned up what was left of his nose as Alex relaxed.

"Anyway, we still have to do some work to reinforce the pauldron so it will function as actual armor instead of just a costume piece. But for now it will at least stay in place and give you some extra mana. I would have tried to transplant the enchantment into something new, but I didn't want to weaken its effect in the process. I'll try it later when I've ranked up my transfer spell more."

"You've done a fine job…" Digby paused before adding, "Alex," rather than calling him boy like he usually did. It wasn't often that someone had put in so much effort for him, so it came as a surprise when a dull ache formed in his deceased chest. Glancing to the floor, he tried his best to form a genuine smile before looking back up. His usual crooked grin just wouldn't do. "Thank you."

"Ah, you're, um, welcome." Alex scratched at the back of his head, clearly unprepared for such sincere gratitude.

"Now." Digby spun and slammed the end of his staff down with a sense of finality. "Where's Rufus?"

CHAPTER THIRTY-SEVEN

The sound of arguing echoed down the hall of the castle as Digby approached the library with Alex and Parker in tow.

"Welcome back." Mason waited just outside the door, leaning against the wall beside Sax.

"What's the commotion in there?" Digby stopped in front of them.

"See for yourself." He gestured into the library.

"Rufus, you're not going out there and that's final. Good god, I can't believe we're even arguing about this." James rubbed at his eyes as Mathew paced behind one of the sofas. The rest of the castle's inhabitants filled the room around them.

"Oh, Digby. Perfect timing." Rufus marched toward him as Digby entered the room. "Tell James that I must go out there and turn myself over. If there is a chance that these people will leave with just me, then we have to take it."

"Hmm." Digby leaned on his new staff and stared at the elderly zombie. "Unfortunately, I have to side with James, here."

"What?" Rufus' mouth fell open. "Surely, you of all people would not let some sort of misguided sense of sentimentality prevent you from—"

"On the contrary." Digby leaned his head to one side. "I don't think it's a secret here that I don't approve of your way of doing things. Now that you have an army waiting outside your doors, I hope you can see that maybe I had a point."

"Exactly. That's why—"

"But I was also wrong." Digby blew out a breathless sigh. "You may lack a realistic idea of what it will take to survive in this new world, but that's only because you see too much of the good in people. And it's for the same reason that we can't hand you over to Bancroft."

"But why?" Rufus' milky eyes stared straight at him.

"Because, there is simply no way in hell that Skyline simply destroys you and just lets the lot of us be." Digby raised his staff and dropped it back down to the floor, appreciating how many faces looked to him at the sound. "For that matter, it's unlikely they will destroy you in the first place. No, they will likely muzzle you and drag you back to one of their bases to be used for another one of their nefarious schemes. Hell, we might as well be handing them another tool to use for world domination. So, no, we shan't be handing anyone over to them tonight, or any other night."

James and Mathew relaxed as Digby backed them up. The rest of the room, however, exchanged a number of fearful looks.

"Then what would you have us do?" Rufus dropped into one of the chairs with his face in his hands.

"Well…" Digby looked around the room at the people as they stood; they gave him their full attention to hear his plan. "I think we should run the hell away."

Everyone groaned at once.

"But you literally just agreed outside that we need to fight back." Alex leapt forward.

"That's true, I did say that. As much as I wish we could go back to hiding, it simply isn't an option. There's no way we make it through this night without revealing the fact that we didn't perish in Seattle. At this point, fighting will be our only option. But that being said, I don't think I need to remind you what's waiting for us out there."

Digby gestured to the room around them. "The people in this castle aren't soldiers, and a fight with Skyline right now would be entirely one-sided. I think I speak for everyone when I say they didn't sign on for a war. Nor are they prepared to fight one. So yes, for now. We must grab whatever supplies we can, shove the sun goddess statue into my void to take with us, and then, flee like cowards."

He raised a claw to keep his apprentice from arguing. "There will be time to take the fight to them later. Once we have escaped and found these people a place to stay. Then, and only then, can we strike back with all the fury that we heretics can muster. I can't guarantee that we'll win, but at the very least we can make Henwick's life as difficult as possible."

"I can get on board with that." Mason stepped forward. "We get everyone to safety, then we go back to being soldiers."

"Why not?" Sax added.

"Aye, ye can count on me." Hawk joined in.

"How 'bout no? Kids stay off the battlefield." Parker grabbed his shirt and yanked him back into one of the chairs. "And quit pretending to be British."

Digby turned to Rufus. "I am sorry, as much as I don't want to sacrifice the horde, I don't see a way of taking them with us."

"I understand. They have done well so far. At least they might be able to rest in peace when this night is through."

"I think you're all conveniently glossing over the part about figuring out how we're going to escape." Rebecca stepped down the stairs that lead up to her room.

"You caught that, huh?" Digby deflated a bit. "Could we use the kestrel up there?" He pointed a finger up toward the ceiling.

"Maybe." She shrugged. "But the only reason no one has noticed it yet is that it's hovering so far above us. Even with its camouflage, Bancroft's men will spot it if I bring it down to land. Hence why I made you jump out earlier."

"What if, between myself and Rufus' horde, we could create enough chaos to cover your escape?" Digby held up a claw.

"It would be tight, but we could fit most of the non-combatants in the passenger bay. And obviously, I would have to fly it. So you would be down a heretic in the fight. That being said, whoever stays behind would be trapped."

"We could make a run for it in the van." Alex shrugged. "That's better than nothing."

"And what, you're just going to ask them politely to let you through." Rebecca rolled her eyes at the suggestion. "How will you cover your escape?"

"I think you underestimate the amount of chaos I can manage." Digby grinned back to her.

"Really, Dig?" She glowered at him. "Because I don't see your loyal army of rats around right now."

"Army of rats?" Mason leaned his head to one side.

"Oh, I raised ten thousand rats from the dead back in Seattle and laid waste to Skyline's camp." Digby shrugged as if it wasn't a big deal.

Parker furrowed her brow for a second before her eyes bulged. "That's horrifying."

"Yes, it was a whole thing." Rebecca waved away the subject. "But back to my point. The odds of landing the kestrel, getting it loaded with people, and not getting shot down, are slim. Plus your van idea is pretty much suicide." She finished her rant by folding her arms as if putting an end to the thought.

"Welp, a bad plan is better than no plan." Digby elbowed Mason in the side. "Am I right?"

"Stop that." Mason stepped away. "And no, I'm not a fan of this plan either."

A chorus of nervous whispers filled the room. Even Hawk looked concerned. Though, a moment later he tugged on Parker's shoulder to whisper something in her ear.

"Well, I don't see you lot coming up with anything better," Digby growled back at Mason as he brought the room's hopes down.

"Mason's right, we need to come up with something to make this plan a little safer." Rebecca crossed the room to stand next to the soldier.

"Can we take out Bancroft by surprise?" Sax interjected. "That would throw off their leadership."

"And what will we do for food if we do escape?" Kate spoke up, adding to the confusion.

"And where will we even go?" Mathew added.

That was when the last person Digby' expected to put a stop to the questions spoke up.

"Oh shit!" Parker slapped a hand on the arm of Hawk's chair as the child leaned away from her ear.

"What?" Digby eyed the woman as she snapped her eyes to his.

Parker gestured to Hawk. "Tell him what you just told me."

"Umm…" The child dropped his horrible British accent as the entire room looked at him all at once. He opened his mouth to speak, but stopped to shove his hand in his pocket. A second later he pulled out the squishy red ball that he'd shown Digby back at the campground when they'd met. Hawk proceeded to execute the same trick as before, this time, with a bit more proficiency.

Holding the ball in one hand, Hawk showed the room before closing his fingers around it. Everyone stared at his closed fist for a moment before he opened it, revealing an empty palm.

"What if…" Hawk flipped his hand back over to show the ball wadded up between two fingers "…we trick them?"

Digby grinned.

The child really did remind him of himself.

———————— ◆ ◆ ————————

Charles Bancroft checked the time on his pocket watch. The hour that he'd given that Mason fella was almost up. About damn time too. Honestly, the fact that Henwick had ordered him to personally fly all the way out just to take a zombie into custody was irritating. Though, something told him the man was just trying to keep him busy and away from Autem's people back at the base.

Bancroft had made his contempt for the empire clear on more than one occasion and he wasn't about to hold back now. Henwick had never pushed any form of belief system on him, but seeing how the people from Autem wore their faith like an identity was unsettling.

Never having a need for religion, Bancroft thought it pointless. Sure, it was possible to use it to manipulate people, but it was far simpler and more efficient to do the same through simple economics. After all, a populace couldn't rebel against its upper class if they couldn't afford to. His feelings aside.

Then again, Autem had bankrolled Skyline at its inception, so going along with their plans wasn't much of a choice. Bancroft ran his eyes over the inscription on the inside of his pocket watch.

To Charles
Love Annabelle
-1898

He snapped the watch shut and dropped it back in his pocket. Obviously, he could have just checked the time on his smartphone, but he preferred the familiarity of the watch. There was an element of comfort in the timepiece, even if it felt like it was judging him with every quiet tick.

The memory of everything he'd given up when he'd accepted the power that Henwick offered drifted to the surface of his mind for a moment before he pushed it away. Standing up from where he sat in the back of his kestrel, he nodded to his men and headed back out to wait for an answer from this zombie master he'd been sent to collect. It wasn't long before the horde began to part to let someone through.

"Cutting it close." Bancroft let out an irritated sigh as he took up a position between two of his men. Both were new recruits. A fighter and a mage. "Another minute and I would have been forced to kill everyone inside."

The new recruits bracketing him chuckled at the comment as a ragged looking zombie shambled its way out of the horde. Bancroft checked his mana, just in case.

GUARDIAN: LEVEL 60, TEMPESTARII
MP: 786/786

Bancroft debated on electrocuting the monster right then and there. It wouldn't take more than a few bolts of lightning to burn the abomination to ash. He refrained. Coming back empty handed would only put him on Henwick's bad side.

Suppressing his distaste for the conversation to come, Bancroft stepped forward to approach the zombie master. The monster was male and looked like he'd already been dead for years. Clearly the apocalypse had not been kind to him. He didn't even have a nose and walked like he was barely able to stand. Each step seemed to take an immense amount of effort.

The unfortunate monster wore a simple black trench coat and a dirty rag wrapped around his head. His right arm hung limp in a sling, as if the creature had lost the use of it. The only thing the zombie wore that might pass for armor was some sort of rough shoulder guard.

Bancroft suppressed a smirk at the monster's appearance. It was difficult to believe that something so frail could control thousands of undead at once.

Such a pitiful existence.

"That's far enough." Bancroft held up a hand, causing the zombie to stop twenty feet away, nearly tripping over itself in the process.

The creature may have been weak on its own but it was still capable of transmitting the curse. Considering the sun was nowhere to be seen, he didn't want to risk becoming a revenant. Bancroft was sure he could hold off Henwick's modified curse long enough to cleanse it, but he wasn't so sure about the rest of his men. The magic acted fast and, at night, most of them wouldn't last a minute.

"Sorry, can't be too careful. You understand, don't you?" Bancroft lowered his hand. The guardian beside him tossed a muzzle to the ground at the zombie's feet.

"Wha—what?" The monster stuttered while looking down at the muzzle. "You mean, you're not going to destroy me?"

Bancroft arched an eyebrow at the shambling form's accent as he carefully picked up the restraint from the ground and held it in his hands. He hadn't expected the creature to be British.

"No, we don't have orders to destroy you." Bancroft tried his best to reassure the frail monster.

"What will you do with my horde?" The zombie's hands shook.

"We'll need you to order them away from the area. As long as they disperse, then we won't have reason to destroy them."

"But they'll just return and attack my friends in the castle. I won't be able to stop them if I'm not here." The zombie stepped forward as if pleading.

"You need to stay back." Bancroft held up his hand again.

"Sorry, sorry." The zombie bowed his head repeatedly, stumbling forward another step when he lost his balance.

"You need to take a step back and put that muzzle on." Bancroft raised his voice.

"Of course, of course." The zombie started to place the restraint over his mouth before pulling it away again. "But you didn't answer me. What will happen to my friends?" The creature took another step forward.

"Listen, I am not going to warn you again." Bancroft refused to take a step back in response, trying to maintain a position of strength. In business, giving up ground in a negotiation was unforgivable. The same was true in the apocalypse. "You need to get that muzzle on and take a step back, right now."

"I know, I'm sorry. But my friends, I need to make sure they will be safe when I'm gone." The monster picked up his foot as if taking a step back as he was told, but proceeded to place it back down without actually moving.

Bancroft would have suspected that the creature was up to something, but its voice cracked as if he might cry, making him seem more emotional rather than suspicious.

"Your friends will be taken into the protection of the Autem Empire." Bancroft gestured with both hands. "You need to step back and put on that restraint, or I will have to tell my men to open fire."

"Then who will stop my horde from tearing your men apart?" The zombie's voice stopped shaking.

"My men will be fine."

"Will they now?" The zombie inched closer as a smug tone entered his words.

Bancroft froze to process the situation. It was becoming obvious that the zombie master was trying to do something, but he didn't know what. He had read up on everything Skyline knew about the different types of zombies, and the only thing a master could do was command others.

There was nothing it could do alone and the horde would never be able to back him up in time to attack. It was more like the monster was just trying to force him into destroying it. That was when he realized he'd never analyzed the walking corpse, he'd just assumed it was a master by the horde it commanded.

Bancroft's mouth fell open as soon as the Guardian Core revealed his error.

ZOMBIE RAVAGER: RARE
HERETIC: LEVEL 25 NECROMANCER

A crooked grin spread across the dead man's face as he took one last giant step forward. "You know, I often forget to analyze my enemies too."

CHAPTER THIRTY-EIGHT

Digby opened his maw the instant he was within range of Skyline's unsuspecting commander. The shadow of his void swept across the ground around Bancroft's feet as well as the two guardians standing on either side of him.

"What the—" Bancroft dropped down a few inches before magically lifting back up to float just above the inky surface of Digby's void. The guardians standing on either side of him dropped straight down, flailing as they sank. One caught hold of Bancroft's boot, nearly pulling him down as well. Skyline's commander simply kicked the man's hand away.

Digby stared at his enemy, unsure how he was remaining aloft in mid-air. Of course, he had already analyzed the man. He wasn't an idiot, but unfortunately, he didn't know what a tempestarii was.

No matter.

Digby wasn't finished. No, not even close.

He tore off the fake sling and rags he wore to cover the bone that formed his gauntlet and horned crown. Then, with a flourish, he slammed his maw shut to kill the two guardians that had fallen in, getting an experience message in return.

Guardian: Level 5 Mage defeated, 450 experience awarded.
Guardian: Level 3 Fighter defeated, 250 experience awarded.

Opening his maw again next to his own foot, he called forth his staff. The diamond shaped head rose from the black shadow on the ground, covered in the necrotic blood that filled his void. He snapped his claws around the weapon and pulled it free while simultaneously casting forge. The black fluid coating the staff flowed up to its head to form a wicked looking spear, leaving the rest of the weapon clean.

Checking his HUD, he noted the decreased cost of the spell.

MP: 214/242

Digby grinned. After using twelve mana to widen his maw, forge had only cost him sixteen points. Then, right on cue, Rufus appeared, standing tall in the castle's entrance at the top of the hill behind him. The ancient zombie raised his cane high and sent the horde into battle.

"Attack!"

Bancroft's eyes bulged as a realization of what was happening fell across his face. He canceled whatever spell he was using to float in the air, and dropped back down to stand on solid ground now that the pool of darkness below him was gone. With a raised fist, he answered the oncoming horde in kind.

"Destroy the dead and take the castle!"

All at once, three thousand snarling zombies shambled forward as Skyline's army charged up the hill to meet the horde. Hearst's Castle loomed over the scene, the moon hanging in the sky behind it.

Total chaos followed.

Dozens of fireballs lit up the night as a shower of icicles struck down corpses left and right. Gunfire echoed here and there along with the occasional explosion of a grenade. From the horde, chunks of flesh and shrapnel of bone flew into the air with each burst of fire and smoke. Not even the surrounding trees were spared as the guardians set them alight to stop the horde from using the surrounding landscape for cover.

Digby was just glad he'd told Asher to wait in the castle. He didn't want her taking any unnecessary risks. He didn't need her in the fight anyway. Not with Rufus on his side. The old zombie master would die before he ate anyone.

Digby struggled to keep Bancroft in his sights. Killing him would give them a chance. The man stood, issuing orders to everyone around him. Black blood from his brief dip into Digby's void still covered his boots and pooled around his feet.

Why not? Digby chuckled as he cast another forge spell to reshape the puddle into a few spikes that stabbed through the sides of Bancroft's boots. Skyline's commander shrieked as he struggled to rip his feet free from the ground. Digby let out a wild cackle while Rufus' horde pushed forward around him to keep the pressure on. Fighting broke out on all sides as screams filled the night. He just hoped Lana had received his message to stay out of the way.

Bancroft swore as he tore his feet free from Digby's spikes. Once he was loose, the commander limped in a small circle while continuing to swear. Apparently, whatever a tempestarii was, it wasn't suited for physical combat. Digby took the opportunity to stalk closer to his prey. Several low-level guardians rushed forward to cover their leader as he slipped away. A few of Skyline's men drew swords from the magnetic sheaths on their backs while some of their mages cast Fireballs to keep Rufus' zombies at bay.

Digby dove into the fray, basking in the freedom of movement that his agility provided now that he had a real foot again. Spinning on one heel, he deflected a sword aimed at his neck and kicked a foe away into a passing zombie. Teeth clamped down on the guardian's throat as he fell in the grasp of the dead. Digby ran him through with his spear to put him out of his misery before another two members of Rufus' horde fell upon the unfortunate man's corpse.

Guardian: Level 10 Fighter defeated, 950 experience awarded.

Ducking down, Digby dodged an enchanted crossbow bolt that hit a zombie ten feet behind him. The poor monster cried out and swelled before exploding in a burst of gore. While crouched close to the ground, Digby opened his maw to call forth one of the skulls he'd originally prepared for the fight with Tanner. Snatching it up, he spun in the direction the bolt had come from to launch the improvised explosive. A Cremation spell lit up the night with flickering green light just before it crashed into one of Bancroft's men.

Guardian: Level 8 Enchanter defeated, 750 experience awarded.

Before Digby had a chance to celebrate, several shards of ice flew straight for his head. He raised his gauntlet to block as spikes of frozen water shattered against his bone armor. A second attack came from behind, plunging into his lower back. Discomfort swelled from the wound as Digby turned and looked down to find an enchanted bolt sticking out of his side. A second later a sizable chunk exploded from his body. Digby fell to one knee, giving thanks that the spell hadn't been fully ranked up. He cast Necrotic Regeneration as he searched for the threat.

An enchanter stood on the grass to the side of the road.

There you are. Digby cast Burial. A sudden yelp confirmed the kill as the earth claimed the foe. Next came the mage that had distracted him with an Icicle. Digby caught them with the corner of his eye, before also dropping them into a freshly dug grave.

Guardian: Level 4 Enchanter defeated, 350 experience awarded.
Guardian: Level 3 Mage defeated, 250 experience awarded.

Just as his wound finished regenerating, a fighter cut through the horde, slicing three zombies at once with their sword. Digby raised his spear to block. The guardian's blade slammed into the crystalized edge of his weapon, chipping away a bit of hardened blood on impact. The fighter proceeded to swing wildly, as if determined to stop him from countering.

Digby couldn't help but chuckle at the idiocy. Didn't the man realize his spear wasn't the only thing he had to worry about?

"You must be new."

Digby simply opened his maw in the palm of his left hand and cast forge. A blade of black blood erupted from the small shadow, impaling the man. Closing his maw, he gripped his spear and swung it in a wide arc to take the fighter's head clean off. It landed at his feet as another experience message flashed across his vision.

"Waste not." Digby snatched the convenient body part up and pried the man's head from his helmet, nearly dropping it when the fighter blinked up at him.

"Gah!" He gasped in horror that the head wasn't dead yet.

Digby immediately cast Cremation and launched the head in the direction of the nearest guardian. It didn't seem to hit anyone, but still, at least it was out of his hands. Glancing around, he tried his best to gauge the flow of the battle. The horde was taking ground, but aside from the guardians that he'd killed, Skyline was holding their own. At best, the horde would only buy them time.

That's alright. Time was all they needed.

That was when Digby spotted Bancroft, falling back toward one of the kestrels.

"There you are, my dear commander."

He stalked through the battle toward his prey. If he could end the man, then maybe they might be able to turn the tides. As it was, the tempestarii didn't seem as dangerous as he would have expected considering the man's high level. Digby flicked his eyes across the chaos, finding the armored brute that had followed him through Santa Barbra a few days prior.

"Perfect. A little back up never hurt anyone." He cast Control Uncommon to override Rufus' commands and take the brute as his minion. His mana dropped below half remaining. The spell's cost was steep even with his staff's reduction. Still, he couldn't afford to be stingy.

Digby called his minion to his side and pushed through the chaos toward Skyline's general. The brute barreled forward, tearing one guardian in half and crushing another under its feet. More experience came in as embers drifted through the air from the burning trees that surrounded the battle.

Bancroft locked eyes with him as he emerged from the horde, the brute at his side releasing a furious roar. The tempestarii threw out both hands as if grabbing onto some unseen force. Digby immediately felt the flow of mana in the man's blood. It was massive. The wind around him began to blow as he realized the danger he was in. A layer of dark clouds flowed in above followed by a deep and foreboding rumbling.

"Oh damn." Digby sighed just before several bolts of lightning ripped through the sky. Converging above him, they crashed down. Digby fell back as his armored brute rammed him out of the way, breaking one of his legs in the process. His minion roared as the spell tore through its body.

Armored Brute, lost.

Digby reread the Heretic Seed's message in disbelief. His brute was dead. It had happened so fast. He snapped his eyes back up to his enemy just as he felt the same intense sensation of mana flowing through the man.

"Best you learn your place." Bancroft's eyes glowed white with power.

"No, no no no." Digby grabbed for his staff, snagging the end with his gauntlet just in time to cast Absorb. Lightning crashed down again, turning his world white. The air crackled around him as energy poured into his spell. It felt like his entire mana system was on fire. He cast Emerald Flare the instant Bancroft's attack was finished, making sure to throw the power he'd just taken in back at him.

Green streaks of sickening energy flowed through the night toward Skyline's general. He leapt back from the epicenter just before the resulting explosion rocked the landscape. A wave of radiation swept out to poison the area along with a surge of emerald lightning that erupted outward to strike everything around it.

Escaping the initial blast, Bancroft got a taste of his own medicine as a sickening current of electricity connected with his chest. He immediately clutched a hand over his mouth and staggered to one side. Clearly, the added power Digby had absorbed had increased the potency of his flare's ailment effect. Still, though, it wasn't nearly enough.

Digby glanced at his HUD.

MP: 38/242

Less than a third of his mana was left. Bancroft regained his composure and raised his hand to the sky again, this time casting something else. For a moment, nothing happened. Then everything did. A hail of ice shards pelted the horde from the clouds. Most shattered on contact but some shattered skulls.

Digby took a cluster of ice to his bone crown, dazing him for a moment. Bancroft probably wanted to drive him away, not wanting to call down another lightning bolt on him while he was still in range to throw it back. It was just as well. Digby didn't have enough mana to absorb much more.

It was time to run. He just hoped he'd caused enough chaos to create an opportunity for the others.

Opening his maw and casting Blood Forge, he thrust a post of crystalized blood up from beneath his feet to launch himself back toward the castle at an angle. Below, the battle raged as Digby soared over the horde. Expecting to crash into the ground, confusion swept over Digby as his fall was broken by a dozen zombies reaching out to catch him. They raised him up for a second, giving him a glimpse of Rufus shouting toward him.

A brief spike of guilt stabbed at him from all the names he'd called the elderly zombie. The horde set him back down on his feet and surged forward to cover his escape. Another barrage of hailstones peppered the area as Digby checked his mana again. There wasn't enough left to do much with and meditation was out of the question.

Understanding the situation for what it was, he did the only thing he could. He left the fight up to Rufus and cast Burial. The ground beneath him opened up to swallow him before filling his grave back in. Darkness engulfed him as the vibrations of battle reverberated through the earth.

He just needed a minute to rest and regain his mana. One single minute to be back up to full.

How much could possibly happen in a minute?

CHAPTER THIRTY-NINE

Lana Moore sat in the back of an empty kestrel with one hand shoved under the visor of her helmet, chomping on her nails with the ferocity of a rabid gopher.

How did I get here?

It was only a month ago that she'd turned eighteen. She hadn't even finished high school, but yet, there she was, a level four mage in the zombie apocalypse. On top of that, she was a founding member of a two-person resistance movement within Skyline against her employers and the Autem Empire. Plus, her only ally outside was a dead man that didn't know how to zip up his fly two weeks ago.

Lana chewed on her fingernail harder and reminded herself who she was fighting for. Her father was dead. She assumed her mother was gone as well, but Alvin, her brother, was still out there. He may have been taken in by Autem, but she was going to get him back. He was all she had left and she would fight anyone who stood between them, even if that meant throwing in with Digby and his heretics. As things were, her two pathetic spells weren't going to get her very far alone.

The sounds of battle raged outside, making her glad that

she didn't have any offensive magic. The fact that she was near useless in a fight had prompted her squad leader to order her to remain aboard the kestrel. It wasn't that she was afraid. No, far from it. She just didn't want to fight against her secret allies in the castle.

On top of that, she had received a warning message from Easton on a smartphone that she'd smuggled in while out on patrol. Apparently, Digby was causing some sort of diversion outside and couldn't guarantee her safety if she was amongst the rest of Skyline's troops. For now, hiding in the kestrel was exactly the right place for her.

That was when a random zombie staggered its way up the kestrel's open ramp.

"Get out!"

She pulled her pistol from her holster and fired. The creature lurched to one side, taking the round in the shoulder.

"Shit!"

With literally one week of training, she wasn't a good shot. Guns just weren't her thing. She fired again, blowing a hole in the corpse's neck. It didn't even slow down. Backing up, she began to run out of space in the cabin. Taking a deep breath, she waited until the zombie got close enough that even she could land a hit. Then finally, she put a round right between its eyes. The monster sprayed blackened gray matter across the ceiling before dropping to the floor in a heap.

"Holy shit." She kicked the corpse repeatedly. "I hate, this, god damn, apocalypse."

Of course, that was when Commander Bancroft stormed up the ramp.

"Ah…" Lana froze mid-kick before eventually regaining her composure and standing up straight. She made a point of giving that ridiculous Autem salute. "Sir, I, ah—"

"Don't just stand there." He ignored the corpse on the floor. "Give me a heal and set up a link."

"Of course." Lana immediately cast Regeneration on him before rushing to the side of the compartment where a pane of plexiglass had been mounted. She reached out to place her hand on the surface. "Where do you need to connect to?"

"Just open the line." He pulled off a glove and placed his hand against the glass as well.

Lana did as she was told, casting the spell Mirror Link. She was glad he couldn't see her face under her helmet, considering the suspicious look that must have been plastered across it. The spell was simple, it just created a visual and audio link between two reflective surfaces. The one requirement being that the user or someone with them had to have touched both sides of the connection.

Back when she'd been given her guardian ring and gained the spell, an officer had taken her on a tour of every major link point on the base. That begged the question, where was Bancroft trying to access? It was either somewhere she hadn't been shown, or it wasn't even on the base.

Bancroft dropped his hand back to his side as the pane of plexiglass lit up to show a fancy-looking office covered wood paneling and framed paintings. A rugged yet well-dressed man sat at a desk at the center. He ceased writing something and looked straight at them.

"Charles, what seems to be the matter?"

"Henwick, sir." General Bancroft stepped closer to the glass. "It's that zombie, the necromancer from Seattle. He's alive."

Lana's ears perked up at the name Henwick. Wasn't that the guy that Digby mentioned? The guy behind everything?

"Alive?" Henwick arched an eyebrow.

"Yes... well, no. He's still dead, but he wasn't destroyed in Seattle like we thought." Bancroft sounded worried. "He's standing with a horde of three thousand and has the help of the zombie master that you wanted me to capture."

"Interesting." Henwick gave an amused chuckle. "I wonder how Graves survived the bomb."

"It seems he's gained some sort of absorption ability that we don't have access to. It's able to throw back the power of spells that are directed at him as part of his own magic. He must have used it to take the brunt of the blast when the bomb fell."

Henwick tapped a finger on his desk. "That would explain the radiation present at the scene of that hotel explosion in Santa Barbara. It seems our necromancer has been getting around."

"It seems so." Bancroft hesitated. "After seeing him in action, I recommend a surgical air strike to take him out. My men can hold him here until——"

"How many men have you brought?" Henwick interrupted him.

"Two hundred. Though, we've lost around ten percent. Mostly lower levels. We will inevitably sustain more losses if we continue this fight as it is."

"You brought that many guardians with you, and you can't handle one necromancer?" Henwick slapped a hand to his desk. "Honestly, Charles, Graves is not a mastermind. At best, he's an opportunist. The only thing he has going for him is that he's slippery. Which is why I worry that he might find a way to flee like the coward he is if you give him too much space and wait for an airstrike. You need to get in there now and take him down with everything you have."

"Yes, I know. I'm sure that with the forces I have now, we can ensure that he and his followers are thoroughly crushed." Bancroft shook his head. "But still, I estimate that throwing our men at him will result in at least half being killed. Most of which are new recruits that will have tactical value in the future as they gain more levels."

"That may be true, but most of Skyline's current troops only joined with the intent of securing food and shelter for themselves, so I wouldn't exactly call them devoted followers to our cause. Obviously it's different for the recruits that are being indoctrinated by Autem, but for now, losing a few men from Skyline's ranks here and there will be fine. Besides, Autem is growing every day and in time we won't even need Skyline."

Bancroft flinched at that last statement before glancing at

Lana beside him. Clearly, she wasn't meant to have heard any of it. Not only that, but Alvin had been taken in by Autem and she didn't like the thought of her brother being indoctrinated by anyone. She clenched her jaw, unsure what any of it meant.

Eventually Bancroft nodded. "Alright, sir, I'll see to it that the necromancer is destroyed."

"You do that." Henwick cut the connection without another word.

Bancroft stood still for a moment, glancing at her again like he was debating on saying something. It was obvious that she had heard something she wasn't supposed to. Actually, she couldn't believe Henwick had spoken so freely in front of her to begin with. It was like he didn't even care about secrecy.

That was when a surge of panic streaked through her mind. Henwick didn't care about what she heard, because he didn't need to. He didn't expect her to live.

Lana froze, afraid that Bancroft might simply kill her right then and there. It would certainly be easy enough. Before she could react, his fingers moved toward the pistol on his hip.

Then he stopped, shoving his hand into his pocket as if that was what he had intended all along. Lana was sure it wasn't. The commander dropped his eyes down to the zombie's corpse that still lay on the floor before turning away to head back to the kestrel's ramp. He stopped halfway down to change her orders.

"Rejoin your squad, we need everyone in this fight." Bancroft continued down the ramp and out of sight.

"…What?" Lana stared at the open ramp as she realized what the general's command was.

A death sentence.

Her mouth fell open. Bancroft had just ordered her execution. With her obvious lack of combat skills and offensive spells, there was only one outcome for her if she went out into the fight. She would die out there. He didn't need to kill her himself, not when there was a horde of zombies outside that would happily do the job for him.

Obviously, she could ignore his orders and continue to hide in the kestrel, but that would only delay her demise. Her squad leader or another guardian would make sure she didn't live through the night.

The realization left her with only one choice.

Escape.

I can't save Alvin if I'm dead. Lana shoved a hand up the bottom of her chest armor to find the smart phone she'd hidden there and opened her conversation with Easton. She couldn't communicate directly with Digby while he was fighting, but maybe Easton could get a message to him.

After sending her coconspirator a summary of everything Henwick had said, she asked him to tell Digby she was making a break for the castle. Somehow, she had to run her ass through the horde to her allies. If she was careful, there was a chance she could make it.

"Shit, who am I kidding? I'm so going to die."

That was when she received a message from Rebecca.

It started by telling her to make a break for the castle and that they would open a path in the horde near the edge of the battle to let her through. Apparently, they needed to use her Mirror Link spell to set some sort of plan into action.

"Maybe I'm not going to die." She nodded before reading further.

What followed was a rough breakdown description of a plan for escape. She read it over three times, unable to believe that Rebecca's words were coming from someone older and probably wiser than she was. Eventually, she dropped her hand limp at her sides.

"Oh god, we are so dead."

CHAPTER FORTY

Digby relaxed within the calm of his grave, letting his mana tick back up. He cast Blood Forge the instant it reached full, erupting from the ground the same way he had during his fight with Tanner. He landed back on the surface amid a scene of chaos. The horde moved all around him, though they had lost nearly a third of their numbers. Bancroft's continued hailstorms had taken their toll.

That was when a torrent of bullets tore through the night.

Leaping to the side, Digby dodged a barrage that cut a swath through the horde. A dozen zombies were shredded to pieces in an instant as a light shined down from above.

What the hell?

Digby shielded his eyes with his gauntlet. A kestrel passed by overhead, its guns blazing. Two more flew over the horde further away while another headed for the castle.

"Damn it!"

Digby got moving. He had expected Bancroft to send in his airships, but he'd thought there would be more time. Rufus' horde parted to let him through as the guardians waged war behind him. Madness greeted him as he reached his home.

The castle was under siege.

A squad of guardians had already gotten inside and were rushing for Rufus who stood amongst a group of zombies with the wall of one of the guest houses at his back. A pair of brutes stood firm to shield him. Fireballs soared through the air as their enemies attacked, setting the guest house aflame. Digby cursed Skyline for ruining his new home. He'd had so many plans for the place.

Down by the makeshift forge, Mason and Sax were doing what they could, each swinging away with their imbued short swords at whoever got near them. The implanted mana in their weapons was the only thing keeping them from being killed outright.

Searching the scene for his apprentice, he found Alex sitting on the ground with his legs crossed and his eyes closed as Parker stood guard with her daggers at the ready. Digby glanced at his HUD, noticing how low Alex's mana was. Clearly the young artificer was meditating to regain what he could. Apparently, he had figured out how and was putting the ability to use, despite the chaos around him.

Digby didn't bother looking for Rebecca; she still had things to do before they made their escape. As for the rest of the castle's inhabitants, he hoped they were safe and already in position. There wasn't time to worry about anything more.

Skyline's men slid down from above on ropes as a kestrel hovered overhead. The aircraft lit up the night with gunfire, obliterating one of the castle's towers and carving through the building toward where Rebecca's room was.

"No!" Digby thrust out a hand to cast flare while the kestrel floated in place. Energy streaked toward the craft just before the airship detonated in an explosion of emerald light. The wreckage crashed down into the pool where he had landed earlier. Digby hoped the blast had been high enough to keep the poison effect from hitting any of his allies on the ground.

His concerns were forced out of his mind as two guardians rushed toward him while he made his way up the lawn to the side of the castle where they intended to land their escape craft. Digby swung his spear to deflect a sword, his weapon's Blood Forged edge snapping in the process. The construct had taken far more punishment than it would have been able to if it had been forged by the spell's previous ranks, but still, it wasn't unbreakable. Without giving his enemy a chance to take advantage of the opening, Digby opened his maw on the ground and sent a black spike straight up to skewer the man.

Guardian: Level 7 Fighter defeated, 650 experience awarded.

Before he had time to read the message, a blade pierced his back just under his bone armor as the other guardian lunged for him. A familiar numbness began to spread up through his chest. His mind flashed back to the fight with Captain Manning just before he'd escaped Seattle as the wave of magic threatened to banish the curse that animated him from his body. Fortunately, the shard of the Heretic Seed chased the spell away.

His attacker ripped their weapon to the side, tearing it through Digby's body in the process. He fell to the ground with a wide gash in his back. A regeneration spell was all that kept his entrails from falling out. Looking up at the burley guardian that had attacked him, Digby confirmed what he feared.

Guardian: Level 27 Holy Knight

His enemy was the same class and level that Manning had been. He'd nearly died at the hands of that man. Digby gritted his teeth and gripped his broken spear. He wasn't as weak as he'd been back then. Opening his maw, he attempted to swallow his enemy whole to end the fight before it began.

The knight thrust his sword downward into the shadow as it grew, somehow destabilizing the gateway to his void. His maw vanished in an instant. Digby growled. It made sense; the spell empowering his blade was strong against the dead. The same must have been true about his abilities.

"Fine, if I can't swallow you whole, I will just have to save you for later." Digby gave a wicked laugh as the knight let out a yelp, the earth below his feet opening to drop him into a fresh grave. The hole rolled back in to remove all traces of the man. Digby nodded to the patch of dirt and walked across it, making sure to stomp extra hard. "Well that's one less thing to worry abo—oh hell!"

A meaty hand burst up through the ground to grab his ankle before he could finish gloating. Digby toppled over, kicking at the knight as he began digging himself out of his grave. "Hey, stop that! It's not fair if you just climb back out."

Clearly, his enemy didn't care about what was fair or not, his level granting him enough strength to push his way through the layer of earth that covered him. Digby made a note to remember the limitation of his Burial spell.

"Alright, fine." Digby opened his maw by his feet and used the blood to forge himself a new spear. "We can do this the hard way."

Before he could make a move, a pile of glossy black bones clattered to the ground behind the knight. The burly man turned to look at the sound, staring at the pile of bones for a few seconds with his head cocked to one side. After nothing happened, he brought his attention back to Digby. That was when Tavern, having jumped from the kestrel above, reassembled and leapt onto the knight's back.

The guardian let out a confused shout as the skeleton wrapped their bony hands around his chest. Digby chuckled at the display just before casting Cremation to set his minion alight. Then, he took several steps back.

A blue protective barrier shimmered across the knight's body to keep the emerald flames at bay. It wasn't enough. The hollow cavity in Tavern's skull sloshed with necrotic blood, releasing a high-pitched whine that blended with a muffled battle cry from the skeleton's mouth, where they held a grenade in their jaws.

Digby dove behind a statue just as his minion exploded.

The knight's barrier winked out in an instant as burning blood covered his upper body. Digby thrust his staff in the man's direction, opening his maw to jam a spike of blood straight up through his chin.

Guardian: Level 27 Holy Knight defeated, 2,650 experience awarded.
You have reached level 26.
4,346 experience to next level.

Digby dropped his extra point into intelligence to boost his maximum mana and ignored the rest of the message. He opened his maw to summon Tavern back to the fight, using the numerous skeletons within. His minion rose from the black pool of necrotic blood, assembling themselves again.

Digby cast forge to armor his minion in a layer of glossy, black blood while filling their skull with enough fluid to create another explosive for when he needed it. Footsteps tore his attention away as soon as he was finished.

Another guardian, much smaller than the knight Digby had just killed, ran toward him with their hands raised as if attempting to cast a spell. Digby checked his mana.

MP: 130/253

Damn, only half left. I'll have to be conservative. Digby readied his spear and prepared to do some stabbing.

"Wait, wait, wait!" The guardian flailed their arms before pulling off their helmet to reveal a familiar woman. Her hair was pulled back, save for a number curly locks that had escaped to stick out on one side.

Digby tilted his head at her before finally placing the face to the photo on her dating profile, having some trouble on account of her somewhat disheveled appearance.

"Lana?"

"Yes, it's me, you jerk!" She didn't stop running, opting to rush straight up to him and hit him in the arm with her helmet. "Rebecca told me to run through the horde to meet you here and you just tried to stab me without a second thought."

"Oh yes, that's right. We still need you." Digby swatted her away.

A number of curse words, some of which Digby hadn't heard before, flowed from the young woman as she stomped in a circle. Eventually she settled down.

"Hey, you got any beer?" Tavern crept up behind her at exactly the wrong time.

"Fuck-shit-why?" Lana leapt away from the skeleton.

"Umm, alright." Digby gestured to his minion. "Allow me to introduce Tavern, my newest minion."

"You make skeletons now?" She shook her head. "I thought zombies were your thing."

"I do that too." Digby nodded.

"Why does it want a beer?" She eyed the skeleton for a moment.

"We like beer." Tavern shrugged.

"Who's we?"

"Who cares!" Digby threw up one hand in frustration at the conversation. "We don't have time for questions. Just get behind me and stay out of the way. We're almost ready to make our move."

"Sure, fine, whatever." She fell in line behind him as he continued up the hill to the kestrel's landing site.

Glancing around for Rebecca, Digby caught a glimpse of her through the windows of the castle's suite, sitting at her laptop. The kestrel came into view a moment later as the air above them rippled. The craft's camouflage deactivated, revealing the airship to their enemies; that was, if they hadn't noticed it already.

Guardians rushed up the hill, clearly realizing he and his heretics were close to making their escape. Mason and Sax ran to block their path as Alex leaped into the fray, firing an enchanted bolt from one of Skyline's crossbows. He must have taken the weapon off one of the fallen guardians. Parker backed them up, along with Rufus, who hobbled his way to join the effort. A few zombies followed close behind, though his brutes had already fallen in the battle.

From his elevated position on the hill, Digby could see the entire horde below as it struggled to fend off the siege. The majority of the guardians seemed to be lower levels, but the few that had clearly advanced further were destroying zombies by the dozen. Less than a thousand of the dead remained standing.

It wouldn't be long before their home fell. They had to make their move now.

That was when Rebecca emerged from the castle's main door, followed by the entire group of survivors that Rufus had been protecting. The ramp on the kestrel lowered as the people ran across the lawn. The crowd was nearly twice that of the craft's occupancy, but for what they had planned, it didn't matter.

Then the hail came.

Chunks of ice the size of dice pelted the area. The castle's windows shattered as frozen shards crashed against the stone walls. The people in the kestrel cried out in fear.

Bancroft wasn't about to let them leave.

The wind picked up as the sky began to rumble again. Digby stepped forward, his coat billowing behind him as the others fought against the guardians that rushed forward. It all came down to this moment. Digby raised his staff, standing before the kestrel, ready to absorb whatever Bancroft threw at him. He let out a wild snarl as lightning shattered the night.

Swirling before him, a purple vortex drank in the power that threatened to tear the craft behind him apart. Just as the bolt of electricity surged through his mana system, another kestrel flew into position with its guns ready to fire. A torrent of bullets carved across the castle grounds toward their escape craft, throwing dirt and stone into the air. Digby raised his staff high, only to slam it back down as he cast Emerald Flare.

Radioactive streaks of energy converged before detonating at the center of the attacking airship. Debris fell across the lawn. One of the craft's rotors even crushed an unsuspecting guardian unlucky enough to have been caught underneath. Digby ignored the experience messages that came in, only glancing at his HUD to check his mana.

MP: 106/253

Somehow, he had to hold out.

Digby watched as the survivors piled into the kestrel behind him. James helped Kate across the lawn as Mathew guided the others. The children fled the castle all at once with Hawk in the lead. Mason and Sax guarded the effort, keeping a few of the low-level guardians at bay. Even Lana did her part by throwing her helmet back on and drifting away from the center of the fray to hide. While out of sight, she made use of the magic that Skyline had granted her to support the others. A healing spell on both Mason and Sax kept them in the fight.

"Is this really going to work?" Alex joined Digby at his side just as thunder rumbled through the sky again.

"It's going to have to." Digby raised his staff to take in the attack he knew was coming.

Lightning struck down, again filling his mana system with a jolt of power to be used later. Digby glanced down at his hands as smoke wafted up from his singed fingers. The white bone of his claws had been burnt black along with the wooden handle of his staff. He wasn't sure how much he or the weapon could take.

They were so close.

CHAPTER FORTY-ONE

Bancroft marched forward as his men carved a path through the horde to the castle's entrance. He took no joy in destroying the place. It wasn't his first time there, after all. Back before he'd joined up with Henwick, he had actually visited the castle just after it had been built. As a member of America's high society of the time, he had been a welcomed guest.

He never expected to return to the place as a conquering army. Then again, it was all still just business.

The necromancer came into view as Bancroft entered the castle grounds. The dead man, Digby Graves, stood with his back to the kestrel he'd stolen. A small group of people stood with him, desperately fighting to give the aircraft behind them time to take off. He almost felt bad for them. Almost.

There was no need to feel guilty. Sometimes people lost everything; that was just how things were. That was the price of doing business.

The stolen kestrel took flight, floating back up into the sky just above the castle.

"Come on, come on." Graves tapped his staff on the

ground as the craft's camouflage rippled across its surface. A moment later it was barely visible.

That won't help. Bancroft raised his hand to the clouds as the sky rumbled.

The necromancer's face fell, clearly realizing that there was no way to protect the kestrel from the ground. It was too late. Bancroft's mana was already moving. Lighting arced through the night as he closed his fingers into a fist and yanked downward to guide the spell to the ground. A dozen bolts converged into one before snaking through the sky toward the space where the kestrel had been visible a second before.

The craft couldn't have gone far. Its camouflage flickered and failed as electricity tore through it like it was made of nothing but paper. The bolt arced off in all directions just before one of the kestrel's rotors exploded.

Graves let out a devastated cry as the craft flipped end over end before exploding into the woods further down on the back of the hill. The pain in his voice was evident. The others around him joined in with shouts and screams of their own.

That was it.

There was no escape for them now.

His business there was nearly complete.

Bancroft stood tall as Graves turned a hateful glare on him. A young man beside the necromancer fired an enchanted bolt into one of his men at point blank range. The man's chest exploded in a burst of gore. Bancroft shook his head. Couldn't they see that it was senseless? There was no need to keep killing his soldiers.

"I'm almost out of mana," the young man shouted, showing a lack of forethought as he announced to everyone around him that he was an easy target.

"We have to make for the van now!" the soldier, Mason, called out as he and a few others struggled to stay standing.

A woman, wielding a pair of crude daggers, rushed to help just as one of Bancroft's men launched a Fireball into her side.

The woman blocked the attack with one of her weapons as the spell burst. Flames splashed against her arm and shoulder. Screaming in pain, she continued forward to thrust both of her blades into the fighter's back. Strangely, the third degree burns that formed on her face, neck, and arms began to slowly heal as she plunged her blade deeper.

That is unexpected. Bancroft arched an eyebrow. *I should make sure to collect those daggers. Clearly Graves has a crafter with some skill among his heretics.* A quick scan of the group told him who it was. The young man, wielding one of Skyline's crossbows, was labeled an artificer. *I will have to see if that one will accept a job on our side.*

The injured woman keeled over in pain an instant later, clearly unable to repair the extent of the damage with the effect of her weapons.

Maybe not then. Bancroft shook his head. Whatever the ability her weapons had, it wasn't strong enough to make the artificer worth the trouble of recruiting.

Mason and the other man with him dropped down at the woman's side. Even the artificer leapt toward the trio. Pulling a flask of water from a pouch, he cast Purify and poured what he could into the injured woman's mouth. Apparently, he'd advanced the spell enough to apply its healing effect. Bancroft almost reconsidered his assessment of the young man, though, as it was, it didn't look like the woman would survive without a real healing spell to pull her back from the brink.

Bancroft sighed; he didn't like to see women get hurt. Even if it was necessary. He stepped forward to put an end to the display.

"I'm sorry it came to this, but you forced my hand." Bancroft pushed up the hill with a dozen of his men at his back.

Graves simply glared down from the top of the hill.

"I would have preferred to have ended this without things getting messy. Now, why don't you all just come down here and surrender?" Bancroft raised a hand to the deceased man. Surely,

Graves had to see that it was over. He gave one more declaration to make sure. "There's no need for any more of your people to die."

CHAPTER FORTY-TWO

Digby glanced at the van, sitting down the hill only fifty feet away. He hoped the vehicle would be able to make it far enough. He snapped his eyes back to Bancroft's stupid face as the man stood there holding up a hand to offer him one last chance to surrender.

For a moment, Digby debated on taking him up on it. He wasn't expecting Skyline's commander to make it through the horde so quickly. Nor was he expecting his allies to take so much damage. As things stood, the plan was falling apart.

Digby glanced to his side as Alex struggled to get more water into Parker. Her burns were healing, but not fast. Mason and Sax did their best to get her off the ground. As it was, she was going to slow them down. He tightened his hand around his staff. He couldn't leave her behind. Not after all the effort she'd put in to helping them.

Surveying the hillside, he took a rough count of what remained of the dead. There were only around five hundred zombies still standing. Even with the last of the horde getting in the way, Digby might not make it to the van with the others.

At the very least, he was going to have to create a distraction.

Digby waved a hand to Tavern, telling the dark skeleton to get moving. There was a chance they could slip away into the shadows without anyone noticing. Next, he checked his mana.

MP: 84/253

Digby winced. It wasn't much. He still had some absorbed power stored up to boost a flare spell but still, it was too slow to catch Bancroft in the blast. He judged the distance, finding the man standing just out of range to open his maw close enough for a blood spike. It was a mistake to show him one of his limitations earlier. Struggling to come up with an idea, he couldn't think of a way to keep the man from dodging. All he could do was try his best.

Digby stepped forward, only to be stopped a second later when Rufus held out a hand in front of him.

"No. I'll go." The old zombie spoke with a sense of finality in his voice.

"What?" Digby's mouth fell open.

"Obviously, we need a distraction." The elderly zombie turned back to look him in the eye. "And I think this is a job for me."

Digby lowered his head, knowing full well what that meant. "But, you'll—"

"I know I have been in denial all this time." Rufus cut him off. "I thought the world could be rebuilt just by keeping those who survived safe. But I had no idea how bad things actually were. After seeing what your enemies are capable of, I realize that this world needs more than a zombie master with good intentions." Rufus stared down at Bancroft as he stood, offering a chance at surrender. "No, for this world to survive, it needs you."

Digby shook his head. "I hardly think I'm the hero the world needs."

Rufus let out a laugh. "I didn't say it needs a hero. I said it needs you." He dropped his cane to the ground and raised his hands as if surrendering. "Against a force as powerful as these Skyline people, heroics won't stand a chance. That's why the world needs someone as sneaky and underhanded as you." He started walking only looking back for a moment. "So do me a favor, Graves, and live up to my expectations."

"I never liked you." Digby clicked his tongue. "But I do respect you."

"Same." Rufus continued down the stairs to approach Bancroft at the bottom. "Now, where were we? Oh yes, you wanted to take me prisoner."

Before any of the guardians had time to react, the zombie master kicked off into a run, or at least, the closest thing to running his frail body was capable of. A Fireball sailed past him as he weaved to one side, stumbling to the ground in the process. Rufus caught himself with his hands and pushed off. An icicle exploded through his abdomen as he struggled to sprint.

Bancroft simply stepped back a few feet to let a pair of fighters move in to block the elderly zombie's path. Rufus crashed into them, biting and snarling. He kicked with both legs, trying to climb over the men with one hand outstretched toward Bancroft, who stood just out of reach.

Digby hesitated, unsure of how to capitalize on the opening. Then Rufus made it obvious.

"Don't you dare let them take me!" The elderly zombie cried out with a fury that he wouldn't have thought possible.

Digby raised his staff without a second thought, casting Cremation on the flailing old master. With Rufus' intent to sacrifice himself, his will made no effort to resist the spell like the dead normally would. Adding the lightning he'd absorbed earlier, Digby set Rufus alight.

The bag of necrotic bones howled in victory as emerald fire climbed his body and electricity arced through the guardians trying to hold him back.

With his last ounce of strength, he yelled, "I leave them in your care, Lord Graves! Don't let me down!"

Then, he exploded.

———————◆ ◆———————

Bancroft leapt back as a bolt of his own lighting lit up every nerve in his body. Fortunately, with his level, the attack wasn't enough to kill him. The same couldn't be said for the two fighters that were guarding his front. The pair lay in a charred heap beneath the burning corpse of the zombie master that had rushed them.

The remaining dead that surrounded the castle suddenly lost their sense of urgency the moment their master had been destroyed. Many began to turn tail and run, clearly understanding that there was no way to kill his men without sacrificing more of their horde.

Bancroft stared down at the burning corpse of the zombie master. The damned thing had actually allowed himself to be destroyed, and for what, to execute a pitiful attempt to kill him?

No. That didn't make sense.

Bancroft swept his eyes across the castle's grounds, noticing the necromancer and his allies were nowhere to be seen. That was when he realized the attack had been nothing more than a distraction. Somehow, Graves had fled during the commotion. His heart leapt into his throat, afraid that the necromancer might actually escape. Then, he caught the foolish group out of the corner of his eye.

His jaw dropped immediately.

They were literally tiptoeing across the lawn and attempting to hide behind various statues. It was the single stupidest thing he had ever seen.

"Get the necromancer!" Bancroft thrust a finger in their direction as they took off at a sprint down the hill toward a cargo van at the castle's side entrance.

The ex-soldier, Mason, was in the lead, followed by the artificer and another man, carrying the injured woman between them. The necromancer brought up the rear, dragging a low-level guardian along with him. The zombie held his spear to the captured combatant's throat as if taking a prisoner.

That was when a white raven flew from one of the castle's windows, cawing as the retreating horde stopped in their tracks and turned back toward the castle.

"What the hell?" Bancroft squinted at the bird.

Animated Minion, Zombie Master, Rare.

"What?" He nearly stumbled in shock as he struggled to work out how a bird could have gained the ability to command a horde of over five hundred zombies. His gaze settled on the necromancer, Graves, as he held the captured guardian like a human shield.

The van's engine started up. For a moment, it looked like there was no-one at the wheel. Then, Bancroft noticed something black and shiny in the driver's seat. He analyzed it as well.

Animated Minion, Skeleton, Uncommon.

"Don't let them escape, damn it!" Bancroft's eyes widened, realizing how much trouble he would be in if he let the heretics get away. Henwick would never trust him again. He might as well hand command of Skyline over to Autem.

Guardians ran and cast spells, throwing everything they could at the group as the remaining horde converged to cover their escape route. Fireballs exploded across the lawn, somehow missing the group as they practically fell into the back of the van. Graves shoved his captive in before climbing in last.

Bancroft locked eyes with the zombie.

Graves shot him a villainous grin as the vehicle pulled away. Then, he flipped him off.

From above, the raven cawed before darting out of sight.

The horde closed in to block Bancroft's men from pursuing the vehicle. Then, the entire horde flipped him off as well.

Bancroft shook his head as the necromancer vanished into the van and closed the door. The vehicle floored it a second later, speeding off down the road. He wasn't sure if the necromancer was insane, stupid, or both. "What kind of enemy did you make, Henwick?"

Letting out a sigh, Bancroft glanced to the side where a few kestrels waited. Then he glanced back to the van, wondering what the point of it all was. There was no way the necromancer was going to escape. He could simply send the aircrafts after them.

Actually, he didn't even need to do that.

Bancroft walked further up the hill to give himself a strong vantage point as he watched the van weave between zombies. The horde parted to let them through while getting in the way just as much. He suppressed a self-satisfied smile, not wanting to seem unprofessional as he raised a hand to the sky. Thunder rumbled through the heavens.

One bolt of lightning probably would have been enough, but after receiving a middle finger from five hundred zombies, he wasn't about to go easy on them.

Emptying his entire mana pool, Bancroft focused on his target. Then, like Zeus himself, he brought down the fury of the heavens. Lightning snaked through the sky before crashing down onto the vehicle and arcing out into the horde around it. The van burst into flames and Bancroft dropped his hand to his side with a shrug.

It was all so pointless.

What did they really expect to accomplish?

In the end, the van quietly rolled to a stop at the side of the road as it burned. Bancroft deflated, looming over the scene. He had been correct in his estimate. A little over half of his forces were still standing. Not that Henwick cared about Skyline's men. No, his employer had his own goals and he didn't care how many men were sacrificed.

Again the horde began to lose interest in the fight. Bancroft had lost sight of the raven commanding the dead, but even if it was still out there, the necromancer had been destroyed. It would have been ideal if they could capture the creature, but with the surrounding trees, it could be anywhere in the area and there was no way to know how much of its ability it would retain without Graves to command it. Even more unfortunate was the fact that he hadn't been able to take the other zombie master prisoner. He shoved his hands into his pockets. It was too late now.

"Get this place cleared out." Bancroft turned back toward the castle's door.

It was a shame, really, to have damaged the property to the extent that they had. Bancroft sighed. At least the castle wouldn't be corrupted by that necromancer and his people any further. From the look of it, they had started building a half-assed forge, probably the work of that artificer. After that, there was no telling what they might have done to the place.

Bancroft took stock of the victory, and reported to Henwick while his surviving guardians cleaned out the area. He even made sure that the young mage that had overheard his conversation earlier wasn't among the survivors, assuming she was among their dead. It took a couple hours to secure the castle, but once his men were done, he sent them back out to prepare the kestrels to leave.

With no pressing matters to take care of, Bancroft headed into the once-beautiful building alone to reminisce about his time there so many years ago. Within its walls, he remembered playing billiards with celebrities and swimming with fashion models.

Maybe one day, when the world was under control, he could return. Maybe he could even fix the place up and claim it as his own manor after humanity returned from the brink that Henwick and Autem had driven it to. He smiled. Something about reclaiming the place felt right.

Stopping in the hall before the open door of the magnificent room that held the castle's indoor pool, Bancroft stared at the tranquil water inside. He stepped forward and leaned against the door frame to admire the craftsmanship of the tile work. It truly was impressive, as if the artistry enhanced the beauty of the water, giving its surface a dreamlike quality. It was almost too perfect to be real.

After staring out at the pool wistfully for a solid minute, Bancroft made his way to the library. Evidence of the castle's temporary inhabitants littered the room. They must have used it as a meeting place. Bancroft grimaced at a half-full container of pastries that sat open on one of the coffee tables. Crumbs covered the arm of one of the sofas.

"Savages." He turned away from the scene, letting his gaze drift toward the stairs leading to the master suites.

Nodding to himself, he headed up. He'd never been up there before, even in his day. Why not have a look now? After all, as wealthy as he had been back then, William Hearst had far more money, and it would be nice to see what he had done with it all. He couldn't help but smile as soon as he pushed through the door of the master suite. Though, he also felt a little jealous.

"I guess that settles it. I must return here someday to stake my claim. At least then this castle will be appreciated." He approached the window to look out over his future domain. "Not like I want to serve Henwick forever."

"That's good to know."

Bancroft's heart leapt into his throat as a familiar, yet horrible voice came from directly behind him. It was the same villainous tone that had irritated him so much earlier that night.

"How?" Bancroft spun whilst reaching for his pistol only to freeze in confusion as his eyes fell upon that insufferable necromancer's image filling a mirror that was hanging over the room's dresser. In the view on the other side, the zombie looked to be standing in some sort of parking garage with a cityscape visible behind him.

"I don't think you'll be needing that." Graves gestured toward the gun in his hand. "I'm long gone at this point."

Surrounding the heretic stood a horde of over a dozen zombies. Bancroft recognized the four corpses in front. They were the humans that the necromancer had escaped with, now apparently reanimated as his minions. The deceased form of that ex-soldier, Mason, held the guardian that Digby had captured in his grasp. Somehow his prisoner was the only one to survive. From the hunger in Mason's eyes, it didn't look like they wouldn't remain alive for long.

Bancroft froze, realizing that Graves must have used the guardian to set up a Mirror Link. "How?"

"Never mind the how. What matters now is the why." Graves gave him a crooked smile. "You know, I was prepared to live out my days without causing you, or Skyline, or even Henwick for that matter, any trouble."

Bancroft holstered his pistol and stood tall, not wanting to look weak in a negotiation. "And now?"

"Now, I want you to deliver a message for me." Graves narrowed his eyes as his lips retracted into a snarl. "Tell Henwick that if he wants an enemy, then he's got one. And if he wants a war, then he's got that too. Because I am coming for him, you, and all of Skyline. Hell, I will tear all of Autem apart just to see how your empire tastes. In short, you will regret what you have done today. I will see to it."

Graves ended the communication spell by signaling to his zombies to tear the captured guardian apart. The corpses of the necromancer's allies fell upon the poor soul without even giving them time to scream. They simply fell out of frame as the Mirror Link ended.

Bancroft stood still for a moment, unsure what to do. How could they have escaped? The van had been destroyed. He'd made sure of it. That was when he clasped a hand over his mouth. What if the van was a diversion? What if Graves had simply dove from the vehicle and hid in the horde around it? He could have slipped away into the trees. There was probably a second vehicle waiting somewhere to take him the rest of the way. He could have even had another kestrel waiting.

His eyes dropped to the guardian ring on his finger. If he hadn't been capped at level sixty by his current rank, he might have realized that the zombie had survived at the lack of an experience notification after striking the van with lighting. Unfortunately, after having reached his maximum level decades ago, he hadn't gained experience for quite some time.

Bancroft grabbed a small ashtray from the dresser and threw it at the mirror. He had been convinced that Graves was a simple idiot. The necromancer even had Henwick fooled. It was all an act. Somehow that fucking zombie had been thinking three moves ahead the entire night.

That was when Bancroft calmed down.

"Think, man, think." His mind flashed back to the image of Graves standing in the mirror with a cityscape behind him. Then, finally, he relaxed. The necromancer wasn't as smart as he thought, clearly unaware of how recognizable some buildings were. Bancroft closed his eyes as he tried to remember the image of a convention center in Anaheim that he'd been to before. The idiot had stood right in front of it. By kestrel, he was only an hour away. Bancroft snapped his eyes open.

"Got you!"

Rushing out the door, he couldn't help but wonder... Why Anaheim?

Then it was obvious.

"You really like castles, don't you?"

CHAPTER FORTY-THREE

Digby held as still as possible, listening for anything that might signal that his ruse was a success.

"This is the dumbest plan. I swear to god," Lana whispered from where she lay on the floor beneath the deceased forms of Mason, Sax, Alex, and Parker as they did their best to make it look like they were devouring the young woman.

"It may be dumb, but it worked." Rebecca shrugged as she ended the Waking Dream spell that she had been casting during Digby's talk with Bancroft. The image of the zombies surrounding him melted away, leaving all of the castle's inhabitants in their place, unharmed. She rubbed at her temples. "I guess there is a downside to casting that many illusions in a row. I am starting to feel one hell of a migraine coming on."

The illusionist had remained hidden throughout the battle despite carrying out the most important role. That being the job of misdirecting Bancroft and his men so that they didn't notice the shell game that they were actually playing. Escape had never been possible from the beginning; they knew that much. After discussing their situation with everyone, they settled on the only plan available.

To hide like cowards.

In the end, the only casualty they had suffered had been Rufus. Though, the plan might have fallen apart without his sacrifice. Aside from that, everything else had been an illusion. The rest of the survivors had never boarded a kestrel in the heat of battle. Hell, the kestrel that Bancroft struck down with lightning wasn't even there to begin with. Instead, Rebecca had combined her Waking Dream spell with ventriloquism to show Bancroft and his men what they wanted them to see. The real airship had been landed a mile away to be used later.

In the moments following Rufus' sacrifice, Digby and the others had simply retreated into the castle to let Rebecca take over. After that, the illusionist created an image of them running across the lawn and diving into the van. She had used the cover of the horde to move along with her illusion and stay in range the entire way.

Tavern did the rest, closing the door and driving the vehicle down the road. Bancroft destroyed it, of course, but that too was part of the plan. With the narrative of their failed escape in place, Digby and the rest of the castle's inhabitants simply hid in the last place anyone would think to look, in plain sight.

Digby glanced behind him at the flat image of a parking garage and cityscape that he didn't recognize. He leaned to one side, watching the illusion distort as the angle changed. It was like Rebecca had slapped a painting behind them that was only meant to be viewed from the front. The image faded to reveal the tiled walls of the castle's empty, indoor pool where everyone had been standing for the last couple hours. A mirror that they had taken from one of the rooms upstairs leaned against one wall.

"Are you sure he didn't notice us?" Lana started to push herself up. "I mean, Bancroft looked straight at us for a solid minute."

"I don't think so." Mason shrugged.

"Yeah, we'd be dead by now if he had," Sax added.

"Oh good, that makes me feel better." Lana went limp in defeat, laying at the bottom of the pool.

"Quit complaining, new girl." Parker nudged at the guardian with a boot.

"Yeah, piss off with all yer moaning," Hawk chimed in with his terrible accent.

Parker let out a laugh. "You have to admit though, this is all pretty funny if you can appreciate the stupidity." She followed the statement by poking at the fresh patch of healed skin on her shoulder where she had received a severe burn during the battle. Most of the hair on one side of her head was singed off as well. "Though, I did get a little crispy at the end there."

"Good thing we had a new healer to help with that." Alex reached a hand down to help Lana up. "And, if you're going to be stuck with us, you'll need to get used to this kind of plan."

"Indeed." Digby stood tall. "What was it Rufus said? We need to be as sneaky and underhanded as we can if we want to beat Skyline. I think this was a good way to start."

"So you really intend to fight back then?" Alex stepped forward.

"I do." Digby leaned to one side. "Well, more like I don't have a choice. Henwick will hunt us to the ends of the earth, and running isn't an option. So yes, I will bring the full power of the Heretic Seed down on him, Skyline, Autem, and whoever else raises a hand against us."

That was when hurried footsteps came from the hall outside the room.

"Quick, Becky, hide us with that water image again." Digby shot the illusionist an urgent look.

"I can't, I used up my mana on that last spell." She shrugged.

"Damn." Digby lowered his head. "Then everyone duck."

"God, this plan is stupid." Lana crouched back down.

"Quiet you." Digby glowered at her as Bancroft ran past the doorway and kept on going straight out of the castle.

Everyone in the pool remained silent for a full minute before speaking.

"Is he gone?" Alex stayed crouched.

"I think so." Rebecca started to raise back up.

Digby stepped toward the edge of the pool and peeked over the side. "I think the coast is clear."

"Hopefully that means Bancroft took the bait." Rebecca nodded. "I made sure to show him a recognizable cityscape that was close to here. As long as it was believable enough, he should be taking his troops there to chase us down."

"Nice." Alex gave her a congratulatory thumbs up.

"Yes, yes, good job, Becky," Digby added as he waited for the sound of aircrafts taking off.

A few minutes later, the kestrels outside were in the air.

"Ah, there we are." Digby headed toward the ladder on the wall of the pool. "Let us be off then."

"Me first! Gotta wee." Hawk darted past him, apparently spending entirely too long hiding without a bathroom break. He only made it half way up before Parker pulled him back down and rushed up the ladder herself.

"Ladies first, outta my way."

Digby shook his head at the soldiers that currently made up a large percent of his forces, unsure how he was going to mount a serious effort against Henwick and the rest of Skyline.

"One thing at a time." He shrugged before repeating, "One thing at a time."

With Bancroft and his men safely on their way, Digby called forth the sun goddess statue from his void to leave it with James and Mathew for protection. Sadly, Skyline's forces had retrieved the guardian rings of their fallen comrades, leaving none to be claimed by his greedy fingers.

The rest of the survivors loaded up the supplies into whatever vehicle was still usable. Taking Mason, Parker, and Sax with them, they headed off to the nearest town to set up a temporary camp. They could last a few days at the very least.

Once Digby found somewhere safer, he would come back for them.

As for his heretics, they had work cut out for them too.

Considering the fight that lay ahead, he needed to do more than just carve out a place for himself in the world. Henwick was building an empire, after all. He was going to have to meet him in kind. He was going to need to build a kingdom of his own.

Digby grinned as Rebecca landed their kestrel in front of him. With it, he would find a domain worthy of his future army. Alex carried a few items into the craft and sat down in the pilot's compartment next to Rebecca as Digby climbed the ramp. It closed behind him just before the airship ascended into the sky.

"So where are we heading?" Alex turned back to look over his shoulder.

"I'm not sure." Digby hesitated, remembering that what little he knew of the world had come from a selection of zombie movies.

"Actually, I had a thought." Rebecca straightened the tiara on her head with a sly smile. "I'm starting to get your appreciation for extravagance, Dig."

"Really?" Digby cracked a smile.

"Yeah. It's ridiculous, but hey, it's the apocalypse. At this point, we can just take what we want." She shrugged. "Who's going to tell us not to? Besides, if we're really going to approach this war in a sneaky and underhanded manner like Rufus suggested, then there's really only one place to go."

"Am I going to like this suggestion?" He arched an eyebrow at her.

"Don't worry." She glanced back to give him a wink. "You're going to love it."

Digby leaned on the door of the pilot's compartment behind his friends as the kestrel pushed forward into the horizon.

"How about some music for the road?" Alex slouched back comfortably in his seat.

"I think I can handle that." Rebecca nodded as Digby felt her move a small amount of mana through her blood to cast her Ventriloquism spell. The sound of a stringed instrument filled the kestrel's cabin a second later.

Alex shot her a sideways look, clearly recognizing the tune as a man's voice began to sing. "Really, Elvis?"

"He's king." She shrugged. "And where we're going, it's the perfect soundtrack."

Digby tapped a claw against the back of Alex's seat, enjoying the rhythm of the song as the chorus filled the cabin.

"Viva Las Vegas!"

ABOUT D. PETRIE

D. Petrie discovered a love of stories and nerd culture at an early age. From there, life was all about comics, video games, and books. It's not surprising that all that would lead to writing. He currently lives north of Boston with the love of his life and their two adopted cats. He streams on twitch every Thursday night.

Connect with D. Petrie:
TavernToldTales.com
Patreon.com/DavidPetrie
Facebook.com/WordsByDavidPetrie
Facebook.com/groups/TavernToldTales
Twitter.com/TavernToldTales

ABOUT MOUNTAINDALE PRESS

Dakota and Danielle Krout, a husband and wife team, strive to create as well as publish excellent fantasy and science fiction novels. Self-publishing *The Divine Dungeon: Dungeon Born* in 2016 transformed their careers from Dakota's military and programming background and Danielle's Ph.D. in pharmacology to President and CEO, respectively, of a small press. Their goal is to share their success with other authors and provide captivating fiction to readers with the purpose of solidifying Mountaindale Press as the place 'Where Fantasy Transforms Reality.'

Connect with Mountaindale Press:
MountaindalePress.com
Facebook.com/MountaindalePress
Twitter.com/_Mountaindale
Instagram.com/MountaindalePress

MOUNTAINDALE PRESS TITLES

GameLit and LitRPG

The Completionist Chronicles,
Cooking with Disaster,
The Divine Dungeon,
Full Murderhobo, and
Year of the Sword by Dakota Krout

A Touch of Power by Jay Boyce

Red Mage and
Farming Livia by Xander Boyce

Ether Collapse and
Ether Flows by Ryan DeBruyn

Unbound by Nicoli Gonnella

Threads of Fate by Michael Head

Lion's Lineage by Rohan Hublikar and Dakota Krout

Wolfman Warlock by James Hunter and Dakota Krout

Axe Druid,
Mephisto's Magic Online, and
High Table Hijinks by Christopher Johns

Dragon Core Chronicles by Lars Machmüller

Pixel Dust and
Necrotic Apocalypse by D. Petrie

Viceroy's Pride and
Tower of Somnus by Cale Plamann

Henchman by Carl Stubblefield

Artorian's Archives by Dennis Vanderkerken and Dakota Krout

APPENDIX

ATRIBUTES AND THEIR EFFECTS:

CONSTITUTION: Attribute related to maintaining a healthy body. Allocating points improves the body's ability to fight off disease and lowers the chance of infection and food borne illness. Greatly affects endurance.

AGILITY: Attribute related to mobility. Allocating points will improve overall control of body movements. Greatly affects speed and balance.

STRENGTH: Attribute related to physical prowess. Allocating points increases muscle destiny to yield more power. Greatly affects the damage of melee attacks.

DEFENSE: An attribute related to physical durability. Allocating points improves skin and bone density. Greatly reduces the damage you take. Defense can be supplemented by wearing protective clothing or armor.

DEXTERITY: Attribute related to skill in performing tasks, especially with hands. Allocating points will increase control of precise movement. Greatly affects control of melee attacks and ranged weaponry.

INTELLIGENCE: Attribute related to comprehending information and understanding. Improves processing speed and memory. Greatly affects mana efficiency. (+4 per attribute point.)

PERCEPTION: Attribute related to the awareness of the world around you. Allocating points improves the collection and processing of sensory information and moderately affects mana efficiency. (+2 per attribute point.)

WILL: Attribute related to controlling your mind and body. Allocating points will increase your dominance over your own existence. Greatly affects resistance to spells that directly affect your physical or mental self. (+1 per attribute point.)

NOTEWORTHY ITEMS

THE HERETIC SEED
An unrestricted pillar of power. Once connected, this system grants access to, and manages the usage of, the mana that exists within the human body and the world around them.

HERETIC RINGS
A ring that synchronizes the wearer with the Heretic Seed to assign a starting class.

THE GUARDIAN CORE
A well-regulated pillar of power. Once connected, this system grants temporary access to, and manages the usage of, the mana that exists within the human body and the world around them.

NOTEWORTY CONCEPTS

AMBIENT MANA

The energy present with a person's surroundings. This energy can be absorbed and use to alter the world in a way that could be described as magic.

MANA SYSTEM

All creatures possess a mana system. This system consists of layers of energy that protect the core of what that creature is. The outer layers of this system may be used to cast spells and will re[plenish as more mana is absorbed. Some factors, such as becoming a Heretic will greatly increase the strength of this system to provide much higher quantities of usable mana.

MANA BALANCE (EXTERNAL)

Mana is made up of different types of essence. These are as follows, HEAT, FLUID, SOIL, VAPOR, LIFE, DEATH. Often, one type of essence may be more plentiful than others. A location's mana balance can be altered by various environmental factors and recent events.

MANA BALANCE (INTERNAL)

Through persistence and discipline, a Heretic may cultivate their mana system to contain a unique balance of essence. This requires favoring spells that coincide with the desired balance while neglecting other's that don't. This may affect the potency of spells that coincide with the dominant mana type within a Heretic's system.

MASS ENCHANTMENTS

Due to belief and admiration shared by a large quantity of people and item or place may develop a power of power of its own.

SURROGATE ENCHANTMENT

An enchantment bestowed upon an object or structure based upon its resemblance (in either appearance or purpose) of another object or structure that already carries a mass enchantment.

WARDING
While sheltering one or more people, a structure will repel hostile entities that do not possess a high enough will to over-power that location's warding.

INFERNAL SPIRIT
A spirit formed from the lingering essence of the dead.

HERETIC & GUARDIAN CLASSES

ARTIFICER
The artificer class specializes in the manipulation of materials and mana to create unique and powerful items. With the right tools, an artificer can create almost anything.

DISCOVERD SPELLS:

IMBUE
Allows the caster to implant a portion of either their own mana or the donated mana of a consenting person or persons into an object to create a self-sustaining mana system capable of powering a permanent enchantment.

TRANSFER ENCHANTMENT
Allows the caster to transfer an existing enchantment from one item to another.

ILLUSIONIST
The illusionist class specializes in shaping mana to create believ-able lies.

DISCOVERED SPELLS:

CONCEAL
Allows the caster to weave a simple illusion capable of hiding any person or object from view.

VENTRILOQUISM
Allows the caster to project a voice or sound to another location.

MAGE
Starting class for a heretic or guardian whose highest attribute is intelligence. Excels at magic.

POSSIBLE STARTING SPELLS:

ICICLE
Gather moisture from the air around you to form an icicle. Once formed, icicles will hover in place for 3 seconds, during which they may be claimed as a melee weapons or launched in the direction of a target. Accuracy is dependent on caster's focus.

TERRA BURST
Call forth a circle of stone shards from the earth to injure any target unfortunate enough to be standing in the vicinity.

FIREBALL
Will a ball of fire to gather in your hand to form a throwable sphere that ruptures on contact.

REGENERATION
Heal wounds for yourself or others. If rendered unconscious, this spell will cast automatically until all damage is repaired or until MP runs out.

DICSCOVERED SPELLS:

NECROTIC REGENERATION
Repair damage to necrotic flesh and bone to restore function and structural integrity.

CARTOGRAPHY
Send a pulse into the ambient mana around you to map your surroundings. Each use will add to the area that has been previously mapped. Mapped areas may be viewed at any time. This spell may interact with other location dependent spells.

CREMATION
Ignite a target's necrotic tissue. Resulting fire will spread to other flammable substances.

CONTROL ZOMBIE
Temporarily subjugate the dead into your service regardless of target's will values. Zombies under your control gain +2 intelligence and are unable to refuse any command. May control up to 5 common zombies at any time.

SPIRIT PROJECTION
Project an immaterial image of yourself visible to both enemies and allies.

ZOMBIE WHISPERER
Give yourself or others the ability to sooth the nature of any non-human zombie to gain its trust. Once cast, a non-human zombie will obey basic commands.

BLOOD FORGE
Description: Forge a simple object or objects of your choosing out of any available blood source.

ENCHANTER

Starting class for a heretic or guardian whose highest attribute is will. Excels at supporting others.

POSSIBLE STARTING SPELLS:

ENCHANT WEAPON

Infuse a weapon or projectile with mana. An infused weapon will deal increased damage as well as disrupt the mana flow of another caster. Potential damage will increase with rank. Enchanting a single projectile will have a greater effect.

PURIFY WATER

Imbue any liquid with cleansing power. Purified liquids will become safe for human consumption and will remove most ailments. At higher ranks, purified liquids may also gain a mild regenerative effect.
Choose one spell to be extracted.

DISCOVERED SPELLS:

DETECT ENEMY:

Infuse any common iron object with the ability to sense and person of creature that is currently hostile toward you.

HEAT OBJECT

Slowly increase the temperature of an inanimate object. Practical when other means of cooking are unavailable. This spell will continue to heat an object until the caster stops focusing on it or until its maximum temperature is reached.

FIGHTER

Starting class for a heretic or guardian whose highest attribute is will. Excels at physical combat.

POSSIBLE STARTING SPELLS:

BARRIER
Create a layer of mana around yourself or a target to absorb an incoming attack.

KINETIC IMPACT
Generate a field of mana around your fist to amplify the kinetic energy of an attack.

SPECIALIZED CLASSES

NECROMANCER
A specialized class unlocked buy achieving a high balance of death essence withing a Heretic's mana system as well as discover spells within the mage class that make use of death essence.

STARTING SPELLS:

ANIMATE CORPSE
Raise a zombie from the dead by implanting a portion of your mana into a corpse. Once raised, a minion will remain loyal until destroyed. Mutation path of an animated zombie will be controlled by the caster, allowing them to evolve their follower into a minion that will fit their needs.

DECAY
Accelerate the damage done by the ravages of time on a variety of materials. Metal will rust, glass will crack, flesh will rot, and plants will die. Effect may be enhanced through physical contact. Decay may be

focused on a specific object as well as aimed at a general area for a wider effect.

DISCOVERABLE SPELLS:

ABSORB
Absorb the energy of an incoming attack. Absorbed energy may be stored and applied to a future spell to amplify its damage.

BURIAL
Displace an area of earth to dig a grave beneath a target. The resulting grave will fill back in after five seconds.

CONTROL UNCOMMON ZOMBIE
Temporarily subjugate the dead into your service regardless of target's will/resistance. Zombies under your control gain +2 intelligence and are unable to refuse any command. May control up to 1 uncommon zombie at any time.

EMERALD FLARE
Create a point of unstable energy that explodes and irradiates its surroundings. This area will remain harmful to all living creatures for one hour. Anyone caught within its area of effect will gain a poison ailment lasting for one day or until cleansed.

ANIMATE SKELETON
Call forth your infernal spirit to inhabit one partial or complete skeleton. Physical attributes of an animated skeleton will mimic the average values for a typical human.

FROST TOUCH

Description: Freeze anything you touch.

HOLY KNIGHT (GURADIAN ONLY)
A specialized class that specialized in physical combat and defense. This class has the ability to draw strength from a Guardian's faith.

TEMPESTARII
A class that specializes in both fluid and vapor spells resulting on a variety of weather-based spells.

AREOMANCER
A class that specializes in vapor spells.

PYROMANCER
A class that specializes in heat spells.

PASSIVE HERETIC ABILITIES

ANALYZE
Reveal hidden information about an object or target, such as rarity and hostility toward you.

MANA ABSORPTION
Ambient mana will be absorbed whenever MANA POINTS are below maximum MP values. Rate of absorption may vary depending on ambient mana concentration and essence compo-sition. Absorption may be increased through meditation and rest.
WARNING: Mana absorption will be delayed whenever spells are cast.

SKILL LINK
Discover new spells by demonstrating repeated and proficient use of non-heretic skills or talents.

TIMELESS

Due to the higher than normal concentration of mana within a heretic's body, the natural aging process has been halted, allowing for more time to reach the full potential of your class. It is still possible to expire from external damage.

ZOMBIE RACIAL TRAITS (HUMAN)

BLOOD SENSE

Allows a zombie to sense blood in their surroundings to aid in the tracking of prey. Potency of this trait increases with perception.

GUIDED MUTATION

Due to an unusually high intelligence for an undead creature, you are capable of mutating at will rather than mutating when required resources are consumed. This allows you to choose mutations from multiple paths instead of following just one.

MUTATION

Alter your form or attributes by consuming resources of the living or recently deceased. Required resources are broken down into 6 types: Flesh, Bone, Sinew, Viscera, Mind, and Heart. Mutation path is determined by what resources a zombie consumes.

RAVENOUS

A ravenous zombie will be unable to perform any action other than the direct pursuit of food until satiated. This may result in self-destructive behavior. While active, all physical limitations will be ignored. Ignoring physical limitations for prolonged periods of time may result in catastrophic damage.

RESIST

A remnant from a zombie's human life, this common trait grants +5 points to will. Normally exclusive to conscious beings, this trait allows a zombie to resist basic spells that directly target their body or mind until their will is overpowered.

VOID
A bottomless, weightless, dimensional space that exists within the core of a zombie's mana system. This space can be accessed through its carrier's stomach and will expand to fit whatever contents are consumed.

ZOMBIE MINION TRAITS (AVIAN)

FLIGHT OF THE DEAD
As an avian zombie, the attributes required to maintain the ability to fly have been restored.

BOND OF THE DEAD
As a zombie animated directly by a necromancer, this creature will gain one attribute point for every 2 levels of their master. These points may be allocated at any time. 7 attribute points remaining.

CALL OF THE DEAD
As a zombie animated directly by a necromancer, this minion and its master will be capable of sensing each other's presence through their bond. In addition, the necromancer will be capable of summoning this minion to their location over great distances.

ZOMBIE MINION TRAITS (RODENT)

SPEED OF THE DEAD
As a rodent zombie, the attributes required to maintain the ability to move quickly have been retained. +3 agility, + 2 strength.

BOND OF THE DEAD

As a zombie animated directly by a necromancer, this creature will gain one attribute point for every 2 levels of their master. These points may be allocated at any time. 7 attribute points remaining.

CALL OF THE DEAD

As a zombie animated directly by a necromancer, this minion and its master will be capable of sensing each other's presence through their bond. In addition, the necromancer will be capable of summoning this minion to their location over great distances.

ZOMBIE MINION TRAITS (REVENANT)

BOND OF THE DEAD

As a zombie animated directly by a necromancer, this creature will gain one attribute point for every 2 levels of their master. These points may be allocated at any time. 9 attribute points remaining.

NOCTURNAL

As a zombie created from the corpse of a deceased revenant, this zombie will retain a portion of its attributes associated with physical capabilities. Attributes will revert to that of a normal zombie during daylight hours.
+8 Strength, +8 Defense, +4 Dexterity, +8 Agility, +5 Will

MINOR NECROTIC REGENERATION

As a zombie created from the corpse of a deceased revenant, this zombie will simulate a revenant's regenerative ability. Regeneration will function at half the rate of a living revenant. Minor Necrotic Regeneration requires mana and void resources to function. This trait will cease to function in daylight hours when there are higher concentrations of life essence present in the ambient mana.

MUTATION PATHS AND MUTATIONS

PATH OF THE LURKER
Move in silence and strike with precision.

SILENT MOVEMENT
Description: Removes excess weight and improves balance.
Resource Requirements: 2 sinew, 1 bone
Attribute Effects: +6 agility, +2 dexterity, -1 strength, +1 will

BONE CLAWS
Description: Craft claws from consumed bone on one hand.
Description: .25 sinew, .25 bone
Attribute Effects: +4 dexterity, +1 defense, +1 strength

PATH OF THE BRUTE
Hit hard and stand your ground.

INCREASE MASS
Description: Dramatically increase muscle mass.
Resource Requirements: 15 flesh, 3 bone
Attribute Effects: +30 strength, +20 defense, -10 intelligence, -7 agility, -7 dexterity, +1 will

BONE ARMOR
Description: Craft armor plating from consumed bone.
Resource Requirements: 5 bone
Attribute Effects: +5 defense, +1 will

PATH OF THE GLUTTON
Trap and swallow your prey whole.

MAW

Description: Open a gateway directly to the dimensional space of your void to devour prey faster.
Resource Requirements: 10 viscera, 1 bone
Attribute Effects: +2 perception, +1 will

JAWBONE
Description: Craft a trap from consumed bone within the opening of your maw that can bite and pull prey in.
Resource Requirements: 2 bone, 1 sinew
Attribute Effects: +2 perception, +1 will

PATH OF THE LEADER
Control the horde and conquer the living.

COMPEL ZOMBIE
Description: Temporally coerce one or more common zombies to obey your intent. Limited by target's intelligence.
Resource Requirements: 5 mind, 5 heart
Attribute Effects: +2 intelligence, +2 perception, +1 will

RECALL MEMORY
Description: Access a portion of your living memories.
Resource Requirements: 30 mind, 40 heart
Attribute Effects: +5 intelligence, +5 perception, +1 will
Units of requirement values are equal to the quantity of resources contained by the average human body.

PATH OF THE RAVAGER
Leave nothing alive.

SHEEP'S CLOTHING
Description: Mimic a human appearance to lull your prey into a false sense of security.
Resource Requirements: 10 flesh.

TEMPORARY MASS

Description: Consume void resources to weave a structure of muscle and bone around your body to enhance strength and defense until it is either released or its structural integrity has been compromised enough to disrupt functionality.

Resource Requirements: 25 flesh, 10 bone.

Attribute Effects: +11 strength, +9 defense.

Limitations: All effects are temporary. Once claimed, each use requires 2 flesh and 1 bone.

HELL'S MAW

Description: Increase the maximum size of your void gateway at will.

Resource Requirements: 30 viscera.

Attribute Effects: +3 perception, +6 will.

Limitations: Once claimed, each use requires the expenditure of 1 MP for every 5 inches of diameter beyond your maw's default width.

DISSECTION

Description: When consuming prey, you may gain a deeper understanding of how bodies are formed. This will allow you to spot and exploit a target's weaknesses instinctively.

Resource Requirements: 10 mind, 5 heart.

Attribute Effects: +3 intelligence, +6 perception.

Made in the USA
Columbia, SC
25 July 2024

8335f1bf-b7fd-4706-99ec-da2c63ae8fbaR01